BOOK STORAGE

DATE		

THE WIDOW
OF
RATCHETS

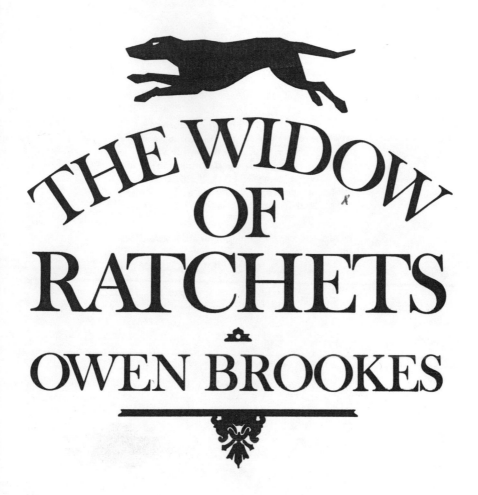

THE WIDOW OF RATCHETS

OWEN BROOKES

HOLT, RINEHART AND WINSTON
New York

Published by Holt, Rinehart and Winston, 383 Madison
Avenue, New York, New York 10017.
Published simultaneously in Canada by Holt, Rinehart
and Winston of Canada, Limited.

Library of Congress Cataloging in Publication Data
Brookes, Owen.
The widow of Ratchets.
I.   Title.
PZ4.B8694Wi   1979   [PR6052.R5815]   813'.5'4   78-12325
ISBN 0-03-040296-4

First Edition
Designer: Amy Hill
Printed in the United States of America
10 9 8 7 6 5 4 3 2 1

THE WIDOW
OF
RATCHETS

CHAPTER ONE

The airplane flew among canyons of cloud which, as the sun rose, took on the iridescent colors of mother-of-pearl. Between their fantastic conformations patches of early blue could be glimpsed. Suddenly the plane glided into the clouds, which resolved themselves into a fine mist, dimming the interior of the aircraft.

Most of the passengers were sleeping, slumped down in their seats. One of the few exceptions was Mrs. Rose Abernathy, a widow from New York City. She was a plump, matronly lady, her heavily powdered face pale beneath a cornflower blue toque which almost exactly matched her eyes. She was watching the young woman who slept beside her. The smile on the older woman's face might have been interpreted as a possessive one, although she had known her neighbor for only a few hours. She'll do, Mrs. Abernathy thought, as the aircraft broke from the cloudbank into a dazzling sunrise.

Mrs. Abernathy was a romantic and the story Lyndsay had told her was nothing short of wonderful. What pleased her most was that the story was going to have a happy ending. Mrs. Abernathy *adored* happy endings. She sighed with pleasure at the thought of it.

Looking past the sleeping woman, through the porthole, Mrs. Abernathy's small blue eyes read fairy castles and towers into the pink and sun-silvered cloudscape. It was to her fanciful mind a dream-setting for Lyndsay and her bridegroom. She had to quell a sudden impulse to wake the girl and point out to her the beautiful colors and shapes which were surely an omen of her future happiness.

Mrs. Abernathy closed her eyes and envisaged the waiting husband, Michael Dolben, whom Lyndsay had so eagerly described to her. She could just see him waiting excitedly in the airport lounge, clutching an enormous bouquet of . . .

The widow's indulgent reveries were rudely interruped by the clatter up ahead of the breakfast trolley. She leaned out into the aisle and frowned at the stewardess. She wanted Lyndsay to sleep on, wanted to prolong the pleasure of watching over her, above all for her to be fresh and rested for the coming reunion. Married just four months and separated by the Atlantic for almost all that time!

They had met in New York, the handsome young lecturer from England, and the lovely young woman from California. Lyndsay worked for some kind of civic planning institution—Mrs. Abernathy was invariably vague about such mundane details—that had organized this big conference. What really made the story so exciting was that Michael Dolben wasn't even supposed to have been at the conference—which just showed that fate had played a part in it all, right from the start. But somehow the professors and people who were organizing the conference heard about him and persuaded him to change his schedule at the last minute. And then—fate again, Mrs. Abernathy insisted—when Michael Dolben arrived, the hostess who was supposed to have met him was off somewhere and Lyndsay's boss, Mr. Mikeljohn, had told her to entertain him instead.

"And you fell in love with him there and then, yes?" Mrs. Abernathy had prompted Lyndsay. The girl's face had grown serious, almost solemn, and then she had said:

"I don't know. Maybe. I guess I must have," finishing with a little laugh.

The rattling breakfast trolley slid alongside Mrs. Abernathy, who immediately pressed a finger to her lips.

"Thank you, dear," she said, taking the plastic tray from the stewardess. "I don't want to disturb my friend here," she explained in a stage whisper. "Would you hold a tray for her, please? She's going to meet her husband at Heathrow. They had a whirlwind courtship in the States and she hasn't seen him since," Mrs. Abernathy burbled excitedly.

"Oh? Coffee?"

The stewardess's indifference deflated the widow for a moment. She nodded, and the girl poured coffee into the plastic cup. She's young and preoccupied, Mrs. Abernathy thought charitably. At her age, she can look forward to so much, but not to a time when, like me, she'll be old and have to live off other people's happiness. Besides, the poor girl was probably exhausted. They worked really hard, these stewardesses, and always had to look good, too. Mrs. Abernathy treated the girl to a bright smile.

"Thank you, dear. And don't forget to hold breakfast for Mrs. Dolben, will you?"

"No," the girl said, and pushed the trolley on down the aisle.

The coffee smelled good and, although Mrs. Abernathy was a ham-and-eggs person, the freshly warmed Danish looked tempting. She added powdered cream and sugar to her coffee, spread the paper napkin on her lap, and picked up the pastry.

Beside her, but unnoticed, Lyndsay Dolben stirred. Her eyes opened and she saw, like something left over from a dream, the mountainous banks of pastel-colored clouds. For a moment she did not know where she was. Her neck hurt. The throbbing of the four great engines, which had not disturbed her sleep, now reminded her. She was on the plane. It was dawn. If it was dawn they must almost be there. Michael, she thought, with a sudden surge of happiness which prompted her to sit up too quickly.

"Ow," she said, feeling the crick in her neck. She reached up a hand to massage the pain and became aware that Mrs. Abernathy, her teeth sunk into a Danish pastry, was watching her bright-eyed. "Oh good morning," Lyndsay said, remembering how kind the woman had been. She had been bursting to tell someone all about her glorious future and Mrs. Abernathy had been really interested.

Mrs. Abernathy swallowed a half-chewed mouthful of pastry and dabbed at her lips with the napkin.

"Did I wake you?" she asked, concerned.

"No. But I really slept, didn't I?" Lyndsay said, still rubbing her neck.

"Like a baby," Rose Abernathy beamed. "I asked the stewardess to hold breakfast for you, okay?"

"Thank you, but I don't think I could eat anything. I feel . . ." Lyndsay made a face and patted her stomach.

"Butterflies," Mrs Abernathy said. "What could be more natural? And do you see what a beautiful morning you have for your reunion?" Impulsively she touched Lyndsay's arm. "I'm so happy for you, honey, I really am."

3

"Thank you," Lyndsay said. She really was a dear and Lyndsay was grateful for her interest, but at this hour of the morning . . . She reached down under her seat and pulled out a small traveling case. "Would you mind if I went and freshened up?" she asked.

"Of course not," Mrs. Abernathy said at once. "You've really got to look scrumptious today. And between you and me, it ain't going to be difficult!" She chuckled hugely and handed Lyndsay her breakfast tray while she heaved her round body out into the aisle. "Now hand it back to me, dear, and off you go. I'll have the stewardess bring yours while you fix your face."

"Thanks," Lyndsay said, and squeezed out into the aisle, where Mrs. Abernathy continued to beam her smile while precariously balancing the tray.

"Take your time. No stinting. Remember who's waiting for you when we land," Mrs. Abernathy called after her.

Lyndsay felt embarrassed by the woman's ebullience and avoided looking at the other passengers. And that's mean of me, she thought, letting herself into the toilet with relief. She really did have butterflies and she needed a while alone to prepare herself, mentally as well as physically, for Michael.

Staring critically at her face in the mirror, Lyndsay knew that Mrs. Abernathy's idea of her marriage was too rosy, owed too much to the images of Hollywood. Lyndsay was a realist, but she had to admit that she had let herself be carried away a little by Mrs. Abernathy's romantic notions of Michael. What she had actually seen that first afternoon at the conference was not some knight in shining armor, nor did she think she'd been waiting for one. He was good-looking, sure, but what had impressed her most was a sense she had of a man entirely at ease in his own skin. He inspired confidence, and she liked that. Quite simply, she felt easy with him. But who could explain these things? Maybe she had been ready to fall in love. Perhaps it was just chemistry. Anyway, it had happened. But they had become friends first, Lyndsay thought. Everything had grown from that. He hadn't made any veiled passes or flirted with her.

It had all been so easy. No *making* conversation, no need to choose bland words to find out about each other. Not that they had exchanged very much information. Even now they knew very little about their respective backgrounds. It had been as though they were the only two people in the world and all that mattered were *their* interests, attitudes, and preferences. Lyndsay had taken leave and flown like a tourist around her own country to be with him. In Chicago, Dallas, and Detroit they had filled in the blanks. Then Lyndsay had woken up one morning and known that she was hopelessly in love with him. Except—and this was the truly miraculous part—it hadn't been hopeless at all. She'd thought, right from the moment she'd agreed to go with him, that this might be a brief, intense affair. She had put the future out of her mind, but that morning it stretched unavoidably before her. She had lain beside him, looking at him and thinking, I don't want you to go. I don't want this to stop. I love you, Michael Dolben. And he'd wakened slowly, kissed her, and pulled her down against his shoulder.

"You must be getting bored," he'd said, "listening to the same old lecture time after time."

"I love every minute of it. Don't you know that?"

"Enough to marry me?"

"Yes."

That's how it had been decided, just like that. They were living in a world of unfamiliar places, of train and airplane schedules, anonymous hotels. It wasn't a world for time-consuming preparations.

"I ought to tell my folks."

"Tell them after the wedding."

She had had to return to New York two days after they were married. He had joined her as soon as he could. Another forty-eight hours together and then she had seen him off. He was running a summer course at the London Academy of Architecture.

"I'll find us somewhere to live. You give in your notice. It won't be long, I promise."

"Why can't I come now? I could live where you live."

"With three other men? Oh no. I'm not sharing you with anybody, Mrs. Dolben."

She had lived for his letters. But he had been so busy that all the arrangements had taken much longer than they had expected. He'd had to go out of London for a while. Then at last he wrote to say he had found them a place to live. Near the river. She would love it. They'd spend the rest of the summer making it just right. She had written back: "When can I come?" His letters, typed on his old portable, had contained no real news and they always seemed rushed. "Terribly busy. I love you." But they *had* been wonderful love letters, and that was all she cared about, really. Yet sometimes she had wondered if everything was all right. She blamed herself. She should have insisted on going with him. But she didn't want to be pushy. Michael was so very English. And then Mr. Mikeljohn had found it difficult to replace her and she hadn't wanted to let him down. Michael wouldn't hear of it anyway. "I want to provide you with a proper home. It's just that I'm so busy at the moment. Soon. I promise." Oh let it be soon, she had prayed. "And there's so much to do. I must go down and see my family." His family. Of course she would have to meet them. His parents were dead, but he had a brother. There was property in the country somewhere. But none of that had seemed important. She, who suddenly had too much time on her hands, had written: "There is so much I want to ask you. That's why I get impatient. Then I remember that I have the whole of my life to badger you and I know I'm being stupid. It's just that I miss you."

There had been bad times, nights mostly, when she had wondered if he had regrets. Maybe, when he got back home, he felt trapped. Perhaps, after all, it had been an affair that had somehow snowballed into marriage. As her parents had said, "You know so little about him."

But she had known all that mattered. Of course it was impossible for anyone to understand, even Mrs. Abernathy. Lyndsay herself could not put a name to it. It amounted to the simple fact that she was sure of Michael. There had been doubts, certainly, but they had vanished with his last letter and were gone forever. As soon as she had read it she had booked her flight and sent him a cable. Her butterflies were just natural anticipation, the growing excitement of knowing that, in a matter of minutes now, she was going to see him again, be with him at last.

He was going to slacken off for a while. In the autumn he would be lecturing at the academy, and in the spring there was a chance of a term at Cambridge. All those dreaming spires, Lyndsay thought. Or was that Oxford? It didn't matter. It was England. With Michael.

Her happiness glowed back at her from the mirror. For a moment it surprised her. She wasn't used to seeing such happiness on her face. Not that she had been miserable before, or had anything to complain about. But her face had looked different. More sober. Sort of private. It was just that until she met Michael, her life had lacked any real purpose or direction. She had been disengaged, a person who stood back a little, seeing what life had to offer.

6

"You were a frump, Lyndsay Kramer," she told herself. Mrs. Michael Dolben stared back at her with open, laughing eyes. She brushed her hair and straightened the collar of her pale green dress. Just a dab of perfume and she'd be ready. Lyndsay did not think she was beautiful, but she thought she would do. And for a moment, before opening the door, she smiled at her reflection and wished it luck.

While she had been in the windowless cubicle, the plane had passed through the great banks of cloud. The cabin was full of bright, dazzling light. Mrs. Abernathy had moved into the window seat in order to enjoy her breakfast without further disturbance. Lyndsay slipped into the seat beside her and accepted the tray which the stewardess brought her. The coffee was hot and strong and good. She drank it, watching the endless blue of the sky and Mrs. Abernathy's undisguised enjoyment of her third cup of coffee.

"Eat your Danish. Try," the elderly woman urged her.

Lyndsay picked up the pastry and suddenly found that she was hungry.

"Mm. It's good," she said.

"That's the way. You've got to keep your strength up now, you know," Rose Abernathy laughed quietly to herself. For a while she stared out of the window, at the sea below. Then, flushing a little, she asked Lyndsay:

"Do you think I could have just one little peek at him when we land? I just want to tell him what a lucky guy he is."

"Of course. I'd like you to meet him," Lyndsay said at once.

"Thank you. But you mustn't let me intrude. You know what an old chatterbox I am."

"Don't worry. I won't," Lyndsay laughed. And later she would explain to Michael how much their story had meant to Mrs. Abernathy and how grateful she had been to have such a willing listener.

"You're a wonderful person," Mrs. Abernathy said emotionally. "Just one peek and I'll vanish."

"It's a deal," Lyndsay promised.

Suddenly, the plane dipped over and Lyndsay, glancing out of the window, caught her first sight of England.

"Oh look," she exclaimed. She'd always wanted to visit England, and now it was going to be her home. At least for a while. A year ago she would never have thought such a change could be possible. She leaned toward Mrs. Abernathy, trying to make out more of the land below. "Do you know, Michael says it's been so hot this summer it's more like California than England?"

"Still looks pretty green to me," Mrs. Abernathy remarked. "But I certainly hope he's right. English rain is disaster for my joints."

"Ladies and gentlemen, your attention please. We shall be arriving at London Heathrow in approximately thirty minutes. The weather is reported hot and sunny . . ." The voice crackled on over the loudspeaker. Lyndsay did not listen. Instead, she fastened her seat belt, handed her tray and Mrs. Abernathy's to the stewardess, and checked her hand luggage. These last thirty minutes, she knew, were going to be endless. She doubted that she could sit still for that long. As if she understood, Rose Abernathy smiled at her fondly.

"Now you just relax, honey. We'll be there in two shakes of a duck's tail."

There was a long line at passport control, but Lyndsay did not have time to get impatient. Mrs. Abernathy, festooned with a camera and three pieces of hand luggage, plus a raincoat over her arm, had mislaid her passport. She *knew* she had put it in the pocket of her bulging purse, so that it would be right at hand. She began to scatter her luggage around her.

"Here, let me," Lyndsay said, aware of the line inching forward.

"Oh I'm such an old fool. If I don't find it . . ."

"Here it is," Lyndsay said. "In the pocket of your raincoat."

"And thank God for that!" Mrs. Abernathy exclaimed. "Whatever would I do without you?"

"You'd manage just fine," she said and helped the old woman to collect her baggage again.

Lyndsay could see ahead to the desk now. There were three men there, one who checked the documents and two who scanned the faces of the passengers with expressions of anxiety. Briefly she wondered why. Were they looking for someone? Had she and Mrs. Abernathy been traveling with a wanted criminal or something? It would be rather exciting if they had, she thought. The line moved forward and Lyndsay clutched her own passport. Only minutes now. Michael would be waiting downstairs. Oh God, it would be so good just to see him again. She closed her eyes for a moment. Whatever happened, she must not cry.

The line had moved on without her and she hurried forward to close the gap. Then, at last, it was her turn. She placed the passport on the desk and waited. The young man took it, flipped it open, and glanced from the black-and-white photograph to the woman who stood before him.

One of the other men leaned forward and looked at her passport, then he turned and nodded to the third man.

"Is something wrong?" Lyndsay asked, her heart beating rapidly.

"Lyndsay Kramer Dolben?" said the second man, taking her passport from the desk clerk.

"Yes. You have my passport there. It's all in order. It must be. I just had it . . ."

"All in order, madam," the man interrupted firmly, "but if you wouldn't mind accompanying my colleague here for a moment . . ."

"Why? Whatever . . . ?" She felt genuinely alarmed. For the first time she realized that she was in a foreign country, and alone. The third man came around the desk and stood beside her.

"What's going on?" demanded Mrs. Abernathy. "Is there something wrong?"

"If you'd just come this way, Mrs. Dolben." The man touched her elbow lightly, prompting her forward.

"Now look here—" Mrs. Abernathy began, but was cut off by a sudden smile from Lyndsay, who didn't want the old lady to cause a scene.

"You just wait for me, okay?" she said. "This won't take a minute, will it?" she asked the man.

"No, madam. Now if you wouldn't mind . . ." She took her passport and let the man lead her across the hall. Behind her, Mrs. Abernathy's voice rose in loud protest.

The man took Lyndsay to a door marked PRIVATE. He opened it, stood back, and waved her in. Confused, Lyndsay looked around her. It was a sort of office, or maybe some kind of waiting room. There was a square table, a washbasin and mirror in the far corner. A young woman wearing the airline's uniform hovered near the door as though she did not know what to do. Lyndsay opened her mouth to speak to her, to demand an explanation, when a tall, gray-haired man rose from a chair behind the table. He was wearing a business suit.

"Mrs. Dolben?" he asked quietly.

"Yes. Would you please tell me . . . ?"

"I'm sorry to bring you here, but I thought . . ." He hesitated a moment and then said: "Look, please sit down."

9

"I don't want to sit down," she said sharply. "My husband's waiting out there and I—"

"I'm a friend of your husband," the man said quickly. "Reginald Pargetter."

The name rang a faint bell. Had Michael mentioned him? He was asking her to sit down again and saying something about the London Academy of Architecture.

"Oh yes. Aren't you Michael's course director or something? I believe you've written to my boss, ex-boss I should say, in New York. Mr. Mikeljohn."

"That's right, yes. Actually, I'm head of the environmental planning division."

"Oh excuse me," Lyndsay said and belatedly offered Pargetter her hand. "Michael has spoken of you, of course. I'm rather confused," she admitted.

"Please sit down, Mrs. Dolben." Still holding her hand, he pulled her insistently toward a chair.

"Michael's not able to meet me?" she said, sitting. "Is that it?"

"I'm afraid not. Unfortunately . . . Mrs. Dolben . . ." Pargetter looked for a moment as though he had lost the power of speech. Lyndsay watched his face expectantly. She felt embarrassed for him and then, suddenly, afraid. She half rose from her chair but he forced her down again, his hand on her shoulder.

"Michael's dead, Mrs. Dolben. I'm most terribly sorry."

At first there was nothing. No sounds, no feeling. She did not even want to cry. Slowly, Lyndsay became aware of the steady pressure of the man's hand on her shoulder and her own loud, startled breathing.

"A glass of water," Pargetter suggested. "Or something stronger?" He glanced at the waiting stewardess.

"No," Lyndsay heard herself say.

But the woman walked to the basin in the corner and drew a glass of water anyway. She carried it to the table and set it down in front of Lyndsay, avoiding her eyes. Lyndsay reached out and pulled it closer, not because she wanted it but simply for something to do. The glass was cool and reassuring under her clenched fingers. By gripping it she could control the tremors which seized her body.

"I don't believe you," she said, and instantly felt better. Of course it wasn't true. Any minute now she would be with Michael. It was an error.

"I know it must be a terrible shock. It was to me. I'm sure there must be better ways of breaking such news but . . . Please forgive me." Pargetter let go of her shoulder and sank tiredly into his chair. His hands were very pale, Lyndsay noticed as he laced his fingers tightly together on the tabletop. "I felt that I ought to tell you myself. I was very fond of Michael. He spoke of you, often. I thought it better to speak to you privately." He glanced helplessly at the young woman who, prompted by this silent cue, bent over Lyndsay.

"Would you like to lie down, Mrs. Dolben?"

Lyndsay looked at her face. It was pretty but she was wearing too much makeup, like a mask.

"No I would not," she said angrily. "Just what is this?" She turned wide-eyed to Pargetter, who looked down at his hands, as though ashamed.

"Michael died two days ago, in a car accident. He was visiting his brother in the country."

None of it was real. None of this was happening. If she closed her eyes this terrible gray man and this painted woman would disappear.

"I don't understand," she said.

"Michael's brother telephoned me. Or rather he got put through to me. He didn't know how to reach you, you see . . ."

Outside, Lyndsay heard a loud, clamoring American voice. To her, it sounded like the voice of sanity. She stood up and pulled open the door.

"What's going on in there?"

The man who had brought Lyndsay to the room seemed to shrink before Mrs. Abernathy, whose whole body quivered with righteous indignation.

"Lyndsay, honey . . ." she gasped, elbowing the man aside. "Why, whatever . . . ?"

No arms could have been warmer, kinder, more comforting. Suddenly she was sitting in the chair again, with Mrs. Abernathy hugging her. Her perfume was familiar. Eyes closed, smelling it, Lyndsay imagined herself safely in the air again, waking from a nightmare. In a moment she would open her eyes and see the colors of the dawn clouds.

"Everything's going to be all right, honey. Everything's going to be just fine. Hang on, now. Just hang on."

She heard the quiet, grieved voice of Mr. Pargetter, repeating the details. With each new shock, Mrs. Abernathy hugged her tighter. She did not know who began to cry first, she or Mrs. Abernathy. They rocked together, weeping, the old woman murmuring words of comfort that Lyndsay did not try to understand. The tone of her friend's voice was comfort enough. Michael was dead. Killed. Dead. It was like ice, this knowledge, and with it came a deadly calm. She pulled gently away from Mrs. Abernathy. Awkwardly, dabbing at her face with a handkerchief, she apologized to the four people who watched her.

The young woman brought her a cup of strong, sweet tea. She drank it gratefully. Michael had been killed in a car crash. This man, Mr. Pargetter, had come to tell her so. That was kind. She must acknowledge his kindness. She must get it all clear in her head and then . . .

"Please, where is Michael now?"

"At Ratchets. Mrs. Dolben, won't you rest? There is a room . . ."

"No. No, thank you. I'm fine now. Mrs. Abernathy?" She felt for the woman's hand and gripped it tightly. It gave her courage.

"Lyndsay . . ." she said softly.

"No, it's all right. Really. I understand and I'm okay. Truly." She turned back to Pargetter. "Where is Ratchets?"

"I don't know exactly. North of here. In the East Midlands, I believe. It . . . was Michael's home. I'm afraid I didn't think to ask the right questions. Stupid of me. His brother was very upset, naturally, and most concerned for you."

"He's to be buried there?"

"Yes."

"How . . . how can I get there? Today. Now."

"Honey, you mustn't . . ."

"No. Please. I have to. Don't you see?" She turned to Mrs. Abernathy. "I've got to go to him. You understand, surely?"

Rose Abernathy nodded.

"My wife Edith and I . . . we'd hoped you'd stay with us," Reginald Pargetter said. "Edith wanted to come with me but I . . ." His voice trailed away. All that he had to say about Edith preparing the spare room for her seemed irrelevant. "You're very welcome," he said.

"Thank you. You're very kind. But I . . . I want to go to Michael."

She did not listen to their well-meant arguments. They urged her to rest, to see a doctor. They could get her a room in the Airport Hotel. Somebody suggested she return straight to America.

"No," Mrs. Abernathy interrupted firmly. "Lyndsay's right. She's got a family here. Her place is with them."

"Thank you," Lyndsay said gratefully. "Thank you all. You're very kind. All of you. But that's what I want. Please try to understand." Her voice was calm and firm. It was all a trick really, an attitude of mind. Once you showed that you were capable, people would listen, help. They all wanted to help, so she let them by organizing their sympathy, directing it onto practical matters.

It took less than an hour to make all the arrangements. She was booked onto a scheduled flight to Birmingham, the nearest airport. The car rental firm in the arrival lounge would have a car waiting for her. All this was fixed by Reginald Pargetter and the young woman from the airline. Her bags would be transferred directly to the Birmingham flight. She bought two maps from the bookstall and set about working out her route.

She needed to be alone. Mr. Pargetter gave her his card. If there was anything, anything at all he and Edith could do . . .

"I'll let you know about the funeral," she promised. "Thank you for all your help."

She looked at Mrs. Abernathy.

"And you," she said, "had better get on to your hotel or you'll miss your reservation. Come on, I'll walk you to a cab."

"You know," the old woman said after a moment, "for once in my life I'm not going to argue. You don't have to be brave with me, honey. I understand. But you'll be okay. Whatever happens . . ." She paused, as though fighting some emotion she did not dare to show. "You remember that. Whatever happens. You'll come through."

"Thanks," Lyndsay said.

Obediently, she wrote down the name and number of Mrs. Abernathy's hotel and then helped her collect her luggage. Impulsively, she stooped to kiss the old woman's soft cheek before helping her into a cab.

"I'll call you. Tomorrow at the latest. And thanks."

"Don't you forget now. And God bless. You hear?"

Lyndsay nodded, and waved as the cab started off into the line of traffic.

They had placed the little room at her disposal, promising to call her fifteen minutes before her flight. Alone in this anonymous room, practically all she knew of England, Lyndsay thought that she was caught in some terrible dream. But in this dream she discovered something hard and certain. The calm that had carried her through the last hour began to leave her. She had a headache and each pulse in her temples said *Michael is alive.* She was aware of her body working. And while her body continued to function, Michael could not be dead.

The evidence was entirely hearsay. A stranger had spoken on the telephone to another stranger. Any one of a hundred misunderstandings could have taken place. Michael had told her that the English telephone system was bad. She could just imagine the static crackling, the muffled explosions on the line. It was so easy to misinterpret. She didn't blame Reginald Pargetter. He would naturally be thrown by a call from a stranger. And, having grasped what he thought the stranger was saying, he would be numbed, perhaps even unable to take in what was being said. Why, on his admission, he hadn't thought to ask for the caller's number. Michael had just been delayed, that was all. Even if he had had an accident, it wouldn't be fatal.

The tears ran down her face, splashing onto her dress. She mustn't let her imagination run away with her. She must stick to the facts.

A few moments later a stewardess tapped on the door. Lyndsay forced herself to be calm again. Eyes hidden by gigantic sunglasses, hair smooth, she held herself erect. The girl, senior stewardess on the flight to Birmingham, had been told the bare facts and charged to look after her. She was surprised but relieved to find Lyndsay so much in control of herself, though she guessed that it must require a great effort of will.

The plane was only half full and the stewardess led her to an aisle seat. The one next to it and those immediately in front were empty, giving Lyndsay a welcome sense of privacy.

"Try to rest," the stewardess advised, bending over her. "And call me if you want anything at all."

"Thank you. You're very kind." Lyndsay was surprised to discover that she could still smile.

"I love your smile. Do you know that it begins in the very center of your lower lip? Just there . . ." He touched the spot with the tip of his finger. "And spreads in a curve . . ." Traced the line of her

14

lips. "And then these muscles here sort of crinkle up." Again the almost imperceptible touch on her cheek. "And finally, through these little lines here . . ." Now the corner of her eye. "It reaches your eyes." Rolling over onto his back so that she had to turn her head to see him. "That's unusual. Most people smile with their eyes first. But not you. I like that." Catching her face gently in his hand, holding it steady. "Your eyes are sad when you don't smile. I want you to smile always."

She could see him so clearly, reproduce exactly every nuance and pitch of his voice. It was the voice of a man who knew and had accepted who he was. His hair, blown by the dry summer winds of the South, or damp, sleek, and curly from the shower. She remembered him swimming, strongly but without much grace. "I lumber through the water," he said laughing. "I know." And he was awkward on the dance floor, too. She remembered him on a series of stages, behind lecterns, or clutching notes, talking in his certain voice. With a sharp pain she recalled his strong profile, caught for a moment in the light of the slide projector he used. Once or twice she had operated the machine for him and afterward he'd joked to some people who had come to congratulate him: "I'm only marrying her because she's the best projectionist I've ever had."

She could still feel the pressure of his hugging arm about her shoulders. All of it remained. Their little time together had been lived intensely, in the knowledge that soon they would have to part. So she remembered it intensely, and with sudden anger. It was too short a time. It wasn't fair. She deserved more than this, had been promised so much more, only to find it all snatched away. Lyndsay closed her eyes against a new surge of tears as the plane circled Birmingham Airport before landing.

The heat seemed to rise up from the tarmac and hit Lyndsay. Even though she wore sunglasses, her eyes were dazzled. For a moment, the row of cleaned and shining cars seemed to shift and waver.

"You all right, miss?" The young man in soiled coveralls, who had been told to show Lyndsay to her car, took her arm.

"Yes. Thanks. It's just the heat."

"I know. It's been something dreadful up here. We've got a standpipe in our street. Even the cut's nearly dried up. Anyhow, here's the motor," he said, unlocking a small, bright blue sedan.

The only problem Lyndsay anticipated was getting used to driving on the "wrong" side of the road. The mechanic cheerfully assured her that she would soon get the hang of it. Michael had, in America, she reminded herself. So she could, too. The car was much smaller than she was used to, but once she was behind the wheel Lyndsay felt quite confident. She unfolded and refolded the maps she had bought and checked through her route. The mechanic gave her basic directions about how to get onto the ring road, and avoid the center of Birmingham. On the map, Ratchets looked a long, lonely way off. Should she try to contact Michael's brother? Call Information and ask for a number? The village looked so small, it ought to be possible. She sat still, considering it. It would be courteous. Maybe there wouldn't be room for her to stay. On the other hand she didn't want to waste time. More importantly, she felt embarrassed about calling him. What could he say to her? And she didn't even know his name.

That did it. She fastened her seat belt and turned the ignition key.

The first part of the journey was easy. All she had to do was follow the traffic, which was so heavy that she could only proceed at a crawl. This gave her time to get used to the car, and by the time she reached the ring road, even driving on the left did not bother her. Prudently, she kept to the slowest lane and handled the intersection quite well.

Soon she found herself able to relax to the rhythm of the car. The traffic thinned out and she drew over into a faster lane. Coasting at a steady fifty, it was not so very different from driving back home. The car handled well. She kept her mind firmly fixed on the road, watching for the turnoff sign she had located on the map. She forced herself to concentrate.

A horn sounding irritably behind her made her aware that she had lost speed dangerously. Signaling, she pulled the car back over into the slow lane and waved an apology to the passing driver. Even so she had to accelerate, which she did cautiously. Her shoulders were shaking and her grip on the steering wheel was too tight. She wanted to stop, but there was no stopping on this road. Even pulling over and resting up for a minute or two was forbidden.

Lyndsay took a deep breath, pressed her shoulders back into the seat, and forced her clenched fingers to relax. For a brief, terrible moment she thought that it did not matter if she did have an accident. With Michael dead . . . But she did not know that. Not for sure. Until she had all the facts, until she was convinced, she had to stay alive. And there, coming up fast toward her, was the first sign warning her of the intersection she wanted. It's going to be okay, she told herself.

In no time at all, she was slowing for the turnoff. The front of the car dipped down a curving, steep ramp. Swinging to the right, she came out onto a grass-verged two-way highway. She drove for another couple of miles and then entered a small town, taking the first free parking space she found.

Her hands trembled the moment she shut off the engine. Her clothes were sticking unpleasantly to her body. She leaned forward, resting her head for a moment against the steering wheel.

It was hot and stuffy in the car. She realized that she had been driving with the windows shut. Annoyed with herself, she got out of the car and gratefully took deep gulps of the fresher air. It was a somnolent afternoon, and very humid. What she needed was some food, to keep her alert.

In the narrow main street she found a little café and ordered a hamburger and coffee. She was surprised when the order arrived without salad or relish, but she did not inquire about it. The hamburger tasted like sawdust. She had to force it down with long swallows of awful coffee. But she felt better for it, and ordered another cup. She watched people passing the windows of the café without really noticing them. The buildings opposite looked old, but at ground level they sported unsuitable new façades. Above the metal and the plastic, the familiar bright signs and lettering, the buildings were built of old, rose-colored bricks. The windows were leaded, the disused chimneys ornate like an illustration from a child's storybook. Michael would have loved the skyline, but would have been outraged by the tacked-on, incongruous shopfronts.

She pushed the thought of Michael out of her mind. It was difficult. It even made her feel guilty, but she knew that she had to do it. If she was going to make this trip, it had to be with her mind free and alert. From here the route got more complicated. She didn't intend to give herself another scare like the one she had had on the ring road. She signaled for the check and paid it.

Outside, the afternoon heat seemed like a physical substance against which she had to push. The locked car was like an inferno. Lyndsay opened all the windows and stood on the pavement, checking the next leg of her route. She had to continue due east and would soon be in open country.

Had Michael never mentioned his brother's name? As she drove through the hedged fields, with a warm breeze hissing into the car, she realized how very uncommunicative Michael had been about his family. For the first time it struck her as odd. She knew that she had told him about her parents, about Jobey, their aging but adored setter, even about Aunt Hester, her father's eccentric spinster sister. In spite of their sense of living on limited time, she had told him something about her background. But what had he said in return? Had she, she wondered guiltily, been too wrapped up in her own feelings to listen?

Parents dead. A brother, yes. Some cousins. Pleased with this scrap of memory, Lyndsay clung to it, searching for names, some details. Nothing came. The village, then. Ratchets. He'd mentioned that. "We live in the Big House." He'd said it as if it had capitals. She'd kidded him about that and he had changed the subject. The family had always lived in Ratchets. For generations. He'd laughed and said, "I'm just about the only one who ever got away." It had not been a humorous laugh. There had been bitterness in it. He hadn't wanted to discuss it. As if he were ashamed or something. And what a strange thing to say. "The only one who ever got away," as though he were talking about some kind of prison or . . .

"You're being stupid," she told herself aloud. The sound of her own voice relaxed her a little. She was imagining things, putting a weight on his words they probably did not have. At the time, his reticence about his home and family had not seemed important at all. She knew even less, when she came to think about it, of his flat in London.

She was scared, or rather nervous, she admitted, of meeting his family by herself. As Mrs. Abernathy had pointed out, they were her family now. She wasn't really going among strangers, but to people who had loved Michael and known him so much longer than she.

She had reached the top of a long hill and there, below her, stretched out like a relief map, was a vast sweep of flat landscape. The car rolled down the hill into a sort of plain, a checkerboard of wheatfields and sun-parched grass, of dazzling streams reflecting light from the sun. There were few trees and nothing that could be called a wood or forest. An occasional clump of trees resembled lonely windbreaks. This was farming country, dotted with spires and towers, so many that even the tiniest hamlet must have its own church. There was something both stolid and graceful about them, even though in the heat they seemed to shimmer and melt into the burning sky.

The road wound in a series of undulating loops across the flat land, drawing her in a dance which displayed the countryside. This was not a road which took the shortest route from *a* to *b*, but one which moved through the landscape with the rightness of a river. Through fields and villages, by farms and solitary churches it wound, leading her on. And it seemed to Lyndsay as she drove that her car was the only moving object in the whole countryside.

As she drove deeper into this country, she became aware of the unmistakable signs of drought. The cracked, moonscape earth, dry ditches, and stagnant riverlets looked sad and out of place. The wheat was stunted. A flock of sheep seemed weighted down by their heavy fleece. Even the few trees she passed were already losing their leaves. Some, diseased and dying, had already been felled. It was horrible, and she shivered, in spite of the heat.

With relief she passed through a large village. Women were shopping, children playing. A dog barked. On the outskirts she pulled into a run-down, one-pump service station and asked a man, who came slowly out of the barnlike garage, to fill up her tank.

"Do you know Ratchets?" she asked. "A village called Ratchets?"

He looked at her with a blank frown.

"No. Can't say I do. It's not hereabouts."

For a moment, as he shuffled off to make change, Lyndsay thought that she must have misread the map, but a quick check confirmed that she was on the right road. Distance, she recalled someone telling her, was relative. At home, a journey of three or four hundred miles was nothing, but on an island like this, a mere fifty miles was a long way off.

"Thank you," she said, as the man tipped coins into her palm.

" 'S'all right," he said and stepped back.

For some miles now the road followed a meandering river. She crossed and recrossed it by means of narrow, humped-back bridges. The water level was low and the stream flowed sluggishly. Occasionally, as she crossed a bridge, a stale, decaying smell reached her. The sunlight glared from the water, hurting her eyes, and she longed for shade.

Gradually the landscape became even bleaker. The fields were now divided by narrow irrigation ditches of drying, cracking mud. Even the sky had changed, had taken on a coppery tone. The sun was a swollen, angry ball, flooding the flat, bare land all around her with an orange light that was almost tangible. On impulse, Lyndsay drew the car, bumping and rattling, up onto the narrow verge and switched off the engine.

The silence was shocking. It pressed against her ears. Lyndsay got out of the car and pushed her sunglasses up onto her head. Wearily she rubbed the bridge of her nose, squinting against the glare. The sound of the car door clicking shut was as loud and sharp as a rifle shot. There was no other sound at all. Shading her eyes with her hand, she scanned the empty, cloudless sky. There was no breeze to ruffle her hair. She walked a few yards from the car, to a pontoon-like bridge which crossed the ditch, into a field. If night fell, she suddenly found herself thinking, there would be no homing wink of light to guide her. She could not see a single habitation. Her mouth was dry and she wished that she had thought to buy a can of Coke somewhere. She hurried back to the car. The silence and emptiness of this place were giving her the jitters. If only she had a radio. She would have given a lot just to hear another voice. She climbed quickly back into the car and started the engine. Its familiar sound made her feel better at once.

It was necessary now to veer north on rough roads which were constantly intersecting and twisting between tall hedges. They were little more than tracks with metaled surfaces, so narrow that had she met any oncoming traffic she would have had to pull up into the hedge and stop in order to let another car pass. She was grateful that there was no other traffic, but she drove cautiously, peering ahead along the twisting lane.

After the openness of the landscape through which she had passed, the tall hedges made her feel confined. She knew that behind them similar flat fields stretched away, but the sudden limitation of visibility made her feel unpleasantly enclosed. The countryside had changed in another way, too. It had become more rolling. The car rose and dipped up a series of small hills. Gradually, she was climbing. Ahead of her, drawing closer at each twist and turn, was a marked promontory on top of which were three oaks, silhouetted against the sky. This must be a high point, she realized, a landmark from which one could see for miles. The road climbed steadily toward these trees and she decided to halt there and check her position.

The trees marked not only the highest point for miles, but a blind crossroad. They actually stood back from the road, separated from it by a patch of grass, but the road she traveled twisted awkwardly so that they seemed, for a second, to block it. To the right, the road fell away to reappear below between cultivated fields. Her view to the left was obscured by the hedge. She tapped the horn, and inched the car forward. The road veered left and then immediately descended a steep hill, much steeper and shorter than the one she had climbed. Lyndsay pulled the car over to the right and stopped by the grass beneath the three trees. It was the only safe place to park, without risk of blocking the traffic from all directions.

Taking the map with her, Lyndsay stepped onto the grass. Walking to the front of the car she could see that the road dropped steeply and disappeared into a tunnel of green. She was looking into a sort of valley or dell, on the other side of which the land rose again to form a bleak ridge and plateau. Her map indicated that Ratchets lay down there, in the dell, and her pulse quickened. She narrowed her eyes and, with excitement, saw a hazy wisp of smoke rising from the trees.

She was drawn to the shade offered by the oaks. Their trunks were black against the sky, but beyond them was an open field dropping down toward the village. She took off her sunglasses and walked toward the trees, noticing a splash of white across one trunk and a large area blacker than shadow on the ground. The grass on which she stood was greener than any she had seen all day, which made her curious about the black patch. It was beneath the largest oak, the one closest to the road. As she drew nearer she could see at once that it was burned. A fine black dust covered her shoes, clung to the mesh of her stockings. The earth was charred as though some-one had used a flamethrower on it. She moved around the area, keeping to the living grass. She realized then that the trunk of the oak was also charred, except for the livid white scar in the wood. Something had torn into the tree, ripping the bark from the wood. Her foot crunched on shards and slivers of glass.

She felt sick and weak with a knowledge she wanted to thrust away from her. Yet she had wanted evidence, something verifiable. She looked around her again. The scar on the tree, the burned grass, the broken glass—all were consistent with a car having crashed into

21

the tree and bursting into flames. She could see it, a gigantic bonfire, blazing in the night. A great *whoomph* as the tank exploded, flames leaping upward. She lifted her face and saw the singed branches, the crisp, dangling black leaves. It would rain ashes in the next wind, she thought, turning her face away. A car coming along the very road she had traveled, accelerating when it should have slowed for the bend, swerving perhaps to avoid an unseen, approaching car, racing out of control headlong into the tree. The fire would have been quick and fierce. A driver, strapped safely and sensibly into the seat, would stand no chance.

Michael had always been very particular about fastening his seat belt.

Lyndsay leaned against the burned tree.

Below, in the village, an elderly woman sat rigid in her chair. Her eyes were closed and she appeared to be listening intently to some distant sound. Her fingers made little flicks of movement on the arms of the chair. Her lips moved soundlessly.

Across the room, a girl watched her with a mixture of awe and fear. She held her breath, as though to aid the woman in her concentration. A large, black dog, curled before the fireplace, suddenly lifted its head and looked at the woman.

The room smelled strongly of herbs. Bunches of them hung on the beams to dry, like sad Christmas decorations. Suddenly they seemed to rustle together, blown by some wind.

The woman let out a long, almost painful sigh.

"She's here."

Her words were part of the sigh. The dog whimpered, rose, and pressed against the woman's legs. Automatically she reached down to curl her fingers in his thick, shaggy coat. The girl, as though released from a spell, moved toward the tiny window which was clogged by potted plants, some of which had fastened tendrils to the old brass curtain rail and grown along the beams.

"The Mistress," the woman hissed.

The girl turned back toward her, startled and afraid. The woman relaxed, opened her eyes.

"You'll be safe now, Emelye," she said, turning her bright, piercing gaze on the girl. Emelye shook her head. She wanted no part of it. "Is Bart coming?" the old woman asked.

The girl peered through the plants, out into the garden.

"Can't see him," she said.

"Then you tell him, when he comes, that she's arrived." Slowly, with obviously stiff joints, the old woman stood up. "D'you mind me, Emelye?"

"Yes."

"Don't you forget, now."

"Where you going?" Emelye asked in a softer voice, her large eyes imploring the woman for something unspoken.

A smile broke on the old woman's face. She was tall and straight-backed. Once she had been handsome, perhaps even beautiful, and her smile proclaimed what once she had been.

"Don't you fret yourself," she said gently. "You just do as I say. I'm only going to see her safely home."

A kind of sob escaped the girl. She turned away again, refusing the old woman's comfort. Watching the girl, she made a dismissive sound, a sort of growl of annoyance and impatience. Emelye wanted to beg her to stay. She was afraid of Bart, to be alone with him. But it was too late. Without even looking, she knew that the old woman was gone. Through the crowded window, she watched the dog trot down the path and into the village street.

Lyndsay had no idea how long she rested against the tree, not crying but fighting the loss of all hope. She did not know that it had been Michael's car that had crashed here. The thought had no conviction. This crossroad was a deathtrap. Something besides the need to take her bearings had made her stop here, she thought wildly. She had been drawn to this place, and she hated it. She hoped the grass would never grow again. She would have liked to tear the trees down with her bare hands, to make of it a memorial as terrifying and cold as her grief.

She shivered suddenly, as though an unfelt wind had sprung up. She moved away from the tree. Her hands and dress were stained with black smears of charcoal. She was not thinking properly. She wanted to lie down and weep. But slowly something penetrated her grief, something that made her uncomfortable. It was as if someone were watching her. She looked surreptitiously left and right, but there was no one. Yet the feeling grew to a certainty. Someone was watching her. She felt panic rising in her. She knew it was ridicu-

23

lous, that she had only to turn round and look for herself, but at the same time she felt a strong desire to scream.

It stood behind her, in the sunlight. She let out a cry of relief. It regarded her with an almost quizzical expression. It was just a dog. A big, black, curly-coated dog, panting from the heat and watching her. At the sound of her voice, her involuntary step toward it, the dog wagged its tail in greeting.

"Hello, boy," she said, walking toward the dog, her hand held out. Its tail lashed with pleasure. Impulsively, Lyndsay squatted down and stroked its big, shaggy head. A moment ago she had been frightened out of her mind and now this friendly, welcoming animal seemed to offer her comfort. He was alive and real. The dog pressed against her, wriggling. Lyndsay gave way to tears, but they were tears of release and relief. The dog whined and pushed harder against her. She threw her arms around his neck and pressed her face to the silky coat.

"It's okay" she whispered. "I'm okay."

High on the ridge, which helped to enclose Ratchets in its valley, a man stood staring across toward the oaks. They appeared as a green smudge against the sky, but he looked at them intently, as though he could make out every leaf. He knew that the old woman would be expecting him, but he had no intention of going to her. She would understand by his absence that the arrival of this foreign woman altered nothing. It was always in this oblique, unspoken way that he dealt with his grandmother. He could not, powerful though he was, risk an open battle with her. They both knew that. They needed each other and, in time, the ties of blood would prevail. The arrival of Michael Dolben's wife would not upset his plans. She was necessary to them, he admitted that, but the old woman must not think that her presence altered anything. His deliberate absence was a warning. In her excitement the old woman might get carried away, might think that it was possible to go back. His lips twitched into a sneer as he thought this, but his eyes remained, narrowed and steady, on the oaks. He had outfaced her before and he would again, if necessary. There was no use in having the power if you didn't use it. Soon now they would all know that he had it and then . . .

His eyes moved from the oaks. The roof of a car, descending the hill, had suddenly caught the sun and flashed a signal to him. She was on her way. He looked around him, at the village below and the great fields which stretched behind him. It seemed changed to him: no longer the land he had known and loved all his life, but a setting for what he had planned so long to achieve. The woman's arrival was the last piece in the pattern. The missing piece. Now all was complete, and his body quivered with the need for action. He felt restless, hungry. In these moods, there was only one person who could console him. His eye picked out her cottage at once. She'd be expecting him, too, he thought. She'd know. He left the ridge and with long, loping strides made for the back door of the cottage. Let them welcome the Mistress. His turn would come later.

Comforted by the dog, Lyndsay had climbed wearily back into the car and driven down the hill. It was time to face up to the fact that she was in shock, she told herself. The sooner she located Michael's brother the better.

At the foot of the hill, she found herself in a narrow avenue of trees. Set among them was a sign: RATCHETS. As the trees thinned, she saw cottages of old stone with quaintly tiled roofs. The tiles were curved, like waves. Green and yellow moss grew on them in vivid patches. She slowed the car as she approached a fork in the road. Ahead of her lay a triangle of grass which ended in a sort of copse beside a high wall. The right-hand fork was clearly marked NO THROUGH ROAD. This must be the village green, she supposed, looking at a couple of ancient, wooden benches. But there was no one there to give her directions. Which way should she go? The marked road was flanked by cottages that in no way suggested the Big House that Michael had mentioned. She decided to take the other road.

The wall beyond the green joined this road and ran beside it. On the other side were trees. She slowed down again as the road made a tight curve, hugging the high wall. As she rounded the bend, she could see fields on her left and a track to her right. Beyond the track was a wide grass border, dotted with white stones and behind that the most extraordinary hedge she had ever seen. She braked hard. It must have taken years of work to shape the hedge, which represented a row of birds. Some upright and sharp-looking, watching the road, others poised for flight. The largest and most impressive of all had their wings fully spread, marking an entrance in the hedge. A white-painted wooden gate stood open between them. Lyndsay leaned forward as the sun gleamed on a brass plate screwed to the wood. She drove until she was able to read it, to read her own name.

DOLBEN HOUSE

A short, fan-shaped driveway of pale gravel led up to a low, plain house. In the evening sunlight, only the roof had any color. Like those in the village it was tiled and in the sunshine was a bright, rusty red. Two wings of the house faced bluntly onto a lawn. These two wings were connected by a central portion which was set back so that together the three walls formed a sort of courtyard. The large front door was guarded by two ornamental boxtrees, clipped to resemble giant toadstools.

Lyndsay got out of the car and stared up at the house. It was not beautiful. It was too solid, too squat for that, and with the sun behind it seemed gloomy. What would she say? How introduce herself? She must look terrible. She brushed at the black smudges on her dress but that only made them worse. She was deliberately putting off the moment when she would have to face Michael's brother. It didn't matter what she looked like.

Two circular and uneven brick steps led up to the front door. Lyndsay, searching for some knocker or bellpush, stumbled on them and fell against the door. It swung open as she regained her balance. She could find neither knocker nor bell. She hesitated. It seemed rude just to march in.

"Hello?" she called, leaning in through the partly opened door. There was no reply. Surely someone would have heard the car? She called again. Still no one answered or came to the door. She stepped tentatively into a great, rectangular room. There was a wooden staircase on her right, leading to a gallery which ran along the back wall of the central wing. Beyond the gallery were three large, arched windows through which the evening sunlight streamed, almost blinding her. The effect of this light, falling in long rays and separated by areas of deep shadow, reminded her of a church or a cathedral. The room was overpowering. She looked away from the light at a round table which stood to her left. It held a bowl of roses whose heavy heads drooped toward the polished wood.

"Hello?" she called a second time. "Is anyone home?" Her voice seemed to get lost in the vastness of the room. Maybe there was another door, she thought, round the back somewhere. She turned to go out again when she heard a noise. Squinting up into the light she could see nothing at first. She heard a step, the rattle of a door latch. She put up a hand to shade her eyes and made out a figure, a black silhouette of a man, moving slowly along the gallery. Because of the blazing windows, he seemed to disappear and then become visible again in the next beam of light. Lyndsay followed him with her eyes. There was something familiar about him, even though she could not properly see him. He began to descend the stairs. He was carrying something, she saw. Something white which held his attention. It was a great sheaf of lilies. In the shadows which cloaked the staircase, their whiteness, against his dark clothes, appeared as strong as the sunlight. Lyndsay could not move or speak. She stared at the flowers, knowing what they meant. Their hard, yellow, pollen-laden spikes jutted bluntly from the curled white petals. Then she smelled them. The scent was sickly. The man stopped suddenly, and she realized that he must have seen her. His face was indistinct in the shadows. She took a step forward.

"Michael?" she said in a hesitant whisper. Then, with growing certainty, she repeated his name, louder. *"Michael!"*

Her foot hit the first tread of the stairs. Something snapped in her head. The stairs rose up to meet her and yet she seemed to be falling, spinning in slow motion. She flung out her right arm. She felt pain and could smell the awful, funereal lilies as everything became black and silent.

CHAPTER TWO

There was a whirling pattern of black and white, of light and dark. It revolved so fast it made her head ache. Gradually the pattern slowed, settled, resolved itself into a face. She shut her eyes tight. She did not want to see. The face hung over her. She was lying down. On a bed. She felt safe. She opened her eyes. The face swam above her, pale and featureless. Hands raised her, supported her back. She did not want to sit up, but the hands were too strong for her. Her headache was worse. A glass was held to her lips. She shook her head. A voice, gentle and consoling, urged her to drink. The liquid was sweet and sticky. She drank it because she wanted to lie down, to hide in the blackness where grief and fear could not reach her. The hands eased her down again. The pillow beneath her head was soft and welcoming. Voices sounded around her as though many people were withdrawing or assembling. She slept.

She was walking with the dog, happy to be with him. He led her into a dark place, like a tunnel. Then, with the peculiar logic of a dream, she was in a vast, lighted place, like a church or a cathedral. There was no sign of the dog. Instead, there were many faces. These faces seemed unaware of her. She was lying down again, on something cold and hard. She shivered and realized that she was naked. Vainly, she tried to cover herself, but there were no sheets or blankets to hide her nakedness.

Everything was very quiet. The light seemed to have dimmed or faded. She heard a rustling sound, as of silken garments. Twisting her head to see, to find the source of this noise, she found that she was restricted in some way. A man's voice spoke, intoning, but still she could not see. The voice droned on and became almost soothing in its rhythm and certainty. When it stopped, a great, collective sigh rose and became part of a chill wind. She felt it move across her unprotected body.

The light had gone entirely and from the darkness a dog bayed. Voices murmured. The dog cried again. Other dogs took up the cry. She heard the snuffling and panting of many excited dogs. An order was shouted and the baying became louder, hurting her head. She wanted to block out the sound, but could not raise her hands. Then the sound of the crying dogs began to fade as though they had taken off somewhere. Very slowly a light came toward her through the darkness. It was carried by a man, and she tried, desperately, to scream.

Her right wrist was bandaged. A heavily shaded lamp cast a pool of light onto the bed. Her bare, pale arm lay in this light. Tentatively, she flexed her fingers. There was a sharp increase in the rhythm of the pain, but it quickly subsided when she relaxed them. Outside the pool of light, the room lay in deep shadow. She could make out no details. Using her left hand to raise herself up in the bed, she discovered that she was naked and, with a start of surprise, that she was not alone. In the shadows, to the left of the bed, a figure rose from a chair. Lyndsay snatched up the single sheet which lay over her and covered her breasts.

"My dear . . ." The voice was low and warm. It belonged to a tall, full-figured woman who, sensing Lyndsay's alarm, stopped some feet from the bed. She wore a pale gray dress with long sleeves and a high neck. It was completely without adornment and for a moment Lyndsay thought that it might be the uniform of a nurse. The high neck accentuated the woman's tallness, while the soft material clung to her breasts and hips. The effect was both chaste and curiously sensual.

"How are you feeling now?"

Her face was large, round, and pale. Her blond, almost white hair was drawn down sleekly over her ears and caught behind on the nape of her neck. Her eyes were startlingly pale, almost the color of her dress. She was a monochrome woman, almost ghostly, yet her voice was warm and reassuring.

"I'm sorry," she said, her eyes flicking to Lyndsay's bare shoulder. "Your bags were locked. I didn't want to leave you to fetch a nightdress of my own. I thought you'd be more comfortable . . . like that."

"Yes." Lyndsay agreed, swallowing. "Thank you. It was just a shock."

"Of course. May I?" With another darting, sidelong glance, she indicated a spot on the bed, beside Lyndsay.

"Oh excuse me. Please." She drew her legs out of the way and the woman sat down. Lyndsay crawled farther under the covers and pulled the sheet up to her chin.

"You must be wondering who I am, where you are," the woman said. "You're perfectly safe, you know. What do you remember?"

Lyndsay frowned, trying to recall exactly. The face hanging over her. This face? And before that . . .

"I remember arriving. This *is* Dolben House?"

"Yes." The woman smiled reassuringly.

"And then I guess I passed out." She did not want to mention Michael, for surely it could not have been he. And again in the dream, she had thought, the man bearing the light, coming toward her. She turned her head restlessly on the pillow.

"I'm afraid you've had a terrible shock. But you're safe here, at Dolben House. I'm Penelope Clare."

The name meant nothing to Lyndsay and the fact must have shown on her face, for the woman said, almost to herself, and in an irritated tone: "Michael was always hopeless about the family. I'm his cousin. Which means that we're cousins, too, I suppose."

"Then you know who I am?" Lyndsay said quickly.

"Of course. You're Lyndsay. Michael's American wife."

Tears sprang suddenly to her eyes. She did not want to correct this statement. On the contrary, she wanted to be reassured, to bask in the comfort it gave her.

"His wife?" she whispered. "Then he's . . ."

"Sorry." Penelope Clare looked away, embarrassed.

"It's true then?"

She nodded sadly. "I'm so sorry."

"Downstairs I thought . . . I could have sworn . . ."

"That was Michael's brother, Patrick. We're all so used to the resemblance we forget how startling it can be to strangers."

30

So it was true. It did not hurt as much as she had feared. Because she had been prepared, had known from the moment she had stopped by the oaks.

"On my way here," she said, closing her eyes tight against the tears, "I passed a place, up the hill . . . I thought . . . I mean it looked . . ."

"Yes. That's where it happened. If we had known you were coming we would have met you, made sure that none of this happened."

"I didn't have a telephone number or anything. I just felt I had to get here."

"Of course."

"I mean I didn't even know his . . . Patrick's name."

Penelope Clare sighed.

"I suppose," she said carefully, "you didn't even know they were twins."

"No," Lyndsay shook her head. "No I didn't know that. Michael hardly told me anything."

"I feared something like this might happen. Of course we knew you would come, but we had no idea when. I came over here to see if there was any news of you. You must think we're terribly clumsy. My dear, I'm so sorry." She reached out and touched Lyndsay's shoulder gently. Lyndsay covered her hand with her own, grasping it. Penelope smiled.

"You don't live here, then?" Lyndsay asked.

"No, I live at the other end of the village."

"Oh," Lyndsay said vaguely. The firm but gentle pressure of the woman's hand helped. She told herself that she had to face it now. It would be better to hear it from this sympathetic woman. "Please," she said, "tell me how it happened."

"Wouldn't you rather wait? You must be . . ."

"No. Please, I need to know."

Penelope Clare watched her for a moment, considering. She drew her hand away.

"Very well. Actually, there's very little to tell. Do you mind if I smoke?"

"No. Go ahead."

Her dress rustled silkily as she stood up and moved back to the chair in which she had been sitting. Lyndsay saw that her pale hair hung loosely down her back from a single silver clasp. From the arm of the chair she took a pack of cigarettes and a lighter and carried them back to the bed. She offered the opened pack to Lyndsay, who shook her head. When her cigarette was lit, Penelope began to speak, slowly and hesitantly, as though choosing her words with care.

"We hadn't seen Michael for ages. You may have gathered that he wasn't very good about keeping in touch." She laughed as though this were a charming failing, but Lyndsay felt that she resented Michael's neglect of them. "So, naturally, we were surprised when he wrote to Patrick and said that he was married." She paused, looking at Lyndsay to see what effect her words were having on her. "Anyway, he said that he was coming here. He didn't give a precise date, of course, but he *did* say when you were arriving, so we had a rough idea of when to expect him. He wanted to talk business with Patrick. I really don't know the details," she said tiredly, brushing a strand of hair from her forehead. "He told us about you, naturally." Penelope smiled rather wanly. "He was on his way here when it happened. Oh he should have started earlier in the day," she burst out angrily. Her face colored and she drew deeply on her cigarette. It seemed to calm her. "And that's all, really. There were no witnesses, nothing. Old Jacob Poole heard the crash. His cottage is at the bottom of the hill. The tank must have exploded at once." She was talking rapidly now, as though anxious to get it over and avoid any details that were too painful. "There was nothing anyone could do. Fortunately Jacob managed to get the car's number. Even then we couldn't be sure that it was Michael until the police had checked. Everything was destroyed, you see."

Lyndsay felt the tears seep out from under her closed lids. She was grateful to Penelope for her silence, for not trying to comfort her. When at last she was able to turn her damp face toward Penelope, she was quietly stubbing out her cigarette.

"I thought when I stopped there maybe he'd swerved to avoid something. You can't see any oncoming traffic."

"Possibly." Penelope sounded tired again. "If he did, the other car didn't stop. Jacob Poole didn't mention hearing one. But then he wouldn't, unless it came through the village. And even then . . ." She shrugged.

Lyndsay closed her eyes again. It was an anticlimax. Now she realized that she had been hoping for some rational explanation, something that would justify her sense of waste and loss. But accidents are not rational, cannot always be explained.

"I wish there was something I could say to help you," Penelope said sadly.

"You have. Thank you."

"I feel . . ."

"Please. You've been very kind."

"We should have met so happily," she said, sitting down again and taking Lyndsay's hand in both of hers. "We were all looking forward to meeting you so much. Right from the moment Michael's letter arrived. I'm sorry. I'm putting this clumsily. What I mean to say is that—"

"I loved him very much. I still do," Lyndsay interrupted. "Being with people who knew and loved him will help me more than anything. Please believe that."

"I'm glad," Penelope said. "I would like us to be friends."

"I feel we are already," Lyndsay replied, and meant it.

Penelope patted her hand and stood up. Lyndsay reached out to her. "Don't go."

"You really ought to rest now. You must be absolutely exhausted."

"No. I'm fine now, really." She tried to sit up, using her right hand. She winced with pain. At once Penelope eased her back onto the pillows. "How did I . . . ?" She held up her bandaged wrist.

"When you fainted. Patrick said it took all your weight. I think it's only a sprain, so I bandaged it, but in the morning, if it's not easier, we'll get Mother Poole to have a look at it."

"I feel such a fool causing all this trouble. I never fainted in my life before."

"You had cause," Penelope said simply. "Don't think any more about it. I'll be over first thing to look at your wrist."

"What about Patrick?" Lyndsay asked, still anxious to keep Penelope with her.

"We thought you should rest first. It's not that he doesn't want to see you. It was a shock for him, too."

"Of course. I guess you're right. Is it very late?"

"Nearly two."

"You must be worn out. I'm sorry."

"I was going to suggest a sleeping pill. Perfectly harmless, but they do help."

"There's just one other thing," Lyndsay said.

"Yes?" Penelope glanced at her as she shook two pills from a small brown bottle into her palm.

"Michael. Is he . . . ?"

"Not here."

"Then where?"

"In the old chancel. You can see him tomorrow. Now please, for your own sake . . ."

"So soon?" She felt alarmed. It seemed wrong, somehow.

"Patrick will explain everything. Please take these now."

"But I don't understand. Wouldn't there have to be an inquiry or something?"

"Everything's been taken care of. There was a great deal of damage."

Lyndsay had not thought of that, and now it was too horrible to bear. She took the pills from Penelope's outstretched hand and put them in her mouth.

"Some water?"

She drank from the glass, spluttering a little. "I'll stay until you fall asleep. Would you like me to get you something to wear?"

Lyndsay shook her head. Penelope moved back to her chair, lit another cigarette. Lyndsay tried not to think about the coffin, what was inside it. What did Penelope mean, "the old chancel"? She turned her head, or tried to, to ask her to explain, but her head felt as though it were drifting off somewhere apart from her body. She tried again and again to frame the question, but the effort was too much for her and the blank gaps between each attempt became longer and longer until she thought she must be asleep.

"Lyndsay?" Penelope Clare stood close to the bed. She repeated the name in her low voice, but there was no response. The slight jerking, flickering movements of her eyes beneath pale lids suggested that Lyndsay was dreaming. Penelope did not envy her those dreams, nor other things that were, she knew, unavoidable. It made her shudder even to think of them. Briskly, she dropped her cigarettes and lighter into her handbag and reached for the switch on the bedside lamp. There were gray marks under Lyndsay's closed eyes. Like bruises. She was very pretty. As Michael had said she was. If only . . . With a sharp click, Penelope extinguished the light and with it the vain, disloyal thoughts that had sprung into her mind. Such thoughts *were* disloyal. She was a Clare and her first loyalty, her best, must always be to the Ways.

In spite of the dark, Penelope walked confidently to the door. Like most of the doors in Dolben House, it fastened with a latch. Years of practice made Penelope able to open and close the door without letting the latch rattle. Then, as she had been bidden, she turned the large key in the lock and walked through the archway to the gallery.

The three great hall windows, each set in a deep stone embrasure, now opened onto thick summer darkness, but the brilliant chandelier in the gallery seemed to her pale eyes almost as bright as the sun itself. It lit her way down the uncarpeted stairs into the hall. As she reached the bottom, Patrick Dolben rose anxiously from his chair. His face was drawn and, as she came closer to him, the black fleck in the iris of his left eye was, she saw, larger than usual. It always was when he worried. It hurt Penelope to see him so anxious and she deliberately avoided his eyes. Her concern could not help him. She knew that.

"How is she?"

Penelope did not answer at once. She went to the large settee beneath the gallery and lit a cigarette. Patrick watched her nervously.

"Well?" he prompted.

She crossed her long legs and stared at him. Every muscle in his body seemed tensed, ready to snap.

"She's asleep now. I gave her two pills."

"Thank God," he said, and his shoulders relaxed a little.

"You'll have to see her in the morning," she reminded him.

"I'm well aware of that," he snapped. His voice had always been higher and lighter than his brother's and now it sounded petulant, like a schoolboy's. It often did, Penelope reflected, especially when he spoke to her. He moved around the end of the settee to a carved cupboard standing against the wall. Penelope heard the clink of glasses and bottles. "Do you want something?" he asked.

"No. Thank you."

Nursing a large whiskey, Patrick sat down in an armchair. Penelope stared at the floor.

"She passed the oaks, of course, and she guessed."

"It couldn't be avoided," he said defensively.

"I know. She asked me about it. She'll want to see the . . . coffin tomorrow."

He said nothing.

"Michael hadn't even told her that you were twins."

He laughed sharply, without warmth or humor.

"No, he wouldn't."

"She'll think it . . . odd."

35

"So? I'll tell her something," he said, a note of challenge in his voice.

"Oh Patrick . . ." she said sadly, "does it really have to be like this?" She looked at him, prepared to beg if necessary. His face, as it often did, seemed to set like a stone against her. It was as though the flesh and skin hardened into a shell.

"You know it does," he said in a voice that matched his expression. "You saw, tonight. What is there to discuss now?"

Penelope knew that he was right, but his words held no comfort for her.

"I like her," she said. "I feel so . . . sorry for her. It would be easy just to . . ."

"And that would be wrong," he said sharply.

She did not argue. She still believed that she could reach him, change him, give him a different kind of courage—if only he would let her. Even the unlikelihood of that did not defeat her. It was this complete rejection of her, the sudden coldness of his voice, the tight, held-in stance of his body that sapped her strength and made her feel hopeless. She stood and put out her cigarette. She picked up her bag, ready to leave. Patrick watched her uncertainly.

"You'll come in the morning?" he asked. "Early?" He was afraid. In spite of his rejection, he needed her just now and was afraid that she would fail him.

"Yes," Penelope said.

"Only I think it would be better if you took up her breakfast. And I'd like you to be here when I speak to her."

If she were to refuse, as part of her wanted to, what, she wondered, would happen to him? Panic? Anger? Or would he simply crumble altogether?

"Don't you want Bart to be present also?" she asked levelly.

"Both of us, of course." He stood up as though to delay or persuade her. This sudden, desperate gesture of appeal was more painful to her than his coldness.

"I'll be here," she said, "but for her sake, not yours. And I think you should speak to her alone."

He looked confused, as if she had slapped him. She regretted her words at once, yet knew that if she took them back she would only be inviting another rejection.

"Good-night, Patrick," she said, and walked quickly to the big front door.

"In the morning," he called after her. "Don't forget."

Lyndsay found the dog again. She was relieved and happy to be with him. She ran toward him, holding out her hand. The dog threw back his head and bayed. The sound halted her. She looked wildly around, to discover what had disturbed him. He howled again, a plaintive but savage cry. She spoke to the dog, trying to comfort him, but he seemed to slink away into the darkness.

She heard a key turn in a lock. She was lying in some dark place. The sound was very loud. She was locked in. Why? Panic seized her. She began to move but her limbs seemed unable to respond properly, as though weighted down. Someone or something was watching her. She had to raise her head to see what it was. It was very important that she see. A black silhouette stood impassively watching her. Or waiting for her. She tried to speak, to move, but both were impossible. She was naked and somebody, a man, was standing, looking down at her.

Lyndsay woke with a start. She was sweating and the sheet lay wrinkled around her ankles. It was only a dream, she realized. She turned her head toward the window. The curtains had not been drawn and it was full daylight. Her head felt as though it had been stuffed with cotton wool, yet she knew at once where she was and what had brought her there. Michael's death was like a dull ache. She would have to face it every morning for the rest of her life. There had scarcely been time for her to get used to waking beside him. If only she had insisted on leaving her job, on coming with him.

Her throat was dry. The pills had given her something like a hangover. She supposed she must have slept very deeply. When she sat up, her head felt heavy and hurt, as though it had been bruised. Sitting up also reminded her of her injured wrist. She flexed and clenched her fingers experimentally. There was only a slight increase in pain. She gripped her good hand over the bandage and pressed. That didn't hurt. Probably it was only a sprain, as Penelope had said.

As she remembered Penelope, she felt instantly better. She was not alone now. Penelope understood how she felt. She looked toward the chair, a large, winged one covered in faded tapestry, where Penelope had sat. It stood in front of the window, facing the bed. The room was paneled in dark wood and was thickly carpeted.

Glancing about it for the first time by daylight, she saw that there were two doors. One of them, she thought, must lead to a bathroom.

The prospect of water to quench her thirst made her get out of the large, high bed. She draped the crumpled sheet around her body and went to the second door. It opened onto an old-fashioned bathroom. The mammoth tub stood on fancy claw feet and looked big enough to drown in. The toilet and washbasin were enclosed in paneling which made them look like a throne and a font, respectively. Cupping water in her hands, Lyndsay drank until she was breathless and her stomach protested. She had got the bandage wet and carefully unwound it. The wrist felt generally sore and was a little swollen, but she didn't think there was any serious damage. Even so, she had difficulty turning on the big, stiff bath taps and had to manage it clumsily with her left hand.

Leaving the bath to fill, she returned to the bedroom and went to the window. She looked down on the lawn and the sculptured hedge of birds beyond. Now that she was raised above the birds, they looked eccentric rather than menacing. She pushed the window wide open and leaned out. The morning smelled fresh, although it was already hot. The air made her head feel better. The view across still fields to a hazy wood was beautiful. She was tempted to linger, but the splash of water in the bathroom prompted her to find her keys and unlock her bags. She pulled out her housecoat and hurried back to the bathroom.

Immersed in the bath, water lapping her chin, she wondered what she was going to do. She would obviously have to stay here for the funeral, but after that . . . ? So much depended on Patrick. She supposed that she would now be involved in whatever business affairs had brought Michael here. Almost here, she corrected herself. There would be documents to sign, decisions to make. All that would sort itself out. What worried her was Patrick himself. What would he be like? What would his attitude be? Involuntarily, she shivered. She was dreading meeting him and that was ridiculous. She was prepared now for his startling resemblance to Michael. It was only because she had not expected it, had been so tired, that she had passed out. She felt embarrassed about that and yet it was crazy. After all, he was her closest relative in this country. That fact ought to comfort her and in a way it did. That and Penelope's kindness.

Wrapped in her housecoat, Lyndsay brushed her hair, looking at herself in the three-sided, dressing table mirror. The bath had made her feel much better, though she looked tired and drawn. She went to her cases and searched for something suitable to wear. She imagined that an old English family like the Dolbens would expect her to observe the traditional forms of mourning, so she pulled out a sleeveless black linen shift and laid it on the bed. It was the only dress she had that was appropriate for a widow.

Somewhere off in the distance a dog barked. It was a mournful sound. It startled Lyndsay and reminded her of the dog who had "met" her—there didn't seem to be any other word for it—when she arrived in the village. The dog she had dreamed about. Then she remembered the sensation of a man looking down at her, appraising her body. But she had not seen his features, did not know that he was appraising her. She just felt it.

Standing up, she told herself that she needed a cup of coffee. Quickly, she exchanged the housecoat for the black linen dress. She went to the door and set her hand on the latch. But what if she ran into Patrick? Well, he had no cause to faint at the sight of her, had he? She lifted the latch.

Just as she did so, she heard the sound of a car crunching on the gravel below. Releasing the latch, she hurried to the window and leaned out. Penelope Clare was getting out of a car, her pale hair shining in the sunlight.

"Hi. Good morning," Lyndsay called.

Startled, Penelope stopped in her tracks, staring up in alarm at the window. Surprised by this reaction, Lyndsay felt her smile fade.

"Stay where you are," Penelope called sharply. "I'll be right up."

Before Lyndsay could say anything, she had run into the house.

Penelope made a late breakfast for them both in the big, flagged kitchen, complaining as she did so about the unreliability of someone named Emelye Poole, who, Lyndsay gathered, came in to keep house for Patrick.

"The house," Penelope went on, "badly needs a woman's touch. You're bound to notice, I'm afraid. Emelye does her best, of course, when she's here, but she really isn't experienced enough—"

There was something brittle about Penelope's chatter, Lyndsay thought. She interrupted:

"Doesn't Patrick plan to get married?" A strange, almost be-reaved look clouded Penelope's face for a moment.

"No," she said, and added quickly, "The house is far too large for one girl to manage anyway. Patrick's so busy with the farm, he hardly notices, of course." She placed boiled eggs and toast in front of Lyndsay, who discovered that she had an appetite.

"Will he be long?" she asked. Penelope had already explained that Patrick had been needed in the fields and had thought it best to let her sleep.

"No. I've sent a message to him. You mustn't feel he's neglecting you," she said, "but there's so much to do right now."

"I guess it's just as well. To tell you the truth, Penelope, I'm rather scared of meeting him."

Penelope's spoon hovered in midair, as though Lyndsay had said something shocking. Her pale eyes widened but not, Lyndsay thought, with simple surprise or curiosity. There was something watchful about her expression.

"Why should you feel that?" she said, plunging her spoon too hard into the egg so that yolk spurted over the side of the shell. Lyndsay laughed.

"That's what I keep asking myself," she confessed. "I suppose because I was so shocked last night. You know, the mind sort of fastens onto things like that. It'll take a while, I guess, to forget it. It's stupid of me, I know."

"Oh really?" Penelope said in a way that indicated her lack of interest.

"And I feel embarrassed. I mean, fainting and everything. I can't imagine what he must think of me."

"He understands, of course. Patrick wouldn't think badly of you because of something like that." She sounded protective, even offended.

"I didn't mean to criticize," Lyndsay assured her, then frowned. There was no avoiding the fact that Penelope was different this morning, sort of on edge and jumpy.

"Look, I'm sorry. I'm aware I'm making too much of things. I just don't seem to be able to stop it."

"What 'things'?" Penelope asked, and Lyndsay wondered if she imagined the undertone of alarm in that warm, companionable voice.

"Oh I don't know." She set her elbows on the table, trying to marshal her thoughts. Penelope watched her attentively.

"For instance, I had a strange dream last night. It was all mixed up like dreams are, but the dog, it was odd how I knew the dog."

"What dog?" Penelope pushed her plate away and reached for her cigarettes.

"Oh I guess I didn't tell you last night," Lyndsay said. "When I stopped up there, where it happened, I met this dog." Penelope's eyes widened perceptibly. "A big black dog, old I guess, with a curly coat. Do you know who he belongs to?"

Penelope shook her head vaguely.

"No. It could be any dog."

"Well, anyway, I dreamed about it. It was very important to me to find the dog," Lyndsay said.

"I really don't see anything particularly odd about that," Penelope replied.

Silently, Lyndsay looked at her second egg. She wished she'd never mentioned the damned dog. She knew it didn't make sense unless she told Penelope about the man, the feeling she had had of a man looking at her body. And even that wasn't important. At least not compared to her certainty that Penelope had unlocked her door before coming in. She had heard the sound of a lock turning in her dream and it was that more than the unpleasant idea of being locked in that made her feel so uncomfortable. Maybe the man had been real. Maybe it hadn't been a dream at all. But she couldn't ask Penelope about it without seeming to accuse her.

"What else?" Penelope asked, getting up and gathering her dishes together.

She sounded as though she really wanted to know, but Lyndsay shook her head.

"Nothing else. I guess I just had a bad dream."

"You said 'things' disturbed you."

"Did I?" Lyndsay was deliberately vague.

"I wish you'd tell me," Penelope said, resting her hands on the table. "I only want to help."

"Do you?" Lyndsay asked, meeting her gray eyes.

Penelope's gaze wavered for a moment and then she said, "I hope you believe that I do."

"Yes. I know. I'm sorry I ever mentioned it. It was just a bad dream, that's all."

"I'm sure it was. You had a terrible shock yesterday. We mustn't forget that. And you must take things easy." Her face was a tight mask as she collected more dishes from the table and carried them to the sink. Lyndsay poured herself more coffee.

Penelope's concern reminded her of the desolation she had deliberately been holding at bay. All her feelings had been numbed. She couldn't really feel Michael's death at all. It was a fact. She understood it, but beyond that she felt hollow, as though with his dying something had died in her. Perhaps that was why she had wanted the dog so badly in her dream. The dog would comfort her somehow. And the man? She suppressed a shudder and turned toward Penelope. She needed a distraction from these thoughts.

"Here," she said, "let me help with those dishes."

"It's all right."

"I'd like to," Lyndsay said firmly and took a cloth from a rack in the corner.

Penelope was leaning against the sink, staring into the water.

"I'm sorry." she said, with obvious effort. "I didn't sleep at all well last night."

"I'm sorry," Lyndsay said, but could not resist thinking: Why? Did you have a guilty conscience about me? About locking me in and knowing that someone might let himself into my room?

For a while they worked in silence. Lyndsay knew that Penelope felt awkward with her. Because of the locked door? And that she suspected Lyndsay of knowing. Why not just come right out and say it, then? Something told her it would be a mistake. Anyway, she had to think about other things.

"There was something I wanted to ask you," she said. "I don't have anything suitable to wear to the funeral. Is there a town nearby where I can get something?"

Penelope turned her head and looked at her as though she were crazy.

"But my dear, there won't be time. The funeral is today."

"Today!" Lyndsay exclaimed.

"It's all been arranged," Penelope said, dismissing the subject. Lyndsay opened her mouth to protest, but Penelope said firmly, "Patrick will explain."

"Now," Penelope said briskly, drying her hands, "let me bandage that wrist again. It's still rather swollen."

The library was a small room at the back of the south wing. Its sole window faced due west, onto a jumble of farm buildings. Such light as there was seemed to be absorbed by the high shelves of books and the worn, leather-upholstered furniture. It reminded Lyndsay of the rare-books rooms she had seen in university and college libraries. Many of the spines were rubbed smooth, their titles indecipherable from much handling, yet the room had an abandoned, unused air.

It was here, after breakfast, that Lyndsay waited for Patrick Dolben. She was in no mood to browse among the books. Penelope Clare's attitude bothered her almost as much as her own uncertainty about what she had dreamed, what was real. Why would they want to lock her in? After all, they must have known that she would sleep, so there was no danger of her stumbling upon . . . what? Some family secret? She must have imagined it, but Penelope's attitude, her questioning, all seemed to confirm it. Still she couldn't help thinking that maybe her dream of a man standing, looking down at her, had not been a dream after all. It made her shiver, just thinking about it. And if it was real, then who? Patrick? The thought made her feel disloyal. She pushed it away. None of it mattered anyway, compared to this business of the funeral. Why had it all been arranged without her? How had it been possible to arrange it all so quickly? She ought to have been consulted. If she had stopped over in London, which she might very well have done, they'd have buried him without her.

She shivered again, this time because the room was chilly. It got no sun until evening. She chafed her arms lightly and looked around her. She felt intimidated, as though she had been summoned to this room to receive a reprimand. God, she thought, I really am letting my imagination run away with me. She moved to the big desk which faced the window. It bore only a scattering of farming pamphlets and magazines, a neat clip of accounts for farm requisites, and a solid ledger. She was about to open this when the latch on the door rattled. She turned around guiltily, her heart thumping.

Patrick Dolben was slight in build though as tall as Michael. Dressed in old work clothes, his trousers stuffed into pale green socks, he looked more like a farm employee than the master of the house. He formed a marked contrast to Michael with his neat, well-cut suits. The face he turned toward her, though, resembled Michael's in every way, except that it was leaner. The flesh seemed to be drawn tightly over bones which were, however, achingly familiar. He stared at her steadily for a moment, as though seeing her for the first time. She felt that he was assessing her. His look made her feel even more uncomfortable.

43

He came toward her, holding out his hand. Lyndsay offered her hand and he gripped it firmly.

"I'm so glad to meet you," he said rather huskily. "And so sorry . . ."

"Thank you," Lyndsay said, and pulled her hand free of his. For a moment she stared into his eyes. They seemed larger than Michael's, probably because of his drawn appearance, and a shade lighter in color. She noticed too the fleck of black, like a stain, on one iris.

"You're very welcome here. Please believe that. I only wish that . . ." He grasped her hand again.

She could think of nothing to say. She felt, for the first time, that someone else missed Michael as much as she did, and yet the feeling did not comfort her. His hand felt too small and shapely for a farmer. Even as she looked down at it, she was aware of his eyes moving over her, as though he wished to memorize every detail of her face and body.

"I'm sorry about last night," Lyndsay said at last.

"So am I, I assure you. Michael hadn't told you we were twins?"

"No. I can't think why."

He seemed about to say something in reply, but changed his mind. He moved past her to the desk and looked down at it. With a gesture that struck her as fastidious, he slightly altered the position of one pamphlet.

"I hope, anyway, that you were as comfortable as possible."

"Yes. Thank you. Apart from some pretty bad dreams."

He nodded as though that were only to be expected.

"And now, I'm afraid, we must talk about unpleasant things."

"I know," she said. "Penelope told me the funeral is to be today. I wanted to ask you . . ."

"Let's sit down, please." He touched her arm briefly, propelling her toward one of the chairs. She sat, feeling stiff and awkward, while he took a chair opposite her, his back to the light.

"Why is it all happening so quickly? I would have thought there would be an inquest or something."

He did not answer immediately. Again she was aware of his eyes regarding her as he lifted his hands and carefully placed the tips of his delicate fingers together.

"These things are often managed more quickly in the country," he explained. "Contrary to popular belief. We are very remote here. Consequently, officialdom is willing to cut a few corners."

"I don't understand."

He sighed.

"We are well known in these parts. We have lived here for generations. The name Dolben means a great deal. Shall we say it gets things done? I assure you that everything is in order. I have the death certificate here . . ." He began to rise from his chair.

"No," Lyndsay said quickly. She did not want to see it. "I'm not doubting . . . It's just that it's all taken me by surprise. I mean, supposing I hadn't got here . . ."

"We would not have buried him without you," he said quickly.

Lyndsay realized that she had offended him. "I'm sorry," she said, flushing.

"There is much," he said stiltedly, "that you will find unfamiliar about us. This is farming country, and remote. We have no other means of survival. The whole village lives off the land and we observe many of the old ways. We live in rhythm with the land. That is how we see it, although you may think we've got our priorities wrong. Nothing, not even something as terrible as Michael's death, can be allowed to interrupt our work. Besides, we don't dwell on death here. We do what is necessary and proper and, I think you'll agree, we do it with dignity; but we do it quickly. Does all this sound unfeeling to you? We believe that it is right and necessary to resume our normal lives as quickly as possible. The land demands our care. But it's not just a matter of our living. We believe that we should return our dead to the soil and get on with our lives."

He spoke with a sonorous certainty, as though delivering a lecture. His voice, though lighter in timbre than Michael's, had a similar authority when he spoke of these things.

"I see," Lyndsay said quietly.

"It is hard for me to see it from your point of view. Your life must have been so different. I've spent my life here. Tradition's in my blood. It's difficult for me to explain."

"Why did Michael leave?" she asked suddenly.

"Ah . . ." He made it sound as though she had touched on something of significance, but when he spoke again, it was almost casually. "Here there was no possibility of his doing the work that interested him. We were very different in many ways."

Lyndsay nodded.

"I am glad," he said quietly, "that he returned to us at the end. It is fitting."

Lyndsay wanted to protest at this. It sounded callous. But as Patrick stood up she realized that he got comfort from such things, from tradition, family life, the land. She found that she could envy him.

"I wish," she said tentatively, "that I could learn your ways. I see that they console you."

"Yes, they do," he agreed. "And I hope very much that you will learn all about us, become one of us. But for the moment, I must beg you to consider . . ."

"Yes?"

"About the funeral . . ."

Suddenly she wanted to have it over with. Perhaps that would help her to accept.

"You're right," she said. "There's no point in postponing it."

"The old ways may seem strange, but there is good sense in them. Human sense. We have learned from the wisdom and experience of our forefathers. It gives us all something to lean on, a sense of continuity."

Lyndsay nodded, agreeing. Patrick laid a hand on her shoulder.

"And now, you'd like to see Michael."

"Please. But, first, when is the funeral?"

"At sunset."

"Sunset!"

"Another tradition. Once it was peculiar to the Dolbens, but now most of the village observes it. You see, we don't believe that loss is to be celebrated. We don't parade our grief in the light of day. It's best done at the end of the day, in the privacy of darkness. But there is also a practical reason. We're no longer a separate parish. We have to fit in with the needs of other villages. Sunset happens to be convenient for Mr. Venables, our vicar, as well. He will be with us this evening."

"I see," Lyndsay said.

"You will understand," he promised. "You must trust us. I know it is all strange to you. But your life and customs are no doubt equally strange to me." He put his arm casually around her shoulders. "One hears such extraordinary things about America."

"It's really not as bad as all that," Lyndsay said defensively. She did not like him touching her.

"Then we must teach each other. Let me take you to Michael."

"We can take my car." Stepping into the bright morning, Lyndsay turned to where she had left her car. It was not there. Patrick stood on the steps, watching her.

"I took the liberty of having it returned," he said. "I hope you don't mind?"

"Returned? But how . . . ?" She did mind. It seemed a downright interference in her affairs. He might, at the very least, have asked her.

"I took advantage of a happy coincidence," Patrick said, sliding his hand smoothly under her elbow and leading her onto the lawn. "One of the farm trucks is being repaired in Corminster. We need it badly and by using your car I only had to spare one man for the trip." He steered her deftly around the north corner of the building. "The car rental agency has an office there. Otherwise," he repeated slowly, as though she had not grasped the point, "I would have had to send two men. One to drive the truck, the other to bring back the Land-Rover."

"Yes, I see," Lyndsay said impatiently. Did the needs of the farm take absolute priority over everything? And was she mad to feel trapped?

Beyond the lawn was a concrete yard, fronting a row of stables. An old, well-maintained Alvis was parked there, beside a battered truck.

"You do mind," Patrick said. His accusing tone startled Lyndsay. It was that of a young boy who had made some special effort to please, only to find that he had done something wrong.

"No. Not at all," she said, surprised into a lie. "It's just—"

"I thought it would help you, too," he interrupted, his voice almost whining. "I thought it would be one less thing for you to bother about. We have plenty of transport here. You're welcome to borrow . . ."

"Please," Lyndsay said, too sharply. "It doesn't matter. I was just surprised, that's all. Let's forget it, okay?"

His bottom lip quivered slightly as he looked at her. Lyndsay tried to smile. Silently, obviously offended, he opened the passenger door for her. As she got in, Lyndsay told herself that they were both on edge, that she was making too much of it all.

A concrete driveway led onto the rutted track Lyndsay had noted the night before. It, in turn, joined the road where the high wall ended. Patrick turned onto that road, hugging the tight curve of the wall. When the car reached the village green, Patrick took the fork marked NO THROUGH ROAD. This was obviously the main street of the village. Stone houses of varying size, but of similar, plain shapes, surrounded by gardens, were set back from the narrow road. All had the distinctive tiled roofs she had noticed before. A weathered sign indicated that one of these cottages served as a general store. Old crates of vegetables stood outside and a group of black-shawled women turned to watch the car slide past. A little farther on, a row of terraced houses faced directly onto the pavement. A scarlet pillar-box stood outside one, with a sign on its top pointing to the post office.

Lyndsay registered all this with only part of her mind. She was trying to prepare herself for the ordeal to come. And she was still perturbed by Patrick's behavior. She wished now that she had not been so annoyed about the car, and yet she did not feel that it was up to her to apologize. Slowing the Alvis a little, Patrick drew her attention to a much larger house on their right.

"That's Clare House," he said, "where Penelope lives."

The house was approached by a stone archway which mirrored the shape of the front door. Roses nodded over the low stone wall which separated the house from the road.

"It's very handsome," Lyndsay said.

"The Clares used to be rectors of Ratchets and the house was the rectory. Look, you can see the old chancel from here."

She leaned forward. A steep, moss-covered path led from the roadside to a lych-gate. On top of a knoll, dominating this part of the village, was a truncated church, a rectangular chancel without a tower, surrounded by old and leaning gravestones.

Patrick parked the car beneath a clump of trees opposite, and Lyndsay let herself out. She stood for a moment, adjusting a white scarf over her head and squinting against the light at the strange church.

"Why is it like that?" she asked, thinking of the many spires and towers she had passed on her drive to Ratchets.

"It was unsafe. We had no choice but to have most of it demolished." He did not seem keen to pursue the subject, perhaps because he was still offended by her. She followed him up the path and through the gate. Standing among the leaning gravestones she heard, from somewhere behind the church, the doleful ring of spades on pebbly soil. It took her a moment to identify the sound. Gravediggers, preparing Michael's grave. She felt afraid and weak.

Patrick, who had drawn ahead of her, was unlocking the plain oak doors with a large key. He pushed them open and stood aside, looking at her. She forced herself to go on, her feet sinking into the cushionlike moss. Patrick cocked his head, listening to the sound which disturbed her. As she reached him, he said, "I'll tell them to stop. I expect you'd like to be alone in any case."

Lyndsay nodded. The rhythm of the spades, striking and wounding the earth, seemed relentless. Taking a deep breath, she stepped into the cool, shadowed chancel. The doors closed with a soft, echoing thud behind her.

She moved forward over old, uneven flags. A rough bier of planks and trestles had been constructed before the impoverished altar. On the bier lay a dark, highly polished coffin, the ornate handles and fittings of which caught and intensified what little light there was. It seemed to Lyndsay a dark, cold, and lonely place. She touched the smooth wood of the coffin and tilted her head to read the brass plate screwed to the lid.

Michael Simeon Dolben
Ratchets
1945 – 1976

This, then, was her reunion. For this she had traveled the Atlantic. Sobbing, she stretched her arms across the coffin, as though to hug the man inside.

When, some thirty minutes later, Lyndsay emerged from her vigil, Penelope Clare was waiting for her. Patrick had been needed in the fields. Penelope announced this as a fact which no one could question. Lyndsay's first thought was that he was avoiding her. She sensed, too, that in Ratchets women were accustomed to deferring to men. The land called them and they went. The women occupied themselves with their own domestic tasks.

She let Penelope lead her to Clare House. She thought that all these traditions, this living in rhythm with the land, would have irritated Michael. She could not help saying so to Penelope.

"Perhaps," she agreed reluctantly. "But then you are seeing us as an outsider. I imagine there are many villages in England where time would seem to you to have stood still. Possibly it's a little more exaggerated here. For one thing we're very remote, and for another, the Dolbens and the Clares founded Ratchets. I suppose it is more of a community than most." She looked at Lyndsay with an amused, quizzical expression. She seemed more relaxed than she had been earlier. "Do we seem very strange to you?"

"I don't know. Yes and no. Patrick made me feel that there is something sustaining about your way of doing things. But sometimes they seem . . . harsh. Tell me more about the village. How was it founded?"

"Nobody knows for sure," Penelope said. Her warm voice, the scent of roses from the garden, seemed as timeless as the story she told. The Dolbens and the Clares had never been able to agree who had settled there first. During the eighteenth century, the issue had caused a bitter feud, lasting two generations. The quarrel had been settled eventually, in the old way, by intermarriage. Now almost everyone agrees the land had first come to a Dolben, as a reward for service in the Crusades. But the Clares had certainly come to Ratchets with them. They were religious men, who had established the church here and had remained associated with it for centuries. The Lords Temporal and Spiritual, then, had been represented by the Dolbens and the Clares. They had tilled the land and built the village. They had watched over the souls of their dependents, chief among whom were the Pooles, who claimed to have accompanied the first Dolbens to Ratchets.

"The Pooles are very proud," Penelope said. "I suppose we all are. We still own the village, you see. All the land here is ours or Patrick's. The Pooles have been given a field here and there over the years, of course, but mostly they work for us, as they've always done. They depend on us and we depend on them."

So it had gone on, a community kept together by a common dependence on the land and intermarriage.

"We're nearly all related to one another," Penelope laughed. "Though nobody bothers about it much. But if you go back far enough, you'll find we're all from the same stock, almost one blood. And each generation passes on to the next the traditions and customs they have learned from their fathers and grandfathers."

"What about your family?" Lyndsay asked. "Are you the last of a line?"

"Heavens, no. There's my brother. Damon. You'll meet him to-

50

night. And we've many cousins, aunts, and uncles scattered around the village."

"I didn't know you had a brother. I suppose he's out in the fields, too?"

"Of course."

"Sorry. I can't get used to this constant devotion to the land."

Penelope's face clouded as it had earlier in the day. Once again, Lyndsay realized she had given offense without meaning to.

"What about your parents?" she asked, anxious to change the subject.

"Dead," Penelope answered flatly, lighting a cigarette.

"I'm sorry. Like Michael's. How odd."

"Not really. Ratchets has its disadvantages. You're seeing it at its best, and in an unusually dry summer. Haven't you noticed how green it is, compared even to places quite nearby?"

Penelope's question reminded her of the baked, dry landscape through which she had passed yesterday. She nodded.

"It's terribly damp here. In winter . . . well, it can be more like a mud bath than a village. You see, being in the dell, here, the land drains into the village. Something our founding forefathers didn't think about," she said wryly. "It's a terrible place for bronchitis and other chest complaints. Then, a few years ago, we had a terrible bout of influenza. There were many deaths that winter," she said sadly.

"But why on earth didn't your parents go away?" Obviously they could have afforded to, and nobody but a fool would remain by choice in an unsuitable climate.

"They were Clares," Penelope said simply. "This is our home. We never go away." Something in her tone reminded Lyndsay unpleasantly of the authority with which Patrick had spoken in the library.

"Michael went away," she pointed out.

"Michael," Penelope repeated softly. "Poor Michael. He was like Rupert Dolben."

"Who?"

"Oh every now and then a restless spirit comes among us. Rupert was one. Michael's great-grandfather. He went away. He wanted to change things, you see. You can't change things in Ratchets." She paused, as though weighing what she had just said. "He made quite a name for himself. He did a lot to improve factory conditions in the

51

Liverpool area. Michael always favored him, or so they said. You don't mind my talking about him?"

"No," Lyndsay said. It helped.

"Like Rupert, Michael went away. It does happen you see. And I'm glad that he did," she said, suddenly smiling. "I'm glad that he met you and that you are here among us. You will get used to us."

"I know," Lyndsay said.

Penelope continued to smile, as though something had been settled.

"Well," she resumed, "now you know all about us, you must tell me about you."

"There's not much to tell," Lyndsay shrugged. "My parents are—" She stopped suddenly, remembering. "Oh my God! They don't know."

"Know?"

"About Michael. Listen, Penelope, can I use your phone? I promised to cable them as soon as I arrived, but it went right out of my head. I remembered this morning but . . ."

Penelope was quick to see the anxiety and rising panic in Lyndsay, and she immediately took charge. Together they composed a cablegram which, at Penelope's quiet insistence, made no specific mention of Michael's death. Such news, she persuaded Lyndsay, would be too great a shock in the terse shorthand of a cable. Lyndsay would write a letter and explain everything properly. She agreed, and allowed herself to be introduced to the idiosyncrasies of the local telephone system. Before any connection could be made, the local operator had to be roused. She would then connect the caller with Corminster, from where, hopefully, the world might be reached. Cloris Poole was the local operator and sometimes her other duties, which included those of village postmistress, caused a delay in contacting her. But at last it was done and the cablegram dictated. This was a novel event for Cloris, who refused to be hurried.

Then Lyndsay remembered Mrs. Abernathy.

"I didn't know you had friends in London," Penelope said at once.

"She's not really a friend. Just someone I met on the plane coming over. She was very kind to me. I promised to call her. I really should. I have the number of her hotel here somewhere."

Again Penelope managed it all, while Lyndsay searched her bag for the slip of paper. Minutes later Lyndsay spoke over a crackling line to the hotel. They regretted that no one of that name was registered with them. Lyndsay hung up.

"Maybe she switched hotels," she said worriedly, and leaned back wearily in her chair.

"Why don't you rest in my room and I'll run you back to Dolben House in plenty of time for the funeral."

Mention of the funeral sapped any will Lyndsay might have had to protest. She followed Penelope meekly upstairs and slipped off her black dress. Gratefully, she stretched out on the soft bed.

"Would you like a pill?" Penelope asked.

"No thank you. I'm fine."

"I've got some for you, by the way. Remind me to give them to you later."

"How did you manage that?" Lyndsay asked.

Penelope laughed and drew the counterpane up over Lyndsay. "Oh easily," she said. "I just went to see Mother Poole and asked for some of her dream-makers. They're made of an ancient herbal recipe that is known only to Mother Poole," she explained in a mocking voice.

"Mother Poole?" Lyndsay remembered hearing the name before.

"A real village character," Penelope explained, straightening the edge of the counterpane. "She's better than any doctor. You'll see. Now, get some rest."

Lyndsay already felt drowsy and when Penelope had gone, she turned onto her side. It was funny but she couldn't make them out. In some ways they were so kind, while in others . . . She just didn't know. Her feelings about Ratchets, Penelope, and Patrick seemed to seesaw all the time from one extreme to another. She thought bleakly of Michael. She could be certain what she felt about him.

Outside the window a bird suddenly burst into song, as though it wanted to charm her to sleep.

CHAPTER THREE

The sun hung low behind the house, in a sky that seemed to be on fire. Layers of pink, orange, and red as deep as blood painted the sky, promising good weather the following day. Patrick led Lyndsay out of the house. They turned toward the village. The sun etched their shadows like black companions on the road as they walked. Even beneath the high wall and its overtopping trees, the evening felt hot and airless. In her hands, held away from her body, Lyndsay carried a wreath of lilies. Their sweet scent rose in a cloud to her nostrils, adding to her sense of airlessness.

The lilies, like everything else, had been provided for her. She had at first protested when Patrick brought the wreath to her, explaining that she had planned to pick some roses to lay on his grave, since there was no time to order a proper wreath. But he had prevailed, insisting that the lilies were traditional: the death flower of the Dolbens. Any deviation from tradition would cause comment, perhaps even offend some of the older villagers who, he explained gravely, looked to the Dolbens to preserve the old ways. And she, he reminded her gently, was a Dolben now. It would grieve him if she were to create a bad impression through ignorance.

She did not have the emotional strength to argue. Besides, she had seen too many squabbles develop into family feuds over the details of burials, which ultimately mattered little. Such rows had always saddened her and she had sworn to avoid them. She had to accept that her modern, urban expectations were different from their ancient, rural way of organizing these things. She did not feel, in any case, being a stranger in their midst, that she had the right to challenge them.

She had found a pair of white cotton gloves, and allowed Patrick to drape her head and shoulders in a black lace shawl. "The Weeds," he called it. It had belonged to their mother. It, too, was traditional. Lyndsay, regarding herself in the mirror, had seen a mourning bride as she listened to Patrick's instructions about the ceremony.

They would proceed through the village on foot. They would be joined, silently and at a discreet distance, by the villagers. It was a mark of the greatest respect. The village people would join the procession directly from their homes, signifying that he who had died was held in sufficient esteem for the cooking pots to be left, the farmers' brief leisure interrupted. She was touched by this and nodded her promise not to acknowledge or look at the mourners. To do so was to give offense. Grief could not be shared, except by the closest members of the family.

He walked beside her in a black suit, his head bared and bowed. As they passed the village green, turning into the fork of the road, Lyndsay glimpsed the first villagers moving from the houses on the hill. Silent, black figures, the women's heads draped in woolen shawls, the men bareheaded. But she kept her eyes properly lowered. In the main street, each house was dark and silent, yet, no sooner had they passed than the soft clatter of a latch, the squeak of a gate hinge told of life within, emerging. Soon the tramp of feet behind her sounded like a hushed, funereal drumming. She was moved by these steadily marching feet. The sound, the weight of bodies behind her seemed to bear her along. Although Patrick had made the ceremonial sound remote and chilly, Lyndsay felt a communality of sorrow, a personal sympathy. There was dignity and comfort in this procession which, she thought, in another village might have been marred by curious eyes taking a peek at her, the stranger widow. She was thankful for the privacy afforded her, knowing that it was not indifference, but a token of respect.

As they drew close to the chancel, she saw a car drawn up under the trees. Penelope Clare and a man who looked to be her brother joined them, walking a few paces behind Lyndsay and Patrick. She had an impression of other shadowy figures swelling the crowd as they left the road and Patrick offered his arm to her on the steep path to the gate. The doors of the little church stood open, a flickering light glowing within. The crowd was silent now behind them. At the doors, Patrick released her arm and indicated that they should wait a moment. She stared into the chancel, which was lit by thick candles set in tall holders. They flanked the coffin on either side. At its head she saw the white surplice of the priest, the heavy black book in his hands.

Together, they stepped over the threshold. Lyndsay, in accordance with the instructions Patrick had given her, proceeded to the foot of the coffin and placed the chaplet of lilies on it. Then she walked backward to stand once more beside her brother-in-law. The doors closed with a hollow booming sound and the voice of the priest seemed to rise out of its echoes, intoning. There was no peroration or eulogy. Simple prayers, the most basic form of service. It was over before Lyndsay realized it. The doors were opened again.

Patrick and a slight, pale-haired young man, whom she assumed to be Penelope's brother, moved to the coffin. The Clares, Lyndsay noticed, were not the only other members of the congregation. As four men passed through the door, their heads lowered, she saw a solitary man standing well back in the shadows. The coffin was lifted and carried out by the four men, assisted by Patrick and Damon Clare. She followed, then Penelope, the priest bringing up the rear. She could not see if the other man joined them.

Outside, a thick, hot dusk had fallen. The villagers stood at the gate, their numbers stretching back up the road. Lyndsay glanced at their pale, uplifted faces. The silence was total, seemed to press on the ears, and was not broken until the coffin bearers briefly trod on the newly turned earth at the back of the chancel. As soon as the coffin was put into position, they took up the slack of the ropes and pulled away the supporting planks. Patrick was at her side again, the priest spoke and, as the first sprinkling of earth rattled on the wood, a sound like a great sigh came from the road. The four men melted into the dusk. Lyndsay stared numbly into the dark rectangle. It was over.

After a brief, silent interval, the priest came to her. He was a small man with a lined, kindly face. He muttered his condolences, pressing her hand lightly. To Patrick he said nothing, but quickly shook his hand. Four identical wreaths of white lilies waited to cover the grave.

"Mrs. Dolben."

She turned to face the priest and saw, over his shoulder, Patrick step quickly forward, as though to divert the man's attention from her. But just then another man appeared at Patrick's side, took his arm, and spoke to him in a whisper. Because it was dusk, Lyndsay could not be certain, but she thought it was the same man she had glimpsed in the chancel. The priest, glancing behind him, drew Lyndsay farther off.

"Mrs. Dolben," he said again, in a low, almost conspiratorial voice, "you are a stranger here." It was not a question. He looked nervously round again.

"Yes," she said.

"If there is anything I can do . . . I must hurry back now. But please don't hesitate to contact me at any time. I want you to know that you can do that. Do you see?" He spoke with a sort of muted urgency. "I can always be contacted at Wellsby. It's only ten miles or so. You will remember?"

"Yes," Lyndsay said, surprised. "It's very kind of you."

He seemed about to say something else but, looking once more over his shoulder, he merely pressed her hand. Then, squaring his shoulders, he hurried away.

"Thank you," Lyndsay called after him.

"Lyndsay?" Patrick stood in the shadows of the chancel wall. She went toward him. "Only a few moments now, then we can go home."

"The priest . . . he seemed very anxious to get away."

"He knows our customs. He must leave before us. He is a stranger."

"Oh," she murmured vaguely, as Penelope and the young man came toward her.

"My brother, Damon Clare," Penelope said formally.

Lyndsay took his hand, smiled into a face which, though shadowed by the dusk, seemed gentle. He looked at her steadily with his sister's pale eyes, and offered his sympathy with an old-fashioned little bow. Beyond the chancel, the priest's car sprang into life. Patrick showed his disapproval as the engine roared and the wheels crunched on loose chippings.

At last the sound of the car faded up the road. When there was no sound at all, Patrick led Lyndsay forward, the Clares falling into step behind them.

The chancel was in darkness, the doors shut, and there was no sign at all of the villagers. They had vanished into the night. Surprised, Lyndsay turned toward Patrick for an explanation, but he shook his head sharply. She understood that their return was to be made alone and in silence.

The houses were completely dark under a distant, silver moon which reduced them to indistinct gray shapes among skeletal trees. As they walked by, lights appeared in the windows behind them, as though their passing put an end to mourning, bringing back light and life to the village.

Lyndsay sat at the foot of the long Dolben dinner table.

She had wanted to stay in her room but Penelope had persuaded her. The ritual would not be complete without the funeral supper.

"No amount of tears will bring him back," she had said, resting her hands on Lyndsay's shoulders. "You *have* to go on living."

"I guess you're right," Lyndsay said. She didn't even feel like crying. Not yet. "Okay. Let's go down."

"Let me help you change first."

She looked down at her dress and supposed that it wasn't suitable for a formal dinner.

"I've only got one other black dress," she said. "I think it's in the large valise. Would you look for me?"

The dress was a film of black lace over a low-cut, satin sheath.

"That will do splendidly," Penelope said, holding it against her.

"I don't know. It's a bit . . . frivolous?"

"Nonsense. Come along."

But now, as she felt Patrick's eyes on her swelling breasts she regretted wearing it. The dress embarrassed her.

Patrick sat opposite her, at the head of the table, with Penelope on his right, across from her brother. The candlelight accentuated the hollows of Patrick's cheeks and made his eyes unnaturally bright. Lyndsay was aware that she looked out of place. Compared to the sober suits of the men, Penelope's severe, high-necked black dress, she was on display. She had never, outside of making love, been so aware of her body. And Patrick's attentive gaze didn't help.

She watched Damon from the corner of her eyes. Over drinks, she had tried to talk to him, but he had answered in monosyllables. He was younger than she had expected, with the gaucheness of youth still about him. It was obvious from Penelope's attitude that she had

58

been placed *in loco parentis*. She treated him as a child, to be indulged yet disciplined. As for Patrick, there was something of the elder in his dealings with the boy. The age difference which, after all, could not be so very great, was exaggerated, but not in a fatherly way. It was more a question of rank, of position, Lyndsay decided. Patrick's manner suggested that the boy was a novitiate, valued but not yet completely accepted. A patrician arrogance, she supposed. It had been there, too, when Patrick had explained how quickly the Dolbens could get things done. It disturbed her. But for all her brother-in-law's secure superiority, Lyndsay sensed that he was uneasy with the boy. Once she saw a frown of annoyance on his face when he caught Damon staring intently at Emelye Poole, who served their meal.

She turned to look at the girl herself. She was ill suited to the task of serving. Her natural clumsiness seemed to be accentuated by shyness. She looked like a frightened animal, Lyndsay thought. Her abundant, wavy black hair was caught back from her face in an untidy bow. It left her features exposed. Enormous eyes seemed— perhaps because of some trick of the candlelight—to peer out from dark circles, suggesting a recent illness. The very thinness of body seemed to confirm this. Her ankles were no thicker than Lyndsay's wrists. She wanted to ask the girl if she felt all right, but she did not because even her murmured thanks seemed to set Emelye in a tizzy of nervousness. Penelope and Patrick managed to seem completely oblivious of her presence in the room, but, when she silently withdrew, Lyndsay saw Damon's eyes following her. Rather obviously, Lyndsay thought, Patrick began to talk to Damon about crops. Penelope listened attentively, her eyes fixed on Patrick's face.

It was not a conversation to which Lyndsay could contribute. She was glad to be left out, left with her own thoughts. She ate her plain, wholesome food and sipped the heavy red wine that accompanied it. The monogrammed silver, the candlelight and crisp napery all suggested richness, a sense of tradition and formality which chilled her. It did so, she realized, because she could not imagine Michael as a part of it. He would have been out of place in this room. Like her, he would have wanted to bring in more candles, throw open the windows to the warm evening. A restless spirit, Penelope had called him, and she, who had found him the very opposite of restless, could imagine these surroundings making him so. Either that or he had changed a great deal in the world away from Ratchets.

Lifting her eyes from her plate, she noticed that all three, Patrick, Penelope, and Damon, were staring at her. She apologized, saying that she had been thinking about Michael. They reacted as though she had committed a faux pas. Was he to be so quickly put out of mind then? She met Patrick's veiled eyes, remembering that he had spoken about their way of dealing with grief, but not about his brother. She would not give up her right to remember.

"I was just saying that we must show you over the estate," Patrick said. "But there's plenty of time. After all, you're not a visitor." He reached for a little silver bell and shook it to summon Emelye.

"True," Lyndsay said, "but I can't stay here forever." This time there was no mistaking their distress. This they had not bargained for. Their faces said so, and a reproving look from Patrick silenced Penelope's protests. It was because of Emelye Poole, she realized. What was obviously a matter of dissent between them was evidently not to be discussed in front of the hired help. Because she would carry tales to the village? Because the Dolbens and the Clares must always present a united front? Their sense of supremacy was almost tangible. Lyndsay could feel it as Patrick's eyes returned to her breasts. It annoyed her so much that even when Emelye left the room she made no attempt to withdraw or soften the remark.

"Then we must persuade you to stay with us," Patrick said at last. "Eh, Damon?"

"Certainly," the boy agreed, dragging his eyes from the door which had just closed behind Emelye.

"You certainly mustn't think of going anywhere yet," Penelope said. "You badly need to rest. We all realize what a terrible strain the last two days have been on you."

Patrick and Damon nodded their agreement.

"By the way," Lyndsay said, deliberately changing the subject, "did Michael leave a will?"

"I don't know," Patrick said. "Our solicitor is looking into that, but it's of little consequence. As his wife you will inherit what is his, and you must let us show you how fine that is. I think you'll approve."

"We have a lot to discuss," Lyndsay agreed, without committing herself. "You've been managing all the land, I suppose? Michael's as well?"

"Yes. But he was kept fully informed, of course. I think I can safely say that he was satisfied."

"I don't doubt it," Lyndsay said. "And whatever I decide to do, I hope you'll continue to manage things. I certainly don't intend to interfere." It had occurred to her that perhaps her inheritance made him and the Clares feel that their kingdom was threatened. Her assurance, however, did not seem to affect them at all. No looks of relief were exchanged between them. It was as though they believed themselves to be impregnable, absolutely certain that no one could touch them or their precious land.

Patrick stood up suddenly and announced that they would take coffee in the great hall. Damon stood aside for her to pass, his eyes lowered. In the hall the chandelier burned brightly and it was to this that Lyndsay attributed a lift in her spirits. Her reactions were not to be trusted. What seemed to her like arrogance was probably no more than a natural trust in the unchanging nature of their lives. To them she almost certainly must appear brash and outspoken. Michael had warned her that she would find the English stiff, and no doubt he had been thinking of his own family when he said it.

"I've been meaning to ask," she said, settling herself on the sofa beneath the gallery. "Who was that man in church?"

Penelope turned to her brother as though she had not heard the question. She spoke to Damon in a low, reproving voice.

"He spoke to you," Lyndsay reminded Patrick. "At the grave."

"Oh you mean Bart Poole," he said casually. "Brandy? Or would you rather have something else?"

"No, that'll be fine," she said. Penelope and Damon were silent now, the boy blushing. "And who is Bart Poole?"

"The farm manager," Patrick said smoothly. "He wanted to pay his respects. Ah, here's the coffee. Thank you, Emelye. That will be all now."

Penelope drew the coffee tray toward her and began to pour. Emelye Poole hurried out of the room, watched by Damon, who, Lyndsay thought, looked as though he wanted to run after her. To cover the awkwardness this seemed to cause, and because she wanted them to talk about Michael, Lyndsay said, "What I really can't understand is why Michael never told me you were twins."

Penelope rattled the coffee cups loudly on the tray.

"I don't think that's particularly remarkable, is it, Patrick? I suppose you're both so used to it . . ."

Lyndsay looked at him expectantly. He handed her a glass of brandy.

"I think there was a perfectly good explanation," he said, returning to the bar. "I disagree with Penelope. I don't think one does become unaware of it. At least not in this family."

"Oh Patrick, please," Penelope said tensely. "I'm sure Lyndsay doesn't want to hear that old wives' tale."

"What?" Lyndsay asked, looking from one to the other. Penelope's face was flushed, but Patrick remained quite calm.

"Is it an old wives' tale?" he asked levelly, holding out a glass of brandy to her. "I would have thought recent events might have changed your mind."

"What?" Lyndsay repeated. The conversation was beginning to make her nervous.

"It's too silly," Penelope said, almost snatching the glass from Patrick.

"Penelope's a skeptic, you see," he said dryly. "What we're talking about is an old Dolben superstition. Twins run in the family, you know. Michael and I are . . . were, let me see, the fifth or sixth pair, I think." He paused and handed Damon his drink.

"Patrick, I really don't think . . ." Penelope began.

"Nonsense," he said harshly. "Lyndsay wants to know. And after all, we're not saying anything so very terrible."

Penelope did not answer, but her annoyance was quite plain to see. She lit a cigarette.

"Please go on," Lyndsay prompted him.

"It's simply that according to family lore, twins are supposed to be unlucky. It is said that the eldest always dies first."

Lyndsay, although she could not have defined what she had been expecting, was relieved.

"Well, that's just nonsense, or logic, depending on your point of view."

"Possibly," Patrick agreed. "But I meant, dies unexpectedly. And Michael was older, by several minutes."

It was like a chill striking her skin, caused as much by the way Patrick spoke as by his actual words. Lyndsay shuddered.

"Of course it's nonsense," Penelope said quickly. "Really Patrick, I wish you hadn't."

"No," Lyndsay said. "It's okay. Patrick was right. I wanted to know. But I agree it's nonsense." She looked at him, determined to show that he had not succeeded in upsetting her. Patrick returned her look coldly. She knew that he was convinced.

"Excuse me," he said, and walked quickly away down the hall. Lyndsay closed her eyes and leaned back on the sofa.

"You're still very tired," Penelope said sympathetically. "You ought to go to bed."

"No, I'm fine, really. Maybe a little jet lag. That's all."

"You mustn't take any notice of Patrick," Penelope said. "He feels Michael's death much more than he shows. He isn't used to considering other people's feelings. I don't mean that he is unkind . . ."

Damon shifted abruptly in his seat as though he disapproved of his sister's words.

"I wish he would talk about Michael," Lyndsay said. "I guess it's difficult for both of us. I tend to forget . . . to think that only *I* care about Michael."

"He will," Penelope said. "I'm sure he will. In time."

"I know I'm not being fair," Lyndsay admitted. "It's just that I can't . . ." She shook her head, unable to express, without the threat of tears, what she felt.

Patrick returned, carrying a long, slim black box. With an almost courtly air, he stood in front of Lyndsay and held the box out to her. She was aware, as she looked from it to his face, of Penelope moving discreetly away, as though this were some private matter in which she must not intrude. At the same time, Damon stood up, apparently in readiness for something.

"You might consider this another piece of family lore," Patrick said reproachfully, "but I don't think you'll dismiss it as nonsense."

"What is it?"

He opened the box deftly and held it toward her. It contained a gleaming black jet collar about two and a half inches wide. Worked into the jet was a design of diamonds which blazed coldly as Lyndsay looked at them.

"A family heirloom," Patrick explained. "It is traditionally handed to the eldest son's wife, if there are no daughters, that is. You must have it now. It is yours."

"It's beautiful," Lyndsay said, "but I couldn't possibly . . ."

"You must. It's yours. Look . . ." He set the box down on her knees and, stooping, lifted the collar from its velvet bed. As he moved it in the light, Lyndsay saw that the diamonds traced the outline of a running hound. A single emerald chip served as its gleaming green eye.

"It's beautiful," she repeated.

"Let me fasten it for you."

Before she could protest, Patrick had moved behind her, and she felt the cold weight of the collar against her throat. It gripped her tightly as he fastened the clasp. Penelope and Damon watched in rapt silence. The young man nodded, as though something necessary and desirable had been done, but Lyndsay saw sadness and regret on Penelope's face. She raised her hand to touch the collar as Patrick smiled down at her.

"Now," he said, "you are truly a Dolben."

Penelope came forward quietly and stooped to kiss her brow, as though she were paying tribute.

Lyndsay could not sleep. She felt guilty. She had stumbled on a truth which was self-evident, which she would have seen had she not been blind to everything but her own grief. She had been clumsy and she had caused pain.

It was after Patrick had clasped the collar about her throat, after Penelope had so strangely kissed her.

"I can't accept it," she had said. "Do something for me, Patrick? Keep it and give it to your wife one day."

"No," he had replied with cold determination. Lyndsay had turned to Penelope for support and saw that her face was lined with longing and pain. Still she had not realized.

"Surely you mean to marry?" she had said, raising her hands to the clasp of the weighty collar.

Penelope had almost shouted, "Leave it." Lyndsay had looked at her questioningly and it was then that she had understood. Penelope loved Patrick. Everything fell into place then: Penelope's nervousness, her quick defense of Patrick, her pleading for Lyndsay to be tolerant of him. Surely nothing could be more fitting. An eligible Dolben and a beautiful Clare. Even then Lyndsay had begun to smile, wanted to press the collar about Penelope's neck. How could she have been so stupid? she wondered, tossing in her bed. Patrick did not love Penelope. She thought that this had probably been acknowledged between them. No doubt they had been sensible about it, rational, but that had not helped Penelope. She still loved him, and he was apparently indifferent to her. Lyndsay recalled how she had let her hands drop into her lap, leaving the collar about her throat. It was a gesture of defeat on her part, she realized.

Patrick's attitude still surprised her. Penelope had told her that the Clares and Dolbens frequently married. The tradition in it, the chance to join the lands together would surely appeal to Patrick. It seemed out of character to Lyndsay, unless this was the one area in which he put personal feelings above tradition and the old ways. If that were so, she was on his side. She could understand that. If he did not love Penelope, then he had the right to choose elsewhere. But poor Penelope. How could she bear to be so much around him, loving him as she did and knowing it was hopeless?

Lyndsay would have given anything not to have hurt her. Sitting up in the darkness, she reproached herself again for her stupidity. Michael would not have wanted her to mourn him to the exclusion of other people's feelings. She, for all that she had lost and was suffering, was more fortunate than Penelope Clare. She had been married to the man she loved, although too briefly.

Snapping on the bedside light, Lyndsay got out of bed and reached for her housecoat. She would make amends, find some way to help Penelope. At least she could get her to talk about it. Her eye was caught by the bottle of pills Penelope had given her. She had not taken any since the first night, convinced that she would sleep without them. Even now she didn't want to rely on them. A book, something to read, to take her mind off her clumsiness. There must be something in the library downstairs that would pass the time until she could sleep. She crossed the room and carefully lifted the latch so as not to disturb Patrick. Silently, she opened the door and slipped out into the corridor.

She hadn't expected to find the hall brightly lit. Patrick had said that he was going to bed as soon as he had finished his drink. She hesitated, not wanting to intrude on him. Except that perhaps now, she thought, he might welcome a chance to talk about Michael. She moved toward the gallery but was stopped by an unfamiliar voice.

"And she looked well, did she, in the Dolben Collar?" said a deep, resonant, masculine voice. He spoke with a slight rural accent and in a way that seemed to demand answers, as though by right.

"Yes," she heard Patrick's tired reply.

She moved closer to the archway which opened onto the gallery.

"Good. At last we're getting on." The man moved restlessly about the room. From his footsteps, Lyndsay guessed that he wore heavy boots. The noise he made obscured Patrick's reply. "Where's your stomach, man?" the voice demanded. "Anyway, there's no turning back now. We're committed. You every bit as much as me. Don't you forget that."

Patrick spoke so quietly that Lyndsay could not make out what he said. His tone, though, was unmistakably whining.

"Don't you bother your head about that. What chance does she stand against me? You've seen for yourself."

The man sounded angry. His voice dropped to a hiss. Again Lyndsay was unable to hear Patrick's reply. She took a step closer, straining her ears. Under her foot an old, loose board creaked loudly.

"What's that?" demanded the voice at once.

Her heart racing, Lyndsay crept back to her room and closed the door behind her. She leaned against the door, her fingers automatically searching for a key. There wasn't one. Of course, she remembered, it was on the outside. She did not dare open the door again. Patrick might come to check on her. She had better look like she was doing something, just in case. The pills, she thought. Yes. She picked up the small bottle and, with trembling fingers, shook two pills out. They were brownish in color and rough-textured. She hurried into the bathroom and washed them down with a long draft of water.

There was still no sound from outside. She got into bed quickly and put out the light. She willed the pills to work. What were they committed to, Patrick and that man? What hold did he have over Patrick that he could speak to him like that? And did he mean her when he asked what chance *she* stood against him? The thought made her cringe. But why should she be so frightened? Firmly, she told herself to calm down. Probably they were talking about some deal, something to do with the farm. That was all the men around Ratchets ever seemed to discuss with any passion.

Lyndsay turned over onto her side. She refused to think about it anymore. Instead, she began to make a mental list of things she would do. When she fancied that her door was quietly, carefully being opened, she knew that she was imagining it, or dreaming.

She was looking for the dog again. It was ahead of her somewhere in the darkness. She was sure of that. There was a square of light in front of her to which she hurried. In the light she would be able to find the dog.

She was confronted by a man. He stood almost at attention. A golden robe hung in stiff, sculpted folds from his broad shoulders. That and the darkness of his hair was all she could make out. She was not afraid, not even startled by coming upon him in this way. Perhaps it was for him that she had been searching, not the dog. She moved toward the man cautiously, her hand held out before her. It was Michael, of course. A great wave of relief swept through her. She collapsed against the man, sobbing with relief and happiness. His arms held her, supported her. She pressed herself against him with the certainty that this time she would hold on to him. This time no one, nothing would take him from her. Then she became aware that the golden robe was open and that beneath it he was naked, that he was pressing against her urgently, demanding.

She was lying down. The naked man hung over her, poised, ready to take her. She spoke his name, shifted her body luxuriously to accommodate him. She cried out that she loved him, wanted him. Wanted him. He entered her fiercely, passionately. It was right and good. His head buried in her neck, she held him and, looking up, saw, as though picked out in stars, the outline of a great, green-eyed dog against the vastness of the sky.

An impression of this dream remained with Lyndsay when she woke. At first it comforted her. She had found Michael and made her peace with him. But then the stark eroticism of the dream embarrassed her. It seemed somehow wrong. Her sprained wrist ached and she realized that her whole body felt sore and used, felt, in fact, as though she had made violent, hungry love.

She pushed the thought away. Probably she had slept restlessly, tiring her body with forgotten turnings and shiftings. She tried to recapture the sense of peace she had felt on waking, but the sexual element stood between her and that precious feeling. She looked at her watch. It was late. She had slept long and well.

The house was, as usual, quiet, except for the muffled sounds of activity in the kitchen. Downstairs, she found that lunch had been laid for her in the gloomy dining room. It was served by Emelye Poole, who avoided her eyes. Her shyness struck Lyndsay as almost pathological. If pressed to speak the girl threatened to burst into tears. Lyndsay abandoned any attempt to make conversation and thought instead of the plans she had made last night, before falling asleep and dreaming . . . She would go for a good long walk, she decided. Soak up some sunshine, blow some of the cobwebs from her mind.

Dressed casually in pants and a shirt, Lyndsay crossed the lawn and went into the old stable yard. Apart from a flock of geese, it was deserted. Far off in the distance she could hear the purr of farm machinery. She went through the open yard-gate onto the unmade track and turned left, away from the road. The track was deeply rutted by tractors, and the ruts were baked hard by the sun. The going was difficult and Lyndsay moved to the edge of the track where the earth was comparatively even next to the high wall which ran beside the village road. She wondered what was behind it. Only trees, as far as she could tell, but who'd put a wall around a lot of trees? Ahead of her the wall stopped. She walked along the track, which began to rise quite steeply until the wall appeared to come to an end. Instead it continued at right angles. Pausing to get her bearings, Lyndsay reckoned that this wall must run roughly parallel to the road. So if she followed it she ought to end up in the village, somewhere near the green. She was sweating already and the path offered shade. The tops of the tall trees growing inside the wall met those of a copse of thinly spaced trees to form a cool, green tunnel. She decided to take the path.

She had gone a few yards when she heard an angry honking behind her. She whirled around and saw two geese, which had followed her. One immediately hissed in a warning way. The other, the larger of the two, spread its great white wings and made a feinting dash along the path. Instinctively Lyndsay stepped back. The bird stopped a few feet from her and hissed. Lyndsay regarded it nervously. Surely it couldn't do her any harm? They must be quite safe or Patrick would never allow them to wander around unpenned. The thing to do was just to ignore them. She felt ridiculous, pressed up against the wall, facing a goose or gander or whatever. Before she had time to move, though, the gander darted toward her, wings flapping. She stepped quickly out of its way and began to hurry down the path, glancing apprehensively over her shoulder. The birds followed her, honking and twisting their long, sinuous necks to fix her with their sharp eyes. She stumbled suddenly on a piece of wood lying across the path and at once the gander rushed her. She felt a sharp peck on her calf, and kicked out at the bird. With a cry, it retreated a few feet, stopped and spread its wings again, hissing ominously. Damn it, she thought, they really were going to attack her. Her eyes went to the stick over which she had stumbled. Well, if they were going to attack, she could defend herself. She stooped to pick up the stick. With a warning cry, the gander rushed at her. She just managed to snatch her hand back from its hard, vicious beak.

"Get out of here," she shouted. "Go on."

Turning her back on the geese, and forcing herself not to look behind her, Lyndsay resumed her walk. The hissing followed her, but they didn't actually attack her. Her first instinct had been right, she thought. Ignore them and they'll ignore you. The path began to curve now, following the wall as the road did. The trees over her head were thicker, making a false twilight. As she approached the curve, she expected to see the end of the path. Once she got to the village, someone would know how to get rid of the geese. Behind her they set up a new clamoring. Forgetting her plan to ignore them, she glanced over her shoulder. Both had their wings spread now and their necks stretched threateningly forward. Damn it, she thought, they're going to rush me again. At once she broke into a trot and, as though this were the cue they had been waiting for, the birds flew forward. She felt one of them snapping at her leg. She ran faster and then skidded to a halt as the gander swept past her, one great wing beating against her arm.

They had her cornered. She was genuinely scared now. Her leg hurt where the big one had nipped her. She thought about her situation for a minute or two while the geese watched her, still hissing. She backed slowly to the wall, flattened herself against it, and began to inch along the pathway. When she got within reach of the gander ahead of her, she would give it a smart kick and make a dash for it. She began to move and, as she did so, the goose behind her came at her again. The gander remained stationary, watching. Lyndsay kept moving, twisting her head uncertainly from one bird to the other. Crazy as it seemed, she was certain they were closing in on her.

"Go away," she shouted, and was surprised at how frightened her voice sounded.

Then suddenly her hand touched wood behind her. Her hand, feeling along the wall, definitely encountered rough wood. She turned around, forgetting the geese for a moment, and found herself facing a small, arched door, set into the wall. Even as she looked at it, she felt a sharp peck on her heel. She cried out. The birds were rushing at her in turns, in a concerted and, it seemed, organized attack. Panic-stricken, she grabbed the metal ring-shaped handle and turned it. The door wouldn't give. She lashed out with her foot at one of the geese and twisted the ring the other way. The door opened and she stumbled through. Her eyes were stinging with tears of pain from her pecked legs, but she managed to slam the door shut against them. To her surprise, they were immediately silent. She looked up quickly, expecting to see them flapping over the wall in pursuit, but they seemed to have lost interest in her. Cursing, she reached down and massaged her smarting calves. It's as if they wanted me to come in here, she thought. It was a crazy thought and yet, somehow, it didn't seem crazy. She straightened up and took a look around her.

A wide path wound through the trees from the little door. She could not see far ahead, but the path was well used and must lead somewhere. She might as well find out where. Anyway, she wasn't about to face those damn geese again. She set off and soon found that the path was much shorter than it had at first appeared. As soon as she rounded the first bend, she could see into a clearing, bright with sunlight.

It took a moment for her eyes to adjust to the sun and another for her to realize that the building on the other side of the clearing was almost an exact replica of the chancel in which her husband had lain. The only marked difference was that this one was much better kept. The large windows reflected the sunlight and sparkled. The ornate hinges and the big handles on the double doors were made of brass and were freshly polished. Even the stone seemed bright and clean, as though recently washed. Everything about the other chancel had seemed neglected, uncared-for.

The clearing extended on either side of this chancel, in a large, irregular circle, and it was used as a graveyard. The path on which she stood led to the big doors of the little church, but on either side, in neat rows, were graves stretching back into the shadows beneath the trees. Something about these graves caught her attention. She looked more closely. They were so small, such tiny graves . . . She stepped close to the nearest stone and bent to read the inscription. It was a child's grave. A baby's. Maria. And the next. The one beyond that. Lyndsay moved anxiously toward the trees, passing among these miniature graves. Many of them were old, the lettering worn faint, or almost obscured by moss, but there was no mistaking the youth, the touching youth of these corpses. Jasper, two years old. Another Maria, barely one. Dorcas, beloved daughter of. . . . Gabriel. Henrietta. Ezekiels and Simeons. Japhets. Ruths. Bartholomew and many Johns. All children. And back in the shadows beneath the trees the stones were still white and newly chiseled. Gabrielle, born and died, 1975. Jonquil, 1971–72. Another Bartholomew, 1973.

Lyndsay could not bear it. She felt as though she had stumbled on something terrible. The place had the fascination of the horrible. All the grief and pain she had been carrying inside her suddenly welled up. She sank down among these tiny graves and covered her face with her hands. Hot tears flowed down her face. So many helpless little children, stretching back over the years. Dead and set apart here in their own, lonely graveyard.

She might have had children. Michael's children. Little Dolbens who . . . No. She reached out and touched one of the stones, tracing the letters with her fingers. They hadn't talked about it, but she had wanted children. It had been there, in her mind, all the time. She had so wanted Michael's children. And now it was all gone. All gone. It felt as though these children were hers. So many babies lay here, dead. They might as well be hers, for now she would never bear any. It was gone, all gone. Michael was dead and their children were little ghosts. All that remained were these stones and tiny crosses, discovered in a silent, walled wood.

"Oh God," she cried.

Her fingers, gripping the stone, were moving over and over some indentation. Not letters. Some design or ornament. Sniffing back her tears, she peered at the mark beneath her fingers. More slowly she traced the shape again and with a start of recognition saw it, felt it to be the racing hound that, last night, Patrick had clasped about her throat. The great star dog in the sky. It was carved there, too, on the next grave. And the next. She got to her feet and began to move back toward the path, checking each grave as she went, pacing between the rows. All the stones, each cross, the oldest and the most recent, bore this emblem of the stretched and racing hound. Why? What did it mean? Some protective god? Some pagan emblem? A dog guarded the gates of hell, didn't it? But that was ridiculous. A sacrilegious thought in this place. She lifted her hand to her neck.

The thought of that collar, clasped about her throat, terrified her. It was as though she had been branded, marked for death. The thought was terrible. She remembered how Damon Clare had looked at her, as if there was some special significance to putting on the collar.

And she looked well, did she, in the Dolben Collar?

That man, asking about it, in his demanding voice. The way Penelope had kissed her, as though in commiseration.

The graves spread all around her. The stark, carved shape of the dog leapt at her eyes wherever she looked. It must be some sign of death, and she had borne it, last night.

According to family lore, twins are considered to be unlucky. It is said that the eldest always dies first.

Lyndsay shrank from the calm certainty of Patrick's remembered voice.

And she looked well, did she, in the Dolben Collar?

"No," she moaned, shaking her head.

I mean dies unexpectedly. And Michael was the older.

This place was inhuman, evil. She took a few, stumbling steps along the path, toward the door in the wall. Then she heard the scream. She did not know what it was. It was possible that she had made it. It echoed in her eardrums. She heard it again, high-pitched, unearthly. The sound of something in torment, caused by some terrible pain. Running now, she realized that the sound was continuous and seemed to be growing louder.

By the time she reached the door her breathing sounded like sobs. She leaned, her chest heaving, against the arched lintel for a moment. There was no other sound now, except her rasping breath. She wrenched the door open and turned back toward Dolben House. She felt too tired to run, but she walked as fast as she could, toward the sunlit track at the end of the wall. Still panting, she burst out of the pathway into the sunlight. And the scream began again.

Careless of the treacherously rutted track, Lyndsay began to run again. The sound seemed to be all around her, to be pursuing her. Tears and the sudden bright glare of the sun off the almost white track blinded her. Through a dazzling mist, she saw the open gate into the yard and grabbed it. She heard voices. Male voices. They were shouting through the screaming. She would be safe in the yard, in the house. That was it. She had to get to the house. She ran across the yard, not looking where she was going. Somebody shouted at her. She bumped into something warm, which swung. There was a great pool of blood at her feet. The swinging thing thumped against her, knocking her back. Blood dripped from it, splashing her trousers and shoes. She stared in horror and revulsion, her mouth stretched in a silent scream.

"Get back. Get away."

She jerked her head up. A man was coming toward her. His breeches and rubber boots were spattered with blood. His thick, muscular torso was naked, gleaming with sweat. His arms were red with blood. He gestured at her with a long, bloodstained knife. At last Lyndsay was able to scream. She fought against somebody's arms. Someone clasped her from behind. She screamed louder. She was dragged toward the house. Her foot slipped in the pool of blood. The man rushed as though to intercept her. She pressed back against the person who was forcing her forward, but she was not strong enough to resist. Almost fainting with fear, she saw the man throw open the back door of the house. His strange, gold-colored eyes were fixed on her with a look of disgust. Then she was almost beside him, weeping and screaming. He stepped closer to her, raised his bloody hand, and hit her hard across the cheek. Her head swung sideways, wrenching her neck. In the silence which followed, when Lyndsay thought that she was about to be killed, she heard the man say, "Get her inside."

He turned away, leaned into the open doorway, and shouted, "Emelye? Look to your Mistress."

And she recognized his voice.

Bart Poole was washing the last of the blood from his arms when Penelope Clare came hurrying into the kitchen. He switched off the tap and watched the pink water swirl into the waste pipe.

"What on earth's happened?" Penelope exclaimed. "Emelye?"

The girl was huddled, whey-faced, on a chair. Bart Poole calmly shook drops of water from his large hands and crossed the kitchen to where a towel hung from a nail in the wall. Penelope swallowed her anger.

"Bart? Why did you send for me? What's happened to Lyndsay?"

He unhooked the towel and slowly turned to face her.

"Nothing's happened to her," he said. "She's just never seen a pig-sticking before, that's all. She's hysterical."

Drying his hands and arms, he walked back to the sink and looked out into the yard. The two pigs hung from pulleys, blood dripping from their slit throats. Damon and two of the men had placed buckets under them and were preparing to sluice the yard.

"Two beauties," he said.

"Where is she?" Penelope demanded.

"Upstairs."

She turned on her heel and went toward the door.

"Penelope," he said softly. She stopped at once, and glanced nervously over her shoulder. "You be careful now. You understand?"

She watched him for a moment, but he kept his back turned.

"What have you been up to?" she asked, her voice shaking a little. "Where's Patrick? And what have you done to Emelye?"

"Done?" he said, swinging round and tossing the towel onto the table. "I've done nothing. She's worse than useless." Emelye winced at his voice and seemed to shrink into herself. "And as for your precious Patrick, he's up on the ridge."

Penelope went toward Emelye, hoping that Bart would not see her relief.

"Come on, Emelye," she said, touching the girl's shoulder. "Go home."

The girl looked at her, then, as though seeking permission, turned her frightened face to Bart.

"Aye, go," he sneered. "Get out of my sight. You're neither use nor ornament."

Emelye scuttled across the kitchen and snatched down a black shawl from a peg. Trembling, she threw it over her head and then hesitated. Bart stood between her and the door into the yard. Penelope understood. She ushered the girl toward the hall.

"Use the front door," she said. "It's quicker."

As soon as the girl had gone, Bart Poole chuckled quietly to himself.

"Why do you taunt her?" Penelope said wearily.

"You know," he snapped. "Go look to your Mistress." He spat out the last word in a half-mocking snarl.

Penelope walked steadily toward the big table and leaned her hands on it, her body bent toward Bart.

"Is that what you're afraid of?" she asked quietly.

His eyes seemed to glow with anger, but Penelope showed no reaction. He took a deep breath and let it out in a long sigh.

"No, Penelope Clare. I'm not afraid of the Mistress, nor of you. Now get to your business and leave me to mine."

In two strides he had reached the door, and she watched him go out into the yard, shouting at Damon. Her body shivered with hatred of him, and with fear. It was an effort to straighten her back. She wanted . . . But what she wanted was impossible. She must go to Lyndsay and do what little she could.

Coming out of the house, Patrick paused on the steps. Lyndsay had not seen him. She was slumped in an old deck chair which Penelope had set up for her on the lawn. He did not know how to approach her. Penelope had been able to tell him little. Lyndsay had been hysterical. She had been sick, but Penelope could not get her to talk about it. Patrick would have preferred to leave it at that, but Penelope insisted. Reluctantly, he stepped onto the gravel and walked toward Lyndsay.

The sound of his steps made her turn her head. Her eyes were wide with fear. Scrubbed and without makeup, her face looked pale and vulnerable. There was a red mark across her left cheek. Patrick had not been prepared for this and he felt inadequate. In fact he was relieved when Lyndsay turned away from him. She was staring at the wall of the old graveyard.

Patrick unfolded the chair he was carrying and clumsily set it up. "Are you all right, Lyndsay? Can I get you anything?"

She shook her head violently and at the same time seemed to draw away from him. Patrick straightened up.

"You've had a bad shock. I'm very sorry. I asked Emelye to tell you that Bart was going to slaughter a couple of pigs this afternoon, but she must have forgotten. She's completely unreliable. I don't know quite what to do about her." He sat in the chair and stretched his legs gratefully. Lyndsay avoided his eyes.

"Bart," she said listlessly. "That man was Bart Poole then?" The man who had asked how she looked in that horrible collar.

"Yes. Not a very fortunate meeting." Patrick's laugh died away. "Anyway, how are you feeling now?" he asked briskly.

"I'm all right."

She didn't sound or look it. Again she seemed to be fascinated by the wall. Patrick twisted round a little to see what interested her. He did not want to mention the mark on her cheek, the blow Bart had given her. The evening sun, which threw the shadow of the house across the lawn, still shone on the mellow bricks of the wall.

"It's a lovely old wall, isn't it?" he said.

Lyndsay's mouth set in a hard line.

"I think it's horrible."

"The wall? But why?"

"What's behind it."

"Ah . . ." Patrick said. So she'd found the graveyard. Mother Poole's doing, he thought at once. Bart wouldn't like that. He wished that he could talk to Bart. Lyndsay was looking at him, he noticed, obviously expecting him to explain. He cleared his throat. "It's only a graveyard. I realize, of course, that just now . . . feeling as you do . . . well, there must be unpleasant associations for you."

"All those babies," she said. "Why?" She still could not bear to think of it. Her eyes stung with tears and she turned her face away again, rummaging for a handkerchief.

"Please don't upset yourself," he said.

She blew her nose and lay back in the chair.

"There really isn't anything unpleasant about it, you know. At least I've never thought so."

"Why are only children buried there?"

"Oh . . . tradition." He knew that he sounded vague. "The little church there used to be the Dolbens' private chapel. There's an underground passage connecting it directly with the house. The Dolben ladies didn't like to get their skirts muddied in winter, especially not on their way to church." He tried to make a joke of it, but Lyndsay only stared at him. "Anyway, eventually it was given to the village. It was a sort of peace offering, really, to the Clares. There'd been a quarrel for years. And it was decided to reserve the graveyard for children. I'm not quite sure why. A sort of memorial, I suppose."

"So many babies," Lyndsay mumbled.

"Well, in those days the infant mortality rate was appalling. Especially in remote country districts like Ratchets. A doctor might have to travel for miles and even then . . ." Patrick shrugged.

"Some of the graves are recent," Lyndsay pointed out.

"Well, of course. Children do still die. Even in America I imagine," he said impatiently.

"But people still . . . bury them there," she said.

"Naturally. Why not? I'm sorry, I really don't see . . ."

"It's horrible," Lyndsay insisted.

"I'm afraid a lot of people would disagree with you. It's entirely up to the parents and if . . ." He paused. Her expression clearly suggested that she did not believe him. "There's no compulsion, Lyndsay. Is that what you thought?" Patrick laughed more easily now. "I know you think we're primitive but I do assure you . . ."

"Those dogs," she interrupted. "Why are the graves marked with that dog? Just like the one . . ."

A tinkling sound behind them made both Patrick and Lyndsay turn around. Penelope Clare was crossing the lawn, carefully balancing a tray of glasses and a chilled bottle of wine.

"I raided your cellar, Patrick. I thought a glass of hock would do us all good."

"Good idea," he said, getting up and taking the tray from her. "I'll get another chair."

Penelope smiled at him gratefully. She felt almost happy. He put the tray down on the grass and went toward the house. Bending, Penelope poured a glass of wine and offered it to Lyndsay.

"Lyndsay?"

She accepted the wine mutely. The glass was pleasantly cold and she cupped her hands around it.

"Lyndsay was just asking about the Gabriel Ratchets," Patrick said, returning with a folding canvas chair, which he opened and set between him and Lyndsay. Penelope gave him a startled look. He shook his head warningly. "I think I've got to the bottom of it. She wandered into the children's graveyard . . ."

"I was chased in there," Lyndsay said, too loudly. "By geese."

Penelope stood up and handed Patrick his wine. They exchanged a look of concern.

"Why are you looking at each other like that?" Lyndsay demanded. "Are you thinking I imagined it?"

"No, of course not," Penelope answered quickly.

"You're sure it was geese?"

"Yes. Just like the ones out in the yard there."

"Did they hurt you?"

"Well, yes. Not seriously but . . . I mean they pecked me. . . . Mostly I was just scared."

"Of course." Patrick sipped his wine. "Mm. This was a good idea."

Lyndsay looked from one to the other. They thought she was

imagining things, she realized. Or at least exaggerating or that she was mad.

"Anyway, it upset her," Patrick said to Penelope, as though Lyndsay weren't there. "It's only natural, of course, under the circumstances."

"And then she bumped into Bart. I see," Penelope said.

Lyndsay raised her glass and drank. The wine was light and cold. She drank some more. Patrick immediately got up and refilled her glass.

"You haven't answered my question," Lyndsay said defensively. "About those dogs."

Penelope laughed and lit a cigarette.

"Gabriel Ratchets," Patrick corrected her. "That's what they're called. And there's only one person who can tell you about them. Isn't that right, Penelope?"

She smiled, "Definitely. I'll call in on my way home and ask her to see you tomorrow. That is if you think you'll feel up to it. Perhaps you ought to rest tomorrow."

"Yes. Have a day in bed," Patrick urged her.

"You mean," Lyndsay said, "that you're not going to tell me anything about these Gabriel Ratchets." She felt angry. She drank more wine.

"That's right," Patrick said complacently.

"We wouldn't dream of spoiling a real treat for you," Penelope added. "And believe me, it will be a treat."

"I'm not a child," Lyndsay said coldly. She knew that they were watching her with indulgent smiles. She drained her glass to avoid looking at them.

"We're only suggesting," Patrick said, "that you put your question to Mother Poole. She's the person to give you a comprehensive answer."

"There's nothing she doesn't know about myths and legends," Penelope said brightly. "She'll keep you enthralled for hours, I promise."

Lyndsay stood up. She was already beginning to feel the wine. For a moment the blandly smiling faces shifted and blurred.

"I think I'll go up to my room now," she said.

"You ought to eat something," Penelope said. "Let me get you . . ."

"No. Thank you. I just want to rest. Excuse me."

Penelope got up and came solicitously toward her. Lyndsay stepped aside.

"It's perfectly all right. I can manage."

The tall blond woman looked hurt, but she did not speak. She remained standing, watching Lyndsay go into the house.

"Was that wise?" she asked Patrick quietly.

"What else could I do?" he asked helplessly. "It was bound to happen anyway. Mother Poole's determined to have her."

"The geese, you mean?"

He shrugged.

"Bart won't like it," Penelope said cautiously.

"He can deal with the old woman," Patrick said, standing up and beginning to collapse the chairs.

"I think . . . Patrick, listen to me . . ." He turned his head toward her, but went on working with the chairs. "I think Bart's afraid of Lyndsay, of what Mother Poole . . ."

"Bart's afraid of nobody," he said quickly. "You know that. You've *seen*."

"All right then," she agreed quietly, anxious to avoid a quarrel. "But you're afraid of him. You know you are. Patrick, please let me help you."

He stared at her pale face for a moment, then brusquely returned to the chairs.

"Thank you for your help, Penelope. I can manage now," he said.

Tears filled her eyes.

"Patrick, *please* . . ." she begged him, but he carried the folded chairs into the house without looking at her, as though he had not even heard her.

CHAPTER FOUR

Emelye knew that she had done wrong, but there was still a spark of angry disobedience in her. It did not show, however, in the quiet early morning as she walked in the shadows and glanced continually about her. In her heart she was defiant as she descended the steep hill from the oaks into Ratchets. There was more that she might do. More and worse, she told herself, but her courage was a frail thing. It began to waver even as she faced the clear, sunlit stretch of the village green. She drew close up under a hedge, hesitating. Anyone might see her and carry tales.

"I saw your Emelye, this morning, crossing the green. That's a bit out of her way, isn't it?"

She would say that she had gone for a walk. It was the truth as far as it went. After all, she knew every corner of Ratchets, every field and stile, even to its farthest boundaries. It had been her kingdom, this village, and yet now she regarded it with a mixture of terror and loathing.

Of all the emotions which assailed her, perhaps the most confusing was this changed reaction to her home. It wasn't just that she had looked outside the village and seen another world, although that was rare enough for a Ratchets girl. As a result, all her life seemed to be called into question, as though she had been living a dream. Love had become hate. Her prospects had dwindled to a kind of death. She had been a privileged daughter of the village, schooled by old Mother Poole to an understanding of her status and inheritance. She had stood proudly on that very green, to be honored as the Queen of the May. That was when the blood that made her a woman had first flown, as the Ways dictated. Garlanded, dressed in white, she had been betrothed that day, and they had sung songs for her future happiness and prosperity. Even Bart had been pleased with her. But now the memory of that day was hateful to her. Now they said that she was just like Maddy Berryman and threatened her with a worse fate.

With a sinking heart, Emelye realized that the longer she waited there, in the shadows, the greater was the chance of being seen and talked about. She pulled her black shawl more tightly over her head, and looked down at her large, ugly, flat shoes. She had been beautiful and now they said her beauty was a curse. Worry and fear had taken it away from her anyway. She knew that she was underweight and walked with a stoop. But what did that matter now? Bracing herself, she moved forward, intending to hurry across the green and take the path beside the children's graveyard to Dolben House. If she didn't hurry, she'd be late. She had only taken a few steps, however, when a movement caught her attention. She shaded her eyes against the sun, looking into the dark tunnel of the road ahead.

She recognized Lyndsay Dolben at once, and instinctively drew back. Bareheaded and chicly dressed, Lyndsay could never pass for a Ratchets woman. Emelye's feelings about Lyndsay were curiously mixed. She felt sorry for her, but she resented her, too. The habits of her short lifetime died hard. She still felt, even though she knew better, something of that fear of outsiders which kept the community so closely knit. The foreign woman was in a hurry, and kept glancing about her as though she, too, feared prying eyes. But she, Emelye thought bitterly, had nothing to fear. For a moment she hated her, yet she had gone out of her way, that morning, to defy them and what they intended. She didn't know what she felt really, except confused and afraid. As she watched Lyndsay turn into the main street, she wasn't sure if what she had done was for her, to tell her, or just to spite them. A bit of both. Perhaps neither. She felt dizzy. Sometimes she thought that it was Lyndsay Dolben who had taken everything from her, but at others she knew it was entirely her own fault.

Lyndsay would draw any prying eyes after her, she realized and, hitching her shawl once more, she scuttled across the green. She was glad that she would have the big house to herself. The chance of Lyndsay speaking to her, asking her questions, frightened them. If anything got out, Emelye knew she'd get the blame, and she had enough troubles already. More than she could cope with.

Lyndsay paced up and down on the pavement outside the post office. She didn't like to knock, but surely it would soon be time for Cloris Poole to open up? She felt better this morning, in spite of the nightmares that had gradually shifted into dreams of such eroticism that she had woken shocked and trembling. The possibility that she was going out of her mind was a very real one. It was even understandable. Making coffee for herself in the silent kitchen, she had realized that Penelope was right. She should rest. She should avoid the emotional shocks of yesterday. She simply wasn't up to them. Not yet. But she would be able to cope, she thought, if only there was someone she trusted, someone sane and sensible to whom she could talk. Mrs. Abernathy had immediately sprung to mind. Lyndsay had felt better at once. Just having something definite to do made her feel safe again. Even though she must have written down the name of the wrong hotel, it had to be possible to track down the old lady. And to her, she knew, she could talk.

At last she heard the thud of heavy bolts being drawn and went toward the two high steps which led to the post office door. It opened inward, with the muffled clatter of an old, tuneless bell. Cloris Poole stared at Lyndsay in surprise. She was a tall, imposing woman with what Lyndsay already recognized as the distinctive, almost gypsyish Poole coloring. She wore an old faded apron which did nothing for her figure, and her thick black hair was drawn into a tight, unbecoming bun. It was, Lyndsay thought, as though she had deliberately tried to make herself look older and less attractive than she was. With a reflex action, Cloris Poole reached up her hand and patted her bun.

"'Morning," she said and turned back into the tiny shop which seemed, after the sunlight, impenetrably dark.

Lyndsay followed her. The room had a red-tiled floor and a counter ran along two walls. The counter immediately opposite the door offered a selection of candy, cigarettes, and newspapers, while the other section, on Lyndsay's right, was barred by an old and heavy grille. In spite of this commercial furniture, the room unmistakably had been converted from an ordinary living room. Faded, leaf-patterned wallpaper reached to a brown picture rail, from which now hung posters and price lists, post office information.

"Yes?" Cloris said, interrupting Lyndsay's inspection of the room.

"Sorry," she smiled. "I . . . er . . . I've never been in a shop like this before."

"It's nothing much," Cloris said flatly, "but it serves its purpose."

"I'm sure," Lyndsay said quickly. She hadn't meant to sound rude. "Actually, I wondered if you had a London telephone directory and a pay phone I could use."

Cloris Poole looked at her steadily.

"There's a phone at Dolben House," she said.

"I know," she agreed.

Of course she knew who Lyndsay was, but it still surprised her. Knew because of her accent, her clothes. There's something hostile about her, she thought. The way she stands there, looking at me. . . .

"There's a phone, of course, but no London directory. I thought you'd have one and that I could call from here. That's all." And why, she thought, should I have to justify myself to her?

"You could have asked for Information, but since you're here you'd best come through," Cloris said, opening a door behind the counter.

"Oh thank you," Lyndsay said automatically. She walked around the counter and into a brighter but incredibly cluttered room. A table stood beneath the window which looked onto a long strip of garden and the fields beyond. It was evidently Cloris Poole's living room, but it was crammed with stacks of newspapers, cartons of sweets and cigarettes and, most incongruous of all, an old and cumbersome switchboard. Lyndsay remained on the threshold, looking around. Cloris Poole, meanwhile, stepped among the clutter, inspecting various piles of books and papers. At last, bending over, she pulled out four thick volumes and blew dust from them as she turned to face Lyndsay. She held the directories almost defensively against her stomach.

"You've found them, good," Lyndsay said, advancing into the room.

Cloris looked down at the pile of directories and then, slowly, placed them on top of the switchboard.

"Thank you," Lyndsay said and took up the third volume. She flipped through the pages until she found the letter *P*. Beside her

Cloris fiddled with the switchboard and then pushed a telephone toward Lyndsay.

"When you're ready, just call up the operator and ask for the number. I'll be in the shop."

"Thanks," Lyndsay called as Cloris went back into the shop, leaving the door open.

For the next fifteen minutes Lyndsay tried all the hotels she could locate with the word *Palace* in their names. None of them had a Mrs. Abernathy staying there. At the third negative reply she felt defeated. Maybe it was "something Palace" and not the other way round, she thought. She asked for London Information, but without further details the girl said she couldn't help her.

"But it'll be a major hotel. In the center of London," she said, her voice sounding desperate. "Can't you think of anywhere?"

The girl sighed audibly. "Just a moment."

Lyndsay waited, staring at the chaos in the room and wondering how Cloris could bear to live like that.

"Hello?"

"Yes, I'm here."

"You could try the Strand Palace and the Metropole Palace." She gave the numbers. Lyndsay jotted them down on the open directory and thanked the girl. She got the Corminster operator again and spoke to both hotels. No Mrs. Abernathy. She was not staying there and they had no booking in that name. Lyndsay replaced the receiver. The switchboard began to buzz loudly and Cloris came back into the room, picked up a headset, and spoke to someone. Disappointed, Lyndsay walked back into the shop. Maybe Mrs. Abernathy had taken off somewhere. Stratford-upon-Avon, or some other tourist spot.

"How much do I owe you?" she asked when Cloris had finished with the switchboard.

"I'll have to get the operator to tell me."

"Will this cover it?" Lyndsay pulled an unfamiliar pound note from her purse.

"I should think so. If not, I'll let you know." Cloris took the note. "Anything else?"

"Oh yes. Do you have any air letters? You know, those blue ones, airmail?" The sort Michael had used, always, to write to her.

Cloris Poole walked round behind the grille and opened a heavy book.

"How many?"

"Two." She pushed another pound note under the grille and took the flimsy sheets of paper.

"You'll be writing home, I expect," Cloris said as she tipped change onto the counter.

"Yes," Lyndsay said. "I must." She fumbled the coins into her purse, thinking about Michael and Mrs. Abernathy, about how she didn't know how to write to her parents. She felt very alone. Cloris watched her impassively. "Thanks for your help," Lyndsay said and turned toward the door.

Cloris said nothing, but her dark eyes followed Lyndsay out into the street, watched her pause, look to left and right before turning back in the direction of Dolben House.

She was still standing there, lost in thought, when a village woman came in.

"'Morning, Cloris," she said. "I see you've had the Mistress in. Fancy!"

Unnecessarily, Cloris tidied the counter.

"There's no such thing," she said dismissively. "You ought to know that by now, Alice."

"Ah, don't you be too sure, Cloris Poole," the woman said, wagging her head. "Such things aren't easily changed."

"Do you want something?" Cloris said rudely, "'cause, I've got lots to do even if you haven't."

With a toss of her head, the woman asked for a postal order and waited, silently, while Cloris stamped it.

Beyond the chancel and its graveyard, where Michael Dolben was buried, the village street became an unpaved track. A high hedge separated it from fields on one side, while the other was bounded by a plantation of trees, a number of which had recently been felled. After about a quarter of a mile, the track petered out into a series of meadows which rose to the ridge. In a corner of the first field, surrounded by a rickety wooden fence, was a wood and tar-paper shack, an ugly, handmade house. It had no garden. The earth inside the fence was trampled hard and strewn with piles of scrap metal, engine parts, discarded bits and pieces from which Timon Berryman scraped his living.

About the time when Cloris Poole was opening the post office,

Timon's wife, Magdalena, crossed the sun-drenched fields and went to her gate. She had walked more than a mile with her eldest children, Christian and Bella. The baby she carried in the crook of her arm. And once she had put the children on the school bus, she dragged herself wearily back again. It was the only safe way and at least this morning, she thought, staring once again toward the ridge, he was not up there watching her. Not that it really made much difference whether he watched or not. She knew in her heart and bones that he was only biding his time, and that it would be soon now.

The baby whimpered, pressed a tight fist into her breast. Automatically she soothed it, shifted it to a more comfortable position on her arm. She unlatched the gate, which squeaked gratingly on its rusted hinges, and went toward the shack that was her home. Halfway across the yard she stopped and glanced warily round her. Her keen eyes had seen a basket, covered with a white napkin, standing in the shadow of the door. She could see no one in the plantation or on the ridge. Best get it inside, she thought, and wished, as she always wished, that she wouldn't bring the basket. Snatching it up, holding the baby awkwardly, so that she began to whimper, Magdalena Berryman let herself into the house.

It was dim inside and the fire, which was the only means she had of cooking, had burned down. Settling the baby in an old crib, she poked dry twigs under the blackened kettle and prepared the baby's bottle. As she sat by the fire, feeding the baby and rocking slightly back and forth, she stared at the basket. All these years Penelope Clare had risked shame and God knew what else, to bring her these little gifts, but she felt no gratitude. It would be better for them all if she didn't do it. He must know, she thought. He has eyes everywhere. And he'll pay her back. Not that Magdalena cared. These were conscience gifts, delivered by a coward. Penelope Clare deserved whatever was coming to her and not one tear would she shed for her. If she lived to see it.

When the baby had drunk enough of the milk, Magdalena rose slowly from her chair and gently placed her back in the crib. Then she went to the table and unpacked the basket. Except, of course, she thought bitterly, they needed this charity. The children needed it. There was a freshly baked seedcake, some biscuits and canned food, all of which she would have liked to throw away but which would, as always, help to keep them going a bit longer. And a note.

Right at the bottom of the basket, folded small. Her fingers shaking, Magdalena Berryman took the paper from the basket and unfolded it.

> I don't know what they're planning, but I'm afraid something will happen now that the Mistress has arrived. I don't think they will forget about you. Can't you get away?

Savagely, Magdalena crumpled the note into a ball and threw it on the fire. She watched it burst into flames and immediately regretted her action. Perhaps if she had kept it, Timon would have believed her at last. Perhaps she could have made him see beyond his pride and his blind certainty.

She turned away from the fire and went to one of the odd, ill-fitting windows. She stared up toward the ridge, which was golden now in the sun. The place haunted her. It always had, even as a girl and a young woman. All the important events or mistakes of her life had happened up there. There, in the long summer grass, she had given Timon her virginity. There she had been trapped and cornered, dragged back into the village, kicking and screaming. There, when they had disowned her, she had met him for the last time.

You'll never get away from me, Maddy. He'll never keep you. If it takes all my life, I'll destroy him and you. You'll pay. Both of you. Aye, and any bastards you bring into the world.

And it was from there now, most days, that he watched her, silent and black against the sky.

She'd been brave then, when it was just her and Timon against the world, but the years had worn her down, sapped her courage and strength. There were the children now. She was so tired that she didn't really care anymore what he might do to her or Timon. As long as the children were safe. *Can't you get away?* Oh it was easy to write, but how? With three children and a man who, when he was not fuddled with drink, thought that he was big enough to stand against the monumental anger of Bart Poole. Timon was an outsider. He didn't know what she did. It was because he was an outsider that she had loved him. He had nothing to offer but his good looks, his red hair, and his chaotically cheerful family. But she had loved him and believed that when they moved on, they would take her with them, that she would be free.

87

Dreams, she thought bitterly. Now the nightmare was coming. She didn't need Penelope Clare to tell her that. What she had suffered in the past was nothing compared to what he would do now. She could smell it in the air, like smoke. She *had* to make Timon understand. They must get away, all of them.

She turned from the window and picked up a heavy, galvanized bucket. Outside in the yard, she pumped water into the bucket and then carried it back into the house. She must get everything clean and ready. At the very least they must take the children's clothes, such as they were. And work, hard work, kept her mind occupied. For whole minutes at a time, if she worked and pushed her body to the limits of exhaustion, she could forget that time was running out.

Lyndsay recognized the dog at once.

"Hello, boy," she called and he came bounding down the brick path toward her. Delighted, Lyndsay squatted in the open gateway and petted the dog, who seemed equally pleased to see her.

The cottage was old and small. The garden was full of the traditional English flowers—marigolds, sweet Williams, black-eyed Susans, and hollyhocks. The dog whimpered as she stood up, and ran a little way along the path, as though asking her to follow.

"See you again, boy," she said.

The dog barked and ran back to her, winding himself about her legs. Laughing, Lyndsay bent to stroke him once more.

"Won't you come in, Mistress? Old dog there seems to have taken a fancy to you."

Lyndsay straightened up and looked at the old woman who stood in the doorway. She was elderly and yet ageless. Her straight back and patrician face belied her years. Her black hair was only dusted with streaks and speckles of gray.

"Come in," she repeated. "We've been waiting on you."

It was true, the old woman thought, as she moved into her herb-smelling, hot kitchen. So long she'd been waiting and now . . . She clasped her bony, arthritic hands tightly together in excitement.

The woman's sudden disappearance left Lyndsay little choice. It would be too rude just to walk away without saying anything. She walked up the path, the dog trotting contentedly at her side. That the woman had been waiting for her seemed unlikely until she remembered what Penelope Clare had said the previous day. This must be Mother Poole. Penelope had made the appointment for her, even though she had not agreed to it.

The door opened into a tiny hall, from which a narrow staircase rose steeply. The door on her left was open and she tapped on it even as the dog pushed past her and went into the room.

"Come in. No standing on ceremony here, Mistress."

Lyndsay had never imagined such a room. It was like a cave, an interior garden. It was hot and full of strange sweet and spicy scents. A fire burned in an ancient range. Something resembling a small cauldron was suspended over the fire. Its contents bubbled noisily. The woman sat in the farther of two chairs which stood on either side of the range. A plain deal table took up most of the rest of the space, and beyond it was a beautiful old dresser, its shelves crammed with bottles and jars.

"You must be Mrs. Poole," Lyndsay said, standing just inside the room. She wasn't at all sure she wanted to go any farther in. The woman's eyes were very black and seemed to glow at her.

"Mother, they call me. Mother Poole."

"Excuse me," Lyndsay said automatically.

"Come, make yourself comfortable. We must have a talk, you and me." She waved a strong, brown-skinned hand at the vacant chair.

Lyndsay hesitated, but no excuse, no polite means of escape came to her.

"I mustn't stay long," she said, knowing that it sounded unconvincing. She perched on the edge of the chair.

Mother Poole did not reply, although there was plenty she could have said. Instead, she kept her eyes fixed on Lyndsay who, embarrassed, looked around the room at the rampaging plants and the drying bunches of herbs.

"I know what you're thinking," Mother Poole said at last. "You're wondering if I'm a witch, with my potions and bits and bobs." She chuckled gently.

"No," Lyndsay said. "I wasn't thinking that at all. First of all, witches don't exist."

With a loud plop Mother Poole uncorked a bottle and poured a pale, pink liquid into two small glasses.

"Isn't it a little early to be drinking?" Lyndsay asked.

"It's never too early for my raspberry cordial," the woman answered quickly and cheerfully. "Besides, it'll do you good. Here." She handed a glass to Lyndsay, who took and smelled it. It certainly

89

smelled of raspberries. "Oh it's not poisoned," Mother Poole said. "My but you're a suspicious one."

"Don't be silly," Lyndsay retorted. "The thought didn't cross my mind."

"Aye, and butter wouldn't melt in your mouth. Cheers." Leaning against the table, Mother Poole raised her glass in salute, and then drained it in one gulp.

Lyndsay couldn't help smiling at this eccentric and, she suspected, calculated show of bravado. She sipped her own drink, finding it too sweet and rather cloying.

"You don't trust me," Mother Poole said matter-of-factly.

"No," Lyndsay said. "I mean, I don't know you."

"Do you never trust on sight? Did you know Michael Dolben before you trusted him? Can't you feel it here—" she clapped her right hand theatrically to her heart—"when you meet those you can?"

Lyndsay looked down at her glass. The old woman's bluntness embarrassed her. And what did she know about Michael anyway? The trust she had had in him could not be compared with any other kind of relationship.

"You can trust me," Mother Poole went on. "I'm the only one you can trust completely. No . . ." She held up her hand, forbidding Lyndsay to speak. "Don't answer back. You must trust me. That's all."

The woman's crazy, Lyndsay thought. She moved back in her chair a little and crossed her legs. Probably she spent most of her time tippling this stuff. She's just a harmless old crazy-lady.

"All right," she said, intending to humor Mother Poole. "So what if I do trust you?"

"Then you will be safe and you will gain your heart's desire. More even. More than you dream of, more than anyone would dare to expect."

Lyndsay suppressed a desire to laugh. Partly it was because the woman was so pompously serious and partly because the so-called cordial was very potent. She felt a little light-headed.

"Do you read palms as well?" she asked defensively.

"Don't mock me, Mistress," Mother Poole said quietly, but with a terrible authority. "And don't apologize, either. This is serious business. You keep your sharp tongue and your spirit for when they're needed."

Lyndsay bent over her drink, ashamed of herself suddenly. To Mother Poole it looked like a sign of obedience and acceptance. She was pleased.

"I thought I was here," Lyndsay said, faltering a little, "to ask you about the Gabriel Ratchets."

The woman's chin went up.

"What about them?"

"Penelope Clare said I should ask you." Lyndsay forced a smile. "She said there was nothing you didn't know about local legends and stuff."

"There's always something a body doesn't know," Mother Poole said. "And Penelope Clare's a great fool. Why do you want to know about the Gabriel Ratchets? What are they to you?"

"I just . . ." Lyndsay stopped. She had been going to say she was simply curious, but it was much more than that and she sensed that the old woman knew it. "I think they're evil," she said, looking the woman full in the face. "I went into that awful graveyard yesterday and I saw the dog on all those gravestones. It scared me. And it's on the Dolben Collar, too. You know about that?" Mother Poole nodded solemnly. "I was afraid. I think it has something to do with death."

Mother Poole looked at her for a long moment, and then inclined her head just a little.

"I'll tell you," she said. "It's nothing but an emblem, like the great people have on their coats of arms, or a country's flag. What else should be the sign of Ratchets but the Gabriel Hounds?" She paused for a moment, looking down at her hands. "It's an old story," she said, "and it comes in many versions. Some say they were geese, others hounds. Some say they exist, and others that it's all an old wives' tale. When a baby dies," she went on, leaning a little toward Lyndsay, "without the blessing of the Church, where does its soul go? Not to heaven, say the priests, nor yet to hell since its only sins are those of the father. Limbo, then. No place. The Church," she said harshly, "brought scant comfort to the grieving mothers. Them with their arguments and rules. Could you have borne it, if you had lost your baby and were told that there was no comfort, no certain resting place? I think you'd have done what the women of old did. They said the souls of their babies took on the shape of great dogs. They came in thunderstorms, up there in the sky, and they lifted up their voices and cried to be let into heaven." The woman's

91

voice rose dramatically, conjuring pictures which made Lyndsay shiver.

"Time back, when the Dolbens and the Clares set themselves up against each other, the priests refused to baptize the babies or bury them in consecrated ground. The women, the mothers, remembered the old tale and took comfort in it. And the men followed the women's lead, but they couldn't leave well enough alone. Not them. Great meddlers, men. They said the babes would rise up out of the graves in the form of hounds and take revenge on those who had condemned them to limbo. And others spoke of using them, of harnessing the power of the hounds. What started out as comfort became a tale to frighten children with. Watch out, they'd say, or the Gabriel Ratchets'll get you. And so they started saying that the hounds came looking for other babes, to be playmates with them in their loneliness and to punish those parents who were against them."

Mother Poole paused, shaking her head over the world's folly.

"I guess I was right," Lyndsay said. "It is evil."

"Foolishness more like. At last, when the stories had got so out of hand that even the stubborn Dolbens and the proud Clares could see the harm in it, they made their peace. Ezekiel Dolben gave the private chapel and the land to the village. He let the Clares take the services there. And so no one should ever forget, they made a memorial of it to all the poor, benighted babes. One day, they say, when all is really as it should be, those poor souls will be released and will fly up to heaven singing with the sweet voices of white birds."

The woman's voice soared and lingered in the hot, stuffy room. Suddenly, she turned to the fire and, taking a piece of cloth, deftly unhooked the little cauldron and placed it on the hob.

"But why do people go on burying their children there? Isn't that macabre?"

"It is if you think it is," she replied calmly. "Are you religious?"

"No," Lyndsay said. "Not particularly. I guess I'm like most people. Hopeful but unconvinced."

"Well then you'll understand. After the feud between the Dolbens and the Clares, Ratchets folk got out of the way of religion. They'd seen enough of the damage that can be done. While the great men quarreled, the rest of us suffered, especially the women. So the old church went to rack and ruin. The Clares preached to themselves about heaven and hell. But the village liked the idea of a memorial to the children. And so it goes on. More out of habit now than respect, I daresay, but what does that matter?" She leaned forward and tapped Lyndsay on the knee. "It's like all legends, Mistress. There's sense and nonsense in it. Good and bad. When it comes to it, it's only what you make of it." She sat back and folded her hands in her lap.

"But why is the hound on the collar?"

"Look," she said, turning round in her chair and unhooking a walking stick from the back of it. It was a beautiful stick, carved and oiled. She held the handle toward Lyndsay. It was carved in the now familiar shape of the hound. "It signifies nothing but habit, tradition. You wear it around your throat to make yourself beautiful, and I lean upon it. All it says is that we remember the children and the old Ways. Perhaps we're hedging our bets. Maybe one day those children'll get into heaven. Is that such a bad thing?"

"No," Lyndsay said.

Mother Poole hooked the stick over the back of her chair. Lyndsay took another sip of her drink.

"Thank you for telling me," she added.

"What frightened you, what ails you, Mistress, is in your own mind."

Suddenly, from some hidden well deep within Lyndsay, the tears began to flow. They were quite unlike the other tears she had shed recently; tears of anguish and fear, of loss and terrified hysteria. These tears were consoling, the ones she needed to shed. Later, Lyndsay would try to make sense of them. Why then? Why there? Because Mother Poole, through instinct or wisdom, had located the source of her fears, that they were all in her own mind, and by doing so had exorcised them a little. But she could not discount the woman herself. The arms which went around her were unexpectedly as warm and comforting as Mrs. Abernathy's had been. She tried to tell her about wanting to reach Mrs. Abernathy, and how she had failed.

"Sh," Mother Poole crooned. "You've got all the friends you need here. Trust me."

And somehow, through her tears, in broken, halting sentences, she had told Mother Poole everything. The geese and Bart Poole's voice. The pig-sticking when she had thought that she would die.

"They lock me in at night," she sobbed. "At least I think they do. Or maybe did. I don't know. And then I have these dreams. Terrible dreams. It all gets mixed up. Do you think I'm crazy?"

The old woman rocked her like a baby. Then she spoke of her

feelings in the graveyard, of the babies she would never have. Throughout the woman was silent, except for soothing, lulling noises.

"Rest now," she said when the tears had stopped. She eased Lyndsay back into the chair and placed her hand on her forehead. "Rest," she repeated. "And remember this. No matter what happens, there is only life for you here, Mistress. Only life."

While Lyndsay slept tranquilly for the first time since she had reached Ratchets, Mother Poole considered her position. Events were moving faster than she had calculated, which meant that Bart might overreach himself, or make some error. But she could not count on that. She knew him too well. Had she not raised and taught him herself, despite the Dolbens? She felt in her bones that Bart would have thought of everything. And if what Lyndsay told her was true then he had already begun to weave the very web which would trap him. She clasped her hands together in excitement, but then a look of worry crossed her aged and handsome face. It meant that she had to invest all in the girl. How much could she take? How strong was her spirit and into what rash acts and dangers might it not lead her?

Mother Poole sighed. The only sure way was to bind Michael Dolben's widow to her completely. She could do that only by telling her everything, by making her commit herself irrevocably. She shook her head sharply. It was too soon. The girl, though right and fitting, well chosen indeed, had too much of the world about her yet. She would laugh or run away. She had to be broken first, like a good horse. She must be broken in order to grow again, become fully and at last the Mistress.

The old lady looked at her sleeping guest. She had no choice but to play it Bart's way then. No two ways about it. And then she smiled, slowly, secretively. Why of course. It was, as it always was, simple. Bart was as handsome a devil as ever walked the ridge. He could be charming, too. He could, when he wanted, be a proper lady's man. The Dolbens had taught him fine manners. And since he wanted to put his head in the noose, Mother Poole saw no reason why he should not do so smiling.

She chuckled gently to herself. Aye, he was clever. But offer him willingly what now he tried to take by force . . . All she had to do was a little innocent pleading. Bart's weakness, she thought with pride and satisfaction, was his love for his old grandmother. Oh he denied it all right, and gave himself many airs, but underneath . . . She felt a stab of pain and gritted her teeth against it, her lips drawn back in a mute snarl. She had given him everything and would seem to give him more. In order to destroy him.

The rattle of teacups disturbed Lyndsay. She opened her eyes and watched Mother Poole moving stiffly from the table to the range. She felt completely at home, she realized, stretching her arms above her head. Mother Poole nodded at her, lifted the lid of the teapot, and peeped inside. She replaced the lid and stood calmly, immobile, waiting for the tea to draw.

"I don't know how to thank you," Lyndsay said. "I'm sorry I broke down."

"You needed to," the old woman said absently, her mind on other things. "Are you rested now?"

"Mm. I feel much better."

"A cup of tea then, and you'll be fighting fit."

Lyndsay laughed.

"I wouldn't go that far, but . . ."

"We'll see." She poured the tea and handed a cup to Lyndsay. It smelled freshly herbal. "Bergamot," she explained. "Freshens you up."

Lyndsay drank the tea in silence, not because there weren't things she wanted to say and ask, but because Mother Poole remained preoccupied and she didn't like to intrude. Her watch told her that it was after two, and she felt that she had already imposed herself long enough. Then, with a sort of preparedness, as though she had reached a decision, Mother Poole sat down and sipped her tea.

"I don't want you to think badly of my Bart," she said directly. "I heard you had a bit of a run-in with him. But don't judge him too harshly. What he did was meant for your own good."

Lyndsay remembered the force with which he had hit her and felt slightly ashamed of herself, yet still sick at the brutality and all that blood.

"Your Bart?" she queried, deflecting what the woman was asking of her.

"Oh that's just a foolish old woman talking," she smiled. "But that's how I think of him still, for all he's so big and manly."

"You aren't foolish, Mother Poole," Lyndsay said. "I know that much. Whatever power it is you have . . ."

She was stopped by the old woman's mocking laugh.

"Oh it's power now, is it? You came in here saying I was a witch and now . . ."

"I'm sorry. Really. But you're wise and kind and that's a sort of power, isn't it?"

Mother Poole stared into the fire for a moment. She seemed to be considering the question very seriously.

"Aye," she said at last. "It is. And it's all you have to rely on just now."

"How . . ." Lyndsay began and then changed her mind. "Mother Poole, will you answer me one question, directly?"

"Yes."

"Am I in some sort of danger? Oh I know it sounds stupid, sitting here so cozy and—"

"No," she cut in sharply. "You're not. But there will be times when you will think you are. That's why you must remember what I tell you."

"But . . ."

"You said one question. That's all I agreed to."

"I don't think that's very fair. I think you ought . . ."

"Trust me," she commanded.

Lyndsay didn't argue anymore. The woman's tone did not permit it and, she thought, I do trust her. To question that trust now would be wrong. She shook her head slowly. Nobody back home would believe in this extraordinary old lady.

"Did you know Michael, my husband?" she asked.

"I knew him. Not well. But he was a bonny lad. Then he went away . . ." She seemed to regret it.

"You know what I think I'll do?" Lyndsay said. "I think I'll go and visit his grave. Put some fresh flowers there."

"Aye, you do that." She set her cup aside. There was something conclusive about the gesture, as though the visit were now terminated.

Lyndsay finished her tea and stood up.

"I've taken up a lot of your time. But thank you," she said, putting her cup and saucer on the table.

"I'll see you to the door," the old woman said, beginning to get up.

"Please don't bother. I can see myself out. You look tired. Can I get you anything?"

"No, no. Be on your way now." She closed her eyes.

Lyndsay looked at her for a moment, then picked her way around the chair and opened the door. "There's just one thing," she said, turning back toward the woman, whose eyelids flickered open. "Why are they called *Gabriel* Ratchets?"

"That I don't know for sure," she said wearily. "Some say the story began here, so they were Ratchets Hounds. Maybe some man called Gabriel thought he had the power to raise them. But most likely it's nothing more than the Angel Gabriel."

She closed her eyes again.

"You're tired. I'm sorry."

The old woman's hand moved on the chair arm, waving her away.

The kind, well-meaning man let Christian and Bella Berryman out of his car at the oaks. Awkwardly, red-faced, Christian thanked him. The school bus had broken down in Wellsby, stranding them. The man had gotten his car and driven them. Christian had asked, politely, as his mother had taught him, to be put out at the stile some two miles before the Ratchets turnoff.

"Whatever for?" the man had said.

"We always go that way. Across the fields."

"Well, today you can save your legs," the man said. "It's much quicker for you this way."

The boy had tried again, but there was no way he could convey to this stranger the fear he did not understand. He had never, ever been into the village. Nor had Bella. Once, when he was very young, he'd toddled along the track, almost as far as the old chancel, and a tall blond lady, as blond as his mother and he, had stood watching him with a funny expression on her face. Then his mother had come looking for him. He could still remember the sting of her flaying hands on the backs of his legs. It was true, though: she had always told him, ever since he could remember, that he must never go there. His father, of course, went through the village in his old truck, very fast, but his mother did not even like that. He was afraid, and he did not know why. All the children at school thought them funny because the bus had to make a special stop for them. None of the other children from Ratchets ever spoke to them, or seemed to be aware of their existence. Sometimes, when they'd been put to bed, if Bella wasn't too sleepy, they discussed together why the village was dangerous. Bella said it was a bad place, full of witches and ghosts, but Christian was too old to believe that now. Occasionally he'd heard his parents talking late at night, and he thought it had something to do with before he was born. The people did not like his mother. Somehow his father wasn't good enough for them, which was also why they were poor and afraid. And why his mother made him work hard at his lessons. He knew, but he hadn't told anyone, not even Bella, that they called his mother "Mad Maddy." Knowing this made him feel guilty, but sometimes he wondered if that was it, if she was mad and just imagined things about the village.

He stood uncertainly at the crossroad, Bella at his side. What would happen to him if he walked down the hill and through the village? In spite of his doubts, he still felt afraid. Besides, he was a boy and the eldest. He had to look after Bella.

"Come on," he said. "We'll go this way, across the fields. If we go far enough, we'll come out behind our house."

Bella looked at him with her big, pale eyes. Her bottom lip quivered a little.

"It's all right," he said.

"Mummy'll be cross."

"No. Not when I explain. Come on."

He walked past the oaks, into the big field which sloped gently down toward the village. In the far corner was a clump of trees and beyond them the chancel roof. They could cut through the graveyard, he decided, and then run the last bit along the track. He turned around, looking for Bella. She was squatting on a charred patch of earth beneath the oaks.

"Bella," he called. "Come on."

"Look, Christian," she said. "Aren't they lovely?"

"Never mind that. Come on. We'll get into ever such a row if we're late."

"But you said . . ."

"I know. But not if we're late. Oh what is it anyway?"

He retraced his steps. If was often easier to get Bella to cooperate if you gave way to her first. She was looking at an old jam jar

98

standing on the scorched earth. It contained three large and beautiful roses.

"Aren't they lovely," Bella said, reaching out her small hand to touch one curled, golden petal. She loved flowers and all they ever had were wild ones, picked from the hedgerows. She'd always wanted a garden, full of real flowers. "I'm going to take them," she announced suddenly, and snatched the roses out of the jar.

"No, Bella. You mustn't. They're not yours."

"I can because they're not anybody's."

"You don't know that," Christian argued. "Somebody must have put them there."

"What for? There's nothing here. You don't put roses on a moldy old bit of earth. They're for anyone who wants," she said firmly, and stood up.

Christian hesitated. It was wrong to take the roses, he was sure, but if he argued much longer they'd be very late. . . .

It was better to risk being told off about the flowers—he could honestly say it was all Bella's fault—than to waste precious time arguing with her.

"All right," he said, taking a firm grip of her free hand. "But remember, *you* took them, not me. *I* told you not to. Now come on."

Bella allowed herself to be hurried along. She thought Christian was stupid. She hummed happily to herself, looking at the roses and dipping her head to smell them. Tomorrow she would take them to school and put them on the windowsill among the other flowers. Miss Barnes would say how lovely they were, and perhaps even give her a gold star.

Tugging his sister along, Christian made a beeline for the little copse of evergreens which marked the churchyard boundary on the field side. Bella's tuneless humming irritated him, but he did not tell her to stop. As long as she was content with her silly flowers, she wouldn't object to him pulling her. Slightly out of breath, they reached the copse.

"Go quietly now," he said, stepping into the shadows.

"Why?"

"Just do. That's all." He trod carefully, moving toward the gravestones. His heart began to thump, just because he was so close to the village. He told himself that there was nothing to be afraid of, but he was afraid all the same. Suddenly, he froze. Bella bumped into him. There was a lady, crouched by a pile of earth, a new grave. Four old, withered lily wreaths were piled haphazardly beside it, and the lady was arranging an enormous bunch of red roses in a stone vase.

"What is it?" Bella asked, peering round him.

"Sh!" he warned, but she pushed past him, staring at the roses in the vase.

"Oh look, Christian. Look how many that lady's got!"

Before he realized what was happening, Bella had pulled her hand free and was hurrying toward the kneeling woman. She glanced up, frowning, and then smiled.

"Hello," Lyndsay said.

"Hello. I've got some roses, too. But you've got more than me."

"Yes, I have," Lyndsay said. "But yours are very pretty."

"Why do you talk funny?"

Lyndsay laughed. "Because I come from a long way away. America."

"Is that why you've got so many roses?"

"No. Just that I picked a lot."

"Why are you putting them there?"

Lyndsay thought for a moment, her smile becoming hesitant. "Just to show I haven't forgotten the person who is buried here."

"Did you put these up by those trees?" Bella asked.

Christian ran from the copse.

"Come on, Bella. We're late. We've got to go now."

"Hello," Lyndsay said to the boy. He didn't look at her. "Is this your brother?"

"Yes. Can I have one of your roses?" Bella asked. "I haven't got any red ones."

Christian, who was afraid to go too near the woman, called to his sister again.

"Sure you can," Lyndsay replied. She pulled a rose from the vase and held it out to Bella, who went toward her.

Terrified, Christian ran forward, grabbed his sister by the shoulder, and pulled her back. Her small, sandaled feet slipped in the loose earth beside the grave, and she fell over, hurting her knee. It was, even so, more shock than anything, Lyndsay thought, when the little girl began to wail.

"Now look what you've done," she said reproachfully to the boy. He seemed to shrink away from her. "It's okay. You're not really hurt, are you?" she said to the girl.

"Get away from her," Christian shouted, red-faced. "You leave us alone."

Suddenly he ran toward Lyndsay and pushed her, hard, in the stomach. He didn't really hurt her, but Lyndsay recoiled, her mouth open in surprise. The boy reached down and grabbed the girl by the arm, trying to pull her up. She, crying and wailing, could not find a foothold. Sharp pebbles grazed her legs as the boy pulled her. Desperately, she tried to gather up the roses she had dropped.

"Stop it," Lyndsay shouted at the boy. "Can't you see you're . . ." She hurried forward again.

"Leave us alone," he screamed, tears suddenly starting from his eyes. "If you don't I'll kill you."

Again Lyndsay stopped, shocked by the sheer force of anger and hatred on the boy's face.

"Go away," he sobbed.

Lyndsay watched, helpless, not knowing what to do. Should she go or . . . ?

"Lyndsay, what on earth . . . Oh!"

A little out of breath, Penelope Clare came around the corner of the chancel and stopped as though horrified. She stared at the children. Bella continued to scream as the boy managed to haul her to her knees.

"I only tried to . . ." Lyndsay called, moving toward Penelope.

"Get away from them," Penelope ordered. "Over there." She waved Lyndsay back, away from herself and the children. "Please do as I say," she shouted as Lyndsay stared at her, bemused.

With a shrug that said she thought the whole world had gone mad, Lyndsay did as Penelope asked. The child's screams, now obviously hysterical, were beginning to hurt her ears.

"It's all right," Penelope called to the children. "We won't hurt you. Come on. This way. Down to the gate. Then you can get home."

The boy looked at her uncertainly, tears streaming down his face. The little girl hit him. She wanted to pick up the flowers which she could not reach because he was holding her tightly.

"For God's sake," Lyndsay said. "What is this? Let her pick up the roses," she told the boy.

"Leave them. Leave them alone."

Penelope whirled round. Lyndsay, forgetting the children, saw a wild-eyed woman running up the path. Her fair hair was unkempt and streaming about her ashen face.

"Mummy," the boy shouted.

The woman stopped short of Penelope, staring at her children. "Get away," she hissed.

As though terrified, Penelope immediately backed away and slowly the woman came forward, her eyes fixed on the children. At a sign from her they ran to her arms. She held them tightly, protectively. The little girl's screams quieted to gulping sobs as she pressed her face against her mother's stomach.

"Now you let me pass," the woman said.

"Look," Lyndsay said exasperated, "all that happened was . . ."

"I don't want to hear," the woman screamed.

"I was only trying to help," Lyndsay shouted back, taking a step toward the woman.

"You? Help?" She made a harsh, hysterical sound somewhere between laughter and a cry.

"Yes," Lyndsay insisted.

"You're a Dolben, aren't you? Then, don't come near my children."

She began to walk away, pulling the children with her. Lyndsay looked at Penelope, who shook her head sharply. Then, speaking quietly to the children, the woman turned around, her arms spread across their shoulders. She hesitated for a long moment, looking at Penelope Clare. Shaking visibly, Penelope met her gaze. Then the woman spat viciously onto the ground in Penelope's direction.

"For heaven's sake," Lyndsay cried, running forward.

"Lyndsay . . . please," Penelope said, her voice breaking.

Lyndsay stopped, bewildered. The woman and the children ran down the path and through the gate. They turned along the road, passing beneath the knoll on which Lyndsay and Penelope stood mutely.

"Are you okay?"

Penelope nodded and drew a deep breath. Lyndsay looked at Michael's grave. The three roses and the one she had offered to the child lay on the ground beside it. One of them had been bruised and damaged by the boy in his panic to raise his sister. Sadly, Lyndsay went toward them, intending to pick them up.

"Leave them," Penelope said harshly. "Please."

She turned and went down the path. Shocked by the violence of all their reactions, Lyndsay followed her.

"I think we both need a drink," Penelope said.

"What was all that about?" Lyndsay demanded, walking after Penelope into Clare House.

"Please," she said weakly. Her hands rattled the glasses on the bar cart.

"Here," Lyndsay said quickly. "Let me do that. What'll it be? Scotch?"

"Thank you," Penelope said, sinking wearily into a chair. She pressed her long fingers to her forehead.

Lyndsay splashed whiskey into two heavy, monogrammed tumblers and handed one to Penelope. She took it and drank, shuddering a little as the alcohol burned her throat.

"Could you pass my cigarettes?" she asked. "They're over there."

Lyndsay fetched the cigarettes and watched, sitting on the edge of the settee, as Penelope lit one and inhaled.

"You're shaking," Lyndsay said. "Should you lie down or something?"

"No. No. I'll be all right in a minute." She picked up her glass and drank again. "I'm afraid," she said, trying to smile, "you've stumbled upon a skeleton in our cupboard."

"Never mind that," Lyndsay said brusquely. "Just tell me, is that woman crazy or something?"

"I don't know," Penelope replied miserably. "They call her Mad Maddy but . . ."

"She looked crazy to me. But those kids were scared to death. Especially the boy. I don't get it."

"What happened, before I got there?" Penelope asked.

Briefly, Lyndsay told her. Penelope had been working in the garden when she had heard the girl's screams.

"You mustn't blame the children," Penelope continued. "She's made them like that. Poor Maddy." She shook her head sadly.

"I think," Lyndsay said, taking her glass, "you need another shot. Then you'd better tell me about it."

"Not too much," Penelope said.

Lyndsay held out the refilled glass and asked gently: "Why did she spit at you?"

103

A look of pain crossed Penelope's face.

"I . . . suppose because she hates me. Blames me. I find it . . . difficult to talk about her like this. She's a relative of mine. A cousin. We grew up together. Well, she's older than me but we were very close once. Poor Maddy," she said again.

Lyndsay remembered the woman's pale hair and eyes. She could see, of course, that she was a Clare. And she had passed the family coloring on to her son. She sat down quietly and waited until Penelope was ready, or able, to go on.

"That branch of the family was very well-off and respected. Albertine Clare, Magdalena's mother—that's Maddy's real name—was a very strict woman and very proud. We all looked up to her. She was like a leader. A village elder. I suppose we were all a little bit afraid of her. She could be hard." Penelope stared into her glass as though she could see the people and events she described floating there. "It was just that she wanted so much for Maddy. Most of all she wanted her to marry well. That was the main thing. And it was all arranged. Albertine set her heart on Bart Poole. I never really understood why. On the face of it, he was not an ideal choice, but Albertine had always had a soft spot for him. He was the same age as Maddy and, of course, it would have been a very good match for him. Mother Poole was all for it, naturally. She was even prepared to settle some money on him. Quite a lot, I believe."

"Does she have any?" Lyndsay interrupted. "It certainly didn't look like it from that tumbledown old cottage."

"Ah," Penelope said, looking at her. "You went to see her, then." Lyndsay nodded. "Well, don't be taken in by appearances. Old Mother Poole's a notorious miser. She's got plenty, and it would all have gone to Bart as a marriage settlement if Magdalena hadn't met Timon Berryman." She lapsed into bitter silence. Lyndsay waited, but Penelope seemed lost in her own memories.

"What happened?" Lyndsay prompted.

"Albertine locked her up. She was only a girl but . . . The Berrymans are a curse," she said, her voice hardening again. "They've always been a curse. Gypsies. Hangers-on. They live like pigs and have no respect for us or our Ways. Timon Berryman was a handsome boy. All the Berryman boys were. But they don't belong in Ratchets. They're outsiders. Thieves and poachers. A marriage between a Clare and a Berryman was unthinkable, of course."

Lyndsay refrained from comment. The pride was absolute in Penelope's voice.

"Somehow they managed to meet," Penelope went on, her voice suddenly flat and expressionless. "After a while they ran away together. It was a terrible blow. Albertine had the men hunt them down."

"Hunt them down?" Lyndsay said. "But how? What do you . . . ?"

"With dogs."

"Dogs!"

"Hounds. It was awful. I shall never forget it." Penelope suppressed a shudder. "I'm ashamed to tell you that even my own father took part. But it's history now. They caught them and brought them back. But it was too late. Maddy was already pregnant. She miscarried the next day."

Lyndsay could scarcely believe that she was hearing correctly. Such things did not happen. And if they did, how could anyone live with the consequences, the knowledge?

"She was half-crazed," Penelope resumed. "But, of course, there was no way Albertine could save the situation. Bart couldn't marry her after that. No man would look at her. Besides, she was obsessed with Timon. When she was better, she ran to the Berrymans' place and stayed there with him and his tribe. They lived in filthy caravans then. Timon's built them a hovel of sorts since. Just up the road from here. Nobody around here would marry them, of course, though Maddy says they are married. It doesn't matter," Penelope said dismissively. "To bear the name of Berryman is her shame."

"Why do you say that?" Lyndsay said. "It's an awful . . ."

"I've just explained. Anyway, Maddy had difficulty bearing children—"

"What would you expect after that?" Lyndsay cut in angrily.

"Yes. Well, that's all done with now. She did have children, as you've seen. She has three actually. Another little girl, I believe. But it all turned her head. She thinks they are in danger. She's incredibly possessive. Oh I can understand it. She's so isolated, you see. Only Timon and the children to talk to. She's driven herself mad."

"But surely people in the village . . ."

"No one. Nobody has ever spoken to her since she ran to the Berrymans. They never even come into the village."

"But that's terrible."

"I can't think what the children were doing in the graveyard anyway," Penelope said, as though she had not heard Lyndsay.

"I said that's a terrible way to treat a person," she repeated.

"It's our way. She broke the rules. She knew what would happen."

"But that doesn't excuse it," Lyndsay argued, standing up. "That just makes it worse. How can you be so cruel?"

"You don't understand, Lyndsay. You don't know the Berrymans."

"So tell me. I'd really like to be convinced."

"What for? I could never make you understand," Penelope said hopelessly. "Anyway, there's only Timon left now. The rest of them have moved on, or died. I wish he'd go, too, and take Maddy with him. It would be best for everybody." She drained her glass and lit another cigarette.

"You said you were close once," Lyndsay reminded her. "How can you bear not to speak to her? To see her kids like that? Even if she has made them . . ."

"I *have* to bear it," Penelope almost shouted. "Don't think it doesn't hurt. It's very easy to judge others when . . ."

"I'm sorry," Lyndsay said. She moved closer to Penelope's chair. "I really am. I have no right to criticize you."

"Just . . . don't let it concern you."

"She seemed to include me," Lyndsay pointed out. "What was it she said? 'You're a Dolben, aren't you?' How could she know?"

Penelope shrugged.

"She keeps her eyes open. She would have known about the funeral. I expect the children hear things at school."

Lyndsay took a deep breath.

"Did the Dolbens take part in the hunt? When they fetched her back?" She prayed that they had not.

Penelope nodded her head slowly.

"Everyone. Every able-bodied man in the village. The Dolbens, the Clares, and the Pooles."

"My God," Lyndsay whispered. "It makes me sick."

"You must understand that if anyone had spoken to Magdalena's children this afternoon, anyone at all from the village, she would have reacted in exactly the same way."

"I don't think I blame her," Lyndsay said, her temper flaring. "But I'm not from the village."

"Don't be silly."

"It's not silly."

"Maddy won't see it that way."

"I guess not, no," Lyndsay admitted, trying for a moment to imagine how the woman must live and feel. Lyndsay, too, hated them all. They were monsters, worse than monsters. She was ashamed to be associated with them. She would have given anything to prove to Magdalena Berryman that she was *not* a Dolben and that she rejected everything they stood for.

"Lyndsay," Penelope said, standing up and carrying her glass to the cart. "There isn't anything you can do. You must believe that. And I'd be grateful if . . ." She turned to face Lyndsay and it required all her courage.

"What?" Lyndsay asked.

"Don't mention this to anyone. Don't say that I've told you."

"Why not?"

"Can't you see how ashamed we feel?" Penelope said, her voice cracking. "The people who really did it are all dead now. We were only children at the time. Can you even imagine how Bart must feel? *Please?*"

Lyndsay couldn't bear to watch her.

"Okay," she sighed. "I promise."

"Thank you."

The two women looked at each other for a moment. Penelope was the first to look away.

"I think," Lyndsay said gruffly, "if you don't mind, I'll be going now."

"Of course."

Penelope turned away, stiff and proud and very frightened.

CHAPTER FIVE

Hunched at the table in the untidy back room of the post office, Bart Poole ate hungrily and with total concentration. If he was aware of Cloris Poole watching him, he gave no sign of it. She leaned against the wall, a mug of tea in her hand, her eyes recording every movement he made. She appeared relaxed, yet she held her body poised to refill his cup or cut another slice of bread from the new loaf, should he want it. Occasionally, he grunted with satisfaction at the food. Cloris sipped her tea.

"She was in here this morning, the widow," she said, almost casually. "She made a lot of calls. To London." At this, Bart glanced up from his plate, his eyes narrowed with suspicion. "It was no matter," Cloris went on quickly. "I got a note of the calls from Enid over at the Corminster exchange. All to hotels, but she couldn't find who she wanted."

Bart nodded, satisfied. Cloris continued to watch him, turning over in her mind how to tell him the rest. She didn't want to make him angry.

"I've made a list of her calls, if you want it," she said. He shook his head. He trusted her. It was of no importance, anyway. "Alice Clare was in here afterward," Cloris began cautiously. She sipped her tea.

"So?" said Bart, frowning.

"She named her the Mistress."

"That's nothing." He lowered his head again and crammed more food into his mouth.

"I told her it was nonsense, but she said, 'Don't be so sure.' Something like that. 'Such things aren't easily changed.'" She waited tensely for his anger to break. He paused in his chewing, as though considering, then reached for his cup and washed the food down with a long swallow of tea.

"What's Alice Clare know?" he asked gruffly. "She's of no account."

"There's plenty more of her mind," Cloris replied. She pushed away from the wall and cleared a space on the cluttered windowsill for her mug. She folded her arms and stood looking out into the narrow garden and the fields beyond.

"They'll learn," Bart said confidently, pushing his plate away.

"Will they? I'm not so sure." Cloris glanced over her shoulder.

"Are *you* worried?" His smile was cool, slightly mocking. "You of all people?"

"Mother Poole wants to see you," she told him. "Tonight, before the meeting."

He looked at her straight back, the tight bun of her hair. With his little finger he dug a fragment of food from between his teeth.

"I'll see her," he said mildly. "Any more tea?"

Sighing, she turned to the table and poured tea into his cup. He studied her face.

"You are worried," he said. "Come here."

Obediently, like a little girl, she walked around the table and stood beside him. He slipped one strong arm around her waist and pulled her body against him.

"They're not convinced, Bart. And the old woman will try to take advantage of it. You've got to . . . persuade them." She felt his arm tighten reflexively around her.

"What more do they want?" he said softly, his face flushing. "Go on, tell me."

"I don't know. I'm just saying . . ."

He turned his handsome face up to her and, impulsively, she put out her hand, pushing the thick black curls back from his forehead.

"It's not like you to worry," he said, his eyes searching hers.

"I'm just saying you should think about it."

"They don't believe, is that it? They don't think I mean what I say, that I have the power."

"It's not that," Cloris said, twisting her fingers in his hair. "They believe all right. But the Mistress . . . They want her still."

109

"And they shall have her," Bart said, between gritted teeth. "On my terms."

"Don't go so fast, Bart, please. Give them time. Persuade them."

He searched her face suspiciously for any sign of weakness. She smoothed his hair and cupped the back of his head in her hand.

"You always give me good advice," he said at last. "I've always listened to you."

She smiled gently. Such power as she had over him meant nothing to her. The smile was not self-satisfied but yearning, loving. He pulled her closer, resting his cheek against her breasts as she put both arms around him, cradling him.

"I'll think about it," he promised.

"Good. I just want you to be . . ." She could not find the word, the right word.

He pushed her firmly but gently away. Her arms fell to her side. He stood up.

"Bart . . ."

"Get ready for the meeting," he said. "I'll go and see the old woman."

All her instincts told her to hold him, to keep him with her. She made herself overcome them and moved away, gathering the dishes automatically from the table. He passed behind her and went to the kitchen door.

"All right?" he asked, pausing for a moment.

"All right," she said tonelessly.

She wasn't a crying woman. She heard the back door close and carried the dishes into the dark little kitchen. It had always been a matter of waiting for him, letting him go without protest, being there when he came back, and all her life it had pained her. She had made herself his slave, gladly. In return, she knew that he needed her. There were times when only she could help him, but more times when he was completely beyond her reach.

She put the dishes into the sink and came back into the living room, pulling the pins from her hair. With a glance at the switchboard, she went upstairs to change.

At Dolben House, Patrick ate the cold supper Emelye Poole had prepared without enthusiasm. Lyndsay hardly ate at all, but pushed the limp salad around her plate while she thought. Something the little girl had said popped back into her mind. Something about flowers up by the oaks. The girl had wanted to know if she had put them there. There were no roses growing there, she was sure. Besides, the child had said *put* them there, and the ones she carried were definitely cultivated.

"Not hungry?" Patrick asked, placing his knife and fork neatly on his plate.

"Not very," Lyndsay admitted. "Would you like some coffee?"

"Thank you."

She stood up and balanced her plate on top of his.

"You don't have to do that," he said. "Emelye can . . ."

"It won't hurt me to carry a couple of plates into the kitchen," Lyndsay said. "Would you get the door, please?"

Patrick stood up and opened the door for her. Slowly, he followed her into the kitchen. She put the plates on the drainboard, and lit the burner under the coffeepot.

"Is something wrong?" he asked.

She shook her head. She had promised Penelope not to say anything about Magdalena Berryman. Therefore, she couldn't ask Patrick about what the little girl had said.

"You saw Mother Poole today?" he asked.

"Yes. We got along fine."

"She told you everything you wanted to know?"

"Oh, you mean about the Gabriel Ratchets? Yes. She told me."

"So you're not upset anymore?"

"I guess not," she said. The coffee began to percolate.

"Did she say anything else?" Patrick persisted.

There was something probing in his tone which made Lyndsay suspicious.

"She said nothing in particular," Lyndsay replied.

"It's just that you seem . . ." He paused a moment.

"I'm afraid I have to go out tonight."

"That's okay," Lyndsay said. She felt relieved.

"I don't like to leave you alone—"

"Are you going somewhere nice?" Lyndsay interrupted him.

"Oh . . . er . . . no. It's just a meeting. Village business. But I do have to be there, unfortunately." Lyndsay sipped her coffee. "You'll be all right?"

"I'll be fine. I have to write to my parents anyway."

"Yes, of course. Well, I'll get back as soon as I can."

Lyndsay smiled a little.

"What do you think will happen to me?"

"Why nothing, of course. I didn't mean anything like that. I just thought . . . well, that you'd like some company."

Lyndsay looked at him directly.

"Do you know what I'd really like, Patrick? Just for once, I'd like to hear you mention Michael's name. I'd like you to talk to me about him."

He looked away, confused.

"Why don't you want to talk about him?" she asked.

"I suppose because I don't really know what to say. We weren't very close, you know," Patrick said with difficulty. "Our lives were very different. He went away."

Lyndsay stared at her coffee.

"Sometimes, listening to all of you talk, I get the feeling that going away from here is some sort of crime. It's as though the moment a person leaves Ratchets, they cease to exist. In your minds, I mean. Do you know what Michael said to me once? He said that he was one of the few who got away."

Patrick shifted in his chair, looked at his watch, and drank his coffee hastily. Lyndsay felt as though there were an invisible wall between them. She spoke, but her words did not reach him.

"I'm beginning to know what he meant," she said quietly.

"That's ridiculous," Patrick said, standing up. "Look, I really must go. Why don't you have an early night? Tomorrow we can talk."

"Can we?"

"Of course. If that's what you want."

"What *I* want? Patrick, don't you have any feelings about him, his dying like that? Is it really that easy for you? You just bury him and that's it? Finished?"

"You're overwrought," he said. "I'm sorry to leave you . . ."

Lyndsay shook her head angrily. She wanted him to go. Maybe she was foolish to think that they had anything to say to each other about Michael.

"Would you like Penelope to come over?" he asked.

"No. Really. I must write home and then I think I will have an early night."

He nodded.

"I'll say good-night, then."

"Good-night, Patrick."

He crossed the kitchen and let himself out into the yard. She saw him pass the window and knew that he was glad to get away from her.

Bart Poole stooped and kissed his grandmother's cheek.

"So, I have to send for you now if I want to see you," she said, teasing him. She was glad to see him. Always.

"I thought you'd have other things on your mind," he said defensively.

"Oh, did you? Like what?"

"Like the Mistress."

"Ah . . ." she said, and went slowly to the table where a bottle and two glasses stood ready. She pulled at the cork clumsily with her large, arthritic hand. "Here," she said, thrusting the bottle at him. "Use your strength on that."

He uncorked the bottle.

"Rheumatics playing you up, are they?" he asked gruffly.

"You know how it is. It comes and goes." She poured dark red wine into the glasses and handed one to him. "Last year's black-berry," she said.

"Smells good. What shall we drink to?"

"Well now, let's see." She picked up her glass and sat down in her chair. "What about to the Mistress?"

"You know I'll not drink to that," he said harshly.

"Why not? What harm can she do you?" The old woman's eyes shone mischievously.

"None. But you can."

"Me? Oh-ho!" She laughed loudly, mocking him. "Still afraid of your old Granny, are you? You remember how it used to be? I could make you tremble and now . . ."

"To you," he said brusquely, raising his glass.

"Aye," she agreed. "And to you."

They drank together, the old woman savoring the wine. Bart Poole sat down.

"So, why did you send for me?" he asked.

"Only so's you can take me to the meeting," she said. "It would be fitting."

He had not thought of that. It would look good. She was crafty, still saw things that he missed.

"That's not all," he said. "I know you too well. And I'll tell you now to save your breath. You'll not change my mind."

"Have I tried? Right from the beginning, have I ever stood in your way?"

"You have your own way of hindering."

"You're too proud, Bart Poole," she said, shaking her head.

"You would have nothing changed," he accused her. "For years its been nothing but the Mistress, the Mistress, and a fine mess you've made of it, too."

Stung, Mother Poole clenched her bony knuckles into a harsh fist in her lap.

"You know there was none fitting. We needed new blood and now we've got it. If you'd only look at her, talk to her . . ."

"It's not the Mistress anymore," he said. "It's me. Just like old Ezekiel said it could and should be." His eyes blazed with conviction and excitement. "But you don't approve," he sneered.

"It's not for me to go against the Ways, nor you. That's the point."

"All right," he said. "What do you want?"

"Only for you to see that you need the Mistress. If you cast her aside, there's no knowing how it will end. No, hear me out. There's plenty in this village who won't have the Mistress put aside. No matter how great your powers are. What I'm saying to you is, *use her.* Like Ezekiel said: the masculine must always be balanced by the feminine. Priest and Mistress. Man and woman. According to the Ways."

He considered her words, frowning at the delicate glass he held.

"There'll be no need for her," he said. "Not once I have the power."

"Oh you're so blind and stubborn, I don't know why I waste my breath on you," she said crossly.

"I told you not to."

"It can't all be done by force, Bart. If you'd just seem to honor the Mistress, you'd carry them with you. Give them a little and you'll have all."

"You mean, seem to go along with it until . . ."

"Aye."

She stood up with difficulty and put her glass aside. Bart weighed her words. They reinforced what Cloris had advised. And Cloris would never betray him. He could set her to watch the old woman, to make sure there was no trick in it.

"I'll say no more. But I'll warn you one last time. If you don't, they'll turn against you. Sooner or later."

"Not once I've shown them . . ." he insisted angrily. She looked at him sharply, her face closed against him. He forced himself to be calm. "I'll think about it," he conceded.

"You do as you please," Mother Poole said, taking her stick from where it hung on the back of her chair.

"You don't mean that," he said, draining his glass.

"I'll walk on your arm tonight and every night. I'll not have anyone say the Pooles are divided among themselves. But that's all I'll do. If you won't see that what I tell you is right and necessary, then you must find it out for yourself."

Bart stood up and put his glass down beside hers, on the table. "I'll think about it," he repeated.

They stared at each other for a long, silent time, two enemies, equally matched. Mother Poole, leaning on her stick, was calm, even haughty, while he had to fight to control the anger and resentment that shook his body. At last, he drew a deep breath.

"We'll see," he said.

He turned abruptly and went to the door. Straightening her back, Mother Poole followed him. In the garden, he courteously offered her his arm and she leaned on it, smiling.

Lyndsay carried her writing case and the air letters she had bought that morning into the library. With the evening sun falling brightly into the room, it seemed less forbidding. She sat at the large, tidy desk and slowly uncapped her pen. She wished now that she had told her parents about Michael in her cable. Because she had not, this promised letter was even more difficult to write. She did not know how to begin, how to break it to them. They seemed so far away. With determination, she wrote the date at the top of the letter. At once she winced in surprise. Her wrist hurt. She had completely forgotten about it. That morning she had removed the bandage and it had not bothered her all day. Now, as she wrote the address, it became painful. And her writing was barely decipherable. She laid down her pen, and massaged the wrist for a moment. A typewriter might be easier, she thought. There must be one somewhere. Patrick was bound to have one. She pulled open the deep bottom drawers of the desk, but there was no typewriter. She got up and looked behind the chairs, in a big cupboard beside the desk, which was full of documents and ledgers. Below the bookshelves was a row of cupboards, at floor level. Bending down, Lyndsay made a systematic search of these. In the third one, standing against the wall was a portable typewriter, in a battered old case. She pulled it out and carried it with her left hand to the desk. The zipper on the case was broken and the machine itself was decidedly the worse for wear. She put the other air letter into the machine and began typing.

> Dear Momma and Pops,
> I'm sorry it's taken me so long to get around to writing you. Now that I have, I don't know how to tell you. So much has happened. I guess there's no way of putting it gently. Michael's dead . . .

She soon became engrossed in the letter, telling them as simply as she could what had happened to her since her arrival. But she suppressed a great deal. She was vague about the funeral and Michael's family. Was she protecting them or herself? she wondered. She certainly didn't want them to think that she was frightened and maybe even a little bit crazy. She leaned back in her chair, trying to thing of something reassuring to say and found herself looking at the half-page she had written, without reading it. It really was a lousy machine, she thought. The *m*'s were out of alignment, the *e*'s blocked by dirt. She could just imagine Mr. Mikeljohn's reaction if she had presented him with a letter like that. She leaned forward and peered at it more closely. Something stirred in her memory. Something to do with New York. Every morning, rushing to her mailbox, snatching out the circulars and bills, looking for that familiar blue air letter, feeling a thrill of pride and pleasure every time she read "Mrs. Lyndsay Dolben" on the front. The *M* in "Mrs." had always stood way up above the rest of the line. If she had thought about it at all, she had put it down to Michael's bad typing, but here, on this sheet she had typed, the *m*'s rose similarly above the line. Had the *e*'s been blocked in Michael's letters? She couldn't remember. Pulling the page toward her, she saw that the capital *s* was damaged, too. The whole of the serif and part of the lower curve were missing. That would be proof positive, she thought. But there was no way this could be Michael's machine. Even if he had brought his typewriter with him on his visit here, it would have been destroyed in the fire, when the car crashed.

She had to put the thought out of her mind, get on with her letter. She managed two more sentences, but her heart wasn't in it. She was so conscious of the machine and its defects. Well, there was one way to check, she told herself. But it was crazy. Upstairs, she had all of Michael's letters. She only had to compare them with this sheet and she would know. She snatched the air letter out of the typewriter and walked quickly to the door.

Michael's letters were the last thing she had packed. Surrounded by boxes and cases, she had sat that last night in New York reading through them once again. She had not minded, then, that there were so few, that they said so little. They brought him close. In a matter of hours, she had thought, she would be with him again, and forever.

The letters were in her traveling case. Her fingers were clumsy as she undid it and pulled out the slim blue bundle. Careful not to rip them, she pulled out three and opened them, spreading them on the bed. She was afraid. For a moment she stood by the bed, her eyes closed. But she had to get it over with, had to know. She placed the half-written letter to her parents beside them and, kneeling down, began to make a careful comparison. The *e*'s were blocked, but then that could happen on any typewriter. Nor did it signify that the typeface was the same. She ran her finger down the letters, looking for a capital *s*. "Soon, my darling. Soon." The serif and part of the lower curve were missing. It hardly seemed worth checking the *m*'s now, but she forced herself to do so. She was trying to postpone what she had learned.

Michael had been here!

She didn't know whether to laugh or scream.

That he had been here, must have been here, hit her like a wave. Happiness, hope, and then fear ransacked her mind. He could have sent the typewriter on ahead. Maybe he'd left it here on some other visit, meaning to buy himself a new one. She searched and found about half a dozen explanations, each one weaker than the last. She rested her head against the side of the bed. The only possible way the typewriter could have gotten to Dolben House was as part of Michael's luggage, which meant that they had been lying to her. He had reached here. Maybe he wasn't even dead. She stood up, shaking all over. But no, that was ridiculous. She'd buried him herself. No he was dead, but they were lying about the time of his death. If he had arrived here and died some other way, that would explain how they had come to do everything so quickly. It hadn't been quick. They'd had the usual amount of time. So how had he died?

Almost worse than this thought was the next. He must have died in some way they wanted to conceal, and people only wanted to conceal things like that when . . . She had to get a grip on herself. She was thinking about Michael's family, his friends. They could never harm him. Her imagination was running riot. There had to be some other explanation. She turned back to the letters spread out on the bed and looked at them again. She had not been mistaken. Then she thought of the postmarks. If Michael had been here maybe he'd written her from Ratchets. She grabbed up the letters, all of them. The New York counterstamp was clear, but yet, yes, here was one. London WC2. She dropped the letter.

Michael must have brought the machine here, her mind insisted. Yet everyone said he had died *before* he reached the village, and that nothing had been saved from his car. If, even if, they had somehow managed to get the typewriter out, it would surely have been scorched, and anyway they would have told her, given it to her as a memento at least. But why should they lie about something as important as this?

A cold fear gripped and steadied Lyndsay. There had to be something terrible to conceal. To conceal from her. But she'd found out about it now, which meant that she, too, must be in danger. Her thoughts were beginning to whirl again. She wanted to laugh at herself, but the sound she made was more like a sob.

There would be times, Mother Poole had said, when she would think she was in danger. Her heart was racing. Was this one of those times? But she would not be in danger, not actually. How did the old woman know? Or what? Lyndsay thought suddenly. Carefully, making herself be calm and rational, she checked the letters again, scrutinizing them to be absolutely certain. She had not made a mistake.

Methodically, she gathered up the letters and made a neat stack of them. Her fear resolved gradually into a hard knot of anger. There had to be an explanation for this, and she meant to have it. Patrick had said that he would get back just as soon as he could. She would wait for him and face him with the evidence. She was not afraid of Patrick, but she was beginning to hate him.

She carried the letters downstairs, into the great hall, and placed them on the big, round table. She did not even think about finishing her letter home. What she needed was a drink while she waited for

Patrick. She poured herself a large Scotch and began to pace up and down, sipping it. She was too angry to sit still and she could not stop her mind from exploring explanations which became progressively more and more frightening.

The meeting was held in the old Dolben chapel, in the children's graveyard. Crescent-shaped pews were arranged in shallow rows, like seats in an amphitheater. They faced a plain altar, covered by a cloth of gold and white. It was a small gathering, confined to the acknowledged heads of the Ratchets clans and their immediate kin. The women, their heads decently covered by black shawls, sat to the left of the altar, the men to the right. Leaning on her cane, Mother Poole delivered the traditional blessing in her strong, vibrant voice, her eyes moving along the rows. All heads were bowed except Bart's. He stared straight ahead of him, refusing to catch her eye. Next to him, Patrick Dolben held his head in his hands, like a man in despair. Justin Dolben, gaunt and lean, sat beside young Damon Clare. Both showed the proper reverence. She could count, she thought, when the time came, on Justin and Damon. The one because he was old and steeped in the Ways, hated change, the other because he was in love.

Among the women, like Bart's shadow, only Cloris Poole stared fixedly ahead of her. Mother Poole's eyes narrowed as she saw this. Penelope Clare's fingers plucked anxiously at the hem of her shawl. Justin's wife, Bryony, herself a Clare, pressed her knuckles to her forehead and leaned forward.

"In the name of the Mistress and of the Priest, welcome," she concluded. After a moment's silence, those who had bowed their heads raised them. Mother Poole moved to her place at the end of the first pew and accepted Bryony's help in sitting. She waited, outwardly calm, both hands folded on the handle of her stick, for Bart to address the meeting. He stood up and walked slowly to a point in front of the altar. He stared at it for a moment, then turned to face them.

"It was agreed," he reminded them, "that we should meet after the burial." He paused, looking over their heads toward the closed doors. "It is written," he continued, "that when there is no Mistress, the Priest shall assume the power and his power shall be masculine, opposed to the softer ways of the female. You agreed to this, all of you. You said to me that we had been too long without a Mistress, that the Ways had been violated and betrayed. Steps were taken. Irrevocable steps. I tell you all this tonight because there can be no going back. We are committed.

"I am the Priest by right of birth and election. None of you challenge that. You know that I have the power, that soon I shall harness the greatest of all the powers mentioned in the Ways. A power which has lain dormant for years and which some said could never be revived. With your consent I shall revive it, to punish the wrongdoers and purge our lands." He paused, raking them with his golden eyes. "At any time you could have forbidden me," he said in a harsh whisper. "When the stranger and the prodigal came among us. When the Ways were threatened. When you saw the corn dying in the fields. At any time you could have said no. But you did not. And what I have done I have done in your name, for the good of us all."

There was a general murmur of assent, which he acknowledged with a brusque gesture of his hand.

"It is work for men with strong stomachs. I have never denied that. We also know what is at stake. Our livelihood. Our way of life, which our forefathers have protected for centuries. It was because you wanted to preserve that, that I acted. Now . . ." He rocked back on his heels, surveying them. All eyes were fixed on him, except Mother Poole's. "Now some of you say that I move too quickly. I admit it. But why? Because it is a matter of urgency, if we are to eat this winter. I want there to be a good harvest, and we who worship the land which nourishes us, know how this must be done."

"Right," said Justin Dolben, firmly and loudly.

"Good," Bart said. "You understand. But you say that circumstances alter. You say that now we have a Mistress and I must trim my sails. . . ." His voice rose to a shout as both men and women began to talk among themselves. At last, Mother Poole looked at him.

"It is thought, I know, that I have not taken this into account. It is even whispered that I do not acknowledge the Mistress and would have her put aside. It isn't so. I acknowledge, before you, that this woman, the wife of the eldest son of the Dolbens, is the true and rightful Mistress. But . . ." He shouted to quiet the babble that had broken out. "But, I also say this. She is a foreigner and unschooled in the Ways. She cannot be the Mistress until she is fit."

"Aye," called Cloris Poole. "That's so."

Mother Poole gripped her stick more tightly, while her eyes seemed fixed to Bart's face.

"And until she is ready, until she is bound to us, body and soul, are we to do nothing? Are we to let pestilence and sin rule us?"

This time he made no effort to stop the burst of talk which answered his question. He stood still and silent, letting them have their say.

"We are all committed," Patrick said. "We can't turn back now."

"Agreed," Cloris Poole shouted.

"And what you do not understand," Bart Poole said when they were silent, "is that only by doing what we have agreed to do can we ever bind her to us. School her, yes, but what will make her one of us?"

They were silent, watching him expectantly.

"Only if we are resolved can we be sure of her. And I will ask you to consider this. If it were not for my allegiance to the Mistress, why would I have stayed my hand this long?" Abruptly, he returned to his seat. He had won them.

Mother Poole said:

"It is agreed then?"

"Aye," they said in a ragged chorus.

She stood up and turned to face them.

"We have a Mistress again," she cried joyfully. "And one that will prove worthy of the name. I give you my word. Tell the people then. Prepare them. And honor her Priest."

Walking slowly, she went to Bart Poole and solemnly bent one knee before him. The others watched tensely, excited and moved. Bart stood, and gently raised her. For a moment they stared into each other's eyes, then Mother Poole moved aside and one by one the rest knelt to honor him.

Lyndsay had drunk three, maybe four Scotches while it grew dark outside. She switched on the chandelier, blinking against its harsh light. The letters lay on the table, where she had placed them. They seemed to accuse her.

She waited, worrying herself sick over what the typewriter meant. She crossed the room and stood looking down at the letters. She touched them, but she could not bear to read them. Her own pathetic announcement to her parents of his death lay beside them.

They were all she had of him. A handful of letters, for the rest of her life. And now they seemed tainted in some way, for they had led her to discover that Patrick, Penelope, everyone had lied to her. Even Mother Poole, whom she had trusted. *Why?* Hugging herself, she walked back across the room and looked down at her empty glass. Maybe Patrick was avoiding her. She looked at her watch. He'd said he wouldn't be late. But if he had something to hide, of course, he would avoid her. But he didn't know that she had found the typewriter, she reminded herself. Why hadn't he thrown it away? A slip, she supposed. An oversight. She picked up the glass and carried it to the bar. She knew that she should not have another, but perhaps the only way to get through a nightmare was drunk, she thought, and lifted the decanter.

Brisk steps sounded on the gravel outside. Lyndsay's hand shook involuntarily as she poured her drink, keeping an eye on the door. Patrick came in. He was blinded by the light, giving Lyndsay a moment's grace to look at him. He seemed pleased with himself, almost elated.

"You're still up," he said when his eyes had become used to the light. "I thought you were going to have an early night."

"I've been waiting for you," Lyndsay said. "Have a drink. I think you're going to need it."

A look of surprise and suspicion crossed his face.

"Thank you," he said. He moved toward the table and glanced down at the letters.

"Take a good look at those," Lyndsay said, pouring his drink. "They're the letters Michael wrote me. The other one is to my parents. Take a good look at them," she repeated.

She picked up both drinks and turned to face him.

Patrick rested his fingertips on the edge of the table and looked down at the letters.

"These are private," he said after a moment. "I'd rather not . . ."

"I couldn't write by hand," Lyndsay said, as though he had not spoken. "My wrist hurt. So I borrowed the typewriter in the library." He looked at her, with a puzzled expression on his face. "You don't have to read them," Lyndsay said, walking toward him. "Just check for yourself that they were all written on the same machine." She put his glass down with a bang on the table. A vein throbbed in his temple as he stooped obediently over the letters once more. "Notice the broken *s*," she said, fighting to keep her voice under control. "The *m*'s are out of alignment. The blocked *e*." Tapping her foot impatiently, Lyndsay drank from her glass. "See?" she demanded.

Patrick straightened and carefully picked up his glass. He walked past her without speaking.

"Patrick?" Lyndsay cried.

"I'm sorry but I don't see what significance . . ."

She snatched up the letters, crushing them in her hand, and followed him.

"These letters from Michael were typed on the machine I found in your library. Now do you see the goddamn 'significance'?"

"Please, Lyndsay, you must calm—"

"Listen to me," she shouted. "I want to know how Michael's typewriter got into this house when he was supposed to have been killed before he even got here. What did he do? Mail it on ahead?" Furiously, she flung the letters onto the sofa and faced Patrick, her eyes blazing. "Come on. I want to know *exactly* what's been going on here."

All the color drained from Patrick's face. Against the brown of his iris, the black fleck seemed to grow larger. "I'm sorry, Lyndsay. Truly," he said.

"I don't want apologies. I want explanations. I want to know why you all lied to me, and it better be damn good."

"For the very best of motives," Patrick said, raising his voice. "To protect you."

Lyndsay laughed hysterically. It was true then, she thought, and wanted to scream.

"I'm his *wife*, Patrick. You owe me the . . . the courtesy of the truth."

"Sometimes, when the truth is very unpleasant, it is kinder to protect people. When you know that they will be distressed . . ."

"Is that part of your 'way'?" she demanded. "Don't you think I know all about 'distress'?"

"Yes I do," he replied calmly, "which is why I . . . We wanted to protect you."

Lyndsay turned away from him.

"You're not going to tell me a damn thing, are you? Who are you planning to get to put me straight this time? Mother Poole? Penelope?" She whirled round again. "Who's going to do your dirty work this time, Patrick?"

"You wanted to know why I wouldn't talk about Michael," he shouted back at her. "I'll tell you why. Because I'm ashamed of him.

He's brought nothing but disgrace on this family and I think it would be better for you . . ."

"I don't have to listen to this. I don't want to hear your lies. It's you who should be ashamed." She slammed her drink down, and went to the telephone. "I intend," she told him, "to have a proper, official inquiry into this." She snatched up the receiver.

"How long did you know my brother?" Patrick asked. "A few weeks? That and a handful of letters. You think you know him better than anyone. I'm sorry for you." She paused, frightened by what he said. Slowly, she replaced the receiver.

"What . . ." Lyndsay had to swallow, hard. "What are you . . . trying to tell me?"

"That Michael betrayed you just as he betrayed and hurt everyone who came into contact with him."

"No," she said. "I don't believe you. You're just saying that to—"

"Ask anyone in the village."

"Their records are not too good when it comes to telling the truth. I don't care what you say. I knew him," she cried.

"For a few weeks," Patrick repeated slowly. "I don't want to hurt you. I didn't know that he had left his typewriter. It explains why he turned back," he said almost to himself. "I don't have to tell you even now, if you'd rather. But you must believe that I would not say these things . . . They hurt me, too."

"You've got to tell me now," Lyndsay said. "Whatever it is, it can't be worse than what I've gone through already."

"Very well," Patrick said, and went to his customary chair. "Michael was here. For three weeks. He sent those letters to a friend in London to post on to you. He didn't love you, Lyndsay. Forgive me. He had no intention of meeting you. He said it was all a mistake. That he had . . . wanted you and somehow got trapped into marrying you."

"Oh God no," she said, covering her face with her hands. Hadn't she known? In her heart?

Patrick said, "Must I go on?"

"Yes," Lyndsay told him, her voice thick with tears.

"Very well," he sighed. "He came here to negotiate the sale of his share of the estate. I couldn't raise the money. He tried to sell to Bart and Penelope. He wanted the money to go abroad, and he wanted it quickly. Before you came. He said something about having had a job offer from Italy."

She shook her head, unable to take it in. Yet she had to believe it, much as it hurt.

"I wish we could have raised the money," Patrick said bitterly. "Naturally, he wanted the top market price. No concessions to family. If we had been able to give him what he wanted, he might not have—" He broke off sharply and when he spoke again his tone was gentle and compassionate. "This will hurt you most of all. While he was here, you see, he . . . slept with Emelye Poole."

Suddenly, and with a feeling of sick disgust, Lyndsay understood why the girl had been so nervous around her. God, she thought, gritting her teeth, how could he have? What could he possibly have seen in her? But she herself had thought that Emelye could be beautiful. She cursed Emelye and was glad, really glad that she looked so drawn and haggard now. It was the very least the cheap little tramp deserved.

"Such a thing is unthinkable, I know," Patrick went on. "The Pooles are naturally . . . well, let's just say that there was a lot of bad feeling. We don't, in Ratchets, take such things lightly."

Lyndsay found his pomposity almost as painful as the truth. But if she had so misjudged Michael, she thought, perhaps she was wrong about Patrick, too.

"I won't conceal from you that we asked him to leave. He was in a terrible temper. We never did understand why he turned back. Presumably, he realized that he'd forgotten his typewriter and . . ." He left the rest to her imagination, but she refused to imagine it. She had done so already, too often. She didn't want to think about Michael—or Emelye Poole, either.

"And when did you decide to keep all this from me?" she asked icily.

"The moment we realized that you would come here and would have to be told about his death. We all thought that it would spare everyone unnecessary pain. You see now why it has been difficult for me to talk about him. I feel more relief than sorrow. I'm sorry," he added quietly.

Lyndsay stared at a spot on the floor. *How could he?* When she had loved him so much, how could he possibly . . . ? Patrick stood up and poured himself another drink. Lyndsay's stood on the coffee table, barely touched.

"You said he was always like that," Lyndsay said dully. "What did you mean?"

Patrick turned and looked at her hunched shoulders, her bent head.

"Haven't you heard enough for one night?" he said. "It's all . . . finished now."

"I think I'd like to know it all."

Patrick sighed and went back to his chair.

"It's not easy to explain. He was always difficult. He could be very charming, of course; I'm sure you know that. But he used his charm in ways which . . . There were other girls. My father only narrowly avoided a scandal. It broke his heart when Michael went away to study, but really it was the only way. He never came back, not for any length of time. Frankly, most of us were glad. None more so than Bart Poole," he finished abruptly.

"Why him?" Lyndsay asked. She wanted him to go on talking. As long as he talked she would not cry, would not have time to take it in and understand completely.

"I suppose you'd better know," he said, as though questioning himself. "Because, apart from anything else, it perhaps explains about Emelye."

"I don't understand . . ."

"No. I'm sorry. I was thinking aloud. The point is . . . I find this rather embarrassing . . . Bart, you see, is my half brother. And Michael's."

Lyndsay looked at him with puzzled eyes.

"Before my parents married, my mother . . . It was a terrible scandal. Of course, I've only heard about it but . . . well, you see why we reacted more strongly than perhaps you would expect, about Emelye. Anyway, my father married my mother, knowing about Bart and everything. He was a kind man, Lyndsay. Please believe that," he said with some emotion. "He felt that he owed Bart something. He wanted to do something for him. He had lessons with Michael and me. We were told about our relationship. It was much harder on Bart, of course, but somehow Michael could not accept him. He never did. Probably for that reason, my father always favored Michael, but he was so cruel to Bart . . ." His voice trailed away as he remembered things that were still too painful to recount. With an effort, he pulled himself out of this reverie. "I never told him that I had made Bart estate manager. He never came here. He never asked. We always paid his share. But when he came back this last time, he was angry. I think that he may have deliberately set out to seduce Emelye, just to hurt Bart. Being as he is . . . because of his own birth, Bart is very sensitive about such things. I feel Michael *may* have used her, simply to get back at Bart."

Lyndsay nodded numbly. What Patrick said had an awful fascination.

"What's the relationship between Bart and Emelye?" she asked.

"She's his niece, but he's always been like a father to her. Now . . ." He gestured helplessly. "He can hardly bring himself to speak to her. Bart, you see," he said urgently, leaning toward her, "doesn't place all the blame on Michael."

Lyndsay sat in bleak silence for a long time. Patrick sipped his drink and stared across the room, not wanting to witness or intrude on her pain.

"I don't know what to say," she said at last. "I just don't know. . . ."

"There's no need to say anything. Just . . . please, if you can, don't think too harshly of us. We lied, but for you, as well as ourselves."

Stiffly, Lyndsay got up. She turned to look at the crumpled sheaf of letters. They didn't seem relevant anymore. She did not want them.

"I'd like to go to bed now," she said.

"Of course." Patrick stood up politely.

Slowly, Lyndsay crossed the big room. At the foot of the stairs she stopped.

"I owe you an apology," she said "This evening, while I was waiting for you, I thought a lot of terrible things. About you. I even thought . . ."

"Please," Patrick said. "Don't upset yourself anymore. Whatever you thought, I'm sure was understandable in the circumstances. There's no need to apologize."

"You're very kind," Lyndsay said, looking at him. "I appreciate that."

"We all want you to be happy," he said simply.

"Thank you." Lyndsay climbed the stairs.

Patrick watched her. He moved out into the room so that he could see her pass along the gallery.

"We all need you very much," he said softly.

And, in a whisper, looking at the floor, added: "Mistress."

CHAPTER SIX

Bart Poole ground the last of the rose petals into the charred earth. Bruised, discolored, and torn, they looked like scraps of tissue paper. He kicked the old jam jar in which the flowers had been placed into the ditch, where it shattered. He was breathing heavily, not from his exertions but from anger. He looked around, almost rolling his eyes, in search of something else to destroy, something more on which to vent his fury. He stood at a loss, staring at the ground, and it was then that he noticed the blood dripping from his hand. He raised his left arm slowly and looked at his hand. The thorns had ripped a jagged line across the fleshy part of his palm, where it joined the thumb. Looking at the wound, the blood, his eyes softened. He bent his head and sucked the blood, cleaning the tear. He felt calmer. Blood, dark red, dotted the line of lightly torn flesh. He held his hand away from his body, palm upward, to stop the bleeding sooner.

When he was a child, his blood had had a special taste. He could remember it. There had always been cuts and grazes, gashes and nicks to be sucked clean, or wrapped in dock leaves until Mother Poole could tend to the worst of them. And it had an individual, slightly salty taste. Now, nothing. Was it because the palate had grown dull over the years, or simply that only the blood of young children had that special savor? He smiled grimly at his thoughts. They were so unusually fanciful. Bart Poole lived in the present, looked always to the future. The battle of his childhood had not ceased, but it had altered, and now victory was almost in his grasp.

He clenched his left hand as though victory were something tangible he could hold and feel. His heart swelled at the thought.

He began to walk, settling his shotgun more comfortably on his left shoulder. There had been a heavy dew—he had noticed it clinging in pearl-like droplets to the petals of the roses—which drenched his boots as he made his way across the field behind the village. Ratchets lay on his left and he stared down on its peaceful roofs, the thick green of its trees. Up here, close by the Corminster Road, the drought was all too apparent. The dew was an illusion of moisture, soon to be evaporated by the sun. It would be hot again, he thought. And all the water drained into the village, to fill the wells and keep the trees verdant. Beneath his feet the earth was cracked, like old and failing plaster. There must be rain soon or the main crops would be blighted. Sometimes he believed that the place was cursed.

He stared down at the village like a king surveying his kingdom and then, with long, almost running strides, descended the hill, skirted behind Clare House, and entered the shade of the clump of trees that grew at the churchyard's edge. He remembered the childhood games he had played here, games he had always won, capturing Patrick and Michael. Only the latter struggled. Patrick had been easy, a born follower, quickly subdued. But Michael . . . Oh the fights they'd had. Not just bloody noses and twisted arms, but a subtler battle, a contest of wills, which at last he had won.

He remained among the trees, concealed by their shadows, but his sharp eyes missed nothing. What he saw was fitting and brought a smile to his stern lips. Michael's widow had dutifully tended the grave. She had set aside the rank, dead lilies and placed blood-red roses there. He smiled, but he did not linger under the trees. He hurried through the graveyard and let himself out by the gate. Crossing the road, he entered a long, tree-lined dirt road. The earth sloped upward, at first gradually, but then quite steeply. It led to the ridge and specifically to the field known as Top Meadow. Fit and strong, Bart Poole made the climb swiftly and without effort. He was scarcely out of breath when he reached the meadow.

His triumph the night before had given him new energy. He had won them over without dissent. Even Mother Poole had been silenced, had honored him. His heart throbbed at the memory. And here, in Top Meadow, was the proper place to celebrate his triumph and savor the future which, last night, Cloris had sweetly planted in his mind.

Only those flowers by the oaks blighted his mood. He knew what they meant and who had put them there. Yet he could not see what she hoped to gain by it. Probably it was nothing more than sentimental foolery. Even so, he would have to put a stop to it. But that could wait. There were bigger, more important things to concern him.

He walked to the edge of the field and squatted down. The early corn had been harvested, leaving a crust of sharp, dry stubble on the parched earth. With difficulty, he crumbled a rock-hard clod between his fingers. It had been impossible to plow and plant again. They needed rain, or something better. He stood up, his face dark and brooding. All these years he had waited and now, one by one, he would have his revenges. The thought of Magdalena Clare was bitter to him. Once he had loved her with all his heart, with the passion and blindness of youth. He stared along the ridge to his right. As always, he had to go there. He could not prevent himself. He set off along the side of the field, walking slowly now. It would be a while yet before she returned. He knew her movements by heart. When she came back he would be there, watching her.

A smile creased his face when, at a distance, he could see the disgusting hovel Timon Berryman had built for her. Some said that it was punishment enough, but he knew that it was not. Magdalena Clare had been promised to him and he, young and callow fool that he was, had adored her. He unslung the shotgun and held it, crooked comfortably in his arm.

The weight of the baby dragged painfully on Magdalena Berryman's aching shoulder muscles. Awkwardly, she shifted the little body to her right arm. They thought she was mad, she knew. Mad Maddy, they called her. Sometimes, she thought it herself. She had taken the children across the fields and seen them onto the bus. She had climbed in after them, explaining to the driver that, if ever the bus broke down again, he was to make sure, if anyone gave them a lift, that they were let off here, at the stile. She heard the crowded bus grow silent as her voice rose, became hysterical. The Ratchets children nudged each other and whispered. The driver insisted that it wasn't his responsibility. She must get off. She was making him late. Christian and Bella stared at their feet, their cheeks burning.

"*Please,*" she had cried desperately. "Please." She backed out of the bus, watching the faces passing, faces mocking her through the windows. She saw them as masks of hatred. Panic rose in her. The children were not even safe at school. Not safe with those little Pooles and Clares, already schooled in the Ways of Ratchets, of their elders. She watched the bus recede. She was helpless, unable to do anything. At last she had managed to shush the baby, climb the stile, and begin the long walk back.

Timon had run off, full of empty promises. She knew in her heart that she had driven him away with her hysteria. But she could not be calm when she told him what had happened. The faces of that woman and of Penelope Clare . . . She wanted to believe in him, that he would, this time, make a real effort. She had to believe it for it was all the hope she had. Yet when she thought of him, all she could see was his angry, bewildered face, screaming at her: "Are you mad, woman?"

Mad Maddy.

"I'll not be driven out," he'd shouted. "I've a right to be here."

"For the children," she had sobbed. "For the children."

But she knew it was too late, and looking up as though to face the God she implored, she saw Bart Poole, silhouetted against the sun on the ridge half a mile away. Her blood ran cold. She knew he saw her, watched her. She forced her aching muscles to stiffen, to stand tall and face him. There was murder in her heart now, a hatred so cold and total it vanquished her fear and panic. She would not run from him. She would not satisfy him by showing, through her stumbling steps, her terror. She waited, facing him, staring up into the sun that hurt her eyes, at his terrible blackness against the sky. At last he moved. Sunlight glinted on the barrel of his shotgun. Magdalena felt no fear. She straightened her shoulders even more, facing him out. The gun flashed light once again and then he turned, disappeared over the brow of the ridge.

Clutching her baby, Magdalena Berryman moved on, stumbling with tiredness and the roughness of the ground, toward her home. There, her eyes constantly watchful, she drew water enough to last the day, carried in logs and kindling, then bolted her doors against the dangerous world.

A pair of geese flapped, hissing, out of Bart Poole's way as he entered one of the farm buildings. The pigs hung headless, their bodies slit open, from hooks in the ceiling. Their scoured skin was cold to his touch.

"Patrick," he bellowed.

He came at once, wiping his hands, his eyes wide with nervousness.

"What are these doing here?" Bart demanded, pushing one of the carcasses, so that it swung. "You want them to rot?"

"Jacob's just coming," Patrick said. "I had them brought out of the refrigerator."

"Then tell him to look sharp about it. And then get back here."

"You . . . got my message?"

"Aye. I got it." Bart turned away and walked out into the yard where he paced up and down impatiently. He heard Patrick talking to old Jacob, telling him to hurry up. Bart went toward an open shed where the tractors stood. Moments later, Patrick joined him. He waited anxiously while Bart surveyed the largest tractor. "I want this one in Top Meadow by sunset," he said, banging his fist against the yellow engine covering. "And I want you there, too." He looked full at Patrick, his eyes blazing like a cat's. "What was his typewriter doing here?" he asked in a low, threatening voice.

"I . . . didn't know he . . ."

"You didn't look, you mean. Christ, man, must I do everything? Would you have me go over the house with a toothcomb? Must I even clean up after you?"

"Not so loud," Patrick said, looking around the deserted yard. "Somebody might . . ."

"What did you tell her?"

"That he was here. That he must have remembered the typewriter and turned back."

"And the rest, as we've discussed?"

"All of it, yes."

"Including Emelye?"

"Yes, Bart. I had to. Also the truth about you."

Bart tilted his head back.

"So, she knows I'm her half brother-in-law, does she?" He smiled. "How did she take it?"

"I don't know. She didn't say anything much. She seemed . . . stunned."

"She seemed," Bart sneered. "Where is she now?"

"I don't know."

"You don't know!"

"I mean," Patrick said, his voice rising querulously, "that she wasn't up when I—"

Bart gestured for him to be silent. He gazed over Patrick's shoulder, his face clouding. Patrick turned to see what caught his attention. Emelye Poole, unaware of them, had stepped out of the house and was emptying a pail of dirty water into the yard drain. Bart put out his hand and gripped Patrick's shoulder, pushing him aside.

"Emelye," he shouted. "Come here."

Startled, the girl dropped the pail in surprise. It clattered on the concrete and rolled away from her. She looked at them, her face deathly pale, her fingers plucking at an old apron made of sacking.

"Quickly, girl," Bart shouted. "I haven't got all day."

She came slowly across the yard and stopped at the entrance to the shed.

"Come closer," Bart said. "This is private business."

Very slowly, she obeyed. Patrick started to move away.

"You stay. I want you to hear this," Bart ordered him.

Emelye could not look at him. She stood before him, her dark head bowed. Gently, almost tenderly, Bart caught her pointed chin in his hand. She gasped at his touch and instinctively pulled back. He gripped her tighter, raising her head slowly. It felt as though her jawbone would crack. She whimpered, but could not speak.

"There were flowers, in an old jar, up by the oaks this morning," Bart said carefully. "Can you think what they were doing there?"

Emelye made a gurgling sound and tried to shake her head. He held it steady. Her eyes rolled toward Patrick, but he refused to look at her.

"I ask, Emelye," Bart continued, "because I can only think of one person who would be so foolish as to do such a thing. You understand?" He released her chin. She put up her hand to rub where he had grasped her. The marks of his fingers glowed red against her pale skin.

"It—"

"No. Don't condemn yourself with lies, Emelye." He caught her thin arm and pulled her roughly against him. "I don't want to hear that it was you, because if it was, you know what I'd do, don't you?"

She stared at him open-mouthed. He shook her.

"Don't you?"

"Please . . . let me go." She twisted against his hand.

"I'd flay you alive," he said and suddenly thrust her from him so that she staggered backward against the big wheel of the tractor. She pressed herself against it. Dry sobs shook her body. "You remember that," Bart said quietly. She seemed unable to move. Bart watched her stonily, enjoying her fear of him. Then, with a jerk of his head, he told her to go. Like a rabbit, mesmerized by a bright light, she remained where she was, staring at him. Only when he took a step toward her did she turn and run into the house. The pail remained where she had dropped it.

"Why would she—" Patrick began, but Bart cut him off.

"Never mind that now. Get this tractor fueled up. And remember, I shall want you tonight."

"What are you going to do?"

"Put the harrowing chains on," Bart instructed him, ignoring his question. "Just the chains. Understand?"

"Yes," Patrick said. "Where are you going now?"

Bart paused in the entrance to the shed. Looking toward the house, he said, "I'm going to make myself presentable for the Mistress."

It had been almost dawn when Lyndsay finally fell asleep and even then she had only dozed. She had scarcely cried at all. She had tried to match her knowledge of Michael with what Patrick had told her. The two images would not fit, but that did not really surprise her. She kept coming back to three things. It was true that she had only known Michael for a short time and she had been blinded by love for him. Then, no brother would so malign another, especially when he was dead. On the contrary, Patrick had gone out of his way *not* to tell her. Finally, there was her own fear, mostly suppressed, but occasionally unavoidable, that Michael might have regretted their spur-of-the-moment marriage. After all, everybody had pointed out how little she knew about him.

She stared miserably at the ceiling. There didn't seem to be any point in getting up. But it was better to face facts. On the plane, after talking to Mrs. Abernathy, she had thought that perhaps she had been too ready to fall in love when she met Michael. He had been handsome and assured. He had lifted her out of her job, out of New York and shown her a good time. A wonderful time. He had been good in bed. Too damn good, she thought bitterly. That was half of it. She'd been infatuated physically. That's why she'd had those dreams when she first got to Ratchets. Dreams which had seemed disrespectful under the circumstances, but which now she saw had been telling her something she hadn't wanted to know. Yet she had loved him as well. Out of the charm and the good times, the marvelous sex which even now made her body tingle with anticipation, had grown love. It is the curse of women to fall in love with men who make them feel fulfilled and important.

Such a crappy, classic mistake. What the hell had happened to her mind? She was glad now that she had always taken precautions when they slept together. That night, after he'd proposed, she'd wanted not to, but now she was glad, really.

She got out of bed and stood by the window. A haze of heat hung over the distant wood. She'd burned her fingers and now it was time to—

A knock at the door.

"Who is it?" Lyndsay called.

"Emelye, miss."

She couldn't face her. Not yet. Her jealousy was like hatred. Where had they done it? In that bed?

"I'm not . . . dressed," Lyndsay said.

"It's Mr. Bart. He's downstairs. He says can you come?"

"Yes. Tell him I'll be right down," Lyndsay said.

Anything to get rid of the girl, her whining voice. She wanted to scratch her stupid, fishy eyes out, when really she should have felt sorry for her. She, too, was a victim, and in a way it must be worse for her.

She washed quickly and brushed her teeth. She didn't want to think about it anymore. There was no point. You learned the facts and you faced them. Deliberately, defiantly, she put on a red cotton dress. It was cool and practical. It was going to boost her morale.

A little while later, Bart Poole watched her come down the stairs. His eyes admired her. She had a good figure, good, long, shapely legs. The full skirt of her red dress flattened against them as she walked, while the bodice clung tightly over her breasts. He liked her coloring. Darker blond than the pale Clares, her skin tanned and smooth. She wasn't like the women he knew. She moved well, economically, and with grace. She had put on enough makeup to hide her tenseness, the marks beneath her eyes.

She said, "You wanted to see me?"

135

"To apologize for the other day. I hope I didn't hurt you."

She had forgotten, she realized. Forgotten it all in the shock of learning about Michael.

"I guess I deserved it," she said and held out her hand. "No hard feelings, though." He took her hand and shook it briefly. "Actually, it did hurt. Quite a lot."

He smiled, showing very white teeth. He looked a little like Michael and Patrick, she thought, but he was altogether larger and stronger. His black curls were definitely inherited from the Pooles. She had expected him to be a country hick, rough or shy with women, but he had an ease about him, a confidence that she liked instantly.

"I can only say that I'm sorry," he said. "And that it won't happen again."

Lyndsay returned his smile.

"Emelye's made some coffee," he said. "Shall we?"

He held out his arm toward the settee. A tray, neatly laid, stood on the coffee table. Lyndsay nodded and moved toward it. His reference to Emelye made her feel awkward.

"How do you like yours?" she asked.

"With milk and sugar. May I?" He looked at the settee, wanting to sit down.

"Oh please," Lyndsay said. She poured the coffee and handed him a cup. His white shirt was open at the neck, showing curling black hair. The rolled-up sleeves outlined hard muscle. Lyndsay sat at the other end of the settee, arranging her skirt.

"I would have come sooner, but . . ."

"I know. You're very busy at this time of year. You see," she smiled, "I'm catching on."

"The land is very demanding," Bart replied, without a smile.

"So I gather." Lyndsay picked up her cup. She felt reproved.

"I wanted you to know, too, that I'm sorry you discovered about Michael as you did. I hope you won't feel . . ." He paused as though the speech were rehearsed and he had forgotten his lines. "I wouldn't like your memories to be damaged by what you've been told. The Michael Dolben you knew was perhaps different . . . I mean sincerely different . . ." Again he seemed to lose the words.

Lyndsay stared at her cup thinking.

"If you really mean that," she said, "that's the nicest thing anyone has said to me in a long time. Thank you."

He nodded coolly, as though her thanks embarrassed him. Lyndsay put down her cup and took a handkerchief from her pocket. Her eyes were shining with unshed tears.

"It's okay," she said. "I'm not going to weep on your shoulder. I am . . . I guess I haven't taken it in yet."

He said nothing. She dabbed at the corners of her eyes, wiped her nose.

"There," she said with relief. Then: "I understand we're sort of related."

"Sort of 's about it," he agreed, smiling slowly.

"Well, I'm glad," she said impulsively. "And I'm grateful to you for coming this morning."

Bart drank his coffee and refused more when she offered it.

"What are you planning to do now?" he asked.

Lyndsay felt that he was making conversation and that it did not come easily to him. His courtesy errand was done, but out of politeness he stayed on.

"I haven't really thought what I'll do. I guess I must do something." The contrast between the savage, bloodstained man who had confronted her in the yard and this man, sitting so calmly beside her, was too great. As great as that between the two images of Michael she could not match.

"Stay here," he said suddenly. It sounded almost like a command. "We would all like that."

His words reminded her of something, but she couldn't quite catch it, bring it to the surface of her mind.

"That's nice of you, but I can't just settle down here. I'll have to do something."

"Why? You're a rich woman now. Comparatively speaking."

That she hadn't considered.

"I guess I'll have to stay to sort that out," she agreed.

"Don't rush into any decision. If you can put up with us for a while, we'd be pleased."

"It's getting easier all the time," Lyndsay said, smiling at him. For a moment, his eyes gleamed at her, then he stood up. "Duty calls?" she asked, teasing him.

"If you'll excuse me."

"Of course. And thanks again for coming, Bart. I appreciate it."

"It's been a pleasure," He turned on his heel, walked toward the kitchen door. "I wonder," he said, glancing back at her, "if one day you'd let me show you round the estate?"

"Thank you," Lyndsay said. "I'd like that a lot."

"Good." He nodded, and continued on his way.

She poured herself more coffee, thinking how easily she could be misled by appearances. Michael had made her feel completely secure. Yet now it was Bart who comforted her, while Michael . . . But he was right, she thought. She had those memories and it was foolish to think that she could just forget them. Whatever Michael had been, for that short time she had loved him and love didn't just go away or stop. She got up and carried her coffee to the front door, which she opened. The sun was hot on her skin. She stood there, staring out at the hedge and the fields beyond and the only thought in her head was that Bart Poole was a very attractive man. She ought, really, to have said something to him about Emelye. But what? She wasn't able yet to be anything like rational about Emelye. It was good of him to come to the funeral, considering how he felt. She understood, too, why he had kept himself apart.

She stood at the door for a long time, letting her thoughts drift. There was something about the Pooles. She had sensed it in all of them, except Emelye. A power of some kind. In the woman at the post office, it had been hostile, but the old woman and Bart seemed to have the knack for saying the right thing. Both of them had reassured her, comforted her in a way that no one else had been able to do. There was something personal about it, as though they understood her very well. Like Mrs. Abernathy, she thought wistfully. Then maybe she had seen a trace of Michael in Bart. Perhaps Michael had favored their mother. Probably it was just an ability to relate well to people. The thought of Michael depressed her. She felt her mood changing. It was one thing to know you had to face facts and another to do it. She ought to do something, she knew. It was no good standing, staring at the view and brooding. The only thing she had to do was to write that letter to her parents, but she didn't feel able to face that. She didn't want to tell them what a mess she had nearly made of her life, and lying was out of the question. She would have to tell them eventually, but it could wait until she felt more at ease with it. It would be better done face to face, anyway. All that in a letter would only worry them. Suddenly she wanted them very much. She wanted America, the things she knew. She did not belong here in this claustrophobic, isolated village. These people, no matter how kind they were, were strangers. In destroying the myth of her marriage—it hurt a lot to admit to herself that it had been a myth—they had made it impossible for her to think of them as family. She knew she was being unfair, but she didn't need a new family. She ought to forget Michael, and that would never be possible here. Every time she saw Patrick, she was reminded of him. And now, Emelye. . . . The best, the sensible thing to do would be to go home at once. It didn't even matter about the legal papers. Someone in her father's law office could handle that. It would take a little longer, but what did that matter?

As she moved away from the door, suddenly excited about the prospect of going home, a dark green sedan car drew up at the gate. Lyndsay had a brief impression of a man peering out of the window at the house, then the car moved on a little and stopped out of sight behind the hedge. She waited, knowing that the driver must have seen her. A moment later he appeared at the gate. A tall man, hastily shrugging on a heavy tweed jacket, complete with leather elbow patches. He looked, Lyndsay thought, as she watched him walk up the short drive, adjusting his collar, like every untraveled American's idea of an Englishman. Rather distinguished, and dressed in defiance of the climate.

"Good morning," he called, raising a hand in salute.

" 'Morning," Lyndsay responded.

He came to the foot of the steps and looked rather diffidently around him.

"Extraordinary hedge you have," he said, patting his jacket pockets as though trying to find something.

"Yes, isn't it," Lyndsay agreed. She smiled at his precise, rather clipped voice, which seemed to contradict his physical nervousness. "To tell you the truth," she confided, "I don't like it very much."

"Oh really? No, well, I do see your point. Look, forgive me for butting in like this, but I'm rather looking for someone and seeing you standing there, I thought . . ." He stuck out his hand, gauchely, like a boy.

"Stuart Donne," he said.

"Lyndsay Dolben." They shook hands. He looked at her with a hopeful, expectant expression.

"The name doesn't mean anything?" he said at last.

"No. Should it?"

"I suppose not," he said. He looked crestfallen and stared down at his shoes as though he had run out of ideas.

"Who is it you're looking for, Mr. Donne?" Lyndsay asked.

"My brother."

"I'm sorry. I can't help you. I've only been here a few days myself."

"Ah . . . I thought so. Recognized the accent. American or Canadian, yes?"

"American," she said. "Look, why don't you come in for a moment. I'll try to find my brother-in-law. He'll be able to help, I'm sure."

"That's awfully good of you. Thanks."

Lyndsay turned and walked into the hall. Stuart Donne followed, wiping his feet elaborately on the mat and glancing appreciatively around him.

"What a splendid room," he said.

"It *is* pretty impressive," Lyndsay said. "Your brother . . . does he live here?"

"No. But I think he may have stayed here. Or visited the village anyway."

"Make yourself at home and I'll see if I can find Patrick."

She went into the kitchen and out into the yard. Apart from the geese, it appeared to be deserted. She called Patrick's name a couple of times, but there was no reply. She turned back into the kitchen and found herself facing Emelye Poole. Lyndsay stopped, her face showing her confused and primarily antagonistic feelings. The girl stood as though petrified in the arched entrance to one of three pantries which opened off the kitchen. In her hands was a laden tray of crockery.

"Do you . . ." Lyndsay swallowed and looked away from the girl. "Do you know where Mr. Dolben is? Or any of the men?"

"They're all up on the ridge, in the fields," Emelye whispered. "Mr. Patrick took the big tractor—"

"All right," Lyndsay cut in sharply. "Maybe you can help." It isn't Emelye's fault, she told herself. She's just a stupid, inexperienced girl and I shouldn't take it out on her. "There's a man just called, looking for his brother. He thought he might be staying here or something. Do you know anyone named Donne?"

It seemed as though Emelye simply opened her hands and let the tray fall. It was made of metal and the noise when it hit the flagstones was deafening. Lyndsay watched the crockery spill and clatter and break as though it were all happening in slow motion. Fragments of china flew across the floor. In the silence that followed, she heard herself shout:

"What on earth . . . ! How could you be so clumsy?"

The girl burst into tears, covering her face with her hands. Lyndsay felt a strong urge to slap her, hard. She pulled herself together.

"I'm sorry," she said tightly. "I shouldn't have said that." Emelye wept helplessly. Lyndsay went toward her, though she did not want to. She certainly didn't want to touch her. "Look, please . . ." she began. "Emelye, will you stop that?" The girl let out a long wail and turned back into the pantry. Lyndsay looked at the debris on the floor. She couldn't just leave her.

Bracing herself, she went into the cool, dim little pantry. Emelye was leaning over a big stone sink, sobbing and retching. Lyndsay made herself go to her, but she could not bring herself to touch her. She watched, pained and disgusted as the girl's thin shoulders heaved and she spat bile into the sink. It made her feel sick, too. Her stomach contracted, and she had to turn away.

"You're not well, Emelye," she said quietly. "You'd better go home." She stood with her back to the girl, fighting the awful thought that had sprung into her mind. "I'll clear up the mess. You just go, okay?" Her voice cracked. Behind her, Emelye became quieter. She sniffed. Lyndsay went back into the kitchen, treading carefully around the broken pieces of what once had been a dinner service, she guessed. After a while, Emelye followed her, wiping her eyes with the back of her hand. Listlessly, she took down her shawl.

"Are you all right?" Lyndsay asked, her voice cold.

"Yes."

"You go right home, now."

"Yes."

She moved on leaden feet toward the back door.

"Emelye," Lyndsay said sharply.

"Yes, miss?"

"You never answered my question. Do you know anyone named Donne around here?"

She did not answer for a long time. Her back shook as though she were going to be sick again.

"No," she said suddenly, her voice uncharacteristically loud and firm. Then she made a dash for the door and ran, on ungainly legs, across the yard.

Lyndsay looked again at the mess on the floor and then tried to compose herself for Stuart Donne. He was examining the great room with the studied absorption of a man who was pretending not to have heard anything of the scene in the kitchen.

"Sorry," Lyndsay apologized. "A slight problem in the kitchen."

"Oh," he said with obvious embarrassment. "Nothing too drastic, I hope?"

"Well, let's just say *I* hope it wasn't the best dinner service. My brother-in-law's out in the fields," Lyndsay explained. "I asked the maid about your brother but . . . Well she was upset about the crockery. I'm sorry."

"Not at all. *I'm* sorry to have troubled you."

"Listen," Lyndsay said, as he moved toward the door. "Why don't you try the post office? I'm sure Cloris Poole—that's who runs it—would know. It's just down the road. Here, I'll show you."

Murmuring his thanks, Stuart Donne held the door for Lyndsay and listened attentively to her instructions.

"Thank you so much," he said. "It's very good of you to go to all this bother."

"Not at all. I hope you find him."

"Yes," he said, frowning. "So do I."

Something in his voice, his frown, bothered Lyndsay, but before she could ask him about it, he offered his hand again.

"Good-bye, Mrs. Dolben, and thank you so much."

"Good-bye," she said. She watched him walk briskly away toward his car. At the gate he turned and saluted her. She waved back and then went into the house.

In another pantry she found a broom, a dustpan, and brush. She swept the clattering pieces into a pile, squatted down and began to place them into the dustpan. The china was old and good. With a start of surprise she saw, on one large piece, the black outline of the hound, the Gabriel Ratchet. She had a feeling that Patrick was going to be very annoyed about this. She dropped the piece of china into the dustpan and carried it outside to the trash can. She could not prevent herself from looking toward the high wall of the children's graveyard, and perhaps it was that, the thought of those babies, that made her think of Emelye and her pitiful retching. She *knew* what the cause might be, and no matter how hard she tried, she couldn't get the thought out of her mind. Wearily, she reentered the kitchen and continued to clear up the broken crockery. It felt as though, at last, her heart were going to break.

It was hot in the room. The air was still and heavy with the accumulated heat of the day. They lay, side by side, naked, sweat lending a sheen to their bodies. When she held her breath, Cloris could hear the ancient timbers of the house creaking in the summer heat. She could not tell if he was asleep or, like her, simply resting, thankful and satisfied. Lazily, she raised an arm and delicately traced the sicklelike curve of his shoulder blade. Her intention was not to wake him if he slept. She did it for the sheer pleasure of touching him. His skin flinched and he sighed, reached his hand over his shoulder and trapped hers, flat-palmed, against him. Responsively, she edged closer to him, pressing her full breasts against his back and seeking to entwine her legs with his. The curls at the nape of his neck were flattened and damp with sweat. Kiss-curls, she thought and, raising herself, kissed them.

At the touch of her lips Bart Poole rolled over onto his back. He inspected the strong face that hung above his. Framed by the tangles of her hair, it was, he acknowledged, the face he would love, if he could love any. Only he saw her like this, with her hair loose, her face soft and warm. He smiled, imagining what a sensation it would cause if Cloris were to show herself as she really was in the post office. Few in Ratchets realized how beautiful she was and none but he knew the depths of her passion. He raised his arms, pushing her away, and stretched like a waking dog. Cloris, unoffended, propped her elbow on the pillow, supported her head in her hand, and smiled at him.

She was a good woman, he thought. She suited him.

For her part, Cloris was proud to be the lover—she ranked herself no more highly, nor entertained any greater expectations—of Bart Poole. She knew that when the time came he would not publicly choose her. Perhaps—the thought increasingly occurred to her—he would take another, but he would always return, using the back door, to spend a few secret hours with her. That was her abiding comfort.

There was a pretense of secrecy about their relationship, but Cloris knew that it was virtually common knowledge. Not that she cared. She was discreet about her love for him, but if she were challenged, she would proclaim it with pride. Yet it was her discretion that Bart valued. That and her loyalty.

"A man came by today," she said, knowing that she should have told him sooner, but she had wanted to have his attention entirely to herself for a while. "A man called Donne," she continued softly, "asking as polite as you please if I'd ever heard of his brother, if perhaps he'd stayed hereabouts."

"And what did you say?" Bart asked, smiling at her.

"Why, I said no, of course. 'There's no place here,' I said, 'for anyone to stay. You must be mistaken.' "

Bart laughed.

"And then?"

"He got into his car and drove off. No. I tell a lie. He bought an ounce of tobacco first."

"That's my girl," Bart said, reaching out and touching her breast. She smiled happily and leaned closer to him.

"I don't think he'll come back," she said casually.

"What if he does?"

A shadow crossed her face.

"Don't be too certain, Bart. Don't be too sure."

"Ach," he said, pushing her away. "You sound like Mother Poole."

Cloris's lips tightened. If there was one person she hated as strongly as she loved Bart, it was the old woman. They were the emotional poles of her life.

"She talks sense sometimes," Cloris reminded him. "And she knows you well."

"As well as you?" he asked, catching her thick hair in a bunch at the nape of her neck and pulling her down, thrusting his tongue lazily into her willing mouth. Moaning, Cloris moved her body so that she lay on him. He bore her weight easily. Breaking free of the kiss, she said:

"I hope not."

"Then don't you lecture me. Leave that to her."

"I won't. I won't," she promised, nuzzling his neck. "I just don't want anything to go wrong for you, that's all," she said.

"It won't," he said. "Now get off me. I've things to do."

"Don't go," she begged, wrapping her arms around him.

"Come on," he said, pushing her easily off him. He sat up.

Cloris lay where he had pushed her, watching him.

"You've made up your mind to do it tonight?"

He made an impatient sound and turned his back on her.

"It was you who put the idea in my head."

"Yes," she said, "but it's so soon."

"Sometimes you don't understand anything," he grumbled, swinging his long legs off the bed. His head almost touched the exposed beams of the ceiling. "Last night," he said, beginning to pull on his clothes, "I promised that I would serve the Mistress. Not

144

in so many words, but that's what they understood by it. Tonight they'll see that the Mistress can never have the power again. Tonight I'll show them," he promised with mounting excitement, "that I am more powerful and stronger than any Mistress. Inside a week they'll beg me not to let the Mistress take my place. You'll see."

Cloris did not reply. She stared up at the ceiling, trying to see what he intended. She brought a woman's caution to it, looked at it from the woman's point of view.

"What's the matter?" Bart demanded, pulling on his shirt. "You don't believe me?"

"No, it's not that." She shook her head on the pillows. "I'm trying to see if there is anything the old woman could do . . ."

"Nothing," he asserted.

"I mean afterward. Could she turn it to her advantage?"

"How?" His eyes narrowed at once. He moved back to the bed, watching Cloris's face closely.

"I don't know. I'm thinking."

"No," he said. "There's nothing she can do. Who'll care about a Berryman? Who wouldn't be glad to see the back of 'em?"

"You," she replied, sitting up and turning away from him. She reached behind and gathered her hair together. Standing up, she walked naked to a plain chest of drawers. Above it, fixed to the whitewashed wall, was a plain square of mirror. She twisted an elastic band around her hair, to hold it back from her face. In the mirror she saw that Bart did not dare to look at her.

"What do you mean?" he asked eventually, fighting to keep his voice steady.

"You don't want Maddy to go anywhere. You wouldn't let her go. It's you that's kept her here all these years. Nobody else."

"She was free to go any time . . ." he began, bending to pull on his boots.

Cloris contradicted him. "No, Bart. Don't lie to me, even if you must to yourself. Timon and the kids—oh you'd let them go to hell, gratefully. But not Mad Maddy."

"Don't call her that," he said gruffly.

"See? You need her. She'll always be here. I know it and I can live with it. Why can't you?" She pulled open a drawer and took a blouse out of it. She turned to look at Bart as she put it on. He was still bending over. She felt afraid suddenly, afraid that she had pushed him too far.

"I'm going to kill her," Bart said softly. "I swear to you that I'm going to kill her. Now say I need her."

Cloris could not speak. Hope choked her throat. Her heart hammered against her ribs.

"Get dressed," Bart said to her, beginning to lace his boots.

Cloris did as he told her, quickly. She could feel the restlessness in him. Did he really mean it?

"You'll have something to eat?" she asked, forcing herself to be calm.

"No. I'm not hungry. I must see that everything's ready."

"Do you want me to come?" she asked, zipping her skirt.

"No. You keep your eyes open down here. This is men's business." He snatched open the door and clattered down the stairs.

"Bart," she called, and hurried after him.

"What is it?"

She stared down at him, her face pleading.

"Don't be angry," she said. "What I said . . ."

"Not with you." He held out his hand to her. She went down the stairs and took it, went eagerly into his arms. He held her tightly. "You're my conscience," he whispered. "I forget that sometimes. The truth hurts, but it gives me strength. I thank you for that."

She pressed close against him, murmuring his name over and over. She loved the smell of him and the strength that lay curled, ready to explode, in his body. She had helped to make him and now she rejoiced in her handiwork.

"I love you," she told him.

He kissed her, briefly but passionately.

"Take care," she said.

"Aye. And you."

He went so quickly. Always. She looked around her own living room as though lost. Her eye fell on the switchboard and she smiled. She had never mentioned it to Bart but it always amused her that, when he chose to make love, all communications with the outside world were shut down. She walked across to the switchboard. She would leave it shut off tonight. He might come to her again, afterward. Even if he didn't, it was better that nobody made any calls tonight.

She turned restlessly to the window. If he killed Magdalena Clare, if he really meant to do it, then he would be free at last. Free as he had not been since they were children. If he were to be free again, he might, he just might . . .

The tractor was silhouetted against the darkening sky as the men climbed toward the meadow. The moon rose behind them.

At the edge of Top Meadow, Justin Dolben knelt, murmuring an old invocation. His action embarrassed the other men, who moved away in a ragged group to a pile of torches, stacked in the shadows of the ride. One of them poured kerosene from a can into a bowl. Several others thrust the rag-bound torches into it.

Bart Poole walked around the tractor and checked the strong chains which met to form a triangle. Squatting down, he pulled a pair of manacles from his pocket and attached them securely to the chains. Grunting with the effort, he tugged on them, to make sure that they would hold. In his mind, it was as though Cloris Poole, his grandmother, the Mistress had all ceased to exist. There was exhilaration, a sense of freedom in the company of men. He felt secure in their cooperation and took pleasure in the silent efficiency with which they set about their tasks.

The moon rose higher, coloring the stubble in the field an eerie silver. Below, in the village, a dog howled, breaking the silence. Bart stood up and watched Patrick Dolben climb the ridge. He arrived slightly out of breath and nodded to Bart.

"I checked with Jacob," he said panting. "Timon went off last night, drunk. He's not been back. There's been no sign of him."

"Good," Bart said. He felt warm and kindly toward Patrick tonight. "What about the Mistress?"

Patrick hesitated. "She seems . . . strange. Depressed. She went to her room."

"Did you lock her door?"

"No. I couldn't, Bart," he said quickly, anticipating criticism. "She was awake. Her light was on."

Bart looked up at the still sky. In the quickening moonlight, his face looked hollowed and tense. Patrick watched him anxiously.

"It's no matter," Bart sighed. "She'll sleep tonight or . . ." He left the sentence unfinished. Briefly, he clapped Patrick on the shoulder. Patrick relaxed a little. Bart left him, walked toward the men preparing the torches at the top of the ride.

"Four of you," he said, "go and fetch him."

147

Damon Clare stepped forward at once, basking in Bart's ready smile. Others followed him.

"Cover your faces," Bart ordered. "And take guns."

Obediently, the men tied handkerchiefs over their faces. One pulled an old muffler from his pocket and wound it around his face. Damon covered his distinctive pale hair with a woolen cap.

"Right," said Bart. They picked up their guns and broke them open with a sharp volley of clicks, then loaded a cartridge into each barrel. "Don't hurt her," Bart said, his voice thick with suppressed emotion. "Remember." They nodded. "Two of you stay behind." Their guns were snapped shut. The barrels gleamed gray in the moonlight. "Go on," Bart said. "Be quick about it."

Silently, like shadows, the men slipped away. He watched them for a moment, only a moment, before they were absorbed into the darkness of the ride. Turning, he called to Justin Dolben.

"You take the tractor. You know what to do."

"Aye," Justin said, with a curt, determined nod.

Bart moved aside.

"Bart," Patrick called, running after him.

"What is it?" he said, his mind obviously on other things.

"Where . . . where are you going?"

"Just to stretch my legs. They'll be a while yet."

"I'll come with you."

"No," Bart said. It was an order.

Blushing, Patrick stepped back, aware of the remaining men watching him.

Bart walked slowly along the ridge. Below him, the plantation of trees caught the moonlight. The chancel, raised on its hillock, was a sharp, black mass against the luminous sky. His thoughts came and went, without sense or pattern. He remembered, with a sharpness that hurt him, Magdalena Clare on her betrothal day. The sunlight on her pale hair, the shy, trusting way she had placed her hand in his. And Albertine, strong and fierce, showing one of her rare smiles. Albertine was Mistress then and, by giving him her daughter's hand, had singled him out for the highest office. She had made him Priest and first of the men. His heart had filled with pride, but then, that day, it was Maddy he most cared about. Then he would have given up his office, risked even the wrath of Albertine and of Mother Poole, just for her.

His expression and his thoughts became bitter. How he despised himself! What a fool he had been! Flouted by Timon Berryman, a peddler's son, a half-witted, unlettered gypsy boy. He had no pity for Magdalena Clare. All that remained now was his duty to fulfill the promise he had made her years ago.

He had no idea how much time had passed before a low, hooting whistle interrupted his solitary communication with the land. He retraced his steps. One by one the men were lighting their torches. They formed a circle around the entrance to the ride. He had heard no sound that he recalled, no screams or cries. Justin Dolben climbed onto the tractor. Silently, Bart joined the circle of men, looking down the dark tunnel of the ride. It seemed a long time before, in the darkness, they could make out approaching figures. The first glimpse of them caused a tense whisper to pass among the men. Three torchbearers moved into the road, lighting the way. The fluttering flame of the torches created gigantic, abstract shadows which reached out toward the climbing figures.

There were three of them toiling up the slope. Two men, each carrying a shotgun, and between them a child, pale and huddled in a blanket. The men gripped the child's shoulders with their free hands, holding him up when he stumbled, always urging him on. The light from the torches dazzled his terrified eyes. He was thrust forward, into the wavering pool of light. He paused, facing the semicircle of people above him.

"Go on," commanded a voice behind him.

Clutching the blanket about him, he started up the last and steepest part of the slope. The men fell back and parted so that he could see the tractor, see, in the moonlight, the chains on the ground. He knew that, in autumn, the harrow was hitched to such chains. He fell, or stumbled, to his knees. The men watched him, tense but impassive.

"Get up," Bart said, without a trace of emotion in his voice. "Get up and prepare yourself."

A single, helpless sob escaped him. He rose, the blanket slipping from his naked body. He stood for a moment, pale and slim, shining in the flickering light. Two men moved from the group and seized the boy's arms. He cried out, struggled. They forced him to the ground, turning him over. The sharp stubble stung and scratched his back. Ignoring his cries, they dragged him forward a little, fastened his thin arms together above his head, and manacled his wrists to the chains. The boy kicked his legs wildly in the air, rolled

149

from side to side, pulling against his bonds. The tractor engine roared into life. The men stepped back. The boy screamed, the power of his voice for a moment drowning the sound of the tractor. Then, as the engine was revved and the big wheels began slowly to turn, his scream was absorbed into the mechanical roar.

Five women listened to the sound of the tractor.

Magdalena Berryman, her body pressed against the wooden door which shielded her daughters, covered her face with her hands and moaned. She could not weep.

Penelope Clare paused in her aimless pacing, and listened. The relentless sound hurt her ears. She hurried to the back of the house, closing all doors behind her, but still the sound was audible.

Cloris Poole clasped her hands jubilantly together and thought: He will be free. At last. Tears of happiness stung her eyes. "Thank you," she whispered into the darkness. "Thank you."

Mother Poole sat bolt upright in her chair. The firelight threw strange shadows on the walls and ceiling of her room. Her face was a mask of stone, ageless and mysterious.

And in Dolben House, Lyndsay turned in her sleep. A roaring mechanical wind filled her dream, engulfing her. In it, swept along by it, she felt powerless and utterly alone.

Thirteen circuits of the field were made. At some point the boy had twisted himself over onto his stomach. For a time he had succeeded in holding his face free of the earth which tore and rent his flesh. By the sixth circuit, he could no longer hold up his head. By the seventh his body jolted and bounced over the ground, tossed onto its back, its front, like a doll. Blood poured down his pale arms from the bite of the manacles where he had twisted his wrists, where now they twisted with the unconscious weight of his body. On the eleventh circuit his head was seen to bounce, like a heavy ball, on the bared and scrabbled earth. At the end of the thirteenth circuit, when the tractor came to a standstill and silence assailed the ears of the watchers, there was no need to check if the boy lived.

The men moved away, melting into the moonlight. They needed no instructions.

Alone, Bart Poole stared at the mangled, livid thing that had been Christian Berryman. An icelike calm gripped his mind and body. After a long time, he spread the blanket the boy had worn on the grass, and then freed his broken wrists. With the toe of his boot, he pushed and nudged the body onto the blanket and tossed the loose ends over it. This done, he walked quickly along the ridge, then descended over rough ground to the plantation of trees. Not caring how much noise he made, he crashed through the wood until, at an area of denser darkness, he could make out the Berrymans' house. He sat down on a felled tree trunk and interlaced his fingers, cracking his knuckles.

His body shook with emotion. His teeth rattled in his head. The house remained dark and silent. Why didn't she scream or cry out? Had they hurt her? He leapt up and stumbled a few yards toward the house. Then he stopped, leaning against a tree. No, he would have heard the sound of a shot. The men would have told him if it had been necessary to hurt her. She was stronger, then, than he had thought. So strong. Moaning to himself, he stretched his arms around the tree, embracing it. The bark was harsh and knotted under his fingers. He had never cried. Even as a child, he had not cried. He gritted his teeth now against tears and sobs of rage and despair. He whispered her name. Pressing his cheek to the bark he rubbed it back and forth, grazing the skin until the blood oozed. She wanted him to go all the way, then.

As the moon waned and the sky became streaked with pink, Bart Poole grew calmer. His sore, tired eyes could make out the house now, gray and lifeless. When the sharp crowing of a cock broke through the silence, he left the tree. The blood had dried to a crust on his cheek. He walked back to the ridge and the loosely shrouded body of the boy. Bending, he lifted the bundle and cradled it in his arms. The sun rose, livid and dazzling. Its first rays spread across the meadow and Bart saw that the earth had responded to their sacrifice. Catching his breath, he walked carefully, almost fearfully, toward the field, where a miracle had occurred. Small, tender green shoots had sprung up among the stubble, from the dry, unplanted earth. The boy's blood had quenched the soil's thirst and brought forth life. He shifted the weight of the body in his arms and smiled at the replenished land.

Then he turned his back on the meadow and descended, carrying the child's body through the still-sleeping village and placed it in the center of the green, for all to see.

CHAPTER SEVEN

Penelope Clare shook her roughly by the shoulder.

"Wh . . . what?" Lyndsay pulled away, as though from an attack. The early morning light hurt her eyes.

"Please, please wake up," Penelope said in a distraught voice.

Lyndsay had been wrenched from a dream in which this woman had no part. Penelope reached out her hand again to shake Lyndsay.

"Okay, okay," Lyndsay mumbled. "I'm awake. What is it?" Her befuddled senses began to work. She looked at Penelope and saw that her pale, straight hair hung loosely over her shoulders, over some sort of black robe that completely swathed her body. There were sharp lines of anxiety on her face and her eyes were enlarged, as though with shock. Lyndsay struggled into a sitting position, pushing her own hair out of her face. "What is it?" she repeated, beginning to feel alarmed.

"Mother Poole wants you. To help us. There's been an accident."

"Mother Poole?"

"There's no time to explain. Will you get dressed and come with me? I'll explain as we go."

Obeying the fear in Penelope's voice, Lyndsay threw back the sheet and scrambled out of bed. She snatched up the clothes she had been wearing the night before and ran into the bathroom, leaving the door ajar. "Mother Poole's had an accident?" she called, splashing cold water on her face.

"No. Not her."

"But I thought you said . . ."

"She wants you to help us. It's the little boy. The one you saw in the graveyard. Christian Berryman." Her voice quavered.

Lyndsay paused, her dress half over her head. They wanted her to help with Magdalena's son? She yanked the dress down and put her head around the door.

"What happened to him? What can I do?"

"He's dead," Penelope said.

"Oh my God, no!"

"Have you got a cigarette anywhere?" Penelope asked, twisting her hands together.

"No. Maybe there are some downstairs."

"It doesn't matter." Penelope went to the window and stood looking out.

Lyndsay fastened her dress and pushed her bare feet into old sandals. She was trying to think how Magdalena must feel. Why did they want her to help, and to help whom? If the child was dead . . .

"How?" she asked, pulling a comb through her hair.

"I don't know exactly," Penelope answered. "We think he must have started up one of the tractors, late last night or early this morning. He must have fallen or something and got caught up in the tackle at the back." Penelope's voice broke.

"What do you want me to do?" Lyndsay asked, pushing the details of his death out of her mind.

"Help us," she repeated. "Help us take him to her."

"Where is he now?"

"On the green. Are you ready? Please, can we go?"

Lyndsay nodded. There were so many questions buzzing in her head that she did not know where to begin. They would have to wait anyway, she thought, as she hurried after Penelope, leaving the house by the back door.

"He was killed on the green?" she asked breathlessly. "But I thought he wouldn't come into the village."

"No. Up on the ridge. One of the men found him and brought him down." Penelope turned onto the track, making for the path beside the children's graveyard.

"But why didn't he take him to Magdalena?" Lyndsay asked.

"That's just it. They won't. I told you how it was."

"But that's awful," Lyndsay protested. "How could anyone be so callous?"

153

Penelope caught hold of her hand and pulled her into the shadowy, tunnel-like path.

"I knew you'd feel like that. That's why I came to fetch you."

"You said Mother Poole . . ."

"We can't manage it alone, and we must do it quickly."

"Who, exactly, is 'we'?"

"Mother Poole, Bryony, and myself. And now you."

Lyndsay stopped suddenly. Penelope turned impatiently back toward her.

"I don't know if I can," Lyndsay said, thinking of the child. He was dead and presumably damaged.

"You *must*," Penelope said, coming closer to her. "If you don't, there's no telling what they might do." She caught hold of Lyndsay's shoulders. "You wanted to do something for Maddy. I know you did. That day when I told you about her, I could see it in your face. Please?"

Was it helping a woman, Lyndsay wondered, to take her the body of her son?

"All right," she said. "I'll try."

"Thank you."

Penelope started along the path again, her robe flapping around her tall body. Clumsily, Lyndsay tried to keep up with her.

The men had left at dawn, backing slowly out of the yard where they had kept their vigil. They had melted silently into the morning shadows of the plantation. Magdalena Berryman had allowed her body to slump to the floor. She was cold and shivering. Her legs were cramped. She half sat, half lay on the floor, her cheek pressed against the wooden door behind which her daughters slept. She felt nothing, nothing at all. A desire to sleep perhaps, which was a luxury she could not afford. She made herself massage her legs until she was able to stand up. Like a somnambulist, she lit the fire and prepared a bottle for the baby. When it was ready, she roused Bella and told her to feed the baby. The little girl's sleepy eyes were alarmed.

"What's the matter, Mummy?"

"Nothing. You just stay here and see to the baby. Whatever you do, don't come out until I tell you. You're not going to school today."

"Why not?"

154

"Never mind. Just do as I tell you." She closed the door firmly behind her. Her face was gray with terror. Perhaps they would send him back, frightened or even mutilated. For a moment something seemed to snap in her brain. Her body would not respond properly to the messages it received. She staggered and fell against the table, upsetting crockery. One way or another, for one purpose or another, they would come. She had been strong so far. She had not given them the satisfaction of screaming or pleading. She had not wept. She must go on for a little longer. For they would come, to torture her further, but this time she would be ready for them.

Slowly, she persuaded her body to respond. She took Timon's shotgun from its place in the corner and loaded it clumsily. It felt like a deadweight in her hands. She had to drag it by its cold barrel across the floor. She opened the window just a crack, and lodged the gun against the sill. Her legs would no longer hold her. She fell to her knees and raised the shotgun, settling the butt against her shoulder, and waited. In the back of the house, the baby cried and then whimpered. The sound hurt her head, like the whine of a saw, like jagged teeth fraying her mind.

The women had gathered like crows at the edges of the green. They were silent, all dressed in black, some with shawls drawn over their heads. In the center of the green, like gaunt sentinels, Mother Poole and Bryony Dolben stood beside a gray bundle. All the faces turned toward Lyndsay as she came out of the path. She felt like an intruder, and hesitated. There was a look almost of happiness on their faces. With horror she saw that there were children present. One woman, her pale hands stark against her child's black dress, bent her head and whispered to the girl, who looked at Lyndsay with a shy smile.

Penelope Clare swept on across the green, as though she had forgotten Lyndsay, who was alarmed by the crowd. How could they bring children to such a spectacle? How could they look so pleased? Why didn't they help?

Her eyes met Mother Poole's, whose face had a sculpted, almost dead look. She wore a cowl over her head, a cape which reached the ground. Her eyes glittered with life. At least she had enough courage, cared enough to do something. She and Penelope and Bryony. Lyndsay walked toward them, keeping her eyes fixed on the old woman.

155

"Help us, Mistress," she said, when Lyndsay was close enough to hear her throaty whisper.

Lyndsay could only nod. She looked down at the gray bundle at her feet. Bryony stooped and took firm hold of one corner of the blanket. Penelope Clare did the same. As they straightened up, the blanket was pulled open. The thin body was gray and yellow with bruises. Streaks of dried, encrusted blood crisscrossed the ruined skin. Here and there fragments of torn flesh hung open to the white of the bone. The exposed flesh was still pink and tender-looking. Lyndsay turned her face away, pressing her hand to her stomach. She was going to be sick.

"You must be strong," Mother Poole whispered. "You *must*."

She swallowed a rush of bile which brought stinging tears to her eyes. Without looking at the body, she took hold of her corner of the blanket, grasped it tightly with both hands. As she did so a murmur ran through the crowd like a sudden wind. Nodding in grave approval, the old woman took the last corner, exposing the broken child completely, and together they lifted him. Christian Berryman was borne in a sort of sling between them. Mother Poole and Lyndsay set off in front, the weight dragging at their arms. Behind them, Penelope and Bryony followed, and when they took their portion of the weight, it became easier. Lyndsay, in order to avoid the eyes of the crowd, looked at Mother Poole. Straight and dignified, she held her head high, staring directly ahead of her. She was an example, Lyndsay realized. This was some kind of necessary ceremony, an expression of humanity toward an outcast. She pushed her shoulders back and lifted her head. She would not be afraid of these women, who, presumably, only wanted to humiliate Magdalena further. The women fell back, parted like a human wall, to let them through. As she reached the edge of the green, an old woman reached out and touched Lyndsay's arm. Her touch was like the brush of a dry and withered leaf.

"Mistress," she whispered.

Lyndsay did not look at her. Matching her step to Mother Poole's, she walked blank-faced up the village street, bearing her share of this terrible burden. She felt proud.

Pressed close against the inside wall of the post office, Cloris Poole watched the women pass by. She kept out of sight, peeping through the window. The door was bolted. An insistent buzz sounded from the switchboard, but she did not seem to hear it. Her body shook with the uncontrollable violence of a fever. She was glad, glad that the old woman had seized her opportunity, was making her own capital out of Bart's betrayal. For betrayal it was. He had promised to kill Magdalena Berryman, but he had been unable to do it. Probably he had lied to her. He would never be able to do it. Magdalena had held his heart from the day Albertine had betrothed them. All her life, Cloris had loved the husk of a man. Even as he lay with her, he had thought of Magdalena.

Her mouth twisted into a bitter line. He had used her, but he had never lied to her. Their relationship was based on implicit trust, which he had betrayed. Cloris stared wildly around the dim shop, looking for something to destroy. She could kill Magdalena Berryman. It would be a pleasure, a fulfillment even greater than her stolen hours with Bart. But if she did—the thought came to her at once—she would lose Bart forever.

The buzzing of the switchboard suddenly grated on her ears. Systematically, she pulled out all the plugs and leaned against the machine, panting. She could not kill Magdalena Berryman, but there was another way to free him. Stumbling over a pile of newspapers, she went to the kitchen and wrenched open a drawer. Her carving knife, honed and polished, caught the sun. She stared at it, trembling.

She could not use it on him. Her heart recoiled, shriveled at the thought. She slammed the drawer shut again, feeling empty and hopeless. There was no way open to her, no way in which she could hurt him as dreadfully as he had hurt her. And that was all she wanted: to hurt him.

Leaning against the little dresser in her narrow kitchen, Cloris realized that it was too late even to go out and join the women. But—the one thought led smoothly to the next—it was not too late to betray him. She could go there, wait for the old woman . . . Before the thought was completed, she had taken down her shawl and thrown it over her loose hair.

She let herself out by the back door and hurried down the garden path. A white painted gate gave onto the field. The dew was like ice on her bare feet. She had forgotten her shoes, but it did not matter. She hurried along the hedge which was, at regular intervals, studded with gates. Panting, her feet numb with the cold, she reached the back gate of Mother Poole's cottage. The bees were busy in the thyme. The whole back garden was given over entirely to herbs which, in the early sun, gave off their sweet and pungent scent.

Cloris opened the gate and ran up the dirt path. She flung open the door into the kitchen, which was as narrow as her own, but darker. She stopped in surprise, hung in the open doorway, her arms spread to steady herself.

Emelye Poole was bending over the old sink. She had twisted her face toward the door. Her eyes seemed to scream at Cloris. A thread of spittle hung from her open mouth. Cloris understood at once. The girl wore an old, loose-fitting nightgown. She turned her face away and retched. A look of curiosity settled on Cloris's wild face. Her breathing became calmer. She folded the ends of her shawl across her breasts and held them in place with her left hand. Then she walked toward Emelye and stood for a moment looking down at her bent head. Swiftly, Cloris put out her right hand and clapped it gently to the girl's stomach. It was tight and swollen. For a second her searching fingers caressed the girl. Emelye moaned and shook her head. Cloris smiled, withdrew her hand, and quietly, calmly went out again, latching the door behind her.

They came to the gate, four of them, carrying her child in an improvised sling. Magdalena clapped her left hand over her mouth to stifle the wail of desolation which rose in her throat. She made a gurgling sound through her fingers. Her right hand still held the gun, the stock pressed against her shoulder, though it trembled with the convulsions which shook her body.

Outside, Lyndsay unlatched the gate. She and Mother Poole, holding the blanket carefully clear of the ground, squeezed through the narrow opening and walked slowly, followed by the others, to the center of the littered yard.

"Set him down," the old woman said.

Silently, the three women obeyed her.

"Magdalena Clare," she called in her strong voice.

Bryony bent down and folded the loose ends of the blanket over the battered little corpse.

"Magdalena," Mother Poole called again. "We mean you no harm. We've brought your boy to you. Come out and let us help you bury him."

The silence from within the house was complete and terrible.

Lyndsay thought that it would be a relief if the woman would scream, or abuse them.

"Maybe she's not there," she whispered.

"She's there," Mother Poole answered with complete certainty. She took a step forward, straight and noble in her black cape and hood.

"Come, Magdalena," she called. "You know who we are. You know the Ways. We have come to help you. Come out and show us where to bury your boy."

There was still nothing, no sound or glimpse of movement. Their shadows lay bleak and black on the trampled earth. The small, misshapen windows reflected the sunlight back at them.

"Let me try," Lyndsay said, moving closer to Mother Poole. "She's afraid of you. Maybe she'll trust me."

The old woman looked at her. Her eyes shone and seemed to bore into Lyndsay's.

"Aye," she nodded. "You try, Mistress. Perhaps she'll heed you."

Magdalena had both hands on the gun. She managed to hold it steady. The foreign woman moved away from the old witch in her black robes and came toward the house. She remembered her, screaming at her children. The foreign woman moved into her sights and she squeezed the trigger, squeezed it gently and slowly the way Bart Poole had taught her years ago.

The sound of the report was deafening. Lyndsay opened her mouth to scream, but before she could make any sound she was spun off balance by the impact of the shot. The earth rose and fell, swayed at crazy angles. Her back was to the house and the sun blinded her. As she fell, she thought she saw a figure, a black silhouette against the light, in the distance.

Mother Poole gasped. Penelope and Bryony went at once to Lyndsay, but the old woman moved forward, her arms raised imperiously in front of her.

"You are forever cursed, Magdalena Clare," she shouted in a terrible, rasping voice. "Cursed," she repeated, "for you have harmed the Mistress." Her voice broke and fell, cracking with grief.

Penelope tried to turn Lyndsay over. Mother Poole swept toward her, her back presented fearlessly to the house.

"Go and fetch your car," she ordered Penelope. "And be quick about it."

Penelope ran off at once, her robe flapping so that she looked like a great broken bird.

159

The old woman looked at Lyndsay, her eyes making a swift examination. Then she turned back to the house.

"You," she screamed, "you can bury your own carrion. It's all you're fit for."

The men had gathered, in small groups at first, but growing quickly to a sizable crowd, to stare at Top Meadow. The newly sprouted shoots were a dazzling green against the dark earth. They stared in awe. A few gave thanks, their hands clasped and their heads bowed. Bart's name was passed from mouth to mouth. The power of the Priest was acknowledged. Someone produced a stoneware crock of wine and handed it around the group. A holiday atmosphere developed. The men felt relieved and justified. They slapped each other on the back and called for more wine. They spoke openly, fearlessly of the Mistress now, and asked each other where Bart was. They had forgotten about the women and the child's corpse on the green. They sang old songs and planned a greater celebration for the evening.

"Where's Bart?" they asked.

"Yes, where is he?"

Patrick, smiling with the rest, drinking the rich old wine, undertook to find him. He set off along the ridge, feeling at peace with himself and with the world.

Bart watched from his familiar haunt as the four women carried the body of Christian Berryman to his mother. He ground his teeth with anger. The splash of Lyndsay's scarlet dress made a startling contrast to the sober black of the others. The old woman had undone his work. She had shown the Mistress to the village and raised the cult of mercy again. His mind raced to find a way of reversing her work. If he hadn't taken the child to the green . . .

You're too proud, Bart Poole.

Blood mounted to his cheeks. He stood there, blushing like a shamed schoolboy. But he had discounted Maddy. He had forgotten that, in a special way, he could count on her.

The shot rang out, echoed like a fading fusillade across the fields, the sound bouncing off the ridge. He saw the red splash of Lyndsay's dress whirl round. For a moment the pale blob of her face was lifted toward him, then she fell.

Maddy had given him back his power.

The shot rang out, stopping Patrick in his tracks. Ahead of him, he saw Bart rise on the balls of his feet and then rush headlong down the ridge. He shouted his name. Raising an arm, Bart waved him on. He could not make out the moving figures below. He ran after Bart, toward Mother Poole's screamed curses.

The shot rang out, cutting off the laughter of the men. Their faces grew solemn. They exchanged looks.

"What was that?"

"From the Berrymans' place."

"Come on."

Like a tide, they surged toward the ride, jostling against one another.

The contents of the forgotten jug of wine spilled onto the earth with a satisfying, gurgling sound.

There was a great ball of searing light over which shadows, dark and flapping, passed. The earth rocked and swung, increasing the pain in her shoulder. She remembered the force of the blow, her body spinning, the earth rising toward her. There was a roaring noise, voices. She was being lifted, borne up, and her head hurt as it swung loose from her body.

Later, cries of "the Mistress" broke into her stupor. She tried to lift her left hand up, but she could not. There was a numbness in her shoulder, no connection between it and her hand, which was being bruised by constant knocking against stairs.

Then her body was still, but figures whirled around her, like puppets in a dance. Something sharp and stinging hurt her shoulder. She struggled against this new pain. Something was pressed against her face. Something damp. A strong, sweet smell. A white, featureless face hung over hers and began to spin.

A knot of people waited on the road outside Clare House. Men, women, and a few children. Silently, they stared up at the blank windows of the old stone house. Bart Poole came out, his brow furrowed. He surveyed them from the stone-arched gateway.

"Get back to work," he said roughly.

"How is she? The Mistress?" a woman asked, stepping forward. Others supported her question with murmurs.

"She's in good hands. Now clear off, all of you. There's work to be done."

He turned his back on them. Muttering, they moved away. He went back into the house and, in the paneled hallway, paused. Penelope Clare, still wearing her robe, was standing at the side window of the sitting room, staring up toward the gloomy old chancel. He watched her for a moment and then went into the room, closing the door behind him. Penelope faced him, a cigarette burning in her fingers.

"What do you want?" she said wearily.

He surveyed her with his cold, golden eyes. With her blond hair framing her face against the black robe, she was handsome. A tall, full-breasted woman, and handsome. Her dislike of him, etched on her face, made him smile.

"Haven't you done enough?" she spat at him. "Get out of my house."

"No," he said simply, though she could not tell whether he meant it as an answer to her question or as a refusal to leave. Suddenly, it didn't seem to matter. She sat down in a chair and rubbed her forehead with her hand.

"Can I trust you?" he asked.

She looked at him in surprise. It would have been funny, she thought, this blunt question, if it weren't for the fact that he meant it in all seriousness.

"You want her to die," Penelope said, in a shocked whisper. He wanted her to help him to . . . "No," she said.

"She's in no danger," he said. "Besides, you're wrong. I want her to live, every bit as much as you do."

Penelope scrutinized his face for some sign that he was lying. He bore her look without flinching or in any way altering his expression.

"I don't believe you," she said, without conviction. "Why should you . . . ?"

"Never mind why," he told her sharply. "Listen. I want her to stay here, in your care. Yours and the old woman's."

Penelope made an exasperated sound and stubbed out her cigarette.

"She's not likely to go anywhere," Penelope said. "You needn't have any fear of that."

"But I want you to take care of her. Do whatever Mother Poole tells you. But no visitors, except me."

"You?" Penelope stood up and tried to move away from him. He seized her arm and forced her to look at him.

"Me and none but me. Do you understand?"

"If you think I'd trust you with her . . ." She pulled against his hand, but he only gripped her more tightly. "You're hurting me," she said.

"Do as I ask and I'll make sure you have Patrick."

Her heart fluttered painfully for a moment. He saw her pale eyes mist over. She looked down at his hand.

"Take your hand off me." He obeyed at once. Haughtily, she moved past him. "That's all we are to you, isn't it?" she said coldly. "Creatures, things, that you can dispose of to suit yourself."

"Think what you like," he answered, "but you know you'll never get Patrick without me. And I know that there's nothing else you want. This is your last and only chance, anyway. Soon you'll be a dried-up old maid, good for nothing."

Penelope kept her back to him, made herself absorb the pain his words caused her. When she felt she could control her voice, she said:

"Get out."

"I'll be back. You think on it. I mean her no harm. And you'll be well rewarded." He waited, wanting her to show some sign of weakness, but she remained quite still, her back rigid. He made a curt nod and went to the door.

Only when she heard his step on the stairs did Penelope Clare give way to her tears of shame and weakness.

The sheet was stained with blood, like a great red flower. Leaning against the door, Bart watched the women at work. Lyndsay was unconscious, but Bryony kept the chloroform-soaked pad ready. Gently, Mother Poole probed the wound with forceps, removing the little grains of shot that had lodged in Lyndsay's flesh. The room smelled of illness and death. He looked at Lyndsay's bared left breast rising and falling in unconscious sleep.

"Ah," the old woman grunted and twisted the instrument she held. Slowly she withdrew it and inspected the stained wad of cotton at its end. "It's clean now," she pronounced.

"Is there damage?" Bart asked as she dropped the forceps and the swab into a waiting bowl of water.

163

"None that I can't see to." She wiped the open wound and, with Bryony's help, placed a pad, smeared with some ointment, against it. Then they bandaged the shoulder, lifting the woman like a doll, and strapped her arm tightly to her side.

He found their work soothing. The quiet competence of their movements, their complete absorption was beautiful to watch. When they had finished, Mother Poole told him to lift Lyndsay up while they changed the soiled sheet. For a long moment he held her naked body in his arms, staring at her flawless skin. The old woman, smoothing the fresh sheet, settling the pillows, missed nothing. She saw the gleam in his eye, the tip of his pink tongue flicking over his lips, the beads of sweat on his forehead.

"Put her down now. Gently."

He placed Lyndsay on the bed and helped his grandmother to cover her. Silently, Bryony gathered up the dirty linen and took the bowl away. Mother Poole and Bart faced each other across the bed.

"What now?" he asked softly.

The old woman's bosom heaved.

"Do your worst," she said breathlessly. "Magdalena Clare is cursed. If you've the heart for it, do your worst."

She turned to the little wooden box, her medicine chest, that he remembered from his childhood. He watched, fascinated, as she took up a hypodermic syringe and wiped it with a sterile cloth. She filled it with a colorless liquid, checked it, and then moved around the bed. Bart stepped back, out of her way.

"What's that for?" he asked.

"To make sure she sleeps. She needs rest." She turned Lyndsay's limp right arm over and swabbed the crook of her elbow. The vein showed blue and prominent. She aligned the needle. "Raise the Hounds," she told him, her voice hissing between her teeth as she plunged the needle smoothly home.

For it was written: "Whomsoever shall raise his hand against the Mistress, or speak ill of Her without full and true substantiation, shall be as a blasphemer; and shall be cursed, cast out forever from Her love and protection; and shall be handed to Her Priest for due and just punishment."

Never, in all her long years, had Mother Poole witnessed such a violation of the Mistress. It shocked and aged her. Sitting in a chair beside Lyndsay's bed, she felt exhausted. The attack could not have affected her more deeply had it been made on her. She had believed Bart capable of something of the sort, but not Magdalena Clare, the daughter of the former Mistress. She had been moved, that morning, by pity for Magdalena. True, her child's death was a gift from the gods, since it provided Mother Poole with an opportunity to establish the new Mistress in the eyes of the village, but her old heart had wept, too. Now it hardened, more so than when she had been angry. Bart would have his way now and she would rejoice in his revenge. Everyone would know that it was undertaken in the name of the Mistress. How it all fell together! The pieces of the old pattern turned and scattered, yet they could only fit together in one way. There was no escaping it.

Mother Poole found comfort in this thought, though the risk still frightened her. She, who was nearing the end of her own time, found death inexplicable and awesome. Its finality was something she could not comprehend. When it came to one so young as the boy, brushed against the Mistress herself, it made her feel helpless and old. All her care and watchfulness were needed now. Lyndsay's illness would delay their plans and there would be less time to school and prepare her. Sighing, the old woman admitted to herself that harsh measures might now be necessary. She knew that she could not contain Bart for long. The tasks ahead of her were formidable. For a moment she felt unequal to them. But weakness she understood less even than death. There was a time for rest as well as for doing. Folding her hands together in her lap, Mother Poole closed her eyes and slept.

Stuart Donne walked the short distance from the new, ugly brick Ketterford police station to The Black Swan, where he was staying. He was already in a bad temper and his mood was not improved by the crowds of people who had flocked into the town for market day. They all seemed, these tanned and stocky farmers and their soft-voiced, package-laden wives, to be intent on bumping into him or on blocking his path. To make matters worse, the actual market was set up in the cobbled square directly in front of his hotel. The all-pervading smell of cow dung and human sweat, intensified by the heat, sickened him. He thrust his way through a group of farmers chatting on the pavement outside the hotel and, with a sense of relief, entered the bar. Waves of raucous laughter and the din of male voices competing to be heard almost deafened him. He had grown quite fond of the bar. It was cool and large and usually patronized only by a few local businessmen at lunchtime. But on market days it was evidently a different story.

The Black Swan was basically a pub: an old, half-timbered building which rented half a dozen rooms and boasted a restaurant. The bar had been opened up to make one large, classless drinking area, even though the two doors opening off the street were still labeled PUBLIC and SALOON. Taken aback by the noise, Stuart Donne hesitated just inside the bar, but the thought of returning to the crowded streets was even less appealing. He was hot and thirsty. He saw that the farmers had gathered at the far side of the room, in what was still, despite the efforts of the brewery's architect, regarded as "the Public."

He went to the counter and waited to be served. The usual barmaid was drawing pints of beer and cider as fast as she could for the clamoring farmers. She was assisted by a young man Stuart had seen around the hotel, but never before behind the bar. He looked hot and uncomfortable in his short white jacket and seemed almost relieved to cross the bar and serve Stuart.

"Busy today," Stuart commented as the youth pulled his pint of lager.

"It's always like this on market day," he said morosely.

"Yes. So I gathered."

"They'll be here till closing time. And half the night, I daresay."

"Still," Stuart said amicably, "it must be good for business."

The boy scooped up the coins Stuart had placed on the counter and hurried away without comment. Stuart sipped the head off his pint and carried it to an old-fashioned, pewlike seat in the farthest corner of the room. He sat down and began to fill his pipe.

As he saw it, there had been no alternative but to go to the police, but the sergeant who had seen him evidently thought the whole interview a waste of time. Perhaps he had chosen a bad day, Stuart thought ruefully, lighting his pipe. Perhaps there was a run on crime in Ketterford on market days. But really he knew that it wouldn't have mattered when he went or whom he saw. To the police, Kenneth, his brother, was just a student. Students were long-haired troublemakers, unpredictable and quite likely to take off somewhere for weeks on end without informing their parents or friends. All

Stuart could say was that Kenneth was not like that. He felt embarrassed, even pompous, trying to explain the difference between the sergeant's stereotype of a student and the hard-working, postgraduate that was Kenneth. All he had achieved was an indirect reinforcement of the police argument. Yes, Kenneth was overage. Yes, he did understand that if a young man chose to be missing, no one had the right to stop him. But, Stuart had argued, Kenneth had planned a serious field-study trip. He had sent letters and postcards to both himself and their parents, until five weeks ago. They had heard nothing of him since he reached Ketterford, which was only twenty miles or so from Ratchets.

Although he had come to know it virtually by heart, Stuart drew Kenneth's last letter from his pocket and opened it, flattening the creased sheets on the table in front of him. Normally they exchanged letters only once or twice a term, and Stuart had solicited this one. He had been planning a trip to the Dordogne. Would Kenneth like to come along, during his vacation?

"It's very tempting," he read, "and thanks for asking, but I've decided to spend the summer doing some *real* work." Kenneth had obviously been enthusiastic about the prospect. An anthropologist who had become interested in folklore and legends, he was writing his thesis on the surviving traces of pagan cults in a Christian society. "The more work I do," he had written, "the more I see, or more accurately, suspect, that it's not just a question of absorption. I reckon there are places where some of the cults actually survive in recognizable 'living' ways, alongside the Christian ethic and practice. And no, I don't mean Morris dancing and Maypoles." This was a joke between them, referring to something Stuart had said when Kenneth had first discussed his thesis with him. Morris dancing and Maypoles just about summed up all Stuart knew of the subject. "For instance," he read on, "there is one place that particularly interests me. It's called Ratchets. I dug up some fascinating stuff on it. My tutor is properly skeptical about it, naturally, but I have a feeling it could be the high spot of my little tour. Anyway, I shall probably get there about the middle of July, unless I find something really good in Lincolnshire, where, incidentally, there's an interesting variant of the Ratchets legend. All this is by way of explaining why I must turn you down. You'll understand, I know. Enjoy France and drink lots of *vin supérieur* for me. I'll see you in the autumn. Kenneth."

167

The sergeant had barely glanced at the letter.

"I expect he changed his plans, sir. Youngsters these days, well, they're very unpredictable. Probably met some nice young girl and decided to have a holiday instead."

It was hopeless, Stuart admitted, and now he did not know what else to do. He had canceled his trip when his parents became seriously worried. They were getting on now, and his father had suffered a minor coronary earlier in the year. His mother was convinced that Kenneth's uncharacteristic silence was making him worse. He'd promised to find him, for he had begun to worry too. The last communication—a postcard of The Black Swan—had come from Ketterford. Kenneth had stayed at the hotel for two nights, and then vanished.

"Why don't you ask over at Ratchets?" the sergeant had advised, standing up. "You see, there's nothing we can do."

Stuart had not even bothered to tell him that he'd already been to the village and drawn a complete blank. Perhaps Kenneth had, too, and had moved on. But where? And why didn't he get in touch?

In spite of Bart's instructions, very little work had been done in the village that day. Neighbor called upon neighbor. The garden in front of the village store provided a gathering point where news and views were exchanged. The "miracle" in Top Meadow was whispered about and brought with it a feeling of well-being and suppressed excitement. The Mistress had been established, too. They had seen her and feared for her life. But when Mother Poole finally emerged from Clare House and told them that she would recover, their excitement grew. Underneath all the talk and speculation was a growing, fervent hatred of Magdalena Berryman. Some were all for lynching her there and then, but the majority insisted that they must leave it to the Elders. It must be done according to the Ways, in the fullness of time. Her history and that of the Berryman tribe was recalled and picked over until the conversation turned again to the meadow and to the Mistress. All day long the gossip flowed back and forth, and in the midst of all this, the fact that Cloris Poole had not, that day, opened the post office was scarcely remarked until Alice Clare regaled all she met with a vivid account of how she had hammered with her fists on the door and had not been able to rouse her. It was a disgrace, she asserted. You couldn't buy a stamp or a newspaper, and no word of explanation. She had banged loud enough to wake the dead, but there hadn't been a sound. And you couldn't see a thing through the window.

Eventually, this news reached Bart, as Alice Clare had intended. It was evening, however, before he found the time to go to her cottage. He went across the field and in at the back door, as always. Cloris was seated at the table, her hair uncombed. She wore a bright yellow dress which dramatized the blackness of her hair and set off her figure. She had been drinking. The stuffy room reeked of wine. Her fingers encircled a tumbler. She seldom drank, but Bart had seen her like this before. He recognized the bright flush of color on her cheeks. He stood in the kitchen doorway, appraising the situation. She gave no sign that she was aware of him, but he knew that she was not that drunk. He leaned across the table and opened the window.

"It smells like a pub in here," he said.

Cloris smiled and raised her glass.

"What is it?" Bart asked, forcing his voice to be gentle, even though he hated to see her like this. "What's the matter with you?"

She shook her head so that her hair swung.

"I took the day off. After all, it's a day of celebration, isn't it?"

"Not that I know of."

"Your great triumph," she said, mocking him. "Or should it be the Mistress? I think I'll drink to both."

He watched her as she emptied the tumbler and reached automatically for the bottle.

"You've had enough," he told her.

"No. I've got more to celebrate." She emptied the bottle into her glass. "You'll have to fetch another bottle if you want one," she said.

"What's made you like this?" he demanded.

"I told you. I'm just celebrating. All by myself."

"Is it that I didn't come?" he asked. "I couldn't. You probably don't know the half of it, shutting yourself up here all day."

"I know you're a liar and a coward," she said quietly. Bart's eyes widened dangerously, but Cloris deliberately did not look at him. "You were going to kill Magdalena Clare, remember? But she's too big for you, isn't she? You can take on a kid, but not your precious Maddy. Poor Bart." She laughed softly.

Bart moved away from her. He was afraid that if he did not, he would hurt her. He faced her across the table.

"She shot the Mistress," he said. "But she'll be all right."

169

"Who cares?" Cloris said blithely.

"I do. Oh you're too drunk to see. The old woman's on my side now. She's told me to do my worst. She'll support me. Don't you see?" He leaned forward eagerly, willing her to understand.

"Good," Cloris said, nodding her head. "That's good. At last the old witch'll get what she deserves."

"You're raving," Bart said disgustedly.

"Am I? I mean that you'll fail the old woman, and that'll break what heart she's got."

"Fail? What are you talking about?"

"You," Cloris shouted. "You won't harm a hair of Maddy's head. You can't. It's all bluff, Bart. You promised me," she finished, her voice rising hysterically.

"Not last night," he said, desperately. "I didn't mean then."

"Never. That's what you mean. You love her. You'll not touch her. You're still eating your heart out for her and I'm glad. D'you want to know why? Because I want you to suffer. She'll make you suffer, and the old woman. It's all down to Maddy, and there's not a thing you can do about it. Only don't come here anymore. Go to her. Go to your slut."

Bart whipped his right hand up over his left shoulder and struck out at her. His knuckles cracked painfully against her cheekbone, snapping her head to the left. She closed her eyes. Panting, Bart stooped over her, his body stretched across the table.

"I will kill her," he said, forcing the words out, as though each one pained him.

Cloris slowly turned her head and pulled the glass toward her.

"I've got a toast for you, too," she said flatly. "Here's to Emelye's bastard." She saluted him and drank.

He smashed the side of his hand into her wrist. The glass flew across the room, spilling its contents and shattering against the switchboard. Cloris clutched her wrist, biting her lip.

"What did you say?" he shouted.

"She's pregnant, you fool." She lifted her eyes to his. "Go and see for yourself."

His mouth quivered.

"If . . . you're . . . lying . . . to me." He raised his hand again, clenching his fingers into a fist.

"But I'm not," she said.

She watched the anger fade from his eyes. That old, uncertain look crept back into them. He was a child again, and vulnerable. Her face softened. He walked to the kitchen door, then turned his head toward her, his mouth opened to speak. Cloris shook her head firmly. She looked at a fragment of broken glass, concentrating her whole mind on it until she heard the back door slam. Then she put up her hand and felt where he had hit her. There would be a bruise in a few hours. She had hurt him more, much more, and it was for this that she began to cry.

At dusk, Magdalena Berryman came out of her house and walked toward her son. Flies had settled on the mutilated body. Falling to her knees, she brushed them away and drew the blanket tightly over him, covering him completely. It took all her strength to lift the stiff and heavy bundle. She carried it slowly to the corner of the house and set it down tenderly. He was her baby, just a baby. And she had to watch over him until he slept. Then she remembered. She went away and fetched a shovel from the outhouse. The ground was hard and she could make no impression on it. She had tried to grow a few flowers by the fence and there she had kept the earth watered. She began to dig, tossing the plants aside. She dug on as the light faded. Her back ached. It was a shallow grave, hardly deep enough. But then, he was only a baby. She dropped the shovel and turned back to the gray bundle. She knelt beside it and, after a while, gathered it up into her arms. Its stiff lifelessness rejected her. She held it tighter, cradled against her bosom. Rocking back and forth, Magdalena Berryman began to sing to her baby. The sound of her voice, cracked and tuneless, disturbed a dog somewhere off in the village. It barked and then began to howl. The moon rose, and Magdalena remained where she was, unaware that her song had become a wail of desolation.

CHAPTER EIGHT

Penelope could not bear to look at Lyndsay. After Mother Poole's visits, Lyndsay's sleep was calm and undisturbed. But she could not bear to look at her. She knew what she was doing, no matter how hard she tried to bury the knowledge in her mind. After all, she had made no decision. She had not promised to cooperate. Her excuses, addressed solely to herself, became weaker with each day. Yet still she tried to make them fit.

"What's troubling you?" Mother Poole had asked her. "You look like twopenny's worth of death warmed over."

"Couldn't she go to Dolben House? If we took care, surely we could move her?"

"And who'd look after her there? Patrick?" Mother Poole snorted and picked up her medicine chest. "Besides," she said in her lecturing tone, "your house is honored. You should know that."

"I'm not very good with sick people," Penelope said. "They make me depressed."

"Bryony will help you. I'll speak to her."

"No," Penelope said quickly. "No I . . . You're right. I must do it."

Mother Poole stared at her. It felt as though her eyes were boring into Penelope's brain.

"Is there something you should tell me? Something I should know?" Penelope shook her head.

172

"What should there be to tell you?" she asked. "I look after her. I do all you say."

"And no more?"

"I don't understand you. What 'more' can I do?"

"Either you know, or you don't," the old woman had said, pushing past her. "I'll be back later to change her dressing."

Penelope stared down into the garden, but she did not really see the roses she loved. It was so hot, so still. The sound of Lyndsay's breathing, regular but shallow, filled the room. It was as though she used up all the air, stifling Penelope.

Why hadn't she spoken to the old woman? Because she was afraid, as she had always been afraid. She could not find the courage to fight back. The risks were too great. So she became a passive, silent accomplice. And when they found out . . . Her heart missed a beat. But he would protect her. Or perhaps it would not matter. By then the situation would have changed, one way or another.

Meanwhile, she could not spend another minute in the room. She went downstairs, leaving Lyndsay's door open. She would like to go out, to go for a walk, but she knew that she would be seen and the old woman's anger would be terrible. So she sat, huddled miserably in her chair, chain-smoking and waiting.

Emelye Poole had not left her room for days. It was a small room, furnished with an old brass bedstead and a washstand with a chipped bowl and jug. A narrow wardrobe and a small chest of drawers contained her few clothes. The room, which had been hers for most of her life, was now a prison.

She had known, the moment Cloris Poole appeared, that her secret was discovered. It had, in any case, only been a matter of time. It was in this room that Bart had found her. She remembered, with a flinch of fear, how he had hurled the door open so hard that it had rebounded from the wall to crash against his upraised arm. She had cowered against the head of the bed, whimpering, while his anger broke over her. It seemed that his abuse would never stop. She had been too frightened to take in the names he called her, the things he threatened. He had seized the rail at the foot of the bed and shaken it until she begged him to stop. But when he had seized her, she had been prepared to fight him, not for herself but for her baby. They wanted to take it away from her. She had known they

173

would. Mother Poole had warned her. But, as Bart drew back his fist, the old woman had appeared in the doorway. Her commanding voice stopped him. He had dropped her so that her head cracked against the brass rail. The pain and the fear and the relief made her dizzy. She wasn't sure how Mother Poole had gotten him to leave the room. The old woman had remained behind, looking down at her.

"How?" she had asked. "How did he find out?"

"It was Cloris," she had sobbed. "She came here this morning. Don't let him hurt me."

At the sound of Cloris's name, Mother Poole had sucked in her breath sharply.

"You should have heeded me. I told you. You'll have to get rid of it. That's the only way."

"No." She had shaken her head violently. "I don't care what you say, I won't."

"Then there's no knowing what he'll do," Mother Poole had said coldly. "You think on it."

"Help me," Emelye had begged, but the old woman had stalked away, latching the door behind her.

Their voices, raised in anger, had reached her for a long time. Bart demanded that the baby be killed. Mother Poole told him that he must not raise his hand to his own kind, against a Poole. Emelye did not know if an agreement had been reached. At last Bart had gone and he had not been back. She could rely on Mother Poole to protect her, but not her baby. Afterward, the old woman would not talk to her, except to tell her to stay in the house.

In the long hours that she had spent alone, her determination had grown. She did not care what happened to her, but she had to save her baby. The shame that Bart spoke of did not matter to her at all. The child she was carrying was all she had left of her lover. His child and his notebook.

For what must have been the hundredth time in the last few days, Emelye took the square, black notebook from its hiding place under her mattress and stared at his handwriting. It was firm and legible. He had given her the book, with clear instructions, but she had kept it, even though she knew that it was dangerous and sinful. She had kept it because it brought him close. Now, she understood at last that the notebook could help her, if only she could place it in the right hands. She could not take it to the post office. Cloris would simply give it to Bart and if he read it, then he would surely kill her. Her and the baby.

Hopelessly, she returned the book to its hiding place. She went to the little window and knelt down, resting her elbows on the sill. She watched people passing, going about their business and knew that there was no one who would help her. Unless . . . The thought set her heart racing for a moment. But she couldn't ask him. Not now. He would betray her at once, for he had cause. Yet she remembered how he had looked at her. Not one word of reproach had he spoken to her. He had cause to hate her and they would have done all they could to turn him against her, but perhaps, even now . . . Besides, what did she have to lose? She would beg if necessary. It was her only chance. A slim one, but she had to take it. How to see him, that was the problem. She would have to plan it very carefully. Her mind began to race. It would be difficult. It might even be impossible, but she had to try. For the baby's sake.

She walked up a long sun-splashed empty street, dragging a great weight behind her. The weight pulled on her arm, so that her shoulder burned with pain. An old woman came from nowhere and brushed her arm with dry fingers. *Mistress.* This single word haunted her dreams. She did not understand it. The word hung and echoed in the still air. It seemed to pursue her as she tugged and pulled her burden. She made herself concentrate on her task. It was very important that she should reach the end of the street. She could not remember what it was she had to do, but it was important.

Then she was standing, looking down into an open grave. It seemed dark suddenly. There was a corpse in the grave. A corpse with lilies strewn all over it. She turned away from it with a sense of relief. She had done what she had to do. She was free now.

There was bright sunlight again. She was standing in an open space, looking up. A man waited for her, on a hill. With a rush of happiness, she began to climb toward him. It was difficult. Soon she had to use her hands to haul herself along. Her shoulder hurt. She was afraid that the man would not wait for her. The gradient was so steep, the climb so difficult. It required a great effort to lift her head to see if he was still there. She was quite close to him. Another few feet and she would be able to see his face. Once she did that, everything would be all right. She redoubled her efforts, but somehow the ground slipped away from her. She was falling backward, spinning, floating into darkness.

Magdalena Berryman had lost all sense of time. Day and night flowed into one continuous waiting. She roused herself only to see to the children, and then she moved and spoke like an automaton.

Bella had become afraid of her mother. She played with the baby and asked, over and over again, when her father was coming back. Her mother shook her head and stared at the fire.

Something terrible had happened to Christian, and Bella was afraid of that, too.

When, at last, the old truck sputtered to a stop outside the house, it was Bella who ran to greet her father. Swaying a little, he scooped her up in his strong arms and swung her round. She laughed, even though his breath smelled funny.

Magdalena stood in the doorway, watching them. Her face was like stone. She seemed a lifetime older. Sobered, Timon set Bella down and told her to run along. Hitching his trousers, he walked toward his wife.

"Hello Maddy," he said. Her eyes were blank and seemed to look through him. "I tried," he said, his voice whining. "Honest I did, There's nothing going. Not even casual work. I've been all over. I swear to you." He drew closer to her, so close that she could smell the beer and whiskey on his breath. "It's not my fault," he said. "You need money to find a place. Times are hard, Maddy." She pushed past him. He lost his balance momentarily and had to steady himself against the wall of the house. Inside, he could hear Bella talking to the baby, telling her that Daddy was home. He smiled. Maddy stopped at the corner of the house. She was staring at something. "Maddy?" he said.

"Come here." Her voice was low and soft. That was better. That was what he wanted to hear. He walked unsteadily toward her.

"What is it, old girl?" he asked, slipping his arm around her shoulders. She swayed a little as he leaned against her. "What is it, eh?" Slowly he followed the direction of her gaze. She'd dug all her pretty flowers up. There was a rough sort of mound there now. Two pieces of kindling had been nailed together and stuck into the ground. "What's that then?" he asked.

"Your son."

He tried to laugh, but her intense, fixed expression checked him. He pulled her round so that she had to look at him. Her expression did not change. "Christian," she said.

"No, no. What are you saying? Maddy?"

She looked like a madwoman. Perhaps, after all, what they said was true.

"I told you," she said, her voice at last taking on some color. "I've been telling you for years. They've killed him, just as they will kill all of us."

He stared at her without understanding. Yet she did not sound mad.

"No," he said again, and shook her. Then he looked back at the grave. "No. It's not possible."

She said nothing. Her face remained set and blank. His hands dropped from her shoulders. He took a few steps toward the grave. She turned to watch him. He looked at the grave, tears welling into his eyes.

"No, God no," he whimpered. He came back to her, holding out his arms. She faced him, lifted her head a little and spat into his face. Then she walked calmly back into the house, closing the door behind her.

He would not go. He would never go. Yet his legs moved, turned back to the truck. He opened the door and climbed in. He was trembling all over. He would not go. He had a right . . . He started the engine and made a bumping, jolting U-turn. Then he pressed his foot down, hard, on the accelerator.

Mother Poole set off for Clare House, carrying her little wooden medicine chest. Emelye watched her leave. She was already dressed and now she slipped quietly down the stairs, clutching the notebook. Almost holding her breath with fear, she wrapped the book in a sheet of brown paper and tied it with string. Laboriously, she printed the name and address which was inscribed on the inside front cover and which she had memorized. Then she took down her shawl and folded it around the parcel, to conceal it. Peeping between the foliage which all but blocked the window, she waited for him to go by. He looked at the cottage, looked up at her window with a mixed expression. She drew back, afraid that he might see her and come in. She waited. She must not be seen with him.

Later, she saw Timon Berryman's truck going toward his house. It was a stroke of luck. That would keep Bart occupied, and probably most of the rest of the village, she thought. She hesitated no longer. Refolding her shawl so that it hung quite naturally over her arm, but still hid the notebook, she went out into the field at the back of the house and hurried along. The field ended in the copse beside the children's graveyard. From among its sparse trees, Emelye could see people on the green, taking the evening air and, no doubt, discussing the return of Timon Berryman. She made as little noise as possible and, when she gained the path, ran as fast as she could to the gate let into the wall. He had left it ajar. For a moment it seemed to Emelye like a good omen. It was as though he were expecting her. She stepped into the graveyard and closed the door firmly behind her. She did not go very far along the path, but took shelter under the trees. They grew so closely together that it was almost dark beneath them. Stooping in order to see better, Emelye searched for a place to hide her parcel. She had planned it all out. If he refused her, it was better that he should not know where it was. She found a spot where the big roots of an old tree had risen above the ground, forming a shallow declivity. She pushed the notebook into this hiding place and then walked away from it. She would wait for him under another tree, in case he should guess what she had done. She chose a place a few feet from the path and covered her head with her shawl.

After what seemed a terribly long time, she heard the chapel door bang shut. For a while there was silence. He would be locking the door, she knew. Then the tramp of feet on the gravel as he passed among the graves. Then silence again as he reached the dirt path. Looking up the path, she could see him. He was walking with his hands thrust into his pockets and with his head bent. Her heart hammered painfully against her ribs. Perhaps the risk was too great? Her courage almost failed, but at the last moment, when he drew level with her, she spoke his name.

"Damon."

He turned, startled, toward the sound of her voice. She could not smile. She tried to, but she couldn't. He stared at her in silence, then, very slowly, he walked a little way toward her.

"Emelye?" he said in an uncertain voice. "Is it really you?"

She nodded.

He came on, pushing a low-hanging branch out of his way. He stopped about a yard from her. She looked down at the ground, blushing. "What are you doing here?" he asked.

"I . . . I was waiting for you," she said.

"Oh Emelye . . ." He sounded so glad, so excited. Emelye wanted to run away from him. "I didn't think I'd ever see you again. Not like this, I mean. Oh Emelye." He walked up to her and, uncertainly, afraid that she would forbid it, placed his hand on her shoulder. "How are you?"

"I'm all right." She couldn't think of anything else to say.

"I'm glad to see you, Emelye. I wanted to, you know, only they said . . ."

She nodded her head and looked at him at last. His face was the same open, boyish face she had always known. Only his eyes were troubled.

"It's going to be all right, Emelye. I promise." He bent his head to hers, but she twisted away from him. "I love you, Emelye. I still love you," he said miserably.

"I know," she said. "That's why I thought perhaps . . ." The words stuck in her throat.

"What? What did you think?"

"Oh you're too good, too gentle," she burst out. "I shouldn't have come here." She tried to walk past him, but he caught hold of her arm and pulled her against him. Emelye struggled instinctively, and then gave way. "It's not how you think," she said, hating the pain which flashed across his face.

He put his arms around her, holding her.

"I still want you. I don't care what you've done. You were betrothed to me and they can't stop us. Nothing can."

"I'm going to have his baby," she said fiercely, "You must know that."

"I know." She felt his body stiffen against her. "But if you'll just do as they say, if you'll . . . get rid of it . . ."

"I can't," she said. "I won't."

"If you don't, they'll never let me marry you."

"I couldn't marry you anyway, Damon. You know that."

He let his arms drop to his sides in a gesture of defeat. Emelye felt ashamed of herself. She moved away from him.

"Why did you come here then?" he asked, fighting to control the quaver in his voice.

"Not to hurt you, Damon. Honestly. I know I've done that already, and I'm sorry. I didn't mean to lead you on."

"Why then?" he demanded, his voice rising.

"Sh," she said, glancing around. "Don't shout, please."

"Why?" he repeated, his hands clenched into fists.

"I thought you might help me," she said in a rush, "I know it's not fair. You don't owe me anything. It was a crazy idea. I should've known better. But there isn't anyone else. I'm sorry." Straightening her back, Emelye began to walk away.

"What is it you want?" he asked.

Emelye stopped. Tears stung her eyes. She turned back and went close to him.

"He left something with me," she said. "A book. He wanted me to send it off for him, but I hung on to it. Will you send it for me? I know what I'm asking. I feel bad about it. But if I take it into the post office, Cloris will only give it straight to Bart." She went up to him and caught hold of his arm. "But you could send it for me. You go into Ketterford now and again. You could do it. Please, Damon. I won't ever ask you for anything again."

He tried to resist her. He wanted to hate her, to push her away. Instead, he seized her in his arms and, murmuring, kissed her cheeks, her eyes, searching for her mouth. She struggled against him, twisting her face from his. With both hands, she pushed hard against his chest.

"It doesn't matter," she said. "I'm sorry."

"I'll do it," he said. "I don't know when. I can't promise, but I'll do it."

She began to cry.

"Is this a bad thing you're asking me to do, Emelye?" he asked gravely.

"No. Honest. I'm crying because you're kind."

"Where is it? Give it to me."

She led him to the tree where she had hidden the parcel.

"It's down there, see?" Damon squatted and thrust his hand into the space beneath the tree.

"I'll leave it there. It's safer that way."

She nodded. "You won't say anything?"

"No."

"I must go now."

"I'll walk with you."

180

"No. You mustn't. Nobody must see us. You wait here a minute and then . . ."

"Emelye . . ."

"I can't, Damon. Don't ask me. Please, don't."

She eluded his hand and ran toward the gate. He watched her go, his chest heaving. She slipped through the gate, leaving it half open.

They would say that he was weak and stupid if they knew. He turned back to the tree and aimed an angry kick at its trunk. He didn't care what they thought. If he did this for her, maybe, in time, she would come round. If it were up to him, he'd take her, baby and all. With all his heart, he did not want them to be like Bart and Magdalena Clare. If he could take her away somewhere, where she would be safe, then maybe she would love him again. Here, in Ratchets, history could only repeat itself.

Bart opened the door and stepped into the mean, unlit room. She held the baby in her right arm. Bella pressed against her left hip.

"It's all right," he said. "I won't hurt them. Put them to bed, Maddy, then come back here."

There was nothing left of her to be afraid. She took the children into their tiny bedroom.

"Where's Daddy gone?"

Automatically, she shushed Bella, made her undress and get into bed. She tucked her in and kissed her, wondering if this was the last time she would see her. Facing the door, she considered bolting herself in, but dismissed the thought at once. It would be useless. If she went to him, as he wanted, perhaps the children at least would be safe. She walked back into the room, pulling the bedroom door shut behind her.

He was sitting at the table, his hands clasped together on its scrubbed wooden top. He looked up at her with his golden, hungry eyes. He looked at her for a long, silent time. It didn't bother her. After a while, she let her gaze move around the room, to the window, the embers of the fire.

"Sit down," he said at last.

Magdalena walked stiffly to her chair, near the fire, and sat down. Her face was in profile to him, her head slightly bent toward the fire.

"You should have done that long ago," he said.

She knew he meant that she should have turned against Timon, who had run out on her. This time, forever. She waited for this thought to bring some pain, at least a twinge of regret, but nothing followed. She sighed.

"Why didn't you?" he asked.

How could she answer him? When he spoke it was almost as though he wasn't there. In silence, she was intensely aware of him.

"You're strong," he said. "I didn't know you could be so strong. There's no woman as strong as you. I admire that. Maddy?" He waited, but she seemed like marble, frozen forever beyond his reach. He quelled the thought because it was unbearable.

When he spoke again it was softly, dreamily, as though from another time and place.

"Why did we call you Maddy? Magdalena is such a beautiful name. I remember Albertine. She had a special way of saying it. Do you remember? Mag-da-*lena*. I think of her often. She was fond of me. I loved her, too. Better than the old woman. That's why she gave you to me. Did you know that? She gave me the best of herself, the thing she cared most about. You. She loved you and she trusted me to take care of you. She knew the cult of the Mistress was dying. She knew what had to be done. But she didn't know that it would be you, whom we both loved so much, who would . . ."

He broke off. There was a chasm between them now. He spoke of a time which seemed more than years ago, a time which perhaps had never been, but which he remembered more clearly than yesterday. There had to be a way back to that time.

"Magdalena," he said again, relishing the sound on his tongue. "How far we've come. How separate we are. I'm not even sure you can hear me."

The light was fading. Her hair was more silver than blond, her clothes as gray as dusk. Like a ghost, she seemed to be fading into twilight, away from him.

"It's not too late," he said with great effort. "I can save you. Even now. Especially now."

She said nothing.

"You nearly killed the Mistress. You know what that means. You heard Mother Poole's curse?"

Nothing.

"I'll not beg, if that's what you think."

She thought nothing.

"He won't come back. You're all alone now. They're all against you. Only I can save you. If you want."

It was her pride, he thought, that kept her still and silent. The famous Clare pride that he had once admired and now so hated. The Clare pride had been fine, magnificent in Albertine, but it had ruined her daughter. Pride had brought her so low that her death would hardly be noticed. Like stepping on an insect, crushing a beetle. He listened to her breathing, the soft drawing in and pushing out of breath. It was now so dark in the room that he could not see her. Ash sifted in the dead fire. He put his hands over his face. He was so tired. His face was wet. Surprised, he licked his fingers, tasting salt.

Magdalena got up. She made no sound. When she opened the door, the room lightened a little. He twisted round in his chair to watch her. There were clouds sailing across the moon. The yard was splashed and stained with shadows, shifting patches of silver light. He saw her pass the window. He sat on at her table, unwelcome. The tears dried, leaving his skin feeling taut. Then he got up and walked out of the house. As he leaned to latch the gate behind him, the clouds broke apart and he saw her, kneeling, stiff-backed, beside her son's grave. She did not look at him. And now it was he who felt like a ghost.

Lyndsay's eyelids flickered open. The room was dark. She tried to move her left arm and could not. Twisting her head, she saw the white gleam of a bandage. Somebody, a man, was standing by the window.

"Patrick?" she said. Her voice was hoarse.

The man moved at once toward her, but she could only see him as a vague, black shape.

"No, it's Bart."

"What . . . what are you doing here?" She felt, obscurely, that there was something wrong in his being there.

"It's my turn to sit with you," he said smoothly. "Mother Poole and Penelope must have some rest."

"Of course," she said, feeling stupid.

"Shall I put the light on?"

She shook her head, although she realized that he could not see. "No."

"Can I get you anything?"

"A drink of water?" she asked.

He seemed to be thoroughly familiar with the room. In spite of the darkness, he moved with confidence. She heard the sound of glass against glass, of water being poured. He came to her and slid his big hand under her back.

"Sit up a little. Gently, now."

"My arm . . ." she said.

"It's strapped to your side, that's all. It's mending."

He supported her easily. Her fingers touched his as he held the glass to her lips. Although she was very thirsty, she found that she could only drink in small sips. She felt weak.

"Lean back now. Rest a minute."

She did as he said.

"Where am I?" she asked, closing her eyes against a slight dizziness.

"At Clare House. How do you feel?"

"Not too good," she said. "What time is it?"

"It'll soon be light."

"You needn't sit up all night."

"Want some more?"

"Please."

Again he helped to raise her. This time, with her right hand folded around his, she managed to drain the glass, but afterward she felt exhausted. He disappeared into the darkness. Lyndsay turned her head and looked at the window, but there was hardly any light. How long, she wondered, how long had she been lying here? What was happening to her arm? Was it okay? Maddy, she thought. *Mad Maddy*. What had happened to her?

"Bart?"

He materialized at her side and caught her hand in both of his.

"You must rest," he said. "You mustn't tire yourself." His voice was very soothing. She felt sleep tugging at her, blurring the questions she wanted to ask.

"I have such . . . dreams," she whispered. Part of her mind knew that this was not what she wanted to say. "Michael's dead," she said. It was a simple statement.

"Yes." He pressed her hand tighter.

"Everywhere I go . . ." She meant in her dreams, but she could not explain this, and the dreams, anyway, were more her world now than this floating room. Only his hand prevented her from floating away. She did not want to do that. She held on tight to him. "Everywhere I go," she said again, "they call me 'Mistress.' Isn't that funny?"

He pulled one hand away from hers and laid it gently on her forehead which was hot and damp with sweat.

"That's because you are the Mistress," he said, as though explaining something very simple to a child. "Rest now. Go to sleep."

The last thing she remembered was the sensation of his weight tilting the bed. He sat beside her for a long time, holding her hand. When his muscles began to ache with inactivity, he very carefully placed her arm beneath the sheet. Moving as silently as a cat, he let himself out of the room and crept down the stairs, avoiding the one that creaked.

Bart paused on the road outside Clare House, like a man who did not know which way to go. The air was fresh and even chill. He looked all around him, as though for a sign, but he found none. He shook his head and started off along the village street. He walked slowly, enjoying the cool, predawn freshness. A lamp burned in Cloris Poole's bedroom, but he barely glanced at it. There was no other sign of life in the village. He crossed the green and took the path beside the children's graveyard. He felt, for the first time in his life, completely and utterly alone. He let himself into the graveyard and walked toward the chancel. He stood for a while on the graveled path between the little graves, with his eyes closed and his fists clenched.

He could feel them, all of them, stirring. It was like the feeling he had when he was alone on the ridge and could feel the power of the earth. This power was greater and much more dangerous. His nostrils flared at the scent of danger. He could feel them moving, preparing themselves. He imagined them clearly for a moment, crouched, ready to spring. He held the image in his mind, experiencing the sensations of dreadful life all around him, for as long as he dared. Then, with a great sigh, he let his powerful body go limp. The sky was streaked with gray. The place was empty, dead again.

Bart walked to the chapel and unlocked the door. The night's efforts had exhausted him. The air inside the thick-walled building felt damp and stale. He walked quickly up the aisle and round behind the simple altar. In a corner was a narrow archway which led to an anteroom. Steps descended from this room to a series of interconnecting, vaulted rooms beneath the church. In the first of these Bart lit an old oil lamp. As the flame grew, his shadow was projected onto the wall behind him. The room contained an ornately carved chest, an old desk, and a narrow, iron cot, covered with a gray blanket. This was his retreat, but tonight it did not give him the usual consolation he expected to obtain there. Tired and numb, Bart stripped off his clothes and carried the lamp to the bed. He set it down on the floor and climbed into the cot. For a moment, as he leaned down to blow out the lamp, his eyes moved to a solid metal-studded door set in the wall behind him. He cocked his head as though listening. There was no sound but his own tired breathing. He blew out the lamp and lay down. In a moment, he was asleep.

When she next awoke the room was light, even though someone had drawn the curtains. White curtains with a pattern of blue flowers. The room was predominantly blue: the wallpaper with a small design of white, flower-filled urns; the bedspread; even the hand-hooked rug on the polished board floor was made up of many shades of blue. Lyndsay thought of the sea. It had been a long time since she had seen the ocean. The sea glittering below her that day in the aircraft. Mrs. Abernathy's blue hat, her periwinkle eyes. The associations of color, of remembered blues led her back to the present. How long had she been lying here? How long since the airplane touched down and her world shifted, shattered? How long since Bart had held her hand and soothed her like a father?

Slowly, carefully, she eased herself up, using her right hand as a lever. Long enough for the sprain in her wrist to heal. Her bandaged shoulder throbbed quietly, but the pain was bearable. Her head felt light, though. Light and somehow fogged.

Magdalena Berryman might have killed her!

The thought frightened her. For the first time she realized how great the danger had been. Mother Poole had been wrong. The danger had been real. A few inches to the right and the shot might have killed her. Perhaps they had fought to save her life. Why hadn't she been taken to a hospital? Or was it only yesterday? Had any time at all passed? Twenty-four hours? What about Magdalena? Had they charged her or . . . ?

Lyndsay's head began to hurt. She wished she could get out of bed, but she felt too weak, and with her arm fastened to her side . . .

She looked at the little cabinet table beside her bed for a bell or something with which to summon attention. Suddenly she was afraid that they had left her entirely alone.

"Hello?" she called. Her voice was weak. Her throat was dry again. Bart had given her something to drink. That's what she needed now. She could remember the feel of his fingers under hers, the pressure of his hand.

That's because you are the Mistress.

Had she imagined that? The *Mistress.* What did it mean? Dreams must have gotten mixed up with reality. If only there were a stick or something she could bang on the floor with. Looking round the room she could not see anything that would serve.

She called out again. And again. Her voice sounded stronger, but there was still no response. Impatient and a little angry, Lyndsay pulled the bedclothes back and carefully touched her feet to the floor. Her head swam and she pitched forward awkwardly, because of her useless arm. She felt very hot. The colors in the rug were dazzling, melting one into the other. It was a good idea to put her head down, between her knees. She closed her eyes but could still see the dazzling, now whirling blues. Quite slowly and, it seemed inevitably, she felt herself falling forward off the bed. Some instinct prompted her to twist her body to the right, so that she would fall on her good side. The rug was thick and soft, like a cushion under her head. If only she weren't so hot, she would have been quite comfortable. Hot and sick, and everything kept whirling, round and round, increasing the feeling of nausea until she lost consciousness completely.

"How did this happen?" Mother Poole swept into the room, where Penelope was bending tentatively over Lyndsay. She and Damon had lifted her back into bed, and then Damon had run to fetch the old lady. He stood uncertainly in the doorway now. "I don't know," Penelope said, moving out of the way so that Mother Poole could take Lyndsay's pulse.

"How was she lying?" she snapped.

"I can't remember. Damon found her."

"On her side. On her good shoulder," he said, coming into the room.

"And what did you want with the Mistress?" Mother Poole

asked, fixing him with her black, glittering eyes. His face turned scarlet.

"Nothing. I . . . I was just passing and I saw her."

"At this time of day? Why aren't you at work?" With surprising speed and energy, the old woman walked round the bed and began to unwind the bandage from Lyndsay's shoulder.

"Stop cross-questioning him." Penelope said defensively. "This is his home."

"And why weren't you with her?" Mother Poole asked angrily.

"I can't be with her all the time. I told you. I don't want her here . . . I don't have time to . . ."

"Ah," Mother Poole murmured, ignoring Penelope as she gently eased the dressing from the wound. There was no damage. The wound was clean and healing well. "Good," she muttered, turning to her portable medicine chest. "Bryony will take over from now on. But she can't be moved. Not yet." Penelope turned away, signing to Damon to leave. "Heat some of that broth I brought over," Mother Poole said over her shoulder. "You can spare the time for that, I hope?"

Penelope's back stiffened.

"I will not take orders from you," she said coldly.

"Yes you will, Penelope Clare," she answered, applying a new dressing to Lyndsay's shoulder. "And don't think you fool me with your so-called Clare pride. It's self-pity and jealousy that speaks in you. Not pride."

"I don't know what you mean," Penelope said stiffly. She could not make herself look at the old woman, who continued with her work.

"Then if that's not what ails you, what can it be? You won't tell me, but I'll find out. And when I do you'll answer to me."

"You think," Penelope said, her voice shaking, "that you're the only one who can give orders. But those days are over, Mother Poole. Just remember that, when you come to judge who's right and who's wrong." She did not give the old woman time to respond, but ran out of the room and down the stairs.

Mother Poole's capable hands continued with their task, but her expression changed to one of anxiety and then cunning. Lyndsay stirred. Automatically, Mother Poole soothed her in a low voice, while she unstrapped her arm and prepared a sling. Murmuring, Lyndsay opened her eyes.

"There, there. All's well. What did you want to go falling for? You're not strong enough yet to be up and around."

"Mother Poole?" Lyndsay said faintly, trying to remember where she was.

"Sh," the old woman said. "There'll be plenty of time for talking later. Just now, you do as I say."

Lyndsay was too weak to argue. With the old woman's help, she was able to sit up, although her head swam again. She drank more water and nodded in answer to Mother Poole's medical inquiries. Her arm felt more comfortable in the sling, which the old lady fixed carefully around her neck. She gave her more water.

"Penelope's heating up some broth. You need nourishment. You must have tried to get out of bed and . . ."

"I couldn't make anyone hear," Lyndsay explained.

Mother Poole pursed her lips in annoyance.

"Well, that won't happen again. Bryony Dolben will sit with you when I can't. You'll be in good hands."

"Bart was very kind," Lyndsay said, aware that she had seemed to criticize.

"Whatever do you mean?" the old woman chuckled, smoothing the bedclothes over her. "Bart's not been here. He's no nurse."

"Yes he was. I remember."

"When?"

Her voice faltered. "I don't know. It was dark. He sat with me. He said it was his turn."

Glancing at the open door, Mother Poole laid a hand on Lyndsay's arm.

"No more talking now," she said firmly. "Here's your broth, made to my own recipe." She walked to the door. "This'll have you on your feet in no time." She held out her hands for the tray Penelope was carrying. "Thank you, Penelope. I can manage now."

Surprised, Penelope hung on to the tray. Mother Poole, who was as tall as she, blocked the doorway.

"How is she?"

"She'll mend. Now be about your business. I know you have a lot to do," she said loudly, pulling the tray from Penelope's grasp. With her shoulder, she closed the door in her face.

"Is that Penelope?" Lyndsay asked, "I'd like to see her."

"No visitors for you yet, Mistress. No excitement. We're going to build you up first. Come along now."

Before Lyndsay knew what was happening, Mother Poole had spread a starched napkin over her and was offering a spoonful of broth to her mouth. She wanted to protest, to say she that could feed herself, but there was something comforting about submitting to this firm, capable woman. It was like having a nanny, to whom she could hand over all responsibility. She drank the broth silently and obediently, while the old woman coaxed and encouraged her.

"There. Now that feels better, doesn't it?" she said when the bowl was empty.

"Mm," Lyndsay said, closing her eyes.

"Does your head ache?" the old woman asked, putting the bowl on the tray.

"No. I feel a bit dizzy but otherwise okay."

"Good. We'll soon have you right as rain." She pulled a straight-backed chair up to the bed and sat on it, her hands folded in her lap. "Well now," she said, indicating that she was ready and willing to talk.

Lyndsay looked at her and smiled with gratitude.

"You're very kind."

"Nonsense. If you hadn't helped me, that madwoman would never have taken a potshot at you. It's my clear duty to see to you."

"What happened?" Lyndsay asked.

"Bless you, don't you remember?"

"I meant to the little boy, and Magdalena. What's happened to her?"

"The child's buried," Mother Poole said briefly, as though it were a matter of no significance. "As for her, nothing's been done. We'll talk of that later."

"I don't want anything done to her," Lyndsay said quickly. "I don't want to charge her or anything."

"That's right. Good." Mother Poole nodded.

"But she needs help."

"You forget about her. We'll take care of everything."

Lyndsay was surprised to discover how much this had been worrying her.

"You promise?" she asked. "She's suffered enough." She didn't really see how anyone could blame Magdalena Berryman. In her position she would probably have done something similar. Yet she had felt proud that morning, she remembered, as though she were performing an almost sacred duty.

"How long have I been here?" she asked.

190

"Nigh on a week."

"A week? I don't remember . . ."

"You were asleep. Rest was essential."

"The doctor . . . what did he say?"

"Why, bless you, Mistress, I'm your doctor." She laughed quietly.

Lyndsay opened her mouth in surprise, but almost immediately closed it. It would only sound ungrateful to protest. And her shoulder didn't hurt at all now.

"I know what you're thinking," Mother Poole said. "And you shall see a doctor if that's what you want, but he'll only tell you what I tell you. You've a good, clean flesh wound that'll soon be healed. And you'll only have a tiny scar. There was no danger once we knew the bullet had passed clean through. Besides, you're a strong, healthy young woman." She leaned forward and patted Lyndsay's hand.

"I still owe you a lot. I want you to know that I appreciate it," Lyndsay said as she gripped the old lady's hand.

"You'll pay me back a hundredfold," the old woman said intensely. "Besides, it is my duty."

"Why?" Lyndsay asked. "Why do you see it as a duty?"

"Because . . ." She paused, staring deeply into Lyndsay's eyes. Her tongue flicked over her lips, moistening them. "Because you are the Mistress and I must serve you, in everything. It is the Way."

Lyndsay was mesmerized by her eyes, the total certainty of her firm, rich voice.

"That's what Bart said," she recalled. "He said that I was the Mistress. What does it mean?"

Slowly, the old woman sat back in her chair, releasing Lyndsay's hand.

"So . . . He named you, did he?"

"Pardon me?"

"That's what we call it. He named you Mistress?"

"But why? What is all this?" She tried to sit up straighter. She did not know whether to be amused or alarmed. She remembered the old women on the green. That hadn't been a dream. The way they had all stared at her, the children as well, that morning.

"Don't excite yourself. You must rest."

"I just want to know . . ."

"You shall know everything in good time. You have much to learn and much to do. But not until you're well and strong."

"Please, can't you explain?"

Gravely, her eyes still fixed on Lyndsay, she said, "The Mistress is the first of our women. Our spiritual leader, whom we honor."

Lyndsay could not help laughing.

"You mean like in a religious sense?"

"Aye. If you will."

"But I . . . I'm not even from here. I don't belong here. I couldn't possibly . . ." She tried to sit forward. At once, Mother Poole was leaning over her, pushing her gently but firmly back.

"The day you married Michael Dolben," she said, "you belonged to us. You are the true and lawful Mistress. None can deny that." Lyndsay tried to protest, but the old woman shook her head sharply. Her hand remained, pressing lightly on Lyndsay's chest, holding her down. "We need you. You cannot fail us." Without taking her eyes from Lyndsay's face, she placed her right arm inside the covers and folded them neatly over her. Raising her, she pulled one of the pillows from beneath Lyndsay's head, then made her lie down again. She pressed her fingertips firmly against Lyndsay's temples, saying: "Sleep now . . . Rest . . . Mistress."

The sibilant, incantatory sound led Lyndsay, like a breath of wind, into sleep.

After a long time, Mother Poole removed her hands and folded them crosswise over her breasts, in a symbolic gesture of thanks. She raised her chin as though listening for something. Her body became rigid. For a moment she trembled, then, stiffly, she extended her arms toward Lyndsay, fingers spread, like spikes, pointing at her head. Finally, very slowly, she raised her hands like a supplicant and let her chin fall forward onto her chest.

Lyndsay murmured and moved in the bed as though something had disturbed her. Mother Poole relaxed.

"Mis-tress."

The word sounded in the air, all around her. She was standing on a paved floor, high stone walls surrounding her.

"Mis-tress."

No visible source of light, yet lit, like a stage. What she saw was a dumb show or mime, presided over by a single, magnificent figure—magnificent in stiff, golden robes, in size and power. A man, she was certain, even though the robes concealed the body and his face was shadowed. With a commanding gesture, he summoned figures from both sides of the "stage."

A group, gray-robed and masked, entered from the right; two men, dressed in trousers and shirts, from the left.

Two more figures, a boy and a girl, detached themselves from the group. They held hands, touched each other's masks tenderly. Behind them, the golden man seemed to bless them. They strolled together, their blank, white mask-faces turned one to the other. Of the two men, the shorter approached them. He was unmasked and unknown to her. He took the girl's free hand and pulled her toward him. For a time, the girl was tugged between them, her expressionless face turned first to one suitor and then to the other. Then the girl shook off her masked suitor and went willingly with the other young man. The crowd hissed. They embraced. The rejected boy looked on forlornly. Their embraces grew more and more passionate until, like an avenging bird, the gold-robed man intervened. He pushed the young man roughly aside, ordered the girl back into the group.

All of this had been watched dispassionately by the other man who now stepped boldly forward to take the younger man's part.

He was Michael Dolben.

There was no question. And he was living, breathing, moving. But she did not move toward him or even try to call out. It was as though she knew that he, and all these people, were beyond her reach, on the other side of some barrier.

Her heart in her mouth, she watched Michael and the golden man join together in combat. The struggle, though stylized, was deadly. It was a duel to the death, presented in ritual form. And Michael was destined to be the loser. Silently, inevitably, he sank to the ground. The robed figure stood astride him, one terrible hand raised to deliver the deathblow.

A woman detached herself from the crowd and seized his wrist. Gradually, he yielded to her. She stood, like a guardian, over Michael, while the golden man appealed to the crowd, pointing at the youth Michael had defended. Under his leadership, they fell upon the boy, who disappeared under a shower of blows. The woman helped Michael up and led him away. Just before he disappeared into the darkness, he turned and faced her directly, his eyes begging, his hands held out in appeal.

She could not move or speak to him. Her body was frozen. She was only allowed to watch and, as she did so, Michael faded, slipped away from her.

The youth was dead. Two figures dragged him ignominiously away. The golden figure ascended a sort of stone dais, on which stood two carved chairs, one set a little higher than the other. He took the lower of the two. The male figures gathered below him, in support and worship. He stood up and opened his arms wide.

The women hung back, their blank faces turned toward the empty chair. The golden man also looked at the chair. He seemed nervous of it, and then covetous. He pointed offstage and the men went running to do his bidding.

Then another woman entered. She, too, wore gold, a robe more fantastic and beautiful than the man's. She was veiled. She stood hesitantly before the women who made obeisance to her. The men returned. The two gold figures faced each other. Backed by their supporters they swayed to and fro as though in battle. The two groups flowed together. Everything became confused and blurred. Then the golden woman ascended to the highest chair and sat. At once the unruly figures became still. They began to leave the stage, in twos and threes. There was a sense of life being resumed, a return to normality and peace.

The veiled woman looked down at the golden man. He turned away from her so that Lyndsay could see, at last, his face. Only there wasn't a face. Nor a mask. And yet it must have been a mask. He had the face of a dog, black silk fur on a pointed muzzle, bared white teeth. It was only a glimpse, for he turned back, raising his quivering muzzle to the seated woman. He began to walk toward her, slipping off his robe as he did so. Naked, his body powerful and gleaming, he mounted the steps slowly. The woman rose and held out her hands to him. The figures were still, wavered, and then were gone.

Lyndsay's eyes started open. The room was dim, full of gray shadows, twilight. Mother Poole leaned over her, her eyes glittering.

"Now do you understand?" she whispered.

Lyndsay could only stare at her.

CHAPTER NINE

"The first Mistress was a very holy woman. When her husband—Piers Dolben, that would be—went off to the Crusades, she lived chaste and gave succor to the people. She nursed the sick and gave alms to the poor. All loved her, that is until news came of her man's death. Then they rose up against her. The Clares said that it wasn't right or fitting for a woman to rule as she had ruled. They confined her to the house, where she cursed them, for she knew they wanted power for themselves. But she had her followers, oh yes. A faithful band, and on her deathbed she made them swear that there would always be a Mistress here in Ratchets."

Sometimes Lyndsay did not listen at all. She thought that Bryony Dolben was the most monotonous person she had ever met. Her gaunt, plain face expressed no emotion whatsoever. Her voice was a drone, without variation or color. She sat, hour after hour, beside Lyndsay, her eyes lowered to a square of tapestry on which, with silks, she embroidered the image of the hound, the Gabriel Ratchet. Lyndsay had, in an effort to stop her ceaseless recitation, asked her about the embroidery. Her work was fine: why didn't she try something else?

"This is needful," she had said, looking at Lyndsay for a moment, and then bending her head again.

"And those that returned brought the pestilence with them. It was that which killed the Mistress. And they, those who had deposed her, could not help themselves. So the line passed to the daughter of the eldest son, and since that time there has never not been a Mistress here, saving but twice. Still, the curse remained. She died before her heart could soften against her enemies."

Sometimes Lyndsay tried to argue.

"You don't believe in curses, surely?"

"Why? Don't you?"

"Certainly not. It's all just superstition."

For a while, Bryony just stared at her embroidery, then, slowly, she resumed, drawing the fine threads through the material and smoothing them rhythmically with her fingers. Soon, this activity would start her talking again, endlessly, without variation of subject or pace.

"And so it continued to Ezekiel Dolben's time and the great quarrel between him and the Clares. The Clares had got above themselves, you see. Old Rector Clare, he said as how all, including the Mistress and the Dolbens, should be subject to the Church. And when Ezekiel defied him, aye and the people, too, for they would not desert the Mistress, he excommunicated all who would not follow him. He called the Ways sinful and castigated the people. They were torn, you see. Afraid. Not knowing who was right. The pestilence came again and he would neither baptize nor bury the children. They were put into the earth unshriven, poor souls. And the women, they turned to the Mistress and to Ezekiel. But that was only half of it. Ezekiel's brother, Rupert, supported the Clares. He wanted to tear up the land and build drains. He said it was not a curse but bad hygiene. Imagine!" For once, just for a moment, Bryony Dolben seemed to experience an emotion. Lyndsay found it difficult to put a name to it, but the woman paused. Her fingers lay idle. Her face was troubled. "Just imagine! He wanted to ruin good land, bearing good crops, for drains."

"Sounds very sensible to me," Lyndsay said, and decided that she had so shocked Bryony that she had won herself a few minutes' respite from the never-ending saga of the Mistress.

They were trying to drive her mad, of course. She realized that. Bryony talked at her, hour after hour. She was allowed no visitors. When she protested to Mother Poole, the old woman put her to sleep. Sleep would have been a relief, if it weren't for the dreams. She had come to dread them. They seemed more like visions.

"Well, Rupert Dolben went away, to make his way in the world, and the time came when the Clares saw that they had no support.

196

But the old rector, he was stubborn. It was not till he died that peace was made between them. Ezekiel drew up *The Book of the Ways,* where it was all set down, the history and the rules of conduct. He established the Mistress and gave her a Priest. The first such, to be drawn from the Clares. And so it's been ever since. Well, more or less." She sighed and folded her embroidery neatly into a little black sack she carried for the purpose.

"I'll just see to your food, Mistress," she said, standing up.

Lyndsay lay back, exhausted and relieved, when Bryony left the room. Sometimes she thought she understood and sometimes not. She tried to tell herself that it did not matter, but she knew that it did because she was trapped in it. Until they let her up and out of this room, she had no choice but to listen and think. What scared her was that they could manipulate her. At least Mother Poole could. She had decided that the old woman must be feeding her some kind of hallucinogens. How else could she control her dreams? For they were controlled, of that Lyndsay was absolutely certain. She had refused most of the medicines, but her food and drink were probably laced with something. And she did not dare refuse food and drink because she needed to get well, regain her strength in order to get away.

What frightened her most, she thought, was that, in spite of everything, she wasn't scared of Mother Poole. Not really, not deep down. Bryony was some kind of idiot, a human tape recorder spilling out legend and mumbo jumbo. Nobody could be scared of her. But the old woman . . . She *ought* to be afraid of her but somehow could not be.

Maybe, she thought, if she could just understand what they were trying to tell her, the dreams at least would stop. That's what it seemed Mother Poole wanted. Every night now she asked the same question: "Do you understand now, Mistress?"

If she could just say yes, really say it and mean it, then maybe it would all stop. She knew that it was useless to lie to the old lady. But if she understood and said yes, would she be committing herself to something? Well, what if she was? Once she'd satisfied them she could get away, get out of this madhouse.

Michael was always present in the dreams and was never dead. He never died. But Michael was dead. She had been at his funeral, had dreamed, when she was in control of her own mind, of his charred corpse. So what could that mean? The young man, on the other hand, always died. Fitting it together, slowly, she decided that the boy was also Michael. Or some leftover scrap of pity for the child, Magdalena Berryman's boy? No, she thought, that didn't make sense, unless her will, her own subconscious became mingled with what the old woman wanted her to see.

Deliberately, clenching her teeth, she made herself go back, follow it through, logically. Patrick had said that Michael had been involved with some girl, years ago. That was really why he left the village. So what she saw was that event. The villagers, that gold man, killed him. In a spiritual sense. In their minds. Yes, she'd thought that before, when she was talking to Patrick. Once a person left Ratchets, they ceased to exist. So Michael had been "dead" for years. But when Michael came back, he did die, again—this time more than just a spiritual or symbolic death.

"Here's your dinner, Mistress."

She had not noticed Bryony return. Absently, she thanked her and placed the tray on her lap. Bryony sat down, took out her tapestry, and began to stitch away, head bent, silent. Lyndsay ate the food automatically.

But what came after that? The veiled woman was the Mistress, of that she was certain. And the golden man must be the Priest Bryony spoke of. But they said that *she* was the Mistress. And the man or Priest or whatever he was climbed toward her naked.

Her fork fell with a clatter onto her plate. Bryony looked up, her fingers poised over her stitching.

They intended for her to . . . marry him?

Aware of Bryony's eyes on her, she picked up her fork. Her hand shook.

But he always, always had that awful dog's head on him.

Her throat was dry. She picked up the glass of milk and drank. She had to keep calm. Keep control. After all, she didn't really know. She was jumping to conclusions.

"Bryony?"

"Yes?"

"What is the Mistress for? What does she do?"

"Why, she protects and guides us."

"How?"

"By example and good counsel."

"But what does she protect you from?"

"Why, everything."

198

"Can't you give me an example?"

"Against pestilence and drought. Crop failure . . ."

"But that's beyond the power of any woman."

"Not the Mistress," Bryony asserted flatly.

"And what else?" There was a drought now, she thought.

"Well, most of all from the Hounds."

"The Hounds?"

"Aye, the Gabriel Ratchets. But one day, it is predicted, she will release them forever, and all will be well."

"How will she release them?"

"That I can't say."

"Okay. But if you've had all these Mistresses, why hasn't it happened yet?"

"Because the time is not right."

Well, Lyndsay thought, it was on such answers that all religions foundered or flourished, depending on your point of view. She was conscious of Bryony staring at her strangely. The woman's eyes actually seemed to register interest.

"Tell me," she said, as casually as she could, "what's the relationship between the Mistress and this Priest you mentioned?"

"Why, he is her Priest. They are polarities. Male and female. The one holding the other in check."

Lyndsay ate more, considering this, and decided that it told her nothing. It never did. But at least there had been no mention of a union. The trouble was that they told her only so much. They kept something back. She sensed there was danger in this Priest. My God, she thought, I'm beginning to think like them.

"And who is the Priest? Right now I mean?"

"I can't tell you that." Bryony shook her head firmly.

"Why not?"

"Because you've not been confirmed yet."

It took a moment for Lyndsay to understand the implications of what she had said. Then she grasped eagerly at this small hope.

"You mean I may not be the Mistress after all?"

"Oh no. You're the Mistress right enough. But there are ceremonies . . ." Bryony stood up.

"What kind of ceremonies?" Lyndsay asked, her voice small.

"That's enough now. You'll tire yourself."

The woman lifted the tray from her knees.

"You must rest now."

Alone, Lyndsay slid down into the bed and lay staring at the ceiling.

"I am not the Mistress," she whispered. "I must not let them spook me. They're mad. Not me. I just have to get out of here."

Outside a dog howled, startling her. There was a world, she reminded herself, outside this village, where all they say would be laughed at, exposed as dangerous nonsense. And no matter what happens, that's where I'm going.

She would be docile, compliant. She would lull them all into a sense of security, and then run.

At last Lyndsay was allowed to get up, first to sit in a chair by the window, watched over by Bryony Dolben, and later to go into the garden, where she sat, mostly alone, among Penelope's fragrant, overblown roses. She was acutely aware that, during her illness, attitudes had changed toward her. People she did not know, the village people, saluted her as they passed in the street. They inquired, smiling softly, after her health and always called her Mistress. Bryony Dolben and Mother Poole had withdrawn from her: she scarcely ever saw them. She knew, though, that this was not an indication that they had given up. On the contrary, the anonymous villagers told her that everyone was sure of her.

This feeling of things having been arranged, of her position having been defined and accepted, was reinforced by two incidents which should have pleased her. The first was the news, smilingly delivered, that Patrick had traced her trunk, which had been shipped by sea from the States, and had it transported to Dolben House. The news felt to Lyndsay like a door closing. The second incident was even worse. A letter came from her parents.

"I took the liberty of writing to them," Patrick explained, sitting opposite her on the lawn of Clare House. "I hope you don't mind?"

She read the crisp airmail sheets scrawled with words of love and condolence. Patrick had explained about Michael's death, her reaction and collapse. They felt she was in safe hands. They missed her and, of course, if there was anything they could do. . . . She stopped reading the letter and stared at the roses.

"I didn't mention the shooting. I thought it would only alarm them, and since you don't wish to pursue the matter . . . formally, I mean . . ."

He wore that expression which had always irritated Lyndsay; that of a little boy anxious, even desperate, to please.

"You obviously made a very good job of it," she said. She did not care if the bitterness was heard in her voice. The letter trapped her. Patrick had convinced them that she was safe and being cared for. And so she was, of course, she thought with a start. If only she had some choice in the matter.

"You're depressed, naturally," Patrick said. "It's only to be expected after all you've been through. We all understand, and you mustn't feel that you've got to put on a brave face."

"I'm not," she said. "Did you tell them about Michael? What he was really like?"

He shook his head slowly. "It didn't seem . . . appropriate."

So everything had been made to seem safe and cozy. Michael remained untarnished. She became the welcomed distraught widow. She felt like a woman who had been presented with a series of costumes. She must choose one. It would proclaim and define her role. It might even look good on her, but she knew that it was not for real.

Patrick sighed.

"And did you tell them that I am the Mistress of Ratchets?"

He smiled slowly.

"No. No I didn't. I hardly thought that they would understand, but I am glad that you do."

"That's just where you're wrong," Lyndsay said, folding the letter and putting it back into its envelope. They could hear the phone ringing in the house. Patrick stood up.

"Well, if you'll excuse me . . ."

"Sure," Lyndsay said offhandedly. "I know you don't like to discuss anything that might put you on the spot. None of you do. You're all so used to having your own way. I wish I understood what it is that makes people, everything, secondary to some idea."

"You will," he said solemnly. "Very soon now."

She shook her head violently.

"I don't mean like that. I would like to understand rationally, not by becoming a part of it."

"But that's the only way you *can* understand. I know it's difficult for you. Of course it is, but you will be glad eventually. I promise you."

He looked at her, smiling, and then walked away. Lyndsay watched him and, when he reached the gate, she called to him.

201

"Patrick, I am not and never will be the Mistress. You'd better understand that."

He hesitated for a barely perceptible second and then walked on, just as though he had not heard, or could not understand.

At least not voluntarily, Lyndsay thought.

"No. Not at all." Penelope's knuckles showed white as she gripped the telephone. "You did quite right to ring me." Her face was ashen. "I'll certainly tell her and do whatever I can." Her voice shook badly. "Yes, yes, I'll be in touch." She replaced the receiver and leaned against the small table on which it stood. She did not know what to do. Go and tell Maddy? But what could she do? She drew herself up, remembering the voice describing her as a relative by marriage of Timon Berryman. It was an outrage. Never, not once, had she thought of herself, of any of her family in this way. For the first time she understood properly how they had all been tainted by Maddy's defection and this gave her the determination to resist the old war of loyalties which had already begun in her.

She moved quickly into the hall and inspected her face critically in the mirror. She smoothed her centrally parted hair with her palms and then went out the front door.

Lyndsay, having noticed her step, turned a little in her chair. Conversation with Penelope these days was cold and awkward. She had not begun to understand why. To her relief, Penelope, who seemed completely oblivious of her, went down the path without glancing to left or right, and walked through the arched gateway onto the road. With an anxious, preoccupied expression, she almost ran up the village street. Glad to be alone, Lyndsay threw off the quite unnecessary rug which they insisted she keep tucked around her legs and went listlessly into the house.

Penelope had heard Patrick's voice in the garden. She had hoped that he would look in. She would, indeed, have ensured that he did so, had she not been distracted by the telephone. Now she hurried after him, knowing that he could not have gone far. When she reached the slight curve in the road by the post office, she saw him ahead of her, walking along the hot road, his head down.

"Patrick," she called.

He stopped and looked back toward her. She could not make out his expression. Panting in the dry heat, she hurried toward him.

"What is it?" he said when she reached him.

"I've just had a phone call." She glanced around her. "Let's walk along," she said. "I must talk to you."

Silently, he fell into step beside her. She wished that she dared take his arm, but knew that if she did, he would only shake her off, or worse, make some clumsy excuse to be free of her touch.

"Well?" he said.

"Let's sit down on the green," she suggested. "I don't want anyone to overhear."

He looked around at the deserted afternoon street, the blank houses, but did not argue. The grass on the green was burned dry. The bench on which he reluctantly sat was hot from the burning sun.

"It was the Corminster police," she said at last. He turned toward her, his face lit with anxious interest at last. She held his eyes, speaking rapidly and quietly. "Timon Berryman has been sent to prison for twenty-one days for drunken driving. And his old truck wasn't taxed or something. I thought you ought to know," she said, searching his face.

"Why did they ring you?" he asked with a frown.

"He wanted Maddy to know. He told them I was a relative." She felt ashamed to say it.

"What are you going to do?" he asked.

"I don't know. I thought perhaps you would . . ."

"We must tell Bart," he said decisively. "It might be just what he's waiting for."

Penelope said nothing. She had hoped that he would see other possibilities, or at least make a decision of his own.

"Should I tell her?" she asked.

"That's up to Bart. No. You shouldn't go near her. Look what happened to the Mistress."

The silence between them was long and strained. "We could go to them," she said softly, but with urgency. "You and I could go to Corminster and put an end to all this. Patrick, you could do it. I know it would be hard but . . ."

He stood up abruptly and took a few steps away from her.

"You're mad," he whispered, his shoulders shaking. He turned on his heel to face her. "I'll forget you ever said that. You mustn't even think it. I'm going to tell Bart," he repeated firmly. "He'll decide what's to be done. I won't listen to this. If anyone knew what you are thinking . . ."

"I don't care." Her voice rang across the green. Patrick glanced around nervously. "I love you. I know you don't care about me but . . ."

"I never asked you for anything," he said coldly. "All I ask is that you do your duty. That's all anyone asks."

She stared at him helplessly. He watched her tense body slump into defeat.

"Don't mention the phone call to anyone. I'll tell Bart. And that's all I'll tell him," he added, "this time."

She did not even bother to call after him as he walked swiftly away from her. She had tried, but there was no comfort in that. Maddy, Patrick, all of them would have to be destroyed. She would stand by and watch, as she had always done. She could not stop it alone. Without Patrick she lacked both will and courage. She crossed the green and went back to Clare House.

Lyndsay heard Penelope's step on the stairs, heard her cross the landing, go into her own room, and begin to sob. Lyndsay had been packing the few things that had been brought for her from Dolben House, for she wanted to return there as soon as possible. She listened to Penelope's crying and after a while, although she felt awkward with her, she went to her door and knocked.

Penelope had been lying on the bed. At the sound of Lyndsay's knock, she sat up, trying to control her tears. Lyndsay opened the door at once.

"Can I come in?" she asked.

Penelope was unable to answer. Her face was blotched and puffy. She searched for a handkerchief. Lyndsay closed the door behind her and went to the bed.

"What is it?" she asked gently. "Can't you tell me? I'd like to help if I can. You've been so good to me."

At this, Penelope snorted laughter, derisive and hysterical. Lyndsay sat down on the edge of the bed. She did not dare to touch Penelope. To save her embarrassment, she did not even look at her.

"It's Patrick, isn't it?" she asked. "Please don't be embarrassed. I've known ever since that night he gave me the Dolben Collar. I meant to say something. If it wasn't for me, that would have been yours, wouldn't it? Somehow I've . . ."

"No," Penelope said, sniffling. "No, it would never have been mine. It's got nothing to do with you. Nothing at all."

"I'm glad," Lyndsay said. "So, won't you let me help you?"

"You can't even help yourself," she said.

Lyndsay looked at her, afraid. "What do you mean?"

"Nothing. It doesn't matter."

"It does to me."

"I can't help you," Penelope said. "One day you'll hate me and you'll have cause."

"No," Lyndsay protested. "Why should I? You mustn't think like that. Listen, I want to help you. Please."

"Leave me alone," she said. She stood up and moved away from the bed.

"Is that what you really want?" Lyndsay asked.

She nodded her head, a crumpled handkerchief pressed to her mouth.

Lyndsay got up and walked to the door, closing it behind her,

Bart, seated at the kitchen table in Dolben House, considered carefully. Patrick watched him, lacing and unlacing his fingers.

"There's no question of bail?" Bart asked.

Patrick shook his head. "Penelope said he'd been sentenced."

"Hm. Well, you'd better go and see."

"Me? Go to the police?"

"There'll be somebody at the court," Bart said impatiently, waving his hand. "Probation officer or somebody. Find out all you can."

"What about Maddy?"

"She doesn't care anymore," Bart said quietly. "Say she's ill. Anything."

"He might tell someone," Patrick pointed out.

"Who'd believe him? The man's a known drunk. They'd only think his brain was affected. Use your initiative, and take the Mistress with you."

"What?" Patrick's mouth hung open in surprise.

"The papers," Bart said impatiently. "She must go to the bank, get everything signed and sealed. Why make two journeys? Besides," he added thoughtfully, "it'll do her good. She's getting restless."

"She said this afternoon that she was not and never would be the Mistress," Patrick told him. "I meant to tell you sooner but this business about Berryman drove it out of my mind."

Bart laughed and tilted his chair back.

"There was a time," he said ruminatively, "when I'd have been glad to hear it. But now . . ."

"But suppose she won't?" Patrick said.

"She has no choice. You leave her to me. Tomorrow, early, you go to Corminster. I'll see she's ready." Bart stood up. "Tell Damon to get the car ready and make sure you've got all those papers."

Lyndsay snapped her small case shut and stood it beside her bed. Outside on the landing she paused, listening, but there was no sound from Penelope's room. Shaking her head, she went down the stairs. When she reached the hall, she heard a car approaching and, with curiosity, stepped out into the still garden. The light was golden now, as the sun moved lower in the sky. A Land-Rover halted by the gate. Bart Poole was behind the wheel. Seeing her, he stood up and waved. She was pleased to see him and went down to the gate.

"How are you feeling?" he asked smiling, his eyes moving over her body.

"Fine. I took the sling off for a while today. Your grandmother certainly made a good job of my shoulder."

He nodded.

"Do you feel up to that tour I promised you? It won't be tiring with the car."

Just to get away from Clare House, she thought. Just to go anywhere.

"I'd like that."

"Come on then."

Lyndsay almost ran around the Land-Rover. He leaned over and opened the door for her. She sat back against the warm leather, watching his strong, capable hands on the wheel. He made a U-turn in front of the old chancel, and drove quite fast up the village street. A warm wind ruffled Lyndsay's hair and brushed her skin. She felt herself relaxing. At the green he slowed down, sounded the horn, and turned toward Dolben House. When they reached the end of the wall, which encircled the children's graveyard, he accelerated again. Lyndsay turned her head to look at Dolben House, squat and solid, with the sun behind it. The strange hedge of birds threw long shadows across the road.

"That hedge," she said. "Whose idea was that?"

"John Dolben's," he answered. "My stepfather. It was his life's work."

"Why?"

He shrugged his powerful shoulders.

"I thought maybe they had some special significance, those birds. You know, like the Gabriel Ratchets."

"Oh they do," he said. "They're guardian spirits, to protect the house."

She scanned his face for a moment and he grinned.

"You're laughing at me," she said. She didn't mind. In fact, she rather liked it. It made her feel human again. He hadn't, she realized, called her Mistress once.

"A little. Maybe," he agreed.

She looked around her. There were fields on either side of the road, but she wasn't particularly interested in the landscape. She was grateful for the breeze, grateful for the illusion of freedom this drive gave her. She watched Bart, the play of light on his arms as he handled the car, the way the breeze ruffled his dark hair.

"I was thinking you looked a little like Michael."

"We favored our mother," he said brusquely, and swung the car to the right, off the road. "Hold on," he warned.

The Land-Rover bumped onto a straight, stony track which rose sharply ahead of them.

"This is an old Roman road," he said. "Or what remains of one. Up ahead's what we call the ridge. It's more like a plateau, really, enclosing the village." He changed gear and the car climbed slowly upward. The field on Lyndsay's right was dry, the wheat stunted and, she thought, dying. At the top of the hill, the view was spectacular. To the left the fields stretched away as far as the eye could see. On the right, the escarpment of the ridge made a false horizon. Ratchets was entirely hidden.

Bart continued to drive along the straight road in silence. Lyndsay was quite content to sit back and enjoy the fresh air, the evening light, and the endless, timeless landscape. Bart suddenly cut off the engine and let the car idle to a halt. The silence gradually asserted itself. Above them a late skylark wheeled and chattered, a scrap of shrill black against the cloudless sky. She watched it, her eyes narrowed against the light, conscious of the fact that Bart was looking at her, appraising her carefully.

"Would you like to get out and walk awhile?" he asked.

She shook her head. "No. I'd just like to sit here. It's so peaceful."

"Aye. It's that all right." He stretched his arm along the back of the seat. Lyndsay braced herself for the touch of his hand on her shoulder, but it did not happen. "All this," he said quietly, "is Ratchets land. This is our life."

"You really care about it, don't you?" she asked.

"More than anything in the world." His eyes shone as though the land gave him some kind of energy, a sort of electric charge.

"It's very beautiful. I can understand that."

"What the drought's left," he said, his voice sharpening.

"It'll break soon, surely?"

"Maybe. If not . . ." He shrugged.

Lyndsay did not know what to say.

"Anyway," he said, shaking off his suddenly bleak mood, "a fair old chunk of all this is yours now."

"I guess," she agreed and, turning toward him, said, "do you mind?"

"No. It's right and proper. Which reminds me. Tomorrow, do you feel up to going into Corminster with Patrick? The papers have come through. You'll have to see the bank manager, get things settled."

"Yes. I suppose so." Her pulse raced a little. If everything was settled there would be nothing left to keep her here.

"Patrick'll pick you up in the morning, then."

She nodded and stared off across the fields. Up here everything felt different. There was nothing to be afraid of. Just good land. Without saying anything, she opened the car door and got out. Bart followed, walking slowly along the track behind her.

Stopping and turning half toward him, she said, "That night you sat with me. You were very kind."

He didn't say anything.

"Though I don't think Mother Poole approved," she said, laughing a little and walking on.

"You told her?"

"Yes. Shouldn't I have? She seemed very interested to know that you called me the Mistress."

She saw a flicker of anger in his eyes, but she wasn't afraid of it.

"But you don't want to be the Mistress, do you?" he said. Surprised, Lyndsay stopped and looked at him. "Patrick told me," he explained.

"Oh." She walked on again. "Patrick tells you everything, doesn't he?"

"Yes. We have no secrets."

"Only from me."

"Why do you say that?"

"This 'Mistress' business. Bart . . ." She suddenly put out her hand and touched his arm. He stopped and looked down at it, his eyes veiled. "It scares me. I don't understand and I don't want any part of it. Do you believe me?"

He said nothing for a long time. Embarrassed, Lyndsay removed her hand from his arm and walked a little farther along the track, kicking at loose pebbles. She felt that she had been presumptuous. Suddenly, she felt his hand on her shoulder. He turned her toward him and she lifted her head to look into his strange, golden eyes. Her heart, she realized, was thumping. She wanted him to say something, or at least to be able to break free of his gaze, but it was impossible.

"Do you trust me?" he asked.

"I . . . I think so, yes."

"Then listen. There's nothing to be afraid of." His fingers moved caressingly on her shoulder. "You must be the Mistress for a while . . . No, listen. You must. But soon, very soon, you can be free. If you want to be."

"Then I'm not free now?"

"Not if you resist."

"And if I cooperate?"

"Then you'll be free. If you want."

"You say it as though you don't think I will want to be."

"I don't think you will."

"That's what scares me. That's why I say I don't want any part of it. Can't you see?"

"What do you want then?" he asked, looking away from her at last. She felt bereft, as though by releasing her, he had taken something essential away from her. And she realized, in the split second before she spoke, that she could not tell him what she wanted. Besides, she was no longer so sure. She moved away from him, to the edge of the field, and stared thoughtfully at the cracked earth.

"If I do pretend to be the Mistress for a while, how will I be free of it?"

"You'll become . . . unnecessary. Not you personally," he added quickly. "The Mistress. But you can't pretend. You have to be."

209

"But I don't believe in it. Any of it. I can't." She turned impulsively back to him. "And I don't believe that you do, either."

He did not answer. His gaze was fixed on the horizon, behind her.

"If you give me the chance," he said slowly, "I can make you believe. Will you do that much for me?" His eyes found hers. They were soft, almost luminous. She wanted very much to touch him.

"I don't know," she whispered. "I really don't."

"We need you. Just for a while," he said, his voice soft and pleading.

"Bryony Dolben told me a lot of stuff," she said. "It was all . . . nonsense. What you, none of you, seem to realize is that I don't have any power or whatever it is the Mistress is supposed to have. I'm just an ordinary person, Bart. None of this makes sense to me. Even if I wanted to, I couldn't do it."

"Of course you have no power," he said sharply. "The power is here, in the land. You will take it from the land and from the people down there"—he jerked his head sharply back toward the village— "who believe in you."

For a moment, Lyndsay felt herself wavering. For a moment, she almost believed. But it was in him, something magnetic in Bart Poole that she could, if she allowed herself, believe, not in the land.

"No," she said at last. "I'm sorry, but I can't."

He took a step toward her and put out both his arms. He held her shoulders lightly. She refused to look at him. Her body trembled beneath his fingers.

"You are the last Mistress," he said in a fierce whisper. "The last of the line. I'm asking only for a little time, to save all that I believe in. I can make you believe and I can set you free. I will do so. I promise you."

With an effort of will, Lyndsay raised her face to his.

"I'm free now, Bart. I intend to keep it like that."

His eyes clouded. His full lips twitched for a moment, somewhere between a smile and a snarl. He let go of her shoulders.

"Are you?" he asked.

With a shudder, Lyndsay knew that he sensed or saw her attraction to him, and at the same time she knew that he would not hesitate to use it.

"I'd like to go back now," she said, moving past him and walking quickly back to the Land-Rover.

"A few days," he called. "And then you can choose."

She got back into the Land-Rover and refused to look at him as he came slowly toward her. By clasping her hands tightly together, she was able to control her trembling body. Her cheeks flamed. Bart got in beside her.

"You're not free, Lyndsay," he said. "You weren't from the moment you arrived here. And that would have been true even if you weren't the Mistress. It's time you faced up to that."

In a small, frightened voice, she said, "Will you take me back?"

He leaned forward and started the Land-Rover. He drove straight on along the track and then turned right. The car jolted along the edge of a great field, toward trees at the edge of the ridge. There was newly sprouted corn in the field, but Lyndsay was too preoccupied to wonder at it. He swung the car to a stop by the trees, but left the engine running.

"Down there," he said after a moment, pointing to a gap in the trees. "That'll bring you to Clare House."

"Thank you."

She got out of the Land-Rover and shut the door. He wasn't even looking at her. She walked quickly to the top of the ride. More than ever now, she thought, she had to get away.

As she walked up the path to Clare House, Lyndsay was suddenly startled by a low voice calling to her.

"Mistress."

She whirled around, peering into the lengthening shadows of the garden. Almost hidden by a clump of tall rosebushes, she recognized Damon Clare.

"Yes, Damon, what is it?" she asked.

"Please . . . Could I talk to you?" He made no attempt to come closer and his voice was, if anything, even lower. "Please. It's very important." He sounded almost desperate.

"Can't we go inside?" Lyndsay suggested.

"No. Please come here."

Slowly, Lyndsay stepped off the path and walked toward him. He had chosen his spot well. Roses screened them from the house and from the road. He looked at her uncertainly.

"Well?" she said, wanting to get it over with, whatever it was.

"Would you . . . will you do something for me while you're in Corminster tomorrow?"

She looked at him with a puzzled expression.

"Sure. If I can. What is it?"

From behind his back, he produced a flat, square package, inside a paper bag.

"Will you post this for me?" He held it out to her.

Lyndsay looked at it for a moment.

"But Damon, there's a post office right up the road," she said.

"No. I mean it can't be posted there. You can do it in Corminster. No one will know."

"Well, I can but . . . Why can't you mail it yourself?" she asked, trying to make sense of the confused and troubled expression on his young face. "Are you in some sort of trouble?"

"No. And there's nothing wrong about it. I promise you. It's just that it's private. Very private, and I don't want Cloris Poole or anyone to know." He swallowed hard, reddening a little. "She gossips," he said.

Lyndsay smiled with relief and understanding.

"Has this got something to do with a girl?" she asked.

Blushing fully, he nodded.

"Yes, Mistress."

"Okay. I'll do it."

"And you won't let anyone know?"

"I promise. Not a soul."

"You'll keep it safe, out of sight?"

"Yes. Don't worry." She took the package from him. "Look, I'll put it inside my sling, okay?" She slipped the parcel into the sling and tugged the material over it. "How's that?"

"I don't know how to thank you, Mistress."

He was so young, so intense. He made her feel a hundred years old.

"It's nothing. Don't worry. Good-night."

"If there's ever anything I can do for you, Mistress," he whispered after her.

She stopped, drew a deep breath and said:

"You can, Damon. You can stop calling me that. My name is Lyndsay."

Lyndsay carried a large, sack-shaped handbag with her the next morning when Patrick, driving the old gray Alvis, came to pick her up. She had removed the sling entirely. In the bottom of the bag was the parcel, just as Damon had given it to her. The boy's embarrassment and gratitude had cheered her a little, but it had not deflected her from her purpose. The bag also contained her passport and such cash as she had. She wore her sunglasses, primarily to hide her eyes, since she was afraid that the least little sign might betray her. She was tense, almost sick with anticipation. She sat stiffly in the car, barely listening as Patrick explained about the papers she had to sign. She held them in a thick brown envelope on her lap, murmuring in what she hoped were the appropriate places. She didn't care what she had to sign. She did not care about anything except getting away.

"We'll arrange a current account for you as well," Patrick said.

"Fine," she said absently.

"Then I'm afraid I've a few chores to do. Will you be all right by yourself? I expect you'll have some shopping to do."

Lyndsay's heart leaped, seemed to stop for a moment, and then beat rapidly.

"Why . . . yes. Yes. There are quite a few things I need. I'll be fine," she said quickly.

"Good. Then I suggest we meet at The George for lunch. I'll show you where it is."

"Fine."

She looked, as he asked her to do, at the documents. The words didn't make any sense. The figures were a blur. She understood that she had inherited outright Michael's share of the estate, at an estimated overall value of some £150,000.

"Is it really worth that much?" she asked, surprised.

"The value of the land, yes. Of course it doesn't bring in anything like that. But on the open market . . ."

"That's what Michael wanted for it?"

"He asked a hundred and sixty," Patrick said bitterly.

"Well, it's a lot of money . . ." she said.

"Then there's the house. That was left jointly to—"

"Oh don't let's bother about that now," Lyndsay said quickly. She forced a tight smile. "After all, there's no hurry, is there?"

"No," Patrick agreed. "We can discuss it later. Just so long as you understand that half of it is yours."

The thought that she would never, ever set foot inside that house again made her want to laugh out loud.

The outskirts of Corminster were dotted with small factories and a bleak new housing development. Patrick explained that recently light industry had been attracted to the town, which had grown and altered. Men and women, especially the young ones, attracted by the larger wages available in the factories, were leaving the land.

"Any from Ratchets?" she asked.

"No. Of course not." He sounded offended.

They left the car in a small parking lot. Patrick took her arm and led her through the shoppers to the bank, pointing out The George Hotel on the way. The bank manager, a Mr. Wilder, saw them at once. Lyndsay acknowledged his condolences and grew impatient as he and Patrick talked gloomily about prospects for the coming harvest. At last he inspected the documents, explained them to Lyndsay, and showed her where she should sign.

"You'd like us to keep them for you? Mr. Dolben already has the deeds deposited with us."

"Certainly," Lyndsay said. She was a very rich woman. Potentially anyway. She asked about a checking account and getting some cash.

"Of course. I'll get one of my staff to arrange it at once."

Coffee was brought in. Lyndsay sat through an agonizing time of small talk, questions, more condolences. At last, Mr. Wilder brought them over to a teller and explained to Lyndsay how to cash a check. She stood in line, sweating. Her throat was dry.

"Are you all right?" Patrick inquired solicitously once they were outside. "You're not overdoing things?"

"No. I feel fine. Really."

"Well, if you're sure."

"Really," she repeated, trying to keep the panic out of her voice.

"Well now. Look, there's The George. You'll be able to find it all right. Shall we say twelve-thirty?"

"Fine."

He looked at her for a moment, searching her face.

"I'll go and look around the shops," she said hurriedly. She began to walk away. With every step she expected him to call after her, or catch up with her. She came to a crossing and waited with a group of other people. She thought, If I can just get across this street, it'll be okay. I know it will. The traffic stopped. She crossed the road. She moved toward a shop window and slowly, with studied casualness, turned and looked back the way she had come. She scanned the people carefully but there was no sign of Patrick. She really was

214

free. She began walking at once and then stopped, causing someone to bump into her. She had no idea where the railroad station was. She stopped the first person she saw coming toward her.

"Well now, go down here about two hundred yards, to Church Street. Straight up there until you come to Station Road, and it's just along there on the right."

"Thank you," Lyndsay said and started off back toward the bank. She hurried now, clutching her bag, pushing her way between the ambling shoppers. Church Street was less crowded. She increased her pace. Then she remembered the package. And there was something else she had meant to do as well. She turned back. A sort of panic seized her. She looked at her watch, but there was plenty of time. When she reached the main street again, she asked another passerby to direct her to the post office. Just down the main street, opposite the police station. She couldn't miss it.

At the police station, Patrick had been directed to the court offices next door. He was shown into an untidy office where an obviously overworked young man produced a file and leafed through it.

"Mrs. Berryman's not well, you see," Patrick explained. "She couldn't come herself. And then she has the children to look after. They live on my land, so I said I'd do anything necessary. It's a very distressing business."

"He's got quite a history," the man said, looking at the folder. "The vehicle being untaxed didn't help. Would you say this man has a drinking problem?" He looked at Patrick with sharp, concerned eyes.

"Oh definitely."

"Well, they'll probably do a psychiatric report while he's in Garston. I can't tell you much else."

"I see. A psychiatric report?"

"Probably. The prison social worker could tell you more."

"He's not exactly very intelligent or reliable. He's a great one for making up fantastic stories. . . ." Patrick stumbled. "I mean, I don't think you should take anything he says too seriously."

"These people know their job, Mr. . . . er . . ."

"Dolben."

"Yes. Anyway, the best thing, I should think, is to get the wife to make a visit. You can ring the prison and find out all about it. And

215

try to keep him off the booze." The young man stood up. "That's about all I can do for you."

"What will happen to him when he's released?" Patrick asked.

"Nothing. Once he's done his time, that's it. Unless the social worker wants to keep tracks on him. But he's got a home and family. No problem."

"Oh."

"It's not really my case, you see. If someone had been here when he was in court, well . . ."

"I understand. I'm afraid we had no idea. Thank you very much." Patrick held out his hand and the young man shook it.

Outside, in the corridor, which smelled of stale wax, he wondered what else he should have asked. Would Bart be satisfied? But it didn't matter, he thought. By the time they let Timon Berryman out, it would all be over. If he came back to Ratchets, Bart would deal with him. Feeling more cheerful, he made his way toward the exit.

While Lyndsay waited for an elderly woman to draw her old-age pension, she pulled the package Damon had given her out of the paper bag. It was neatly wrapped and addressed in childlike block capitals. For a moment the name meant nothing to her. Then she remembered.

MR. KENNETH DONNE

She remembered the man with the pipe who had called at Dolben House. He'd been looking for this man, his brother. But what struck her as odd was that Damon had said it had to do with a girl. Why should he lie?

"Yes, please?"

She glanced up. The man behind the counter was glaring at her impatiently.

"I want to mail this, please," she said, waving the package at him.

"Put it on the scales."

She looked around and then saw the scales, on the counter to her left. She placed the parcel on them.

"Where to?"

"Oh . . . er . . ." She picked it up again and read the address.

216

"Cambridge." Immediately, she remembered what Michael had written. In the spring, a term in Cambridge. All that was dead now, she told herself firmly. Dead as Michael himself.

"First or second?"

"Pardon me?"

"Do you want to send it first or second class?" the man said irritably.

"First, I guess."

"That'll be thirty-seven pence."

He pushed two stamps toward her and waited, tapping his pencil on the counter, while she sorted out the unfamiliar coins in her purse. There were several people behind her now. She stuck the stamps on the parcel and looked about for the mailbox.

"Over there," the man said to her. "By the phones."

"Thank you."

She carried the parcel across to the box and dropped it in. Then, taking out her purse again, she went to one of the phone booths. Setting down her bag, she took out Reginald Pargetter's card, read the instructions on the wall carefully, and dialed his number. She heard the ringing tone. A voice answered and was immediately cut off by a series of rapid pips. She pressed a coin into the slot.

"Hello?"

"London Academy of Architecture. Can I help you?"

"Yes, please. Can I speak with Mr. Reginald Pargetter, please?"

"Just a moment." The line went dead. For a second, Lyndsay thought the girl must have hung up, or that they'd been cut off. She was holding more coins ready in her hand and she felt them becoming slick with sweat. "Mr. Pargetter's secretary," another voice said in her ear.

"Oh hello. This is Mrs. Lyndsay Dolben. Can I speak with Mr. Pargetter, please?"

"I'm sorry. Mr. Pargetter's on holiday at the moment. Can I take a message?"

"When will he be back?"

"Not for another two weeks. Can someone else help you?"

"No. No, thank you." Lyndsay replaced the receiver.

She felt desolate for a moment, and then told herself that it didn't matter. If she hesitated now . . . She gathered up her bag. Calling him had been a superstitious act anyway. She'd just thought that if she told him she was coming to London it would somehow make it more real. More certain. And if anything went wrong, someone would be alerted. But nothing was going to go wrong, she told herself as she hurried out of the post office and turned back toward the station.

She walked with her head down, not daring to look about her. She felt more confident once she left the main street. Station Road was the third turning on the left, off Church Street. She felt a surge of excitement once she turned into it. A humped bridge crossed the railway tracks and there, off to the right, was the small, wooden station. In the train station, she looked at the array of timetables pinned to the wall but she was too excited and nervous to make any sense of them. She went to the little window marked TICKETS and asked the time of the next train to London.

"You can't get to London direct, miss."

"I can't?"

"No. What you'll have to do is go to Birmingham and change there."

"Okay. That'll be fine."

"Now then, let me see." The man disappeared, muttering to himself.

"Could you hurry it up, please?" she called.

"Don't you worry now. You've got plenty of time. The next one to Birmingham's not till twelve thirty-seven. Now, that'll connect up with . . ." He paused, running his finger down a page of small, closely packed type. "Ah, that's right. That'll connect up nicely with the two-thirty to London."

"Fine. Thank you."

"Will that be single or return, miss?"

"Single," she said, reaching into her bag.

"Morning, Mistress."

Lyndsay's heart stopped. She felt the blood drain from her face. Her body slumped against the little window. The man had disappeared again. A hand touched her, supported her. Dry-mouthed, she looked at Bryony Dolben. The woman's face was, as always, impassive. Lyndsay tried to speak, but her panic and shock were too great. Bryony had a firm grip on her arm. She pulled her gently, but firmly, toward the entrance. "Me and Justin came in to pick up some seed we ordered," Bryony said in her flat voice. "You look done in. Must be the heat. Come along now. We'll see to you."

She was outside, on the pavement. A tall man came toward them.

"You don't know my husband, do you?" Bryony said in her awful, relentless voice. "Justin, look who I just bumped into."

"Mistress." He touched the brim of an old trilby.

"Let go of me," she said, tugging against Bryony's arm.

"I think she's got a touch of the sun," Bryony explained. "It's too soon to have that arm out of a sling, if you ask me. We'd best run her to The George, Justin."

"Aye."

He stood on the other side of Lyndsay, like a jailer. They crossed the road to an old car. The trunk was open, showing sacks of seed.

"I'm perfectly all right," Lyndsay said.

"We'll drive you to The George," Bryony said implacably.

Lyndsay got into the car, with Bryony pressed close beside her.

"How . . . how do you know I've got to go to The George?" she asked.

"Why, Mr. Patrick always has luncheon there when he's in town. You came with Mr. Patrick now, didn't you?"

Lyndsay leaned back against the seat, tears misting her eyes.

"You know damn well I did. You were told to spy on me, weren't you?"

Bryony allowed herself a small, faded smile.

"I'm sure I don't know what's got into her," she said, addressing her husband. "If you ask me, it was a good thing we found her. That's what comes of trying to do too much too soon."

It was useless to argue. Lyndsay lay back and closed her eyes. Tears of helpless frustration rolled down her cheeks.

"Here we are," Bryony said as the car slowed to a stop. "And there's Mr. Patrick, look, all ready and waiting."

Numbly, Lyndsay got out of the car. Patrick was walking toward her, his face expressionless.

"Let's go and get some lunch," he said softly, taking hold of her arm.

"I don't want any lunch," Lyndsay said through her tears.

"No? Then I expect you'd like to go home," he said, turning her toward the parking lot. "Yes, that would be best. Let's get you back to Ratchets."

CHAPTER TEN

Justin Dolben's old car dogged them all the way back to Ratchets. Bryony sat bolt upright, staring placidly straight ahead. It was a bad sign, an omen, she thought. She could not share her fear with Justin. His face, she knew without looking, wore the smug expression of the men, of those who gave their allegiance to Bart. She would have to consult the book, Mother Poole. The wise old woman would know if there was any precedent for it. It shocked and pained her that the Mistress should seek to abandon them. These were indeed terrible times. As the cars turned, in slow procession, off the Corminster Road, skirting the oaks, Bryony looked away across the village and saw a small dark cloud hovering in the sky.

"Looks like rain's coming," she said to her husband.

"Aye," he said. "Tomorrow. You can count on it."

Patrick had not spoken. The tears streamed silently down Lyndsay's face. She did not try to check them. They were tears of utter misery, which brought her no consolation. When Patrick parked the car outside Dolben House, she did not move. He got out, taking the keys with him, and walked around the car. He opened the door and stood back, holding it wide. She got out, swaying a little. He held her arm, reached into the car, and picked up her bag, which she had forgotten. Then he led her to the steps and through the front door, into the hall.

Bart Poole faced them across the circular table. Patrick let go of her arm. She hung her head in misery and fear. Patrick started toward Bart, who waved him away with a sharp, irritable gesture. He opened his mouth to speak.

"Leave us," Bart said. "Go on. Get out of here."

She heard Patrick's slow footsteps receding across the room, the clatter of a door latch. She lifted her face to Bart. A nerve ticked high in his cheek, but she could not tell whether he was angry or sad. Tired, she pulled off her sunglasses and dropped them, with a sharp clatter, onto the table.

"I . . . could use a drink," she said.

He made no response. Lyndsay waited, leaning against the table. After a while, unable to bear his accusing silence any longer, she walked round the table and past him. She poured herself a stiff Scotch and sipped it, shuddering. She felt so cold and afraid.

"Well?" she said, turning toward him. "What are you going to do with me?" His broad, stiff back was absolutely still. "What's the ritual?" she asked, her voice rising, barely under control, "for attempted defection?" She drank again, still watching him. "You want me to guess? Well now, let me see." She walked about the room, tapping her fingernail against the glass. She wanted him to think that she was not afraid, that the whole business was an irritating joke. "Do you still have stocks here? That's a good old English custom, isn't it? Yes, why don't you do that? Clap me in the stocks and let them all pelt me." Her aimless pacing brought her closer to him. His silence angered her and made her even more afraid. She gulped down another mouthful of whiskey. "Or have you got something better in mind? Something more refined? Something special to Ratchets? Come on, you can tell me. After all, there isn't very much I can do about it now, is there? You made damn sure of that."

He swung suddenly toward her. His powerful body exploded into action. She saw his hand slicing through the air. The blow made her stagger sideways. The glass dropped from her hand, shattering on the floor. Lyndsay regained her balance. Her cheek ached and stung. She clenched her fist, to prevent herself from touching her face.

"You said," she panted, not looking at him, "that that would never happen again. You promised me." She lifted her blazing eyes to his face, intending to challenge him, but she could not hold back the tears. His arms went around her, pulling her fiercely against him. She let her body become limp. Her raging cheek rested against his chest. She could not see his face. He murmured something, a sort of moan, in her ear. She felt his arms crushing her, heard his labored breathing. She tried to look at him, but his hand pressing against the back of her head prevented her.

"You made me," he whispered. "Don't make me hurt you. Please don't."

She tried to shake her head, but he held it still. She gave herself up, weeping, to the strength and comfort of his arms.

He pushed her away from him but held her by the arms. His mouth worked compulsively as though there were much he wanted to say.

"What do you want from me?" she said.

Slowly, he got his feelings under control. She saw his face become still, composed and hard. He pulled her roughly by the arm toward the stairs.

"You must go to your room," he said.

"Like a naughty girl," she said, and tried to laugh.

"It's no joking matter, Mistress," he said harshly, forcing her up the stairs.

"I can find my own way," she protested, trying to prize his fingers from her arms. "You're hurting me."

He said nothing. She stopped struggling and let him half pull her along the gallery. He threw open the door to her room and pushed her in.

"Just remember," he said, "there's no way you can defeat me."

She turned around and took a step toward him. He was holding the door steady while he fitted a key into the lock.

"I don't even want to fight you, Bart," she said. "Can't you see that? What do I have to do to make you understand?"

He stepped back, pulling the door to.

"Wait," she begged. "Bart, please."

He hesitated, but she saw through the almost closed door that his face remained set in a scowl of anger, yet she thought that his eyes softened a little.

"That night," she said, putting her hand on the door, "when I was locked in before . . . Bart, it was you, wasn't it?"

For a moment his eyes flickered, as though lit by some terrible memory. She thought that he was afraid, and she pressed closer to the door, wanting to reach him and comfort him. He jerked the door shut. The key turned in the lock. She heard it being withdrawn.

"Bart," she called.

Silence.

She beat wildly against the paneling, calling to him. It was useless. She stood with her sore hands pressed against the door.

Bart Poole flung the key onto the table. It skidded along until stopped by a mortar and pestle. Mother Poole kept her eyes resolutely fixed on his face. He stared at the key, his hands twitching as though he wanted to snatch it back.

"What have you done with her?" the old woman asked in a bleak voice.

His eyes flashed at her angrily.

"Nothing," he sneered. "She's all yours now. Now that *I've* fetched her back."

Mother Poole sighed, stretched her knotted fingers, and began to inspect them with concentration.

"Why didn't you let her go?"

"What?" he said. He looked at her guardedly. "Oh no, no, I don't believe it." He shook his head, trying to laugh. "What devilry are you up to now?" he asked, leaning toward her.

"None," she answered calmly. "You fetched her back. You must want her."

He snorted and turned away from her, his mind racing to discover the meaning he suspected behind her words. She kept her silence, staring at her fingers.

"You've not abandoned the Mistress," he said, trying to make his tone more confident than he felt. "Not you. Never."

"A Mistress that runs away?" she said. "One who will not be persuaded? What use is she?" She shifted in her chair, angry and discomfited.

"Tonight—" he began, but the old woman cut him off with a sharp gesture.

"By force and terror?" she said. "You think that'll win her?"

"It'll bind her. I never promised you more."

"And then?" She raised her face to look at him, her lips twisted in a sneer.

"Then I shall have won," he said simply. "The game will be over. The Mistress will . . . cease to be effective."

"And you'll be king of the castle," she chanted in a singsong voice.

"Why not? Don't I have the right?" His stance, his voice, everything about him reminded her painfully of the belligerent boy he had been.

"Ask yourself," she said, turning her face to the fire.

He stuffed his hands awkwardly into his pockets. Her question, her attitude frightened him. He had expected a battle to the last.

"You know what I think?" he said, his head cocked to one side, a cheeky boy now, defying her. "I think the idea of losing the Mistress has turned your brain. You're old. You can't face up to it, can you?" His voice taunted her.

"Where is it written," she asked dully, "that the Priest shall take unto himself all the power? What does a man know of serving the earth?" She turned her terrible black eyes on him. "Where?" she demanded.

He did not flinch but bent down toward her. "In here," he said, tapping his forehead. "From the day I was born. By the Dolbens, Albertine, and you." The last word was a hiss of hatred.

"No." She shook her head slowly from side to side. "John Dolben and Albertine, perhaps. But not me. You can't lay your sins at my door."

"And you can't stop me."

She pursed her lips. Slowly he straightened up, watching her as a cautious man watches a deadly snake.

"It's you that's mad," she said sadly. "Albertine and her daughter saw to that. Go, have your pound of flesh and strut about in your fine robes. The earth will not answer to you for long, Bart Poole. Destroy the Mistress and you destroy yourself."

He laughed quietly.

"Talk sense. I've not destroyed her. There she is, waiting for you to make her ready. You can't say I don't play you fair and square."

"You can say that?" She half rose from her chair, her breast heaving with anger. "You say that to me?" She let her body fall back into the chair. For a moment her hands waved uselessly in the air then, like felled birds, flapped into her lap. "You've defiled her," she said. "You and no one else."

Bart Poole caught his breath. The color drained from his face. His body rocked as though he had been delivered a blow. The old woman kept her face averted, almost as if the sight of him sickened her.

"You . . . don't know . . . what you're . . . saying," he gasped.

"Aye. Aye." She waved him away. "Go, tell them Mother Poole

is mad, the Mistress dead. Go on, go on. Tonight they'll believe anything you say."

Her air of defeat frightened him, but years of habit prevented him from showing any sign of weakness toward her. He forced himself to stand tall and straight, to keep his face arrogantly fixed against her.

"But the nights are short," she said. Her voice was cracked and dry, like old leaves moved by a chill wind. "And the dawn comes . . . the dawn comes." Her head slipped sideways. He saw her eyelids flicker and close. Afraid, he stepped close to her, peering into her face. Her chest rose and fell as though she slept, exhausted. Softly, the old dog, curled before the fire, murmured in his sleep, his skin twitching.

Bart tiptoed toward the door. The old woman's eyes opened as he shut it quietly behind him. She held her breath, listening intently to his step on the path, the old, familiar creak of the gate. Slowly, she reached out a hand to the table and felt blindly for the key. Her strong fingers clenched around it. Holding it tightly, she knew that she had rattled him. But that would only spur him on. Good, good, she thought nodding. She had the Mistress now. He would do the rest. An old sadness swept through her. Leaning her head back, she closed her eyes again.

"Bart, Bart," she cried in a whisper. "Why? Why must you?"

Penelope Clare pulled on the traditional black robe and arranged her loose pale hair over her shoulders. If that policeman or whatever he was had not called her a relative by marriage of Timon Berryman, she might have been able to refuse Bart's last request.

"After this," he had said, standing in her living room, "your work will be done."

She knew that it wasn't true. There would never be an end to it, not until death came. Bart would always find something else for her, his accomplice, to do.

"I trust you, Penelope Clare. I can depend on your pride and on your love for Patrick."

Knowing how she felt, he could make her do anything he wanted. He played on her breeding, education, and the habits of generations. She was the head of the Clares now. It was therefore fitting that she should be the one to start Magdalena Berryman on her last futile race to the grave. She must begin the act that would make the Clare blood pure again.

"This is your last task, and when Patrick has performed his . . ."

And if her sense of family pride should fail, he could always use Patrick to goad and tempt her. But this time, she thought, he had spoken the truth. When Patrick had done what he had to do, Bart would have no further use for him. Then Patrick would have to turn to someone.

"Who else will care about him?" he had asked simply. His cold, golden eyes were frank and open.

Bart was her only rival, she admitted at last. He had always been. Even as a child. Patrick had tagged along behind Bart, trying so hard and so painfully to be like him. Bart had been quick to exploit that, building everything on Patrick's striving, his worship, until Patrick had become blind to all but Bart's needs and wishes. The dependency was total, and when Bart no longer needed him, where would he go, what would he do?

"You'll be there, ready. He'll need you then."

It's true, she thought, staring out of her bedroom window. The single cloud that had appeared at noon had multiplied. The sky above the ridge was ringed now with fluffy, purple-bellied clouds. It would be a dark night. The rain was coming. And even if it wasn't true, her thoughts continued, what did it matter now? She was committed. She had pride, but no dignity. She had love, but no lover. The emptiness of her life seemed suddenly immense. She felt as though she had been dropped down into some limitless desert, in which she was doomed to wander in vain for the rest of her days. Pressing her fingers to her temples, she did not understand how it had come to be. Where had it gone wrong? *Maddy*, she thought, her heart hardening. She had grown up with it, with the curse of Magdalena's defection and betrayal hanging over her. She had ruined them all. Bart, Albertine, Patrick, herself. Even Michael Dolben had to pay for Maddy's sin. They had suspected her, Penelope, of conniving with Maddy. She recalled with vivid, childish terror, the interview she had had with Albertine. The questions, the threats, the cajoling. But beside Maddy, Penelope had been a slow and dull girl who had always known her place and her duties. They had been satisfied at last that she knew nothing. With the rest of them she had sworn to repudiate Maddy, yet, she thought bitterly, she had not been strong enough to keep her vow. It would have been just if the shot had found her heart instead of Lyndsay's shoulder. For that, surely, would have been preferable to this living death Maddy had bequeathed her. If she had only been wiser all those years ago, or quicker, she might perhaps have stopped Maddy. Maddy would have married Bart and he would have had no need of Patrick. Patrick would have become her husband. Albertine . . . She covered her face with her hands, pressing hard against her eyes. There was no future, no hope or comfort in "might have been." The past wrote the future. Maddy, by running away that night with Timon Berryman, had set them all on a course which brought them, logically and inevitably, to this night. And beyond that, Penelope Clare had neither the will nor the courage to look.

She let her hands fall to her sides and straightened her shoulders. She must be composed now. She must do her duty. The past wrote the future, she thought again, clinging to the bleakness of the thought. That, after all, was the very basis of the Ways, and no one could alter it.

Lyndsay also watched the clouds. Like soldiers they came, forming out of the very air and hanging like waiting presences around the village. She had counted them—there was nothing else to do—several times, and each count revealed more, yet she had not noticed new ones arrive. Through the locked windows of her room she could see no sign of a breeze that might blow them imperceptibly in from the sea. They looked heavy with rain. She ought to be glad, for the drought had become a blight not just on the land but on their lives. It seemed that the will, the spirit had been dried up in the endless summer, yet when she looked at the clouds she saw no hope in them. The rain could not wash away her fear.

Nobody had come near her since Bart had locked her in. Perhaps that was all they intended. Just to keep her locked up here. Bart had said he needed her only for a short time, and then she would be free to choose. So, when she had served whatever purpose they demanded of her, they would let her out and she could go. But he had said that she would not want to go, and now she knew why. He had made her powerless to choose already. It was a foregone conclusion. There never had been any choice. And he had not needed *her*, but the Mistress.

"Bart," she moaned, "Bart," pressing her hot cheek against the glass of the window. How much did he understand? There had been an opportunity to tell him but she had pushed it from her.

There is only life for you, Mistress. Only life.

Now, at last, she understood what the old woman meant and it was her secret, her power. She would never tell Bart for it was more important than anything she felt for him. It secured her and would give her the courage to do whatever might be necessary. She turned away from the window and placed her hand gently, protectively across her stomach.

All his preparations were made. Bart Poole stood on the ridge, alone, looking at Top Meadow, with its sharp green shoots. He walked slowly, contemplatively between them, placing his feet with care. In the middle of the field, he stopped. There was a circular area, about seven feet in diameter, where no corn grew. He had not noticed it before, but this was the place he was now drawn to. He felt awed, shocked by the power of the earth and his closeness to it.

He stepped boldly into the circle, knelt down and then, slowly, prostrated himself. He lay on his stomach, legs together, arms stretched out, his fingers curled into the warm, crumbling soil. He made his mind empty, waited. Gradually he perceived the strength of the earth. He could feel it bearing him up. Then he felt its life, the incredible power of it. The ceaseless movement, hidden from the eye, which now seemed to rock and sway his body as though he were cradled in enormous, invisible arms. The earth crumbling, reforming, breaking down. A great heart beating and pulsing, giving life, sustaining, growing, changing. It seemed to him that the field tilted beneath him. He was borne up on a great primeval sigh, and sank down again, trembling against the waiting earth.

"O Mother Earth," he whispered, his lips pressed close to the soil, "hear and receive your son. I have served you. Give me now your power. I have conquered everything in your name. The sacrifices have begun and you have received them. Tonight, the greatest sacrifice of all will be made. I ask only the means to do it." He was silent, pressed to the earth, listening. "Give me," he said after a long time, "give me . . . the Hounds."

A sound like a rushing wind, a sighing heart filled his ears for a moment. The earth grew cold beneath him.

"Deliver up to me, in return for blood, the symbol and embodiment of your power, that I may serve you with the full strength of a man."

The chill struck through his clothes, making him shiver.

"Hear me," he implored. "The time of the Mistress is at an end. Take now your Priest as husband. Let me be wedded to the earth. Give me the Hounds to complete your work."

The silence was shocking and total. Gradually, the warmth returned. He lifted his head and saw the circle of clouds, a continuous black ring bringing a premature night. He had received his answer, cold, terrible, and implacable. He rose steadily to his feet. His clothes, hands, and face were streaked with the earth. He bowed his head solemnly and picked his way carefully back to the edge of the field. He allowed himself one last look at the earth and the lowering sky, before hurrying off along the ridge toward the children's graveyard.

In the dusk, Penelope Clare came to Magdelena Berryman's house. She walked across the yard and opened the door. She paused like a great black bird on the threshold until her eyes adjusted to the shadows within. The hearth was cold, the table cluttered. She listened for a sound, any sound, of life. She sped across the room and opened the door into the children's bedroom. The unmade bed, the crib were empty. Breathless now with fear and excitement, she hurried to the other bedroom. It was empty. She leaned against the door.

They had gone. Maddy had made a break for it, taking her children with her.

Penelope did not know what to do. Should she raise the alarm or hope that they had gotten away?

She pulled the bedroom door shut. Walking slowly back into the main room, her foot kicked against something soft on the floor. She stopped and looked down at it. A child's dress. She picked it up. A scrap of tartan cloth, abandoned in the panic of departure. She clutched it, crumpling it in her hands. It had been worn recently. It would be just like Maddy, she thought, to dress her children in clean clothes before leaving. There was a stain on the dress. Some spilled food or drink that had dried to a sort of crust on the tiny bodice. She smoothed it with her finger. Then, walking toward the door, she tucked the dress inside her robe. She left the door open to the night. Her duty was almost done.

Lyndsay awoke at the sound of the key turning. Light flooded the room, hurting her eyes. She shielded them with her hand, unable to make out the black figures who advanced into the room.

"Come. Get up. It's time."

"Mother Poole?" she asked, squinting against the light.

The old woman's voice was cold and hard. She leaned with both hands on her stick.

"Put this on."

Bryony Dolben stepped toward her, holding out a long black robe.

"What for?" Lyndsay said.

The old woman moved to the dressing table and opened a drawer.

"Be quick now."

"I want to see Bart," Lyndsay said.

"So you shall."

"I must talk to him."

She stood up quickly, watching Mother Poole. Bryony pressed the robe against her shoulders.

"What are you looking for?" Lyndsay asked.

Bryony guided her arms into the loose sleeves.

"This." Mother Poole turned toward her, holding the Dolben Collar loosely in her left hand. Bryony went to her and took the collar.

"I don't want it," Lyndsay said. "You can't make me . . ."

"Put it on her," Mother Poole told Bryony.

She moved swiftly. The cold weight of the collar bit into Lyndsay's neck. She clawed at it, scratching her fingers. The clasp shut tight.

"What are you going to do to me?" she asked.

"Nothing," Mother Poole answered tiredly. "Come now. Come."

Bryony fussed around her, fastening the cloak.

"Leave me alone," Lyndsay said.

"We'll take you by force if necessary," Mother Poole warned. She raised her stick, ready to rap with it on the floor. "Shall I call them?"

"Who?" Lyndsay asked, her eyes dilated with fear.

"The men. To take you."

"No." She shook her head. "No. I'll come with you."

The old woman lowered her stick. Bryony stepped back. Mother Poole surveyed Lyndsay critically, then nodded her head once, apparently satisfied.

"Follow me," she said. "And no tricks, mind. There is nowhere for you to run to now." She turned about and walked to the door. She did not seem to need the stick. She moved with the strength of a young woman, straight-backed and proud. Bryony gave Lyndsay a little push and, obediently, she followed after Mother Poole, along the gallery and down the stairs.

"Mother, wait," she said as the old lady reached the front door of Dolben House. Mother Poole stopped. Slowly she turned her head until she could regard Lyndsay coldly over her shoulder. "I'm afraid," Lyndsay said. "Help me."

"I told you before, the fear is all in your own mind. I can't help you now. You must see for yourself. You must learn the hard way."

"No," Lyndsay said. "What have I done? Please . . ."

Mother Poole turned away from her and opened the door.

"Go on," Bryony said behind her.

She stepped out into the night. Patches of lingering blue showed between the clouds. The air felt damp and chill. She followed Mother Poole down the drive and onto the road. There, they turned toward the village. The old woman placed herself on Lyndsay's right, Bryony on her left. Ahead Lyndsay saw the flicker of torchlight. Each woman grasped one of her arms. She saw the torches disappear.

"Now," Mother Poole said and urged her forward.

They walked in silence down the road, past the wall of the children's graveyard, toward the green. Lyndsay drew back, pulling against their grip when they reached the path, but they pushed her forward. Her heart racing, she walked ahead of them along the path. Despite the darkness, she seemed to have no difficulty in finding her way. Automatically, she turned into the open door. Once again the women fell into step beside her, but they did not touch her. She looked straight ahead. The chancel doors stood open. The interior was lit by the glow of torches.

"Wait," Mother Poole commanded, taking her arm.

They stood on the far side of the clearing, facing the open doors.

Lyndsay shivered. The light increased, came toward them. She blinked. People walked, two abreast, out of the chancel, holding torches. The graveyard leapt into dancing light and shadow as the torchbearers formed a circle around the central graveled area. They were all robed. She could not make out their features in the wavering light. Bryony slipped away from her, hurried forward to take her place in the circle. From the darkness of the chancel a last figure emerged. Lyndsay's pulse quickened. She took a step forward to meet him, but Mother Poole caught her arm and pulled her roughly back. He walked slowly into the light. His eyes glowed like a cat's. Lyndsay opened her mouth to call him, but no sound came. Mother Poole tightened her grip on her arm.

He, too, wore a black robe, open to the waist. Sweat gleamed on his chest as he extended his arms stiffly out from his body. He threw back his head, his eyes flashing. The light flickered on the taut sinews of his throat. A great tremor shook his body. Beside her, Lyndsay felt Mother Poole tremble also, as though in response.

Lyndsay could not take her eyes from him. He was like someone in the grip of fever. His body shook with a terrible energy. The crowd swayed around him as though infected by the force which gripped him. Lyndsay was afraid for him, but unable to do anything to help him. Suddenly, he lowered his head. The light pitted his face with shadows. His eyes burned directly into Lyndsay's. She was unaware of anything but the compelling, beckoning fire of his eyes. She walked forward, toward him. She had no choice. As she did so, she realized that Mother Poole had gone, had slipped away unnoticed while she had been staring at him. The thought drifted through her mind, scarcely noticed. She kept walking. His eyes were enormous, golden, licked with fire that drew her on.

"O Mother Earth," he intoned, his voice a grave, level chant. "Deliver up your unhappy dead. Open, in the name of the Mistress and of her Priest."

The crowd murmured. It seemed that space and perspective had altered. The voices of the people came from a long way off. She was still walking toward Bart, but now he seemed as far away as ever. A moment ago, or perhaps an hour, his eyes had been enormous, close to her. Now they were pinpricks of golden light in the distance.

"Deliver up the Hounds," he cried, his voice ringing and clashing against her ears, echoing against the sky.

"The Hounds. The Hounds."

All around her voices took up the cry.

Suddenly, she was standing a foot or two from him. His eyes were again fixed on her, but he gave no sign of recognition. It was as though he could not see her, had never seen her. She put out her hand to touch him, but he was beyond reach.

Then, all around her, she heard a new sound: a snuffling, a padding of paws on the earth. Something warm and living bumped against her. Looking down she saw a great dog, a black, silk-coated hound. Recoiling in surprise and fear, she bumped against another. It growled at her, deep in its throat.

"The Hounds. The Hounds."

The crowd whispered, swayed. More and more dogs appeared, trotting between the people, milling on the graveled space, sniffing, panting, their great jaws hanging open.

"Bart," she called desperately as he advanced into the pack, like a sleepwalker oblivious to danger. Each hound lifted its great muzzle toward him. Lyndsay watched in horror as he moved among them. One, the leader, suddenly threw up its head and bayed. The sound echoed eerily around the graveyard and just as it seemed about to die away, another dog took it up, another and then another until the very sky seemed to reverberate with the awful, mournful noise.

Bart had passed through the pack now and they turned to follow him. Lyndsay stepped forward, not knowing whether she wanted to prevent him, or to save him. The dogs blocked her way and she hung back, hesitating. Somebody caught her arm, drew her aside. The dogs were flowing now, a stream of black, panting bodies moving after Bart into the darkness beyond the circle of light. The crowd broke. She was jostled by people pushing one another in their eagerness to follow. She was buffeted this way and that. Another, or perhaps the same hand steadied her. Twisting her head she tried to make out who it was that held her arm, urged her to follow the crowd, but in the uncertain light and the press of people, she could not be sure. The crowd closed around her, silent, yet taut with excitement. They seemed to lift her up and carry her along after Bart and his hounds. She was forced through the little door and pushed left. The crowd, once free of the graveyard, gathered momentum. Several people brushed past her. Somebody, treading on her heels, told her to hurry. They came out onto the track which ran beside Dolben House. The clouds broke apart for a moment. The unnaturally bright moonlight dimmed the torches and silvered the coats of the hounds. She saw them bounding up the track, behind

233

the striding figure of Bart Poole. She hesitated, afraid to follow any farther. Hands caught her again, forcing her to run to catch up.

At the top of the track they turned onto the ridge. She glimpsed the hounds, a black ribbon, along the path in the moonlight. It was a beautiful sight. As though in response to some signal, the crowd formed into single file. Someone pushed her into place. She was part of it now, part of this living entity which was the crowd. The pace increased. She could feel the excitement like a tangible thread flowing back from the hounds, through the people, urging them on. As though spellbound, she found herself as anxious as the others to get on, to follow.

They were approaching the head of the ride, the edge of the meadow. The crowd slowed, fanned out. Lyndsay was forced aside as the people fought to get a clear view. She pushed her way forward to see what was happening, what had caused this halt. Penelope Clare stood at the entrance to the ride, the hood of her black gown thrown back.

"They've gone," she said.

The crowd murmured, surged forward. Lyndsay was carried with them.

"Did you get something?" Bart sounded excited, as though her answer were a matter of the utmost urgency.

Penelope Clare's face seemed to flicker and dissolve in the light. A spasm of pain crossed her face, then, with a gesture of contempt and fear, she pulled her hand free of her robe and flung something onto the ground. Bart stooped and picked it up. It was a scrap of cloth, or clothing.

"Here, boy. Here, here, here," he shouted.

Lyndsay saw him, surrounded by the milling hounds. He held the material out to them. At once, the animal she took to be the leader lifted its magnificent head and let out a great bay. It was taken up by the others at once.

"They've taken the scent," somebody said close to her.

"Aye," a voice agreed. "We've got 'em now."

The hounds set off again, along the ridge. The people followed. Penelope Clare joined them, pulling up her hood. They skirted the plantation of trees and suddenly, in the moonlight, the landscape was revealed below them. One vast meadow stretched down. The Berrymans' shack was a distant, silver speck. Beyond lay flat and open fields. With a great cry, the hounds broke into a loping run, streaming down the hillside. The crowd rushed after them. Lyndsay could not help but run. It was downhill and the gradient gave them impetus, so that they were able to keep up with the hounds. When the ground leveled the hounds spread out, sniffing the air, the earth. Breathless, Lyndsay halted with the others, watching in tense fascination. Then, with renewed speed, the hounds took off again, making for the corner of the great meadow. There was a stile over which someone helped her. The hounds forced their way through the hedge. One or two leapt it with ease. Lyndsay stood still, watching. All eyes were fixed on an old, crumbling structure in the corner of the field. It was perhaps an old cow byre or stable. Bart's voice rose, calling to the hounds, who immediately obeyed him. They stood like gun dogs, quivering.

"In there," a voice breathed.

"Yes. We've got 'em now," somebody else said.

"Aye. The chase is done."

"The kill, the kill," a woman shouted shrilly.

"Go on, flush 'em out," another man said.

"Wait," Bart shouted.

There was a moment's terrible silence, then the hounds began to growl. Their hackles rose. They strained forward, rubbing against each other. One, its white teeth flashing, snapped at another of the animals. Part of the crowd began to move again, to form into a double line, torches held aloft. A path of light, of human bodies moved toward the byre. Lyndsay was aware of the others pressed around her. Slowly, she understood that the crowd had divided itself according to sex. Those who strode forward, carrying the torches, were all men. The figures pressed around her, touching her, were women.

One by one the men stopped. They formed two sides of a triangle, the apex of which was the old byre. At its base Bart Poole stood alone, except for the seething mass of dogs whose whines and sharp, anxious barks were like some unearthly musical accompaniment to these awful preparations. Lyndsay twisted and turned among the women, trying to read their faces, to find help. They seemed indifferent to her. Their eyes were fixed on the scene ahead. She pushed free of them and ran toward Bart. The hounds frightened her for a moment, but then she felt certain that they would not harm her. She forced a path through them, pushing their heaving flanks aside with her knees.

"Bart," she said.

He put out his arm to bar her way. She clung to it, the dogs pressing against her, pushing her. Ahead, at the end of the man-made tunnel of light, she saw one man draw back his arm and fling his flaming torch high into the air. It rose, turned over, sank down, and landed among the old, dry timbers of the byre. She felt sick. Gripping Bart's arm, she watched, heard the sharp crackle as the fire caught. In a moment, the byre had begun to glow.

Bart's arm dropped to his side, causing her to stumble forward. As she righted herself, she saw that she was in the avenue of flickering torchlights, ahead of Bart and the restless hounds. She looked at the man nearest to her, but his face was turned toward the byre. A shower of sparks rose into the air and smoke billowed in a great, swirling cloud, masking everything for a moment. As it cleared, she saw Magdalena Berryman silhouetted against the flaming building. She held her baby in one arm and clutched Bella to her with the other. Behind Lyndsay, the hounds set up their eerie, infernal baying.

She understood.

"No," Lyndsay screamed. She whirled around, her hands held out to Bart. He stood straight and immobile, staring at Magdalena. "Bart, no. No, you mustn't. All of you . . ." Her voice was drowned by the sound of the hounds. She knew it was useless. Smoke stung her eyes and choked her lungs. Lyndsay began to run toward Magdalena Berryman and her children, who had begun to walk slowly forward. Magdalena's face was set and calm and beautiful in the light.

"No," she said. "You mustn't. Stay with me. Listen . . ."

Magdalena brushed her aside. Her wide gray eyes were fixed ahead, on Bart.

"I am the Mistress," Lyndsay screamed, turning, snatching at her.

Magdalena suddenly opened her arms. With a cry, the baby fell to the ground and rolled over and over, bawling with fear and surprise. Abandoned, Bella screamed for her mother.

To Bart it seemed, as he released the hounds, that Magdalena opened her arms to him, held them out in the offered embrace she had denied him all those years. He closed his eyes tight as the lead hound, the biggest and strongest, leapt.

To Lyndsay it seemed that Magdalena's outspread, imploring

arms meant to embrace the hound and her own death. The force of the impact knocked her down. Lyndsay saw, and knew that she would always see, the hound's great jaws fasten on Magdalena's throat. The other hounds came racing on. She screamed, adding her voice to those of the baby and Bella. The baby! She had to find the baby. Crawling and sobbing, she searched the ground. The hounds flowed all around her. She was knocked flat. For a moment her stomach heaved as one of the hounds paused, sniffing at her. She was overwhelmed by its rank breath, chill and damp, smelling of long-forgotten, rotting earth. Suddenly it moved on. It was impossible now to tell the human screams from the joyful baying of the hounds. Lyndsay managed to raise herself to her knees. She was weeping. Her vision was blurred by the smoke and her tears.

Everything seemed to be in confusion now. The dogs barked and worried at something on the ground. The air was full of the encouraging cries of huntsmen, of burning, crackling timbers, of the hounds baying. Lyndsay managed to get to her feet. Swaying, she watched helpless, utterly broken, as two of the hounds found a small bundle on the ground. They seized it. She could not turn away or close her eyes. For a ghastly moment, they pulled it between them, fighting over it. It was the baby. One dog won the obscene tussle. Shaking its great head, it hurled the lifeless bundle into the air. As it fell, broken and bloodstained, six or seven hounds jumped, snarling, upon it. From the melee, one hound emerged, dragging something white. It ran toward her. She recognized the baby's shawl, stained with blood. Mindlessly, the dog, thrashing his tail, played with the shawl, barking at it, worrying it, running from it.

Lyndsay clasped her arms around herself and stumbled away from the hound. She heard her own voice, moaning in protest and pain at this terrible, meaningless slaughter. She felt nothing, or felt so much that it carried her beyond ordinary feelings. She stood still, numbed into a sort of living death, a paralysis of pain.

The sounds continued around her. She smelled the smoke and tasted her own bitter tears. A whistle rose above the noise. Once, twice, three times. A shrill, piercing whistle. The hounds, silent, fleet, brushed past her, making her shake with fear and disgust. She raised her head and watched. They moved silently away, were, for a moment, lost to sight in the dense shadows below the ridge. Then she saw them, a moving, moon-silvered mass, rising up the slope of the ridge. She strained her eyes, trying to follow them to the very last moment, but they seemed suddenly to shiver, dazzle, and then to disappear.

Slowly, she became aware of movement in the stillness around her. A last timber crashed to the earth behind her, shooting sparks high into the night air. Flames rose for a moment, illuminating the field, and then died down again. She was the center of a torch-lit circle. They had formed up, men and women alike, to surround her. Panic seized her, making her limbs twitch uncontrollably. It was her turn now. They were going to kill her, for having defied them. This, then, was what it meant to be the Mistress. She tried to resist the thought, but she knew what she had shouted to Magdalena Berryman in her last seconds of life. She had named herself and now she knew what it meant to be the Mistress.

The Mistress was a sacrifice.

Bart. The thought of him pierced her. She was the last Mistress. He had said so. The end of the line. Her death was required, too.

It did not matter. Panic ebbed from her, leaving her calm and strangely strong. She straightened herself, raised her head, and brushed her hair back out of her face. After what she had just seen, there was nothing to be feared. They had taken her, chosen her, and pushed her to the very limits of human endurance. There had been Michael's death and his betrayal. The first of a chain which led to her death. She did not understand why. It no longer mattered. She saw the little boy, dead. His mother, dead. Bella and the poor baby, Dead.

She had known it all along. The source of her fear was clear now. It *was* in her mind. It had been planted there the moment she had first seen Bart Poole advancing toward her, his hands and arms running with blood. She had known then that he was going to kill her, that he was her death. She had seen, in that moment, the shadow of her death, and had been unable to face it.

She lifted her head. The crowd surrounding her parted a little to let Bart through. He held his arms, bent at the elbow, in front of him. The guttering torches showed them red and slick with blood. It was happening again, just as it had happened before, only this time he did not carry a knife. The blood was not pig's blood, but human. She tilted her head back to meet him, offering her collared throat to his bloody hands.

Their eyes met. Hers were wild and hurt. His, somber, golden, regarded her with infinite tenderness. She could tell him now, in this long-as-life moment. She could tell him and save herself. But she would not. Let him do his worst. She chose freely to take her secret knowledge with her. That way, he would be proved wrong. Let him learn afterward, she prayed, and be hurt as much and as terribly as I am hurt.

She did not flinch or close her eyes as, slowly, he reached out his stained hands toward her. She stiffened her body and looked deep, deep into his eyes. I love him, she thought, as he gently cupped her face in his hands. The warm, sticky blood was transferred from his hands to her cheeks. He pressed her face hard. His breath hissed between his teeth. She waited, accepting. He moved one hand to her forehead and traced a smeared line of blood along it.

His hands fell from her face. He dropped to one knee, his black, silky head bent. He caught hold of her hand and raised it to his lips.

"Mistress," he murmured. And kissed her hand.

She stared down at his head and knew that, in spite of all that had happened, she would have done anything he wanted of her. His obeisance, capitulation, whatever it was, was worse than all that had gone before. She felt his lips, dry and harsh on her hand, and saw that she had not understood at all. Impulsively, she clasped her free hand to her stomach. She wanted to kneel with him or to raise him, acknowledge his power over her. He dropped her hand, stood up, and moved quickly aside. Trembling, Lyndsay forced herself not to call out, or try to follow him.

A man in the circle surrounding her lowered his torch, extinguished its flame by grinding it into the earth. He walked forward, knelt on one knee, took her hand and said:

"Mistress."

One by one they came to her, spectral figures in the spreading darkness as the torches were put out. One by one they came to her, those she knew by name and those who were yet strangers. They came, knelt, took her hand, and named her. Penelope Clare and Cloris Poole, Patrick, with sad, haunted eyes. Everyone, except the old woman, except Mother Poole.

It was a long, long time before Lyndsay noticed that she was alone. They had gone, melted away like the hounds, into the night. Only it was no longer night, she realized, lifting her head. The damp, chill of dawn was all around her. She looked at the sky. Light, gray as ash, crept across it. Big storm clouds formed in the first wash of light. Looking down at herself she saw that her robe was torn. With her hand, she felt the dried streaks of blood on her cheeks and forehead. She stared around her. The field was empty. The face of the ridge still lay in darkness. Getting up, she walked to the smoldering remains of the byre. The smell of charred wood lingered in the air. Everything was still, tense, as though the earth itself were waiting for an explosion, a holocaust.

It had not been a dream. She had been a part of it. Of murder, she thought. She turned her back on the burned byre, that last pitiful refuge of Magdalena Berryman and her children. She turned her back on it, dry-eyed; she who had laughed at curses; she who was the Mistress.

There was no sign of the bodies. As the light increased, she scoured the field for any remains. Gone. All of them, everything, gone. Like the hounds. Like birds home to roost. She walked on, her feet and the ragged hem of her robe became wet with dew. She climbed the stile and walked toward the Berrymans' house. Light flashed suddenly across the ridge. She turned toward it. Thunder rumbled, rolled around the sky. She trudged on, tired now. Lightning danced across, hurting her eyes, striking the trees ahead, bringing the field into sharp, fluorescent relief. The thunder cracked, bursting against her ears. It was all over now, she thought. The heavens would rage and storm in answer to the power she had seen at work and felt for herself. Compared to that, the elements possessed no terrors.

The next flash of lightning showed her the black, waiting figure. It stood at the edge of the field, near the Berrymans' deserted house. It waited for her. She did not increase her pace. The next clap of thunder brought a sudden sharp gust of wind which seemed to take her breath away. The open door of Magdalena Berryman's house swung on its hinges, banged, swung open again. The gate, too, was caught by the wind. It creaked in protest as it swung back and forth, as though letting ghosts in. The clouds massed, ready to unleash their burden of rain. Lyndsay walked on, listening to the empty banging of the door, the creaking gate. The increasingly frequent flashes of light illumined the implacably waiting figure. Tall and straight, without expression, it was the figure of Death itself. Death, the reaper, come to gather his rightful harvest. Or rather hers, Lyndsay thought. Death, like luck, the earth itself, was a woman, and against that omnipotent sisterhood no one could prevail.

It was as though she had needed the exceptional, magnificent light in order to see and understand. She stopped short of the waiting woman, whose features faded as the lightning died away.

"Mother," she said.

The old woman opened her arms. The great loose sleeves of her black robe were like wings. The wind caught at them, made them flap. Lyndsay ran the last few feet into her arms. Mother Poole enfolded her daughter, the Mistress, in her arms, hugging her.

"I understand now," Lyndsay said. "I understand."

The old woman patted her back consolingly.

"Come," she said softly. "We must hurry from the storm."

"It will break my heart. I thought, out there, last night, that I had reached the end of suffering, but now I know that it's only just beginning. Will you help me, Mother?"

"Always," she promised.

"It will break my heart," Lyndsay repeated.

"Aye. But it will mend. There are always consolations."

They moved off, their robes tugged by the wind. Mother Poole's strong, sustaining arm lay across Lyndsay's shoulders, supporting and warming her.

"I killed them, too."

"You could not stop him. But you will."

"No," Lyndsay said, her heart flinching.

"Even though it breaks your heart," the old woman reminded her.

Lyndsay began to cry then, leaning against Mother Poole, who led her into the village, lashed by rain and wind. In a matter of minutes they were both soaked to the skin. They clung together, their robes sculpted to their bodies, against the force of the wind.

Lyndsay stopped and turned her ravaged face to Mother Poole.

"Was it really necessary?" she asked. "Magdalena and her children? Did that really have to happen?"

"Aye. It was necessary. And there was nothing you could do to stop it." Mother Poole looked away from her, looked up at the black and raging sky. The rain—not tears—stung her face, ran in rivulets down her old, creased skin. "But she will have her revenge," she said softly. It was a promise to Lyndsay. "Through you, Mistress, she and her poor babes, all the poor babes, will rest."

Lyndsay nodded. Bart had been right. When the time came to choose, there was no choice. She bowed her head and let the old lady lead her on, accepting.

CHAPTER
ELEVEN

A small pulse of light scratched the erratic rhythm of a heartbeat on a miniature television screen. Stuart Donne watched it wearily. It was the only sign of life. Without it, anyone might think that the person in the bed, his father, was dead. But as long as the frail pulse continued there was hope. He rubbed his eyes. It was already light. Soon his mother would come to relieve him.

There was no question in either of their minds that this second heart attack had been brought on by stress, by growing worry about Kenneth. Stuart had been so confident when he set off to find him. His empty-handed return had only made matters worse, but what else could he do? The local police had been more affable than those in Ketterford, but the same argument had prevailed. Kenneth was an adult. If he chose to go off somewhere by himself, not to communicate with his family, there was really nothing they could do. Of course, if there was the slightest suspicion of foul play . . . Stuart had moistened his lips, preparatory to telling them. But what could he tell them? That he didn't like Ratchets? That there was something about the place that made him feel uneasy?

He had not told the police, just as he had not told his parents. In the latter case, he wanted to avoid alarming them. In the former he knew that it would be useless. Groundless suspicion, mere "feelings." It was madness. In their shoes he would not have taken any notice either.

Now, with the cooperation of the doctors, an S.O.S. call would be broadcast by the BBC. Perhaps that would work. Perhaps, if he heard it, Kenneth would be reminded of his filial responsibilities. But Stuart could not believe that he had ever forgotten them. They were a close family. Kenneth knew not only that they would worry about him but that they were all interested in what he was doing. Perhaps too interested. Lately Stuart had been forced to consider this. Had his parents been quick enough to recognize Kenneth's independence? Maybe this silence was a gesture, asserting his right to an adult life of his own. In their eyes, he was still the little boy, the favorite.

A young staff nurse came into the room and, smiling at Stuart, took his father's pulse.

"There's a cup of tea outside," she whispered. "You look as though you could do with one."

"Thank you," Stuart said and got up, stretching his limbs.

Outside, in the still dimly lit corridor, he claimed a cup of tea from an elderly woman patient who wheeled the early morning trolley. Gently, she inquired after his father.

"It's always a good sign if they have a quiet night. Try not to worry, love."

"I won't," he lied and drifted off to a seat in the corridor. All around him the hospital was waking up, the day's routine beginning. He sipped his tea.

He would wait for his mother and tell her what he had decided. It was nothing much, he thought, and he must be careful not to raise her hopes. But anything, no matter how slight the chance of success, was better than this helpless, endless waiting. It might help his father, too, to know that he had returned to the search.

He had telephoned Kenneth's college yesterday and ascertained that his tutor, Daniel Carr, was back from his holiday. He had also obtained Carr's phone number. Just possibly he might know something, some scrap of information which might indicate a change of plan, a new tack. And if not? Anyway, Carr had agreed to see him. He stared bleakly into his cup. Instinct prompted him to go to Ratchets again. He could make more determined inquiries. But he would only mention Cambridge to his mother.

The hospital allowed him to use a little bathroom at the end of the corridor. There he washed his face in cold water and shaved with an electric razor. His eyes felt raw and tired, but he was determined to set off straightaway. He could catch up on his sleep when he'd seen Carr.

Promptly at eight his mother arrived. He told her how the night

243

had passed. She nodded. The worry lines seemed permanently etched into her skin now, scoring her forehead, the corners of her mouth.

"I've decided to go to Cambridge, Mother. Kenneth's tutor is back from his holiday. I spoke to him briefly yesterday. He will see me. He might know something."

"What?" she asked, raising her blank eyes to his face.

"I don't know," he said. "I just . . . You'll be all right. I'll only be gone a day at the most. I'll telephone."

He could see that she did not want him to go, that she needed him. He wavered for a moment.

"Oh well, if you think it will do any good," she said. "But shouldn't you wait to see what happens when they broadcast the S.O.S.?"

"What difference will it make? If he hears it, he'll be here before me."

"Well, if you're so set on going," she said, turning toward the little room where his father lay.

"I think anything is worth a try," he said, and stooped to kiss her cheek. Tears filled her eyes. She pressed his hand.

"You will be careful?" she said.

"Of course. And I'll telephone. This evening at the very latest." She managed a quivering smile.

"Go on then, and do drive carefully. You've had no sleep."

Outside the morning was not yet hot, but the clear, familiarly empty sky promised that it would be. He was tired of the heat, this long, dry, un-English summer. He walked slowly to his car and got in, opening the windows. He did not set off immediately, but filled and lit his pipe. As he smoked, he tried for the hundredth time to understand what it was about Ratchets that bothered him. There must be some rational explanation beyond the fact that the trail went cold there, but if there was, he soon admitted, he could not put his finger on it. He tapped out his pipe and started the car.

Cloris Poole let herself quietly into the chancel. Pulling her shawl from her dark head, she shook it vigorously. Raindrops spattered onto the flagstones. It was cold in the chancel. Looking around its gray, unadorned interior, she shivered. Then she walked toward the altar.

"Bart?" she called. "Are you down there?" She waited, but there was no reply. As far as her ears could tell there was no sound at all. "It's me, Cloris. I'm coming down, all right?"

Her footsteps echoed in the little anteroom behind the altar. One hand pressed against the rough stone to steady herself, Cloris descended the dark steps. It seemed even colder as she went farther down. At the foot of the stairs she peered nervously into the gloom.

"Bart?"

She heard a noise, but it came from behind the big door on the opposite side of the room. Her hands held out in front of her, she groped her way to the narrow cot. She felt his warmth beneath the rough blanket, heard his steady breathing.

"Bart? Are you awake?"

He sighed.

"What do you want?"

"Oh thank goodness," she said, pressing her hand to her heart with relief. "I thought you'd taken ill or something."

He said nothing, but she heard him move, turn over.

"Where's the lamp?" she asked, leaning against the bed and searching for it.

"Go away," he said.

She acted as though she had not heard him. Her fingers traced the outline of the lamp. Resting one hand on the chimney, she searched the floor for matches.

"Ah," she muttered. "Here they are."

She struck a match, removed the glass chimney, and lit the lamp. As the flame steadied, she straightened up and looked at him. He was unshaven, and beneath the rough black stubble his skin was sickly pale.

"What's wrong?" she asked, reaching out to feel his forehead. He jerked his head away from her, as though her touch were unclean. Cloris sucked in her breath sharply. "What's the matter with you?" she asked fiercely.

"Nothing," he said. "What do you want?"

"What should I want?" she answered. "Bart, it's been almost two days. Do you realize?" She leaned over him. Her face was pale with worry but her eyes were angry. "And longer," she added reproachfully, "since I've seen you."

"I'm fine." He closed his eyes.

She watched him for a while, wondering what to do.

"Shall I get in with you?" she asked.

He opened his eyes and saw her hands move eagerly to her sweater, ready to pull it off.

"No," he said sharply, and hitched the blanket up over him, as though to protect himself from her.

He looked at her, Cloris thought, as though he did not remember what had been between them.

"It's her," she sighed, "isn't it?" Out of years of habit, she pushed his legs aside and sat down on the bed. "I knew it was, but I had to come and see for myself."

"You've seen me now," he said tiredly. "You can go."

"Thanks very much," she said. "And what about the rest of them? What are they to think?"

"They can think what they like."

"I'll tell you what they think. They think that you've lost your nerve. They think that you've overreached yourself, just as the old woman said you would. They'll turn to the Mistress."

"Well, they'll be proved wrong," he said. His voice showed no interest. Like an old, sick man he rolled onto his side, away from the light.

"You're giving up then, are you? You're going to throw it all away?"

"Leave me alone. I'm tired."

"Tired? You? No." She shook her head. "It was all for her, wasn't it? All bravado. You tried to frighten her into . . . what? What did you want? You must have known that even if she cared for you, you couldn't have her. You must have been mad," she said, her voice trembling. "And you dragged us all . . ."

He sat up slowly. His face twitched as though with some nervous, muscular spasm he could not control. Only his eyes, blazing with anger, remained unchanged.

"Get out of here," he said, his voice full of loathing. "Get out of here before I kill you."

Staring at him, open-mouthed, she knew that he meant it. She shook her head once, almost to deny it, but she stood up, pulling the shawl around her.

"And don't come back," he said, flopping back onto the single, uncovered pillow.

"No," she said. "I won't. It's all over then. I must shift for myself now." Tears stung her eyes. Embarrassed, she dabbed at them with the corner of her shawl. Her teeth chattered. "What about me?" she whispered. "What am I to do now?"

He stared at the vaulted ceiling where her shadow danced.

"All right, I'm going," she said. "What shall I tell them?"

"Nothing."

"You'll lose everything," she said.

He smiled. He heard her fighting to control her breathing, her longing to weep and plead. After a long time her shadow wavered and faded. She said something else to him, but he didn't listen.

He could alter it in his mind. He could make it different. He could see it. So clearly. He, not the hound, ran toward her. She ran toward him. Her face so pale, so beautiful, so still. And then, then he felt her arms so tight about him. Those frail-looking arms. So white her skin. They belied her strength. Such strength. He held her, her body of bones, swung her up against the summer sky. She steadied herself by holding on to his shoulders. Her pale hair fell forward. She laughed wonderfully down into his face and he said, relishing each perfect syllable:

"Mag-da-le-na."

But she became a shadow, slipped away from him when the chancel doors banged shut. The booming sound echoed above him, reminding him that everything was empty and cold. He huddled under the blanket, trying to sleep, to find her again.

Daniel Carr lived on the outskirts of Cambridge, in a large, ramshackle house with an untidy garden. The door was opened by a child of indeterminate sex—at least to Stuart's unpracticed eye— who immediately ran off, shouting for its mother. Stuart Donne felt embarrassed, abandoned on the doorstep. After what seemed an age, a large woman in a shapeless, vaguely Eastern garment, came slowly down the corridor, wiping her hands on a scrap of towel.

"Yes?" she said vaguely.

"Mrs. Carr? My name is Donne. I telephoned your husband."

She looked impassively at his outstretched hand. Blushing, Stuart withdrew it.

"You've got an appointment," she said. "Is that it?"

"Yes. Well no. Not exactly. Your husband said it would be all right to come over. I telephoned," he repeated.

"I didn't hear. It's the kids. They make so much noise. Half the time I don't hear it. Dan thinks I just don't answer it but it's not that. You'd better come in." She turned away. Stuart followed her, wiping his feet and shutting the door, though he felt certain that she would not have noticed if he had failed to do both. She went into a large room full of children and shabby furniture. There were open, half-unpacked suitcases on the floor. Two children were fighting noisily and, Stuart thought, viciously, over some board game on the floor. Another sat cross-legged in front of a blaring television set. A fourth, male and older, sprawled on a settee, a pair of headphones clamped to his ears. He regarded Stuart coldly.

"Where's Daddy?" the woman shouted.

"Mummy, Tina won't let me have . . ."

"Dominic, turn the telly down, darling, *please.*"

"Mummy, it's her. She took my . . ."

"I said turn it *down*, Dominic, not *up.*"

Stuart, standing awkwardly just inside the room, looked through the open French windows. A slight, bespectacled man was standing on the dried-up lawn, apparently lost in contemplation.

Stuart cleared his throat.

"Er . . . is that Mr. Carr?" he shouted.

The woman looked at him as though she had completely forgotten him. He repeated the question, pointing to the garden.

"Oh yes." She picked her way sedately through the clutter. Stuart followed, murmuring apologies to the children as he passed. "Dan," she called. "Someone to see you."

"It's terrible," he said. "Everything's died. We should have got someone in to water at least. All those pansies we put in. They've all died. It's the drought I suppose."

"They weren't pansies," Mrs. Carr said, drifting serenely back into the chaos of the room. "They were violas. They don't have faces." Her voice wafted after Stuart as he stepped into the garden.

"Mr. Carr?"

"Yes." The man blinked, pushed his glasses up onto the bridge of his nose.

"My name's Donne. Stuart Donne. I rang you about my brother, Kenneth."

"Ah. Yes. Of course. That's right." Carr regarded him blankly. "You said you'd drop by."

"Yes."

"That's right. Well . . ."

"I explained to you about Kenneth. How he seems to have disappeared?"

"That's right. Yes. So you did. I say, do you mind taking a turn round the old garden? It's a bit noisy inside."

"No. Not at all," Stuart said with relief. "I'm sorry to bother you."

"Not at all. It's a very puzzling business."

"I hope that you might be able to help me clear it up," Stuart said, falling into step beside Carr, who morosely regarded the dried-up garden.

"Only wish I could."

"Well." Stuart took a deep breath. "As I told you, he got as far as Ketterford, which is the nearest place of any size to Ratchets. He told you he was going there?"

"He sent me a card. I picked it up at the college yesterday."

"Where from?"

"Ketterford. But it didn't say anything. Just a couple of lines. Good trip. Have a good vacation. That sort of thing."

"I see." Stuart's voice betrayed his disappointment. Carr stopped and looked at him intently.

"You're really worried."

"Yes," Stuart agreed. "I am."

"How can I help?"

"I don't know. I have a feeling—it really is only a hunch, I suppose one would call it—that he did go to Ratchets. He had high hopes of the place, according to the letter he wrote me about the trip." Carr nodded. "I went there, of course, but nobody knows anything about him. I wondered if you had any idea what he was looking for, what he expected to find there? It might . . . help."

"Mm. Look. Sorry. Do you mind if we go inside after all? I've got some notes in my study. Better have a look at them."

"Thank you."

The study was dark and dusty, but relatively quiet. Carr sorted vaguely through his untidy desk.

"Oh yes. Perhaps you'd better have this." He tossed a flat, brown paper package in the general direction of Stuart.

"Thank you," he said automatically, picking it up. It was addressed to Kenneth. "I don't understand," he said.

"I went down to the college after we spoke yesterday. No one's seen him. He hasn't been back there. Anyway, that had just arrived for him, so I took it. I thought, you know, you could give it to him or . . . ."

"Thank you," Stuart said quickly. He turned the parcel over.

"Now then." Carr settled himself in an ancient swivel chair that squeaked at even the slightest movement. He held a manila folder in his hands. "His itinerary. A few notes. You understand," he said, peering at Stuart over his spectacles, "that I only had to rubber stamp this trip? I saw no reason to go into it thoroughly. Kenneth's very reliable, and in postgraduate work . . . ."

"Quite. I understand."

"Wish that I had asked a bit more now." He poured over the notes again. "Mm," he said after a while. "This thing about Ratchets. Apparently, it was an entirely etymological guess on his part. The Gabriel Ratchets, you see. An old legend. Quite widespread in those parts and he thought that a village so named . . . He checked on the history of the place . . . Heaven knows how. Anyway, he was pretty certain there was some valid stuff to be dug up there."

"Have you any idea what kind of 'stuff'?"

"Pagan, undoubtedly. Totem animals. Possibly fertility cults. That sort of thing. Kenneth was writing his thesis on surviving traces of such things in present-day society. The idea is to—"

"Yes," Stuart interrupted. "I know. He talked to me quite a lot about it. Do you think he could have found anything like that?"

Carr shrugged.

"Who knows? I had doubts. I admit it. Said as much to him. But then, you see, it's my job to be skeptical. I believe in letting my students find out for themselves." Carr let the folder drop onto the desk. "What do you think has happened?" he asked directly.

"I . . . honestly don't know. It's just completely out of character for Kenneth not to keep in touch. Especially as my father had been ill."

"Girl friend?"

"Not that I or my parents know about."

"Nor me. And I asked around. Nothing serious anyway."

"I just feel that something is preventing him getting in touch."

"You've spoken to the police?"

"Yes. They can't or won't do anything. Except now that my father is ill again, we are putting out an S.O.S."

"Really? Well . . . If there's anything I can do . . . ."

"Thank you." Stuart stood up. "I'll keep you informed."

"And needless to say, if I should hear from him . . . I'll give him a rocket. Full blast." Carr smiled.

Stuart nodded. "And thank you for this." He held up the parcel.

"Not at all. Anyway, I wish you luck."

They shook hands. Carr obviously did not know what else to say. As they went out into the hall a horde—or so it seemed to Stuart— of children descended upon Carr, clamoring for his attention.

"I can see myself out," Stuart said. "Thank you again."

"Not at all," Carr shouted.

Stuart let himself out of the noisy, untidy house, feeling, despite his deliberately controlled expectations, thoroughly let down. And tired, he thought, tossing the parcel onto the passenger seat and starting the car. He must check into a hotel and get some sleep. When he felt fresher, perhaps he would be able to think of something else to do.

Lyndsay had woken briefly in the dark. The rain was still falling, rattling against the tiny windows of Mother Poole's cottage. At the old lady's insistence and with the aid of her pills, she had slept again. When she woke for the second time, it was just light. Water dripped mournfully from the eaves. Instead of a dressing gown, Lyndsay put on the black robe and opened the window. She saw Ratchets then as Penelope and others had described it to her. The thick, damp air seemed choking. The trees dripped like sad fountains. The street ran with water and the sky seemed to press close, imprisoning the village. She shivered and closed the window.

She rubbed her arms to warm them. It seemed as though the whole village had withdrawn into itself. In shame, she thought, or out of guilt. Were they guilty though? Yes, insofar as they had allowed it to happen. But she too had played her part and could not now pretend otherwise. It was up to her to stop it. She was surprised at her own determination. But perhaps—she glanced quickly out the window again—perhaps the villagers were simply biding their time, waiting to see what would happen next. She smoothed her hair back. It was time to do some straight talking, she thought. No more riddles, no more half-truths. Mother Poole would not evade her now. She went down the steep, creaking stairs and pushed open the door of the living room. The old dog waddled forward to greet her, thumping his tail. Mother Poole was kneeling before the fire, blowing on a pale flame. Stiffly, with a wince of pain, she tried to get to her feet. Lyndsay went to help her.

"It's the damp," she explained, panting a little. "It's disaster for my joints." Lyndsay glanced at her strangely. "What is it?"

"Oh . . . nothing," Lyndsay smiled. "It's just that someone else, Mrs. Abernathy—you remember, I told you about her, the woman on the plane?—she said exactly the same thing. That's all."

Mother Poole drew away from her.

"I'll make the tea," she said, lifting cups and saucers down from the dresser.

"Do you have any coffee?" Lyndsay asked.

"Acorn coffee, aye."

"No. Thank you. Tea'll be fine." Lyndsay sat down and held out her hands to the fire. Mother Poole continued with her preparations.

"Mother," Lyndsay began, "I've got to have a serious talk with you."

"Aye."

"Something has to be done about what happened the other night."

The old woman carried a teapot to the range and tipped a little water into it from the singing kettle. She held it in her crooked hands, swirling the water round.

"I know your ways are different from mine," Lyndsay went on, "but I think, well, the only way to clear this up, once and for all, is to send for the police." She watched the old woman's face carefully but it remained impassive.

Mother Poole took down an old tea caddy and opened it.

"I'd be interested to know what you think you'd say to them."

"Why, I . . . we must tell them everything."

"Everything?"

"We were accessories to a murder out there."

"We?" the old lady cut in sharply. "*You* were, Mistress. Not me."

Lyndsay felt her mouth go dry. It was true, she remembered. Mother Poole had not been there. At least, she hadn't seen her. She took a deep breath.

"Okay. But you knew it was going to happen."

"Did I?" She picked up the kettle from the fire with an old pot-holder and made the tea. "And how will you prove that, or any of it? How will you convince the police that this murder ever happened?"

252

"Well, heaven knows there were enough witnesses. The whole village was out there watching."

"And not one of them will remember it."

"Okay. So there's just me. And the bodies."

"What bodies? Where will you find them?"

"I don't know. But they must be somewhere."

"They'll never find them," the old woman said with absolute certainty.

"In other words," Lyndsay said in exasperation, "you won't help me. On the contrary, you'll block me every step of the way."

"Don't jump to conclusions," Mother Poole said haughtily. "I just want you to understand what you're saying and what will happen."

"There's still the little boy."

"But everyone knows that was an accident. It will have been reported and seen to."

"But was it?" Lyndsay asked.

"That you'll have to ask Bart."

"Then there's the dogs, those hounds. Where does he keep them?" Mother Poole banged the teapot down and looked at her with a mingled expression of annoyance and disbelief. "All right. You won't tell me. But they'll find them. A pack of dogs that size can't just disappear."

Mother Poole laughed suddenly, her old body shaking with amusement.

"I don't see what's so funny," Lyndsay said. "Look, if we don't do something about this, don't you think Timon Berryman will?" At the sound of his name, Mother Poole laughed louder. "Stop it," Lyndsay said. "Please, stop it."

Slowly the old woman got control of herself. Chuckling, she pushed a cup of tea along the table toward Lyndsay. "You promised to help me," Lyndsay said.

"Aye. But that was when you talked sense. That was when you spoke like the Mistress."

"What do you mean?" Lyndsay asked, feeling afraid.

With difficulty, Mother Poole sat in her armchair.

"Hand me my cup," she said. Lyndsay obeyed. "I've listened to you, now you hear me," she said. "You can check every word I say for yourself. You can go out there this morning and search wherever you like. Every door will be open to you, but you won't find any bodies or any graves. You won't find a kennel full of hounds. You won't find one person to stand with you. In fact they'd probably kill you if they knew what was in your mind. They are looking to you now to do your duty. The women demand it and the men . . . well, you must hit 'em while they're down."

Lyndsay drank some tea, considering. It felt as though everything were closing in on her again and she was determined to resist it. "These hounds," she said. "Are you trying to tell me they aren't the ones you all used to hunt down Maddy and Timon all those years ago?"

"They weren't," she said promptly. "Those were ordinary village dogs. There's one of them sitting at your feet right now," she said.

Lyndsay looked down at the old dog, so peaceful and still. She felt a shudder of revulsion.

"You know as well as I do," Mother Poole went on, "that the hounds he set on Magdalena Clare were the Gabriel Ratchets. The Gabriel Hounds. You can find them easy enough. You know where they are."

"The children's graveyard," she said. "But that's impossible." Her voice lacked conviction and she knew that the old woman heard it.

"It's always been written," she said, "that they would be raised. And when they were, that the Mistress shall release them, once and for all. It makes little difference in the end whether you choose to believe it or not. But this you must believe. If you bring in the police, it will be the same as handing this village and all in it to Bart and his lackeys." She spat out his name as though it disgusted her.

Lyndsay looked at her. She did not want to believe it, but she felt herself unable to argue.

"You felt his power for yourself," Mother Poole said softly. "That you won't deny."

"But it's only . . ." She stopped, confused. She had felt it but she could not say, could not actually assert what it was or where it came from.

"There is only one way to fight a power like that."

"How?"

"With an equal, an even greater power."

"I don't have that."

"You won't let yourself have it. You won't trust."

"In what? You? Magic?"

"Ha," the old woman snorted. "You don't know what you're say-ing. Magic, indeed! Oh Bart would like to hear you say that." She leaned forward suddenly, her face intent, her eyes glowing. "It's real. A real power. A power that the world has forgotten. The Mother Earth. In olden times that power was respected and used. Here in Ratchets we've never lost touch with it. We have lived close to the land and served her. So it will always be." She sat back. Her face looked tired. "But like all power, it can be used for good or evil. And time, time," she said wearily, "is running out."

"Please," Lyndsay said. "Make me understand."

The old woman's eyes were closed.

"Out there," she said flatly, "when I came to fetch you in, you understood then. Remember what you felt then."

Lyndsay tried. She remembered the cold, the flickering lightning, the stillness before the storm. And a feeling of rage and fear, a certainty that the world was out of kilter and she could put it right again.

"It was the women," she said with difficulty. "I felt that I was a part of them, like a sister. Magdalena's sufferings were mine. I had shared them and carried the sorrow they left behind."

"Yes," Mother Poole said quietly. "And what else."

"That I could stop it. Somehow, I felt this great, terrible burden of sadness, like the whole world was in pain. Maddy and her kids were only a part of it."

"The earth's pain. Centuries of suffering," the old woman intoned. "And who was responsible?"

"Bart. The hounds. No. Bart. But all of them . . . the men," she said, hearing her own voice as though it belonged to someone else. "And if I didn't stop it . . . it would destroy me." Mother Poole nodded. "But why me?" Lyndsay asked.

Slowly, Mother Poole seemed to regain her energy. She held out her cup to Lyndsay.

"Pour me another cup while I tell you," she said. Lyndsay took the cup from her hand and refilled it. "Ever since the great quarrel I told you about, there has been a danger of this happening. During the bleak time, the women sought comfort in the old legend, as I told you. Ezekiel Dolben, the peacemaker, saw the possibility of using the power for himself, though. He gave the Mistress a Priest, supposedly to keep the Clares happy. The idea was to balance the power, to share it. The Mistress balanced by the Priest and vice versa. But he intended more. He sought ways to seize the power. He knew that it was possible to raise the hounds. Fortunately, he died before he could do it. But he bequeathed us the danger, the possibility of a man taking the power. The Mistress, you see, maintains peace with the earth. She is the bearer and assuager of sorrows. But the men, they only want to pervert the power, to use it to kill and destroy.

"When we had no Mistress, the opportunity was created. Sometimes I think," she said wearily, "that they planned it all along, Albertine Clare and Bart. They were close. Too close, perhaps. She wanted him to be Priest, you see. She was the Mistress then, and Magdalena should have succeeded her. But it is forbidden for the Priest and the Mistress ever to marry."

Lyndsay felt cold suddenly. Her hand trembled, rattling the cup against the saucer. The old woman paused, watching her carefully.

"Please go on," Lyndsay said. "I'm listening."

"Anyhow, that was what Albertine wanted," she continued after a pause, during which her eyes had grown suspicious.

"She turned his head by making him Priest and deposing her daughter. She fed his ambitions. Then, when Maddy ran off, it turned her brain. She became so crazed with it, the shame, that she let the power slip away. She let Bart see and know more than was fitting. She encouraged him in things I'll not speak of. At the end he took advantage of her, the same as he's taken advantage of everyone. He probably helped her to die. No one knows for sure. She did away with herself, and he knew more about it than anyone. Still, that's all over now." She sighed and relapsed into silence for a time.

"Who was the Mistress after her?" Lyndsay asked.

"Emelye. But she was only a child. We traced the line—it's not easy. It goes according to the blood and the cycles of the earth. But there is no doubt that Emelye was the right and proper Mistress. But too young. She had to be a woman first. She would have been blooded and dedicated this summer, when the harvest was in. Aye, and married, too." A look of deep, almost unbearable sadness settled on her face. "But she . . ."

"I know," Lyndsay said, feeling ashamed. "Patrick told me about her and Michael."

"Ah," the old woman breathed, nodding her head. "Well then, you see . . . She could not be Mistress, having brought shame on herself and on her family. The Ways forbid it. So we had to trace the line again."

"And you got me?" Lyndsay said. "But there must be some mistake . . ."

"We got not you personally but the wife of the eldest Dolben boy. And then . . ." Her eyes became clouded, as though she were remembering something very strange and wonderful. "And then, after all those years, Michael came home and told us that he was married."

"Coincidence," Lyndsay said at once.

"I don't believe in coincidence. It was a sign. No sooner had we traced the line again than he appeared and told us of you."

"Is that what he was running from?" Lyndsay asked. "He wouldn't have wanted . . ."

"It didn't matter what he wanted. It was so," she said with cold authority. "But Bart saw his chance. He knew that when you came here, there would be the perfect conjunction of circumstance. He'd worked on the men, he used Emelye's shame . . . But there has to be a Mistress, you see, for him to get the power. But you were weak and unschooled. He seized his moment. You've seen for yourself."

"But why kill Maddy and her kids?" she asked.

"Because it was necessary. It all began with her. If she had not run off, shamed herself and the Clares, driven him half mad with bitterness, we should have held the balance. Magdalena Clare had to pay for the curse she brought on us. And her children. But now you can absolve them," she said fiercely.

"No," Lyndsay said. "I can't. I don't know how."

"You're a fool," Mother Poole said quietly. "Who has suffered more at the hands of men than you? Who hates all that you have seen and learned here more than you? Yet you set your face against us. You don't care if they murder and kill and slaughter . . ."

"That's not true. You know it isn't. It's just that I'm not sure . . . I don't know . . ."

"Michael Dolben used you. Bart's used you. Maddy nearly killed you. And still you say you don't know."

She shook her head. It was beyond her comprehension.

"I do hate it all. It's got to stop . . . but what you say is nonsense."

"Were the hounds nonsense? Was Maddy's death nonsense? Do you think Bart will stop at nonsense?"

"I don't know," she repeated miserably.

"You do. But your head's turned. The war in you, Mistress, is the war we're all fighting. You want peace and life. He stands in direct opposition to you and only you can stop him, but he fascinates you. Even you are weak, weak as only a woman can be."

"It's not as simple as that," Lyndsay said. "You don't know . . ."

"I know this much. You've felt the weight of sorrow in this place. You feel it now. You know its cause. Only the women can bring comfort to this place and placate the earth. Yet still you side with the men. Still, you give way to the old weakness."

"No," Lyndsay said.

"I'll tell you something," Mother Poole said, leaning forward and gripping her wrist tightly. "While you hesitate, Emelye's upstairs with Michael Dolben's baby in her belly and Bart's sworn to do away with it. You just think about that," she said, tossing Lyndsay's arm from her as though it burned.

Something snapped inside Lyndsay's head. She had known it, feared it, ever since she had seen the girl being sick that day in the pantry. She had refused to face it. Then, her anger had been directed at Emelye. Now a much stronger wave of hatred swept through her. It turned her heart to steel.

"I . . ." she began, but the old woman shook her head.

"Sh. Listen."

"What?"

There was a sudden, loud knock at the door.

Stuart Donne stretched out on his bed. It had not been easy to find a room in Cambridge, at the height of the season, especially since he lacked even the respectable minimum of luggage. He looked critically around the room he had finally managed to secure and found it wanting. But it was a place to sleep, he thought, and that was all that mattered. He turned over onto his side, preparing himself for sleep. He stared at the package Carr had given him. He must have thrown it onto the bed when he entered the room. He pulled it toward him. The postmark was a black smudge. It seemed wrong somehow to open it, like prying. But Kenneth would understand, he thought. And then he became afraid.

This pretense of a search, he realized with bitterness, blinded him to the certainty that Kenneth was beyond minding. There could be no other explanation and it was time that he faced the fact. His parents would have to face it, too. He sat up, no longer tired. He knew, and he forced himself to think it through properly, all the way through.

He knew that Kenneth was dead.

And that it would fall to him to sort out Kenneth's things, his personal effects. Compared to that, he told himself, opening his post was nothing.

He slipped the string and paper from the parcel and found himself holding a square, black notebook. He flipped through the pages, blank at the back, but covered with Kenneth's handwriting at the front. He opened it properly, read the neatly inscribed name and college address on the inside front cover. It was a diary of some sort, a record of his trip. Stuart sat up straighter on the bed and let his eyes run down the pages. Notes about Morris dancing. A stream-cleaning ritual in Northamptonshire. The notes were in a personal shorthand which meant little to him. He turned the pages over quickly. The notes were undated. He smiled involuntarily to see the words *Good ale*, heavily underscored at the bottom of one page. There followed a sketch of an inn sign and a group of corn dollies, with brief, elliptical descriptions. Then, right across the top of one page he read with intense excitement the single word: Ratchets.

So he had been there. But then Stuart had always known, without being able to explain how, that he had been there. Just as he knew with equal certainty that Kenneth was dead.

"Exhausted. Never knew manual labor was so tiring. Good for my social conscience if not for my aching bones. Have got a job for two weeks. Casual farm laborer. Can just imagine how that will amuse the family. Wonder if I shall last the two weeks? If this stiffness doesn't wear off . . . Must stop feeling sorry for myself. I'd give anything for a bath. I asked my landlady, Mrs. Dolben, who said I would have to wait until Friday. Priceless! And then in a tin bath in the back kitchen. And she's my boss's aunt! The village incredibly primitive. Only two houses have baths as far as I know. The big houses. Manors. One's the old rectory. Not even a pub. The only way I could get to nose around here was by taking a job. There are two churches. Both *incomplete*. A good sign, that. Everyone very protective about their history, village life. So far I've discovered precious little. I'm sure the chancels (all that's left of the two churches, if there ever was more. Try to check.) are significant. Especially—this will make old Carr's hair curl—as one of them is specifically reserved for the burial of children. Put that together with Ratchets—Gabriel Ratchets—child death cult??? But how to crack it?"

The first note ended there. On the facing page was a list of names. "Poole: Bart, old Mrs., Jacob, Emelye (!). Dolben: Justin and Bryony (landlady). Patrick and Michael. Clare: Penelope and Damon. Bryony D. née Clare." And underneath: "The names recur. Over and over. There *are* no others. Incredible inbreeding. Incest? My

259

informant is deliciously vague about *exact* relationships. My informant is delicious—period. Am not allowed to write down her name. She is 'spoken for,' 'betrothed.' I am a foreigner and therefore mistrusted. Save by her. Bart P. overreacted to finding me in children's graveyard. He and Patrick had big row. B. does not approve of casual labor—period. Why?"

The next page contained a rough sketch of a dog. Kenneth was an imperfect draftsman. It looked rather like an overmuscled Doberman pinscher, its legs stretched in an ungainly gallop. It was labeled: "The Gabriel Hound."

On the following page Stuart read:

"Have stumbled on goldmine in Emelye. Have to remember it all. She clams up at idea of my taking notes. There is v. active Earth Cult here and my Emelye is destined to be its Mistress! Incredible. She's completely serious. Also v. afraid. She's sworn to absolute secrecy. It's a female cult. Men are excluded? Yet the men appear to be incredibly dominant. B. Poole runs everything. Yet E. insists on female superiority. Pagan Women's Lib. If half she tells me is true, then it would make some of the liberated ladies at Cambridge sit up.

"Am allowed to stay on. Why? The early harvest is in. They don't need me. Perhaps E. put in a word? She denies it. It's crazy I know but I want to stay for her more than anything. She's extraordinary. With her I feel in touch with something intense. I can't express it. Lying up on the ridge with her, watching the sunset . . . it's like going back in time. She's very wise. Uneducated. Very simple. But wise. She's not what Mother would call 'suitable' but there's something beyond all that. Some knowledge. An inner stillness and power. I don't know. I suppose I'm in love."

So, Stuart thought, in a sense the police had been right. There *was* a girl but, glancing ahead at the remaining few pages, there didn't seem to be any suggestion of taking off somewhere with her. He turned back to the next entry.

"Long talk with Michael D. V. civilized bloke. Architect. Says he's frightened. Certainly v. tense and nervy. Says he hates Ratchets. Warns me to get out. I told him about E. Followed by big row with Damon Clare, E.'s intended. Anyone would think I'd done it deliberately. There is much more at stake than his *amour propre*. But what?"

The next entry was headed *Wednesday* and was much longer.

"M. Dolben leaving Friday. Has offered to take me. Bart and

whole village seem to know about Emelye and me. M. says I'm in danger. She is quasi-sacred to them. The Cult is real. M. knows all about it and has promised to loan me a book from family library which tells all. He says something big is brewing. He doesn't know what. My guess: E.'s initiation? Apparently, I've thrown spanner in the works. Tried to see E. and get everything sorted out. Mrs. Poole v. firm. (They say she's shape-changer!) She's at the bottom of whatever's going on. I'm certain of that. Don't like her. E. at top. All lines lead back to Mrs. P. She really looks and dresses like a witch. But *am* worried about E. Must see her. Want to take her out of here, if she'll come. M. says o.k. if I can fix it."

Stuart closed his eyes. Why hadn't he listened to Michael Dolben? *What* danger?

"Managed to see E. at Dolben House. She was in terrible state. Frightened out of her wits. At first wouldn't even speak to me. I never knew I could be so cut up. Finally got through to her. She'll come with me on Friday. Then Patrick came in and I had to hop it. The stupid thing is, all these jitters are making *me* nervous. I wish I understood what is going on. The important thing now is————"

Kenneth had never completed that sentence. There was a gap of a few lines and then the notebook continued.

"Have been summoned to a meeting. All v. pompous and solemn. The village elders, no less. To discuss my relationship with E. I'm relieved. I said, there wasn't much to discuss. I love her and want to marry her. She ditto me. They said I could see E. this evening, before the meeting. No sign of M. today. Nothing much for me to do. I feel too restless to make up my notes properly. I shall rely on E. to tell all/refresh my memory when we get home. God, won't the family be surprised? It's ridiculous I know, but I shall be glad when we're on our way. Fear *is* contagious."

Yes, Stuart thought, slowly turning the remaining blank pages. He was afraid. This blankness, the abrupt end of his brother's notes was somehow terribly final. He'd gone to the meeting and . . . He pushed the thought away, got up from the bed, and began to pace up and down in the narrow space between the bed and the window.

Emelye would know, he thought. He must find her. Somebody had sent the notebook. Somebody from Ratchets. Because they thought it was unimportant? Or because they wanted to alert somebody to what was going on? But that was too slim a chance, he decided. Yet it was just the sort of chance a desperate person would take. Should he take the book to the police? He dismissed the idea at once. Even if they would act on it, it would take too long. He must go to Ratchets and find Emelye Poole. It was slightly eerie. He had known that he would have to go back there, even when he set out again, before he knew anything about the notebook. Now, he told himself, he was being ridiculous, too. As Kenneth said, fear is contagious.

He sat down on the bed and picked up the telephone. When the switchboard finally answered, he gave the number of the hospital, thinking that he would have to be very careful what he said. How much time did he have?

For the first time in her life Cloris Poole had no one to turn to. Her independence was a sham, since it was an exclusion of all other relationships, a total dependency on Bart. Now she felt blinded, lost. She could almost wish Magdalena Berryman alive again. At least when she had been there he had had some time for her, Cloris. Now Maddy's claim on him was total, and Cloris was left with nothing.

She walked through the dripping village and knew that the time for schemes and stratagems was over. No plot would reach Bart now. Nothing, no act or claim, would bind him to her. She had been put aside but she could not bear the loneliness. She, who had stood firm against Mother Poole and the women, had nowhere else to go. She wondered if Bart had thought of that. By putting her aside, he had taken her pride, too. He wouldn't care. That was certain. So, on that terrible bleak morning, Cloris walked to Mother Poole's cottage and knocked on the door. All her strength went into this final act, into the hope that Bart would know and be hurt by her defection. She knocked, seeking revenge and shelter.

She faced with courage the cold mask of dislike Mother Poole presented to her when she opened the door. They were enemies of old about to be thrown into an alliance that was entirely beyond their control.

"Can I come in?" Cloris asked. "Please. It's about Bart."

She knew that the old woman wanted to slam the door in her face and, as surely, that she could not afford to. Bart was her passport.

"Aye," Mother Poole said after a long time. "You can come in." She saw the deadness in Cloris's eyes and knew that she was broken. She would make what use of it she could, but she would never trust or like her. Never. She swore it even as she turned her back on her.

Cloris followed her into the kitchen with a feeling of emptiness. Mother Poole warmed her crooked hands at the fire. The way she stood, refusing to look at Cloris, made it clear that she intended to give no quarter. Cloris pulled her damp shawl more tightly round her shoulders.

"It's Bart," she said in a low, broken voice. "I think he's sick. Will you go to him?"

The old woman was silent, staring into the flames.

"What's wrong with him?" Lyndsay asked.

With a start, Cloris turned her head. She had not noticed her in the shadowy corner by the window. Her face was pale and drawn. Cloris felt a flicker of dislike, of jealousy, but knew that she had to hide it.

"I don't know," she said. "I think perhaps he has a fever." She addressed this to Mother Poole. Both women waited for her to say something, but she was resolute. "Please," Cloris said.

"Where is he?" Lyndsay asked, coming to her side. "Are you all right? You're trembling. Take off that damp shawl."

Cloris protested feebly, but Lyndsay pulled the shawl from her and made her sit down. Her teeth chattered and a fit of trembling seized her. She felt so cold, as though she had crossed into the grave itself.

"I'll get you some tea," Lyndsay said. The old woman stepped aside, allowing Lyndsay to reach the kettle. She poured more water into the teapot. The old woman stood behind her chair, gripping its back. Her eyes moved from Cloris to Lyndsay with unconcealed scorn. Lyndsay poured a cup of tea and handed it to Cloris, urging her to drink it. She nodded gratefully.

"What a pair you make," Mother Poole said with bitterness. "If you could only see yourselves."

"Will you go to him?" Lyndsay asked, ignoring the taunt in the old woman's voice.

"Never."

Lyndsay gripped Cloris's shoulder. It shook beneath her fingers.

"What do you want?" Cloris said, her head bent over her cup. "Tell me and I'll do it."

"I want nothing from you."

"What's happened?" she asked Cloris. "Can you tell me?"

Cloris shook her head miserably. Lyndsay looked helplessly at Mother Poole.

"Don't you have any pity?" she asked. "Have you forgotten how to—"

"I can't afford it," Mother Poole snapped. "Not while you are weak. You must fight him with hatred every bit as fierce as his. As for her . . ." She looked disdainfully at Cloris. "She's only got what she deserved."

Cloris began to cry. "I'm begging you," she sobbed, holding out her hand to Mother Poole.

"No," she said. "I've cut him out of my heart. You must do the same. Both of you. You will never know what misery is until you do it."

Somehow Cloris managed to raise her head and control her tears.

"I know all about that," she said. "I came to warn you. He's not . . . like himself. I can't tell any longer what he might do. I don't know him anymore."

Lyndsay watched the old woman's face for some sign of alarm or concern. She regarded Cloris unmoved.

"There's no trusting you, Cloris Poole. Your heart's as black as his. He won't change now. He can only be stopped." Her eyes moved to Lyndsay, challenging her.

Lyndsay straightened her back and faced the old woman. She felt strong, certain of what she was doing.

"If you won't go to him," she said quietly, "I will."

She kept her eyes fixed on Mother Poole, even though she knew that Cloris was looking at her. The old woman pursed her lips. Her eyes narrowed for a moment, as if she suspected some trick. Then she nodded her head.

"Very well. But you can't go to him. I'll bring him to you."

Cloris touched Lyndsay's arm.

"Thank you, Mistress," she whispered.

"And you, Cloris Poole, get home," Mother Poole commanded, moving around the chair with a sudden burst of energy. "Keep yourself to yourself but, to show you're sincere, you'll attend the Mistress when the time comes."

Cloris seemed to flinch, as though the words were blows, but she managed to control herself sufficiently to bow her head in assent. With unexpected speed Mother Poole propelled her out of the door.

"Be on your way now," she said gruffly. "And remember what I've told you."

The front door closed behind her.

"Why are you so cruel to her?" Lyndsay asked when she returned.

"Never you mind," she said. "I know her. You don't."

"You can be as cruel as Bart," Lyndsay said. "Maybe he learned it from you."

"Listen to me," Mother Poole said, rounding on her. "You'll understand very soon now why I am as I am. You can afford to be merciful. That's how it should be, but if I do not protect you, all the mercy will be burned out of you. She'd kill you as soon as look at you. Bart will destroy you completely if you let him. I can't afford to be merciful. For your sake."

"Bart can't hurt me now," Lyndsay said levelly. "You can count on that. I hated Emelye when Patrick told me, but I know now that I was wrong. I've learned my lesson better than you know. Her baby must be protected. If for nothing else . . . Now I can face him."

"Good."

Lyndsay felt a sudden rush of protectiveness toward Emelye and her child. She was a part of it now, completely and utterly. She accepted it. She was part of the chain leading back into history, to those dead children, a chain that caught and killed Christian, Bella, and the baby and which led, without deviation, to Emelye.

"The first Mistress cursed *us*, didn't she?" Lyndsay said, her eyes shining. "The women deserted her. And she cursed them. And this is our reward."

"Aye," Mother Poole said solemnly.

"Well then," she sighed, "fetch him. Let's get it over with."

The old woman turned away, took down her cloak, and picked up her stick.

"Go to the top of the ride," she said. "He'll come to you there."

Lyndsay nodded and slowly climbed upstairs to dress. All around her she felt the great weight of sadness, pressing against her. It was something, a force, to which she must submit. It would engulf her, she knew, but she would survive it. She had everything to live for now. Everything.

With fixed, glazed eyes, she lifted the Dolben Collar and fastened it, voluntarily, about her neck.

After he had spoken to his mother and learned that there was no change in his father's condition, Stuart Donne told her that he planned to drive on to Ratchets.

"What good will that do?" she asked.

Stuart hesitated.

"I don't know. But I think it's worth a try. Trust me," he added quickly and hung up before she could protest. He did not dare to tell her about the notebook, not until he knew for sure. But he had to tell someone, get some advice. He found Daniel Carr's number and asked the switchboard to connect him. Carr's voice swam out of a sea of noise. After a moment, he said, "Just a minute. I'll go to the other phone."

Stuart held the receiver, listening to Carr remonstrating with the children. Their voices clamored tinnily against a blurred background of music. Stuart waited, tapping his finger on the table.

"Hello. Ah, that's better," Carr said. The background noise continued. "Sorry. They haven't put the other receiver down. Just a minute."

Again Stuart waited. In the distance he could hear Carr shouting to the children. With a crackle, the noise was blotted out and a moment later Carr came back on the line, panting apologies. Briefly, Stuart told him about the notebook.

"Does it make any sense to you?" he asked.

"Not much," Carr admitted. "Of course folklore isn't really my field. There are lots of versions of the Gabriel Ratchets story, but I've never heard of a cult built around it."

"What about witches? Kenneth does seem to think that a Mrs. Poole might be, well . . ."

"There *are* covens, of course," Carr said. "You must have read about them in the Sunday papers. But mostly they're harmless. An excuse for a bit of rural wife-swapping, as a rule. But of course if they were *serious* . . . I mean if Kenneth stumbled on something illegal. Or if they really valued this girl as some sort of totem . . ."

"I see," Stuart said. "Have you any advice? Anything you think I should look out for?"

"My advice is to put it all into the hands of the police."

"I don't think they'd be very impressed," Stuart told him. "I'm going to go there myself. I have to. I don't think my father . . . Well, let's say the sooner I can get to the bottom of this the better. I intend to talk to the girl, Emelye."

"Well . . ." Carr sounded doubtful.

"Thanks for your help anyway," Stuart said. "I'll be in touch."

He hung up and sat for a moment looking at the receiver. He

couldn't think of anything else he ought to do. There was no point in putting it off. He slipped on his jacket and checked his pockets. He'd keep the room. He felt tired again, but shook the feeling off. Outside, the sky had clouded over. It looked like rain. He walked toward the car with a heavy heart.

Lyndsay saw him coming along the ridge toward her. She had been waiting fifteen or twenty minutes, with only the doleful sound of dripping trees to keep her company. There were frequent gusts of cold, damp wind which promised more rain. He walked with his usual confidence, the easy loping stride, but she saw when he came closer that he had changed. His face was pale yellow beneath the stubble of beard. His eyes were restless, darting, never still. He looked older, much older.

"Well?" he said.

Lyndsay walked slowly toward him, her hands in her coat pockets. She did not know why she had insisted on seeing him, nor what she could say to him. She felt drained of all emotion now. Liking, fear, love, even the knowledge that he was a murderer meant nothing to her.

"How are you, Bart?" she said at last.

They stood side by side, not looking at each other, but staring away across the ridge.

"I'm fine. And you?"

"Okay, I guess."

"Good."

"I want you to know that I'm glad for what you did to me the other night. I'm glad I'm the Mistress."

"I only did my duty," he said stiffly. "The Priest must always blood the Mistress."

"And then doesn't he have to obey her?" she asked slyly.

"Not if he is stronger than she."

"Are you?"

"Of course." He laughed a little.

"I wouldn't be so sure of that. They might accept that Maddy had to die, but I don't. And they'll follow me now."

"The old woman's put you up to this," he said, looking at her for the first time. A smile twisted his lips cruelly.

"No. She didn't want me to see you. I insisted. I don't want to fight you, Bart. But I will if you make me."

"You know nothing."

"I know you killed Maddy Berryman."

"Her name was Clare," he said viciously. "And her death was nothing."

"And her children," Lyndsay said relentlessly. "You even killed the boy, didn't you?"

"Yes. I killed her bastards. As I'd promised her."

"And now you want Emelye's baby."

At this, he showed something of his old anger. His face twitched, his hands clenched. Lyndsay pressed her advantage.

"And mine?" she asked.

He watched her for a long moment, his eyelids blinking rapidly. Then he began to laugh. She turned away from him, bewildered, and walked a little way along the ridge. His laughter followed her. She wouldn't listen to it. She heard the wind and the rain, like a murmur of voices, calling to her. She felt him standing behind her, his laughter finished.

"You really don't care, do you?" she said. "You really are a monster."

"I care," he said, his voice shaking with emotion. "I care about all this."

She turned to see what he meant. His left arm was swept out from his body to embrace all the land, stretching away to the cloud-darkened horizon.

"What good is land without people to care for it?" Lyndsay asked.

"There are plenty of people."

"I don't think so. Not unless you listen to me. They won't take much more. You're ahead at the moment, but you've forgotten the women. If necessary, I'll lead them and the children out of here. You won't last long without them."

"No," he said, shaking his head. "You still don't understand. You will keep them here for me."

"Oh no. I've got too much at stake. You don't matter anymore."

"I'll tell you a secret," he said, his eyes glittering in his ravaged face. "You're the key to it all. They all thought I was against you. They banked on me failing because I held the Mistress in scorn. But I don't. I know how essential she is. You are the one who will make everything possible for me. But you will serve me. That is the difference."

Just for a moment Lyndsay was afraid. The power she had felt before flickered into a brief, renewed life. She turned her head away from him, avoiding the danger of his eyes.

"And how are you going to manage that?" she asked.

"You'll see."

"When?"

"Whenever you're ready."

"The sooner the better."

He took a long, deep breath.

"Tell Mother Poole to make you ready then. It'll be tonight."

Gravely, swallowing her fear, Lyndsay nodded her head in agreement.

"That's it then, I guess. I feel sorry for you, Bart. I somehow loved you, you know."

"Don't talk to me of love," he snarled. "That's your weakness. You think it's a strength, but it isn't. It's the very opposite. And it's the only weapon you've got. But I know. I *know*."

"What?" she challenged him. "Tell me what you know."

"What it is to love," he said, his voice falling, flattening, becoming drained of all color. "For seventeen years I loved a woman and a night ago I destroyed her. So don't you talk to me of love."

"God help you, Bart," she said.

"She'll help me," he said.

"Who? Maddy?"

He shook his head sadly. "No. Not her. The earth. The Great Mother."

Lyndsay looked down at the dark, rain-damp earth. She had to get away from him. The earth gave under her feet. It was soft and yielding, feminine. It welcomed her. She walked slowly toward the ride, with a feeling that the earth consoled her.

"Mistress."

She stopped.

"Yes, Bart."

"It's not too late to change your mind. You could still go now."

Lyndsay shook her head, firmly but sadly, and walked purposefully under the trees, drops from their weeping branches scouring her face. At the bottom of the ride she looked back, just for a moment.

CHAPTER TWELVE

Mother Poole rose to greet Lyndsay as she came hurrying into the cottage. Her pale face looked as though the flesh had been drawn tight against the bones, but what impressed the old lady most was the collar, the Dolben Collar, gleaming at her neck.

"Well?" she asked as Lyndsay stood, panting a little, against the door.

Lyndsay hesitated because she noticed Emelye, sitting at the table, near the dresser. She was stripping dried marjoram leaves into a jar and pretended to be completely absorbed in her task. The sight of her filled Lyndsay with a confusion of emotions which she forced herself to put aside. She looked at Mother Poole.

"He said I should tell you to get me ready. For tonight. It's to be tonight."

"Ah," the old woman said. It sounded like a sigh of relief, of contentment. Her thin lips drew back into a satisfied smile. "Good," she said. "Cloris was speaking the truth then."

"What do you mean?" Lyndsay asked, taking off her coat.

"It's too soon. He's moving too fast."

"That may be my fault. I told him I wanted to get it over with as soon as possible."

"Good. You did well. It's not too soon for you. Only for him. But we must hurry. First—"

"First," Lyndsay interrupted, "I think you'd better tell me what's going to happen. I let him think I understood, but I don't."

The old woman nodded.

"You're right. Sit down."

Lyndsay sat by the fire, glancing at Emelye, who seemed oblivious of their conversation.

"You have been blooded," Mother Poole explained quickly. "That is the first stage. Now you must be dedicated to the Earth. You must be formally proclaimed Mistress."

"What do I have to do?"

"You will know that when the time comes. No," the old lady said, holding up her hand to silence Lyndsay's protest. "I'm not keeping anything from you. What will happen tonight depends on what Bart decides to do. You will have to react according to what he does. I can't tell you because I don't know."

Lyndsay felt alone then, but she was not frightened. It seemed that she had known all along that it would be just Bart and her eventually.

"He will perform the ceremony?"

"As your Priest, aye."

"He said that I was the key to everything. That after tonight I would serve him and that the women would follow me, but only to do what he wants."

"We'll see," the old woman said dryly. "Now you must return to Dolben House and we must see to your gown."

"Why? I'd rather stay here."

"You are a Dolben," she replied levelly. "You must leave from your home, like a true bride. And you must wear the traditional gown of the Mistress. The wedding gown. Each family has one, for when the line is traced to them. It will need alterations."

"Is that really necessary?" Lyndsay queried.

"Certainly. Everything must be done according to the Ways. Bart may choose to ignore them, but we must not. And you must be attended. Everything must be done correctly and quickly." As she said this, she pulled on her cloak. "I'll go and see Cloris. We'll have our work cut out, but we'll manage it." Passing Lyndsay's chair, she touched her shoulder briefly. "You did well, Mistress. But then I always knew you would."

Lyndsay turned her head, wanting to ask more questions, but Mother Poole flapped her hands impatiently and hurried out. A log shifted in the grate, making Lyndsay more aware of the silence. She looked at Emelye, trying to decide what she should say, how she could begin. Obviously aware that Lyndsay was watching her, the girl stopped stripping the tiny, brittle stalks.

"Emelye," Lyndsay said, "I want you to know that I'm sorry for . . . the way I've behaved to you. I was angry. I'm sure you can understand why. But I'm not angry anymore. Not with you. I'm sorry it happened, but really I'm glad about your baby. I really am. I want you to know that and that I won't let anything happen to it."

Very slowly the girl raised her head and looked at Lyndsay. Her enormous gray eyes were troubled. Two bright spots of color burned on her sunken cheeks.

"Emelye . . ." Lyndsay said, and moved toward her, to comfort her.

"Lies," Emelye said. "Oh the lies they've told you, Mistress." She shook her head sadly. "I'm so ashamed."

"Sh. There's no need to be, Emelye. Please, you mustn't feel like that."

"You don't understand," she said, her eyes brimming with unshed tears.

The door opened suddenly, startling them both.

"Emelye." Mother Poole commanded. "Put on your things and go and find Patrick. He must be prepared."

With an apologetic glance at Lyndsay, Emelye stood up. Lyndsay had to fight hard to control her reactions to the roundness of the girl's stomach, pressing against her dress.

"You see," Mother Poole said to Lyndsay, "Patrick will have to present you. There's no one else now."

"What does that mean?" she asked, her eyes following Emelye as she put on her shawl and moved awkwardly across the overcrowded room.

"It's like being given away at a proper marriage. Normally it would have fallen to Michael, but as it is . . ." Emelye reached the door. "Go on, girl," Mother Poole said. "And look sharp about it." She came farther into the room to allow Emelye to pass. When the girl had gone, Mother Poole said to Lyndsay, "You mustn't pay her any mind, Mistress. She's off her head with worry."

"I just wish I could make her understand that I don't blame her," Lyndsay said.

"There'll be plenty of time for that later. You rest now. You've a long day ahead of you."

The old woman went out and Lyndsay, alone, sat beside the fire and closed her eyes. With the fingers of her left hand she traced the outline of the diamond hound in the collar, and thought about Bart.

Word spread quickly through the village. All normal work was immediately suspended. Like components of a well-maintained machine, the villagers went to their allotted tasks without instruction. Everyone knew what had to be done.

Justin Dolben led a party of men to the chancel in the children's graveyard. The curved pews were carried back to the walls to make a series of loops along the sides, defining the empty, central space. Six-feet-high candlesticks, so heavy that each one required two men to maneuver it into position, were placed the length of the hall. The altar was carried forward, down from its raised dais, and set at the foot of the shallow steps. It was covered in a black velvet cloth, the folds of which fell to the stone floor. A border about a foot deep, depicting the hounds in golden thread, with gleaming green eyes, ran around all four sides of the cloth. Wooden framed hassocks were fetched and placed before the pews. Each one was covered in black material and emblazoned with the Gabriel Hound, like the one Bryony had embroidered when she was sitting with Lyndsay at Clare House. The men worked quietly and with industry. Last of all they fetched out the mask and suspended it like a great screen behind the altar. Then they hurried away under the gray sky to their homes, to prepare themselves.

One of the last to leave was Damon Clare. His pulse quickened when he saw Emelye slowly crossing the green. He ran to catch up with her.

"Emelye," he called. "I did it. Just like you asked."

She looked at him blankly, as though she did not understand.

"The parcel, Emelye. I gave it to the Mistress, that day she went into Corminster. I asked her to post it for me."

"And did she?" Emelye asked, a flicker of hope lighting her face. Damon blushed.

"I haven't seen her alone since, but she said she would," he added quickly.

Emelye's heart sank.

"It doesn't matter," she said in a tired voice. "It's too late now, anyway."

"Too late? What do you mean?"

"Nothing. I've got to go. Mother Poole wants me."

They walked along together. Damon could not ignore her swollen stomach. There was no hiding it now, no possibility of pushing it out of his mind.

"You said there was nothing wrong in sending it . . ." he began.

"It doesn't matter," she said. "Thank you anyway, Damon."

"Emelye, listen . . ."

"No. Damon." She shook off the hand he had placed on her arm. "There's nothing more to be said." She hurried ahead of him and darted into the cottage gateway.

He let her go, walking slowly past the cottage, past the village shop and the post office, both of which were closed. Overhead the sky began to lighten a little. Tonight, he felt sure, Bart would make it all right for him. Emelye would, eventually, see that she had to marry him. It wasn't a hope but a conviction. He began to hurry then, toward Clare House.

Penelope, standing in the window, saw him come excitedly up the path. He waved to her.

"We've got the chancel ready," he said, bursting into the room. "You know the Mistress is to be dedicated tonight?"

"I know," she said listlessly.

"Aren't you pleased?" he said. "She'll help me. I know she will. She already has."

"How?" Penelope turned away from the window, her face suddenly alert.

"Oh . . . it's no matter. But I know it will be all right. For me and Emelye, I mean. I *know* it will."

Her face clouded. She wished that she could make him understand. No matter what happened, Emelye would never marry him now. But his excitement, his certainty saddened her unbearably. They were both, she and Damon, in the same hopeless situation. Impulsively, she went to him and put her arms around him. He drew back in surprise.

"What's the matter?" he asked.

"Nothing," she said quickly. "Can't I . . . wish you well?"

"Of course." He returned her embrace. "I must go and get ready," he said.

"Yes. All right."

The door slammed behind him and she heard him whistling happily as he ran up the stairs.

274

From her pocket she drew the bottle of sleeping tablets on which she had relied on for so long. She stared at the bottle with a fixed expression. It was more than half full. She did not know how many she would have to take. She sat down and lit a cigarette. She could not bear to watch Patrick fail, to witness Damon's disappointment. It was better to follow Maddy, peacefully, in her own way.

But she was afraid. She looked at the bottle again. Afraid that it would not work and of what it would be like if it did. But the alternative, the only positive alternative, demanded even more courage. More, certainly, than she had. She began to daydream, to wonder how it could be done. The car was out of the question. Somebody would be sure to hear it. Even on foot it would be dangerous, and might be too late. But she owed it to Patrick, and to Lyndsay. Perhaps most of all to herself. But when, how could she get away? She knew it was hopeless. Putting down her cigarette, she uncapped the bottle and tipped the pills into her left hand. She began to count them, pushing them around her palm with her finger. Then she tipped them back into the bottle and put it in her pocket. She stood up, lit another cigarette from the smoldering butt in the ashtray, and walked slowly through to the kitchen to get a glass of water.

She was accompanied to Dolben House by Mother Poole, Bryony, and Cloris. These last, she understood, were to be her attendants. They both carried large bags, containing all they would need to prepare her and themselves. They would stay with her until it was time for the ceremony.

"I don't want to see Patrick," she told Mother Poole as they drew close to the house.

"You won't," she said confidently. "No man must look on you until tonight."

She was relieved. These woman, her women, she realized, were all she needed. They would sustain and guide her until the moment she would have to stand alone, and then she would be able to trust in her own strength, in the power she knew she had. Bryony went ahead, as a scout, to make sure that there had been no violation of the customs. She returned almost at once and waved them into the house. Lyndsay was hurried straight to her bedroom where she noticed at once that a large, dusty, cardboard dress box had been placed on her bed.

"Is that the dress?" she asked.

"The gown, aye," Bryony said, lifting the lid.

From a mass of yellowing tissue paper, she lifted out an old but exquisitely made white silk dress. It had a high collar and leg-o'-mutton sleeves. The bodice was decorated with seed pearls and fastened with a long row of tiny, silk-covered buttons. The skirt billowed as Bryony, with a rare smile of pleasure, shook it out. Lyndsay had never seen anything like it outside of a museum.

"It's beautiful," she said, touching the soft, cool silk with an almost sensual pleasure.

"Make haste now and slip it on," Mother Poole said.

"It's sure to need altering," Bryony said. "I fancy it'll be too long."

Lyndsay undressed quickly. Cloris Poole unfastened the Dolben Collar for her and placed it on the dressing table. Carefully, Bryony helped her into the dress. It was too long and a little tight at the waist, but otherwise it fit well. Lyndsay could not help admiring herself in the mirror while Bryony, her mouth full of pins, busily marked how much should be taken up.

"It's funny, you know," Lyndsay said, "but I really wanted a proper wedding dress. Of course there wasn't time."

"For that marriage, what difference did it make?" Mother Poole said sharply. "But the Mistress," she added in a softer, warmer tone, "deserves a beautiful gown."

"There," Bryony said, getting to her feet. "Now let me see the waist. Mm. Yes. I'll let out these two darts here." She pressed her fingers lightly against Lyndsay's back. "That should do it."

They unbuttoned the dress and lifted it over her head. At once Bryony went to the window and began stitching, completely absorbed in her work.

"You should rest," Cloris said to Lyndsay.

"I'm fine."

"Do as she says," Mother Poole advised. "I must leave you now."

"Where are you going?" Lyndsay asked, her voice revealing her alarm.

"I have to get ready, too," she said. "Rest." Moving to the door, she beckoned Cloris to follow her. The old woman whispered in her ear. Lyndsay turned back the bedclothes and climbed onto the bed. The door clicked shut. Outside, a thin, watery sun broke through the clouds. Cloris pulled the bedclothes over Lyndsay, and then said to Bryony, "Do you need me?"

"No. You go and get ready."

Picking up her bag, Cloris went into the bathroom. Lyndsay let herself be soothed by Bryony's neat, rhythmic stitching. The pale yellow sunlight struck the wet leaves of the wood outside, making it shimmer and shine. She recalled what Mother Poole had said, that she would have to react to whatever Bart did. For that she would need to be alert, so she closed her eyes and tried to sleep.

It had been a long journey, a long *crazy* journey, she thought. But now there seemed to be only the most tenuous connection between herself as she was when she stepped off that plane with old Mrs. Abernathy, and the person she had become. When had she changed? When Patrick had told her the truth about Michael? When Maddy had shot her? When she realized that Bart haunted not only her dreams but her waking life? None of these events in isolation had changed her, but all of them in conjunction. They seemed now like beads on a thread, a connected series of bewildering incidents which, in fact, led her to this moment, to the next few hours. Yet she felt that the moment of her blooding had been the true climax. It was then, after her desperate but vain attempt to stop Magdalena Berryman, that she had completely committed herself to them all, to Ratchets itself. This was her home now. She belonged in a way that she had never belonged anywhere before. She belonged to the women and the children. Whatever she had to do later that night, she would do it for them, for life and the future. Her life, her future was here, for she was tied to the place by a man.

Only life. There is only life for you here, Mistress.

Mother Poole had not lied.

She dozed for a while, seeing the village transformed. Autumn, with a smell of woodsmoke in the air. A soft, slightly misty light. Each tree was a gold and brown lantern. There was the sound of children's voices, raised in laughter and play. She saw the cottage doors brightly painted, the women moving about the street and the green in flowered dresses. At the end of the day the men came back from the fields, stamping the mud from their boots and stooping slightly to greet their women. She saw the chimneys sending up little curls of smoke against the pink sunset. She saw Michaelmas daisies and chrysanthemums in abundance. She saw Dolben House, aired and cleaned. It shone with polish. The light of a big fire was reflected in the boards of the hall. The house would be serene. There would be people to stay. Her parents perhaps. Mrs. Abernathy, if she could contact her. And the sound of children.

She opened her eyes and turned onto her back, stretching. Bryony snapped a piece of white thread between her teeth. In front of the dressing table, Cloris Poole brushed her silky black hair. She wore a long, full, scarlet gown. It fell in soft, loose folds from her breasts. Lyndsay smiled at what she saw. She rememberd those excited preparations for a college dance. Girls gathered together, making the best of themselves, talking and laughing. But this was more serene, mature. There was an air of purpose, of strength, beneath these exclusively feminine preparations.

"There," Bryony said, shaking out the dress.

Cloris put down the hairbrush. "Finished?"

"Yes."

Cloris came to the side of the bed and looked down at Lyndsay. "Come, Mistress. It's time for your bath. You must get ready now."

"You're very beautiful," Lyndsay said. "I hadn't realized."

Cloris smiled, accepting the compliment.

Bryony disappeared into the bathroom. She heard water running. Cloris switched the light on. Steam began to swirl out of the open door, bringing with it some sweet scent. Lyndsay got up and removed her underclothes and then walked naked into the steam. They had placed some sort of oil in the water, rich and scented. Lyndsay sank into the bath, the water immediately relaxing her. She saw her skin take on a gleam that was beautiful even to her own eyes. She gave herself up to the water and the heady perfume which rose from it.

The weak sun was soon engulfed by clouds. The sky gradually became leaden as Penelope Clare slipped out of the back door. The tense silence which covered the village emanated from the sky itself. It was as though the earth were holding its breath in terrible expectation. She glided diagonally across the field behind Clare House. Her feet slipped on the wet grass as she climbed, hurrying now toward the oaks. Her route was exposed. She knew that she was vulnerable and did not dare to look back. Her ears strained for a shout, a cry of pursuit, but only the silence pressed, throbbing, against her ears. It took her less than five minutes to reach the oaks at the crossroad, but it seemed to her much longer. She felt as though she had been walking for hours yet somehow, when she reached the road, she found enough strength to run.

Patrick prepared himself according to the Ways. Glowing from the bath, he felt pleased with himself. He would do well. Bart would be pleased with him. Tonight, in the loosely belted black robe and white tabard of the Presenter, he would face his greatest test. He would pass it. He *had* to, for then Bart would clasp him round the shoulders and call him Brother. Suddenly, for no reason at all, an old memory popped into his head. He'd been about ten and afraid of Bart. He'd stolen some candy and offered to share it with Bart, who then laughed and took the precious sweets, dropping them one by one on the ground, where he smashed them to sugary splinters with the heel of his boot.

"You can't buy me," he said, grabbing Patrick and twisting his arm painfully toward his shoulder blade. "You've got to obey me, without question." Then he'd flung him away. Patrick had stumbled, fallen, and grazed his knee.

He trembled with anger at himself for recalling that stupid, trivial incident now. Bart was his brother and friend. All that was long ago and the result not of Bart's nature but of his equivocal position in the Dolben household. Tonight, all that would be altered. Bart would never again feel unaccepted, and he, Patrick, would be directly responsible. All old scores would be settled, the wounds of a lifetime healed. He peered at himself in the mirror. The robes became him. Only his pale, sunken cheeks and the enlarged, black fleck in his left eye betrayed his agitation. It was just that he was excited, he told himself. He tried to think of afterward, of Bart's joy and the honor it would confer on him.

"Mistress."

Bryony Dolben stood beside the bath, holding out an enormous towel, read to wrap her in it. She, too, had changed, into a severe gray dress with white collar and cuffs. Lyndsay stood up, the water sliding from her skin, leaving droplets of oil on it like blue-lit pearls. She stepped into the enveloping warmth and softness of the towel and allowed Bryony to guide her out into the bedroom. There, swaddled in the towel, she was handed, like some precious object, to Cloris Poole.

279

Cloris's hands moved over her body, pressed the towel against her, drying her. She knelt, lifted Lyndsay's feet onto a towel spread across her lap, and carefully dried them. An act of penance, Lyndsay thought. Cloris's hands moved up her legs, patting with the towel, which absorbed the oily moisture. It was like a caress. Lyndsay's mouth hung open a little while Cloris touched her, dried her, gently, with care and patience.

She stood naked, her skin giving off the perfume of the bath. They made her sit down. Bryony Dolben brushed her hair with long, soothing strokes, her left hand following the passage of the brush. For a moment she was transported back to her room at home and childhood tales of princes and princesses.

They put the dress over her head, over her naked body, and let it fall into place. The silk was softer than her skin. Indeed it felt like a second, living skin. As Cloris stood before her, fastening the long row of silk-covered buttons, she saw the material cup and lift and strain across her breasts, outlining them, giving her an appearance more erotic than nudity. Bryony knelt and fastened the long cuffs of the gown. They placed satin slippers on her feet. Cloris fluffed out her skirts in a white, shining cloud around her. She saw herself for what she was: a woman, proud and ennobled by the gown. The wedding gown of the Mistress transformed her, proclaimed that she was above all women, was all-powerful.

Bryony went to the dressing table and picked up the Dolben Collar. As she held it in her hands, the door opened and Mother Poole came in. Tall and stately in watered black taffeta, her cloak thrown loosely over her shoulders, she smiled at Lyndsay. Silently, she took the collar from Bryony and passed behind Lyndsay, who stared at her altered self in the mirror. As the stark black, flashing collar was fitted around her neck, she said, "It's not just for the Dolben women, is it? The collar is for the Mistress."

"That's right," Mother Poole said. "It is her badge of office."

A tiny white frill of silk rose above the upper edge of the collar. The diamonds struck fire in the brightly lit room, the emerald glowed coldly. Mother Poole surveyed her critically from all angles, nodded, and went to stand by the door. Cloris lifted Lyndsay's hair and arranged it smoothly on her shoulders. From the box, Bryony drew a veil which was draped simply over her head, anchored by a few carefully placed pins. The two women, working together, arranged it to fall over her shoulders, and spread it out around her. Looking at it closely, Lyndsay smiled when she realized that the

280

beautiful, handworked lace was composed of a single, repeated motif: that of a great hound in full cry.

"There," Cloris said, stepping back and admiring her.

"What happens now?" Lyndsay asked.

"We must wait awhile. Not long," Cloris answered, turning to arrange her own hair in the mirror.

"Well, Mother?" Lyndsay asked, turning toward the watching woman.

"You'll do," she said. "You'll do very well."

"Wish me luck?"

She looked deeply into Lyndsay's eyes, then she kissed her forehead in blessing. Lyndsay's throat contracted with emotion, but Mother Poole released her before she could speak or embrace her. She glided, upright and magnificent, out of the room.

Bart Poole, alone in the cold room beneath the chancel, carefully honed a knife. Its blade was a ripple of silver light, some nine inches long. The handle, of black ebony, was shaped like a hound and fitted the palm of his hand to perfection. The knife was beautifully balanced, and he had made it sharp as any razor. Holding it reverently, he placed it on a black velvet cushion in readiness. Above him, he could hear people arriving in the chancel. With a set, almost remote expression, he removed his clothes, shivering in the cold. Then he covered his naked body with the stiff, golden robes of his office. When this was done, he went to a small, arched door in a corner of the room, set back in an embrasure so that it was barely noticeable. He unfastened it by drawing back three heavy bolts. Ahead of him lay a long, dank-smelling passageway. Into the wall were set iron sconces, containing fresh white candles. With a taper which he lit from the oil lamp, Bart moved slowly along the passage, lighting each candle in turn. As he did so, fire sparkled from his robes, making him appear to be a walking, ethereal column of light.

"Come, Mistress. It is time," Cloris said.

She led the way. Lyndsay lifted her silk skirt and followed her down the stairs into the deserted hall. Bryony carried the trainlike veil behind her. She followed the scarlet splash of Cloris's dress into the kitchen, into the pantry where a door stood open. Bunching her skirt around her, tended before and behind, she descended into a vaulted cellar. They passed from this chamber to another, where they came to an open door. Beyond it she could see a long, damp passage which danced with candlelight. The private Dolben passage to the chancel, she realized. Patrick had told her about it, how the Dolben women liked to keep their skirts clean for worship. But Patrick had told her a lot of things, she thought bitterly, and stepped into the passage, which smelled of candle wax and cold, fetid air. Bryony bunched the veiling up in her arms, to keep it clear of the moss-covered floor. In front of them the passage curved toward a stream of light. They emerged, through a small door, into an underground chamber. The room contained a narrow bed and another door, much larger, in the opposite wall. A flight of stone steps led up from the corner.

"Wait a minute," Cloris said, and hurried up these steps.

Lyndsay looked around her. The room was lit by an old oil lamp. She recognized Bart's clothes on the floor by the bed and the blood beat in her temples. Bryony carefully adjusted her veil. After a few moments, Cloris returned and beckoned her to follow. She climbed, her skirt held high. The steps led into another small room, and then into the chancel itself. She could see little in the dim candlelight. She let her skirt fall. Cloris arranged it, while Bryony spread out the veil. Then they led her forward, past the black, covered altar, into the empty space of the chancel. People sat, robed, on the curved pews. Her women led her to an empty space on one of the pews and sat beside her. The women were on one side, the men on the other. Directly opposite her, staring at her, was Patrick. He looked pale and ill. She did not want to look at him. Turning her gaze toward the altar, she gave an involuntary start. Suspended above it was an enormous mask, fashioned to resemble the snarling muzzle of a hound. She remembered it from her dreams. Only then it had been worn by . . . the Priest, she realized. Bart. Now she saw that it was suspended from wires and held steady by others, which fastened to rings, let into the floor. She stared at it wonderingly, remembering the hounds in the field, the night she had been blooded and named. He was going to use the hounds again, she thought. That must be the significance of the mask. But there was nothing to be afraid of. Not even the hounds.

She waited, looking at the mask. The silence was almost total. Occasionally someone stifled a cough, or shuffled a foot on the stone floor. Time did not seem to have any significance.

In solemn magnificence, Bart Poole stepped from behind the

mask at last. He paused as though relishing the shock of acknowl-edgment and awe which his appearance caused. He wore a stiff, golden robe, encrusted with gems which sparkled and glowed in the light. Beside her, Lyndsay felt Cloris Poole stiffen and strain toward him. The robes, the strength and majesty of his appearance did not move Lyndsay. They confirmed only that he had used her and despised her for being his passive victim. He walked forward. The robes rustled in the silence. He stood before the altar, his hands folded together, his dark, curly head bowed. Lyndsay had to fight to distance herself from him. She felt something of the impulse, the magnetism which drew Cloris under his spell. In the long, tense silence before he spoke, she laid her hand on Cloris's arm and was grateful for the distraction she provided.

"We are gathered here to dedicate the Mistress to the Earth, according to the Ways. But first . . ." He seemed then like an actor who is uncertain of his lines. There was a murmur, a shifting of bodies on both sides of the chancel. The men were excited, but the women, her women, she knew, were afraid. She did not know what to do. She looked for Mother Poole but in the uncertain light could not find her. Bart, she realized, was staring at her. For a moment, she returned his look, but only for a moment. Chin high, she looked straight ahead, ignoring the man who wanted to dominate and use her.

"First," he repeated, his voice sounding small and uncertain, "the Hounds."

Cloris and Bryony shifted besider her. The men rose as one body and stepped forward. Linking hands they knelt on the little hassocks before them, but the women remained seated. They turned to her, seeking instruction. Bart's glittering eyes commanded them. A shiver passed through Cloris and Lyndsay sensed that she was going to obey him. She tightened her grip on the woman's arm, digging her nails into the soft, warm flesh beneath her sleeve.

None of the women knelt.

"O Mother Earth," he said in a dry whisper. "Deliver up your unhappy dead, your children. Give me your thirsty Hounds, the souls of the unshriven." His voice grew stronger. Like a puppet he raised his hands, his head. "Give me the Hounds." He swung round violently to face the great black muzzle suspended from the roof. The tremor which had seized him in the graveyard caught him again. He rose on the balls of his feet and then seemed to pitch forward. Lyndsay gripped Cloris more tightly. He fell to his knees with such force that his whole body was jarred. He was worshiping the hound, she realized, for its own sake, and not as a symbol of the Earth's power. Was this the moment to intervene? And then, as though in answer to her thought, she saw Mother Poole, who stood back in the shadows, beside the mask. For a moment her eyes met Lyndsay's. It was too dark and too far for Lyndsay to make out her expression, but she saw clearly that the old woman was shaking her head. It was not time, not yet.

"Great Hound of Gabriel," Bart cried. "Come, come to me."

His voice throbbed and shook with such intensity that no man, no human being could sustain it for long. Suddenly he fell forward, lay prostrate before the black altar, the black muzzle of the hound. The silence was intense, complete, and then it was shattered by a sudden, awful baying. Lyndsay turned with the rest toward the doors of the chancel. They were bolted, she saw, and guarded by two men who also stared at them in surprise. The sound chilled her blood. After a moment she heard, they all heard, a snuffling at the doors, the scratch of terrible claws. The door shook, quivered. Barks and yelps mingled with snarls and a pitiful whining. The hounds wanted to come in. Then the baying began again, one voice leading, the other taking it up until there was a choir of unearthly, evil voices clamoring at the doors, the high, vaulted windows.

"The Hounds are singing."

Bart had risen. He stood facing them all. Lyndsay was shocked by his bloodless face, the demonic glitter of his eyes. They burned like flames, while the rest of him seemed already dead. He held out his hands, which trembled with exhaustion or fear.

"We can proceed," he said quietly.

The men rose and shuffled back to their seats. The singing of the hounds gradually ceased, but again the door shook and rattled with the creatures' demands. Lyndsay was glad of the stout bolts. Whatever else happened, the hounds must not get in, she thought. She could see them, streaming into the chancel, the floors running red with blood, with the slaughter. She stood up, her eyes blurred by the vision of carnage, of impending death.

"Who presents this woman to be the Mistress of Ratchets?"

Bart's voice cut through her vision, snapping her back to reality. Her breasts rose and fell beneath the taut, confining silk. Patrick stood up and walked toward her.

"I do," he said, holding out his hand to her.

Gathering her skirt about her, Lyndsay stepped over the embroidered hassock and walked to Patrick. She took his hand. She seemed to know what to do. His hand was cold and damp in hers. She gripped it tightly, for his comfort. Together, moving as one, they turned to face Bart.

"The Hounds are free," he said. "Tonight they attend the dedication of the Mistress for the first time." He continued to speak over the rising murmurs of the congregation. Lyndsay supposed that their agitation was caused by this and other forms of deviation from the established ritual. "And to honor them, symbol and embodiment of the Earth's power, the dedication will be made in blood," he shouted. The crowd was instantly silent. "I say that the union of the Mistress with the Sovereign Earth will be made in blood."

Each time he cried the word *blood* the activity and noise of the hounds outside seemed to increase. Lyndsay looked at Patrick, but his gaze was fixed immovably on Bart. He led her forward so that they stood, like bride and groom, only a few feet from Bart.

"You," he said, "the Presenter, will make the necessary sacrifice."

Patrick released her hand and stepped forward eagerly. Lyndsay tried to work out what Bart was going to do, but he stepped aside and looked impassively into the shadows beyond the mask. With a feeling of panic, Lyndsay realized that Mother Poole was no longer standing there. She was tempted to call her name, but then she remembered that she had to do what must be done alone.

She heard sounds on the steps leading up from the chamber. Indistinct figures appeared. Two men dragged another, slumped, between them, toward the velvet-covered altar. With a concerted heave, they swung the body up, stretched it on the altar. It seemed only half alive. Its pale, naked arms were bound at the wrists and held in a triangle above the head by one of the men, who pulled the free end of the rope taut. She saw that it was a man, naked to the waist, gaunt-ribbed. Suddenly he stirred, his face turned, twisted, so that the light fell on it. She felt the ground shift under her feet. The face swam before her eyes, then steadied. Inside her head she heard a long scream of pain and unreason. She swayed where she stood and then spoke his name into the silence.

"Michael," she whispered.

Outside, the silence of the deserted village was shattered by the rapid arrival of three vehicles. Led by Stuart Donne's car, they screeched to a halt at the village green, close to the point where the path to the children's graveyard met the road. Penelope Clare flung herself out of Stuart's car and ran to meet Sergeant Burroughs of the Ketterford Constabulary and two police constables who scrambled out of the following car.

"This way," she cried. "Quickly."

"Just a minute, miss," the sergeant said. Some half a dozen other policemen were climbing from a black van, topped with the familiar blinking light, which completed the convoy. "Hurry up, gather round," the sergeant ordered. "You, Johnson, stay here. The rest of you come with me and the lady. Now, miss, you think they'll be in the church itself?"

"Yes, I told you," Penelope exclaimed. "But there may be Hounds . . . In the graveyard." She seemed about to break down. Stuart Donne laid a hand on her shoulder.

"Steady," he said.

"We may be too late," she protested. It had not been easy to convince Sergeant Burroughs and she knew that she would never have succeeded without Stuart Donne. The notebook he had, his ability to keep his head had persuaded them. That and the fact that she had been able to confirm and describe his brother's death. But it had all happened so quickly. Her head was reeling. She kept thinking, If he had not been driving along the Ketterford Road, if he had not seen her, not stopped and listened . . .

"Come on then," Burroughs said. "Let's move. As little noise as possible. Right, miss, lead on."

She pulled herself together and hurried into the pathway. Police flashlights pierced the gloom beneath the trees. Penelope was aware that she was panting, and of the solid, comforting presence of Stuart Donne behind her. Thunder rolled suddenly in the west, distant but menacing. At once, as though in answer to it, the hounds set up a grumbling barking which caused Penelope to stop in her tracks.

"The Hounds," she said weakly.

"We *must* get on," Stuart said, taking her arm.

"It'll be all right," she said. "They won't harm you. But . . . I . . . I'm sorry but I can't go in there."

"Better not anyway," Stuart said.

She knew that they did not really believe her about the hounds. She prayed that they would trust her. They came to the wooden door in the wall. Penelope flinched back into the shadows of the trees. More thunder sounded. A solitary hound bayed.

"All right, men," Burroughs said. "Watch out for these dogs. Ignore them and they should ignore you. But take it easy."

"I'll come, too," Stuart said.

"Shouldn't you . . ." Burroughs nodded toward Penelope.

"I'll be all right," she said, leaning against the trunk of a tree, her legs shaking. "Only please hurry."

Burroughs stepped up to the wooden door, opened it, and went through. The policemen and Stuart followed, closing the door firmly behind them. Penelope shut her eyes and tried to remember a prayer. She heard no sound but the snuffling of the hounds and the approaching, intermittent thunder.

"Michael!" The second time she screamed his name and lurched forward.

Patrick threw himself in front of her, holding her back. She could not tell if Michael said anything. His mouth was open, his eyes fixed on her face. She moaned his name again. She did not understand anything except that she had been tricked. Mentally, she was thrown back several stages in what she now thought was an elaborate, deadly game. Her attitudes shifted and became confused. She was not the Mistress. With Michael alive, how could she be anything other than his wife?

"Patrick," Bart commanded.

Thunder rolled ominously in the distance and the hounds bayed. Patrick walked slowly, like a drunken man concentrating on a chalked line, toward the altar. With a flick of his fingers, Bart summoned an acolyte who bore in his hands a velvet cushion on which the gleaming, serpentine knife lay. He held it out to Patrick, who stared at it as though mesmerized.

"Lynd-say." Her name broke from Michael's pale lips in a hoarse whisper.

She felt unable to move or speak but seemed to be suspended between Michael and the women whose eyes burned into her back.

"In the blood of the brother, spilled by the brother shall the Mistress be solemnized," Bart intoned in a hollow voice which was answered by a rumble of thunder. Patrick extended his hand toward the knife.

"Patrick, no, you can't," Lyndsay shouted. With all her strength she pulled free of the force which held her. "You mustn't, Patrick. I forbid it."

His hand closed around the ebony handle of the knife and lifted it free of the cushion. The acolyte stepped backward into the shadows. Bart Poole suddenly glanced toward the doors. Lyndsay caught the fear on his face. The hounds were silent. She listened, breathless. Thunder rolled, but the hounds were silent.

"Patrick," he said. "Hurry."

Holding the knife up, Patrick stumbled to the altar. Lyndsay saw Michael writhe against his bonds. Patrick placed both hands on the knife, held it poised above his brother's heart. Then a new sound came from the hounds outside. It was a whimper, as of a cowed or beaten dog, yet it was made by so many that it seemed to swell and fill the chancel.

"Now," Bart shouted, and Patrick raised the knife a little higher. The wailing outside sounded almost human, like the plaintive voices of a hundred babies. It seemed to make the building shake and reverberate.

"*Now,*" Bart repeated, stepping closer to the altar.

"No," Lyndsay shouted and dashed forward.

The doors shook again but not as they had been shaken before. Bart and Patrick turned toward them. Somebody, several people were hammering on the doors. Amid the noise of the hounds, Lyndsay heard human, commanding voices.

"Open the doors," she shouted over her shoulder as she threw herself against Patrick. She caught him off balance. He fell sideways, across the altar. The knife clattered on the stone floor.

"No," Bart shouted to the men who stood hesitating, bewildered at the doors.

Lyndsay looked at Bart and saw his face twist into a mask of agony. She knew then what he was going to do. They ran for the knife together. Lyndsay, moving faster than she had ever moved in her life, swooped down and grabbed it up. She swung away from Bart, eluding his snatching hands. She was standing at the side of the altar now and he faced her, his back to the congregation. She got a firmer grip on the knife, held the carved handle with both hands. She held it at waist level, the long, cruel blade pointing upward. She did not dare take her eyes off Bart.

"Let them in," she shouted to the men.

"Too late," Bart said with the ghost of a smile. He began to move steadily toward her. Instinctively, Lyndsay backed away. She had no choice but to go behind the hound-mask. As he walked, following her like a shadow from which she would never be free, he unfastened his robe. She saw his chest, gleaming with sweat in the candle-light. She stopped. He came on, walking determinedly. She advanced the knife toward him, threatening him.

"Get back," she said.

He smiled. "You don't understand."

Lyndsay braced herself, closed her eyes, and lunged forward with the knife. She thrust it upward with all her might. He grunted and fell onto her, clinging to her. She opened her eyes, staggered back beneath his weight.

"There was no need," he whispered, his face twisted with pain and disbelief. "I would have . . . done it . . . No need . . ."

A terrible gurgling sound escaped his throat. She saw his eyes roll wildly, showing the white pupils. She pushed against him, her hands warm and sticky, then she stepped aside. He hung for a moment, swaying. Blood spurted from around the knife, splashing her skirt. He fell. Looking down at him, she saw that her bodice was stained crimson, her skirt spotted and splashed with his blood. His legs twitched in a last, compulsive dance.

Lyndsay turned away from him. Straightening her shoulders, lifting her head, she began to walk back to the main part of the chancel. Then, standing against the wall, she saw Mother Poole. Tears streamed down her face. She did not look at Lyndsay, but at Bart. Lyndsay thought that Mother Poole alone had seen everything that had happened. She looked defiantly at the old woman who continued to weep, her mouth silently forming his name.

Lyndsay walked down the central aisle of the chancel. Everything was in confusion. Men and women milled together, screaming, shouting. As she passed through them, looking neither to left nor right, they fell back, silent.

"Open the doors," she ordered.

The two men shrank from her in terror, but one reached up and drew back the bolts. The doors swung open. Men ran into the chancel, shouting orders.

"Oh my God," said one, staring at her bloodstained dress.

Hands tried to restrain her, but she pushed them away. She was outside, in the graveyard. She kept walking. The hounds were pressed close to the earth, cowed, whimpering. She moved fearlessly among them. They scented the blood on her dress, her hands, and gathered around her, whining. She touched their heads, one by one.

Reaching down, moving like someone in a trance, she touched one silky head after another.

And then there weren't any hounds.

Lyndsay stood alone in the center of the graveyard. Her mind was empty, her body cold as ice. After a while, she raised her face to the sky. There was a rush of wings, a honking sound, piercing the damp, silent air. The police at the doors, Stuart Donne, the villagers who pressed stricken against the cordon of linked blue arms, saw a vast skein of geese flying white and beautiful against the night sky. They flew back and forth, tracing patterns above the graveyard. Lyndsay watched them for a long time and then turned, walked slowly back to the chancel. The police made a path for her through the waiting, awed people.

It was dawn when, at last, the police began to lead people out of the chancel. For hours now Stuart Donne and Penelope Clare had waited, watching the continually flying geese. With the first hint of morning, they swooped low, their wings thrashing. It seemed that they were going to settle in the graveyard, but then, with a sudden swerve, they rose and disappeared into the east. Penelope stood up and watched them until they were just specks and then nothing at all.

When Patrick was led out, handcuffed to a constable, she went to him and took his other, free arm. He did not seem to notice. She spoke to him, told him about the geese. She was crying and smiling all at once. Patrick did not acknowledge her, but he did not shake her off. Thinking that she might need him, Stuart Donne followed her, at a discreet distance.

Inside the chancel, Michael Dolben sat on the altar and watched Lyndsay. She stared dumbly at the covered corpse of Bart Poole. A policeman led her away, saying that the ambulance men would soon be arriving. And the photographers. She unpinned the veil from her hair and let it drop onto the floor. Michael stood up, signaling to the policeman that he would take care of her. He held out his arms to her, but Lyndsay, her face closed, her eyes glazed, turned away from him as though she could not see. Bewildered, he watched her walk out into the morning light, followed by Mother Poole's old dog.

CHAPTER THIRTEEN

A bright, cold morning in October. The leaves had already begun to fall and the wind had blown them in drifts against the tiny graves. The whole graveyard had a forlorn, deserted air. Weeds sprouted among the gravel and the brass fittings on the chancel doors were filmed with dirt and neglect. It was a sad place. Surveying it in the cold autumn light, Stuart Donne could not repress a shudder.

"Are you sure," Michael Dolben asked, "that you want to go on with this?" He had seen and understood the shudder.

Stuart nodded. He could see that his curiosity might strike Michael—anyone—as morbid, but he felt strongly that only by seeing for himself, piecing the fragments together, would he be reconciled, be able to put it behind him and think of the future. Staring around the graveyard, he noticed, here and there, freshly turned earth.

"What's been going on here?" he asked, pointing to the disturbed graves.

"The police," Michael said. "They opened one or two."

"But why?" Stuart asked. "What were they looking for?"

Michael shrugged. He was wearing an old sheepskin coat, his hands buried in the pockets. What he had suffered still showed like a stain on his face.

"I don't know," he said. "Anyway, they didn't find it." Michael walked along the path, his feet making the gravel crunch.

"How do you mean?" Stuart asked, following him.

"Precisely that. Nothing. There was nothing in the graves." He looked at Stuart fully. He was frightened, Stuart thought. A frightened man. "Not a bone . . . nothing."

"That's . . . extraordinary," Stuart said. "Is there any explanation?"

"Many. As you can imagine," Michael said and turned away. "At least it means that we can plow it under. That's the best plan." He thought, If Lyndsay will agree. She, he was sure, subscribed to the opinion that of course there would be nothing in the graves now the hounds had been released.

"Yes," Stuart agreed and, more to change the subject than because he was really interested, he asked: "What's the form on something like that? You have to get the Church commissioners to agree, I suppose?"

He shook his head. "No. It was never consecrated, you see."

Stuart felt the chill strike into his bones.

"It must have been about here," Michael said, nodding to a spot on the ground, just outside the doors.

Stuart stared at it. Michael meant where Kenneth had fallen, been knocked down. Stunned or killed? Stuart wondered.

"I couldn't see, of course . . ." Michael's voice trailed off apologetically.

But according to Penelope Clare they, the men, had felled Kenneth as he ran out of the chancel. That meeting to which he had been summoned, about which Stuart had read with a feeling of helpless panic, had been a trap. Stuart looked over his shoulder. There was something terrible in the fact that Kenneth's last sight of earth had been this dismal place. But there was irony in it, too, for all that had happened here would have fascinated him. Indeed, it was precisely for this that he had come to Ratchets. Sadly, Stuart thought that Kenneth might have made some sense of it.

"And nobody saw who struck him?" he asked.

Michael hesitated, staring at the ground. Stuart regretted the question at once, but could not withdraw it. He had a right to know. He owed it to his convalescent father, his mother, to pursue it as far as he could.

"Somebody must know, obviously," Michael answered, "but no one can or will say for sure. You know. You were in court. And, difficult as it must be, I think you have to accept what the judge said."

Person or persons unknown, acting together in a fit of collective hysteria, under the influence of one man . . .

"I know," Stuart agreed. "I'm really not out for revenge. I'd hate you to think that. It's just . . ." He hunched his shoulders.

And afterward they had taken him and placed him in Michael's car. It must have taken many of them to fake the accident. The car driven or pushed into the tree, then set on fire.

"I liked him," Michael said. "He was a very bright, cheerful young man." He also felt guilty. It was a strange, eerie feeling knowing that Kenneth had been buried in his place, in a coffin bearing his name. The body had been exhumed and forensic evidence had established, beyond any reasonable doubt, that it was the body of Kenneth Donne. Besides, what doubt could there be, with Michael Dolben sitting there in court? He had given evidence, of course, had explained how, when Kenneth made a dash for it, two of Bart's men had seized him and dragged him down the steps beneath the chancel. He had told the court how he had hoped, as much for his own sake as for Kenneth's, that the boy would get away, and how Bart had returned later, gloating, to tell him what they had done.

"It would be convenient," Stuart said, shaking himself slightly, "to think that Bart Poole had done it. But then life is seldom so neat and tidy. Shall we?" He gestured to the doors.

"If you want," Michael said, producing the key from his pocket. "In the final analysis, he did do it," he said, fitting it into the lock.

"This may sound strange to you," Stuart said, "but in a way I wish I'd met him. A man who could dominate so many, who could wield such power . . ."

Michael pushed the doors open and stood aside, motioning Stuart to go in.

"Be grateful that you didn't. He was mad. During those last weeks, I felt that I knew what it must have been like to know Hitler. It was a madness that was almost irresistible."

"Except that he must have had charm in some degree. I can't persuade myself that Hitler had much of that."

"He never had any charm for me," Michael said bitterly, following him into the chancel. "Even as a child I hated him. And I was afraid of him. I saw what he was doing to my brother even then. But I didn't understand it. If I'm honest, it was because of him that I was so keen to leave here, and so reluctant to come back. If I had . . ."

"You really mustn't blame yourself, you know," Stuart said. "It's a gloomy-looking place, isn't it?"

He walked, his footsteps echoing, down the almost empty chancel. The pews remained, a fine film of dust covering them, and the altar, stripped bare.

"You can't imagine," Michael said, following him slowly, "how we've been badgered by newspaper people wanting to photograph the place. They even offered money. Quite a lot."

Stuart made a sympathetic noise.

"You were wise to prevent them."

"The alternative was to turn the place into a sort of black museum," Michael said.

"Look, I'm sorry," Stuart said suddenly. "I shouldn't put you through all this."

"No. It's all right. I understand your . . . need to see it. It's got to be faced. All of it." Michael walked past him, hurrying now. Shaking his head, Stuart followed. The man had been through so much . . . "There's a flashlight here. You'd better keep close behind me." Michael reached up to a ledge beside the entrance to the anteroom and took down a powerful torch. He switched it on.

The stone stairs curved downward in a spiral. Stuart followed the pool of light. The room below was empty. Michael moved the light slowly around the chamber and brought it to a stop on the large, wooden door.

"In there?" Stuart asked quietly.

"Yes," Michael said in a neutral voice.

Together they went to the door. Michael held the light and Stuart opened the door. Behind it was a small, windowless room. It contained a bed and a bucket and four chains hanging from rings in the wall. Stuart could not begin to imagine what it must have been like to be kept a prisoner, chained, in this cell.

"I'm sorry," he said.

"It wasn't too bad. Mother Poole saw to it that I was drugged most of the time. Apart from Bart's midnight tirades and the endless worry about Lyndsay . . ." He stopped. "Do you know what she said when she saw it?"

"No." Stuart looked at his shadowed face.

"She said it was just like something out of a Vincent Price movie," Michael said, chuckling.

"She's a remarkable woman," Stuart said.

"Yes," Michael agreed. It sounded perfunctory, as though her courage and resilience could be taken for granted. The light suddenly swung away. "That's the door to the secret passage," Michael said, mockingly. "We could go back that way if you like."

"No," Stuart said quickly. "I think we both need some fresh air." Michael shone the light at the foot of the stairs.

"How many of them knew you were here?"

"Apart from the men who brought me down here? They had mufflers wound round their faces—I still don't know who they were. Apart from them, Bart, of course, and Mother Poole. Emelye. Penelope and Damon. My brother."

"It was good of you not to press charges. I'm not sure that in your position I would have been so forgiving," Stuart said. And one of them, he thought, placing his feet carefully on the twisting steps, must have killed Kenneth. If they were all who were present in the chancel that night, it must have been one of them. For the first time, he realized that it could have been a woman who struck the blow.

"There was no point," Michael said. "Unlike you, I knew Bart. I knew what power he had over them. I genuinely agree with what the judge said. To turn the whole thing into a witch-hunt . . ."

"An unfortunate turn of phrase, all things considered," Stuart murmured dryly.

"I suppose. I hadn't thought of that. Anyway, my brother has been punished. I can't see any purpose in pursuing it. Nothing can alter what happened. I don't want to store up more bitterness. Somehow this community has got to go on living."

"You're set on staying here, then?" Stuart asked as he stepped into the anteroom.

"To be frank," Michael said, switching off the torch, "Lyndsay is. Personally . . ."

"I rather thought as much last night," Stuart said. Lyndsay had seemed determined to stay. She had talked excitedly of her plans for the village. Her enthusiasm had struck Stuart as overplayed. There was a hint of desperation in it, he felt. But it was none of his business, he reminded himself as he walked into the chancel. Personally, he would have gotten out of Ratchets as quickly as possible, but perhaps she was right. "What about your work?" Stuart asked as Michael replaced the flashlight on the shelf. "Will you be able to work from here?"

"Oh yes. It'll mean being away quite a bit, but it's possible. Fortunately, I hope to be teaching in Cambridge in the spring, so that will be relatively easy. In a way it is better to stay here," he went on, as though speaking to himself. "I've been running away from it all my life."

"If you don't mind my asking," Stuart said, taking out his pipe. "How much did you know?"

"How do you mean? This time or generally?"

"Both, really. Look, do you mind . . . ?" Stuart moved to a pew near the open doors and sat down, tamping some tobacco into the bowl of his pipe. Somehow, he did not know why, he did not want to leave the chancel. Not yet.

Michael joined him, but did not sit down. In a way he wanted to talk about it. Not to the uncomprehending, disbelieving ears of solicitors and policemen, but to someone impartial yet involved. With Lyndsay . . . He stopped himself before he could finish the thought. Anyway, he owed Stuart Donne what explanation he could give.

"I grew up with it," he said, staring out into the graveyard. "We all did. But children were excluded. I mean we knew that Albertine Clare was the Mistress, but we didn't question it. We didn't know any different, you see. Children accept what they are presented with. And we were so protected. We never left the village. My father educated us. He was a very remarkable man. It just seemed a part of life. The grown-up part that we regarded, on the whole, as boring. It was more fun playing up on the ridge. Do you understand?"

"Mm," Stuart said, sucking on his pipe. "Of course." He crossed his legs and waited for Michael to go on.

"The cult only impinged on us in very pleasant ways. The sort of thing Kenneth was looking for. There were the harvest suppers, the May Day celebrations. Things like that. To us, they were all very jolly. We looked forward to them. And I should stress that the cult was fairly inactive then. My father did not encourage it. And then, being young, we were excluded anyway from the finer details."

"Tell me about your father," Stuart said.

"He was a good man. A rational man. Educated but not developed. He was cushioned by money, by the rather pleasant life of a country squire. He had plenty of time to indulge his passions—"

"Topiary," Stuart interrupted.

"Among other things, yes."

"I noticed the hedge has been cut down."

"Yes. Lyndsay didn't like it."

"A pity. For all it was a little bizarre, it was magnificently done."

"It was his life's work," Michael said bleakly. "That and trying to make up to Bart for . . . well, his birth."

"I gather he was illegitimate."

"He was my mother's child by her brother," Michael said, his voice shaking a little.

"Oh I say I . . ." Stuart blushed. He did not know what to say. He felt graceless, a blunderer.

"My mother was a true Poole," Michael said. "And my father wasn't strong enough to . . . well, it's over now."

"I'm terribly sorry," Stuart said. "It must be very painful for you."

"At the time, yes. Bart, what he was, affected me much more deeply than the Ways."

"I can see that it would."

"It fascinated Patrick. But I . . . Oh I suppose I was jealous of Bart. I was always closer to my father, and he felt such an obligation to Bart. He wanted him to have the advantages we had. Yes, I was jealous. And when I found out . . . I'm not very proud of this, but I loathed my mother. I've often tried to sort it out, but the honest truth is that I hated her. And still do."

Stuart puffed smoke into the still air. He felt cold and chastened by what he had heard.

"So you see why I kept away from Ratchets," Michael went on. "Why I never wanted to come back here. When my father died I considered that all my ties with the place were finally cut."

"Yes, of course." Stuart stood up.

"You have no idea, growing up as I did, what an incredible thing it was to go to Cambridge, to live a normal life. My instinct was to push Ratchets out of my mind. I should have known . . ."

"How could you?" Stuart said. "You left a disastrous, even horrible world for a good one. Why should you think—"

"But that's the crazy thing. I did think about it, after I married Lyndsay. I can't explain why. It just came back to me. I knew, you see, that my wife would automatically be involved in the cult. I'd been away from the place for years. I'd married a woman I met on the other side of the Atlantic, and yet I was afraid. That's really why I came back here." He lapsed into a sad, reflective silence.

"Shall we?" Stuart said, nodding his head at the open doors. "It's not very warm in here."

"Yes." Michael walked to the doors. The sun had come out, mak-

297

ing the earth steam. They stood on the threshold, glad of the sun. "You see, when I said all ties were cut, I was really fooling myself. My father left the house, the estate, which, I may say, amounts to about two-thirds of Ratchets itself, to Patrick and me jointly. Patrick ran everything, or so I thought, but I still lived off it. I received my quarterly check. I had the land, the house to fall back on if I ever needed it."

"What I don't understand," Stuart said, interrupting, "is why your father left nothing to Bart, feeling as he did about him."

"By then he knew what Bart was like. At least, I think he did. You see, there was all this fuss about Magdalena Clare and, well, I'm sure my father knew more than he ever said. Albertine, the Mistress then, was determined to make Bart her Priest. In order to do it she deposed her daughter. Madgalena would have been the next Mistress. It was no secret that she did it because she . . . well, to be blunt, because she fancied Bart. She thought that by marrying him off to Maddy she'd have him in her pocket for life. He used to boast to us, Patrick and me, about things he'd done with Albertine." His voice sounded choked.

"Don't," Stuart said gently. "I can imagine."

"But she miscalculated. Bart fell in love with Maddy. Head over heels. Only she was her mother's daughter."

"Berryman," Stuart said.

"Right. She wanted him and she was going to have him, no matter what anyone said. The Berrymans were a thorn in everybody's flesh. They were poachers, thieves. My father tried several times to get them put off his land, but somehow they always managed to wriggle out of it. Bart succeeded though. When Maddy went to live with Timon, he went berserk. He made life so unpleasant for the Berrymans, they soon left."

"But she didn't leave."

"He wouldn't let her. Meanwhile, Bart was virtually living with Albertine, who was getting more and more crazy by the day. And this is the result. All this." He gestured toward the graveyard, the chancel.

"And that's when your father decided to cut him out of his will?"

"If he was ever in it, yes. And Bart never forgave him. I think that must have contributed to his . . . to the way he was."

"I interrupted you," Stuart said. "I'm sorry. You were saying about when you came back."

"That's right. Well, as I told you, I don't know why I thought

298

about it all but I did. I tried to ignore it, but as Lyndsay's arrival came closer and closer I felt that I *had* to sever all my relations with Ratchets, even though I was afraid. So," he sighed heavily, "I came back here a couple of weeks before she was due to arrive. I was only planning to stay for a few days. I wanted to sell my entire share in the estate, the house and everything. My great mistake was to tell them that I was married. God, if I'd only . . . Well, anyway I did, and that's that. At first I thought my cool reception was because I wanted to sell my portion to cut all ties. To leave is the ultimate sin," he explained. "And, I admit I was annoyed that Bart had taken over the estate management, but since I wanted to sell . . . well, it was Patrick's business. However, to cut a long story short, they kept stalling. Patrick refused to talk about it properly and eventually I threatened to put the whole thing on the open market. I wasn't serious, of course, but I thought that it might make them see that I meant business. And that's when I discovered that Patrick had signed everything, every stick and stone, over to Bart. He was a tenant in his own house. Well, you can imagine how I reacted."

"Quite," Stuart said, knocking his pipe out on the heel of his shoe. "But did you realize what else was going on?"

"No. I was hopelessly slow. In fact, it was your brother who alerted me to it. He asked a lot of questions which I was perfectly happy to answer. But I did so as though I were recalling old times, you know? He told me that far from being history, it was all going on now, right here, under our noses. Emelye and he, by then, had fallen for each other and she'd told him a lot. Not all of it, but enough to make him feel anxious. I realized then that the fear that had made me come here, the fear for Lyndsay, which I had thought was irrational and superstitious, was very real indeed. I should have left then but Bart suddenly said that he would buy. He and Penelope Clare together. So I hung on. I still didn't know what Bart was planning. By then they were all up in arms about Emelye and your brother. As far as I was concerned, if they loved each other, fine. I offered to take them with me. I should have become suspicious when Bart stopped shouting and became rational. He called this meeting. We were going to discuss the sale and your brother. I honestly thought it was just a bit of face-saving. Bart would huff and puff, Emelye would be made to feel terrible, but that would be it."

"Instead of which, my brother died and you were held to ransom, as it were."

Michael nodded.

"What happened at the meeting?" Stuart asked.

Michael pressed his fingers to his head, as though in pain. "I can't remember too clearly. All the drugs they fed me afterward . . . I can tell you, Mother Poole's herbal possets really do blow your mind, as Lyndsay would say.

"Bart was all got up in his gold robes. That put the wind up me, I don't mind admitting. And Mother Poole sat there like some enigmatic avenging angel. They denounced Emelye. All the old stuff about shaming the blood, blackening the good name of her family. It was just like Magdalena Clare all over again. I couldn't believe it, but I had to. And Kenneth, of course, was condemned as the violator, the foreigner who had abused hospitality. It was unbelievable, madness . . ." He shook his head again as though trying to clear it. "And then they pronounced sentence of death on him."

"And they carried it out," Stuart said somberly.

Michael nodded again. Stuart looked away across the graveyard, breathing deeply.

"For what?" he asked. Then: "Shall we be getting back? I think I've had enough of this place."

Michael pulled the chancel doors shut behind him and locked them. Side by side, they began to walk slowly down the gravel path.

"And Bart's motive was really to get his hands on all the land, everything?" Stuart asked after a while.

"I wish I could believe that," Michael said. "Unpleasant though it is, at least it's a human motive, something one can understand. But Bart . . . Bart wanted . . ." There were no words for it, he realized. "Power, but a power which lay beyond the bounds of reason, which was so terrible and, ultimately, so incomprehensible, that the rational mind shrinks from it, confused."

"Collapse of the rational man, eh?"

Michael stopped and looked slowly around him, at the autumn trees, the tiny graves, up to the high walls of the graveyard.

"You were in court for the inquest. You've no doubt read the various newspaper reports." Stuart nodded, confirming that he had. "They all sheltered behind the civilized phrases. Megalomania. Mass hysteria. The grip of a dominant personality, his will, imposed upon a whole village. Blood, superstitious belief in . . . What did the judge call it?"

" 'The dark and impenetrable side of the human soul,' " Stuart quoted gravely.

"But when you think about it," Michael said, "when you've been

300

a part of it, there comes a point when you come up against a great big question mark. You have to choose between sense and irrational belief."

"And you believe," Stuart said quietly, "that something . . . What do we call it? Supernatural? Occult? Something like that occurred here?"

Michael did not answer for a long time, but then he said, "The autopsy on Magdalena and her children—they were buried up on the ridge, you know. The police found them—was quite conclusive. They had been savaged, mauled beyond belief by . . . animals."

Stuart could not believe it. It was too terrible to contemplate. Slowly, Michael looked at Stuart, who was shocked by the expression on his face.

"I'm afraid," Michael said, and Stuart believed him.

After lunch Michael leaned against the stone mantelpiece in the great hall of Dolben House. A log fire burned in the grate. Lyndsay had rearranged the furniture to make the fireplace the focal point of the room. A great copper bowl of chrysanthemums stood on the table; gold and yellow and a bronze almost as dark as the brandy in Michael's glass. He looked silently at his guests and thought that this really was the end of something. The feeling, he knew, was prompted by Stuart Donne's questions, his desire to "to get everything straight," but the feeling went deeper than that for Michael. He did not know how to express it, except as a certainty that they would never all meet again like this. It was as though they had gathered solely in order to cut the bonds that tied them.

Emelye was leaving that afternoon with Stuart Donne. It was what she wanted and Michael was pleased for her. She had put on weight, partly, of course, as a result of her pregnancy, but also thanks to Lyndsay's determination to "build her up." She had lost that haunted look and her skin had regained its natural bloom. Her long, dark hair shone. She looked, Michael thought, like a beautiful ripe fruit. He was glad for her and grateful to the Donnes for wanting to give her a home. They were looking forward to their first grandchild and Michael hoped that the baby and Emelye would in some measure console them for Kenneth's death. Sometimes Michael wondered if Lyndsay wasn't especially glad that the girl was leaving. It was an uncharitable thought insofar as Lyndsay had insisted on her staying at Dolben House and had cared for her attentively. But sometimes, especially when she entered a room and found Emelye and Michael alone together, a certain look crossed her face that made him wonder if, despite all the protestations and assurances, she still did not quite accept that he was not the father of Emelye's baby. The idea that he could be had shocked him. He had never, ever thought of Emelye in that way, but then they had endowed him with a fictitious past that no man, except possibly Bart himself, could live up to. But Lyndsay had been convinced of it all. Naturally it would take time for her to adjust. But perhaps, having Emelye off their hands would enable Lyndsay to make the other, essential adjustments more rapidly.

But if Lyndsay had succeeded with Emelye, he mused, pushing other, unpleasant thoughts aside, she had signally failed with Penelope, whose pale hair was suddenly, dramatically streaked with gray. Her strong face looked as though it had collapsed inward. Her clothes hung on her bony body, making her look perpetually untidy. She sat now a little apart from Stuart and Emelye, chain-smoking, clutching her glass and pretending to listen to the conversation. Michael was tired of asking if she was all right, not because he did not feel sympathetic toward her, but because her answers were predictable and unconvincing. He did not know whether she rejected help, or if he and Lyndsay were simply unable to help her.

She lived, he knew, for her weekly visits to the hospital where Patrick had been placed by the court. He thought that she must think it unfair that Patrick had been punished when others, herself included, had not been. But Lyndsay insisted that it was not a punishment. It was obvious to everyone that Patrick needed help. Everyone except Penelope, he corrected himself. After her visits she dutifully reported on his progress. Michael actually wished that she would not. There was something terrible about listening to her making mountains of hope out of nothing. Patrick had sat out in the garden. Patrick had gone for a little walk with one of the nurses. Patrick had seemed pleased with something she had taken him. Recounting these incidents, she became vivid, alive again. Her eyes shone and she punctuated her accounts with bursts of desperate laughter. Michael wondered if she hated him for not visiting Patrick, but Lyndsay said he was being paranoid even to think of it. The doctors insisted that it would not be a good idea, neither for Patrick nor for Michael. Besides, Lyndsay sometimes went with her—she insisted that it was her duty—and returned feeling flat and helpless. She pretended, though, for Penelope's sake, to echo her certainty that he was getting better. Michael sighed. Perhaps Lyndsay was right. Perhaps if Penelope were deprived of her slim hopes, made to face the truth, it would destroy her. But then, what was the truth? he thought. Patrick might recover, in time, but would he then be able to love her and live with her, here, in Ratchets?

"Cheer up, old man," Stuart said. "It can't be as bad as all that."

They were all looking at him, he realized, their attention caught by his sigh. Penelope's eyes were cold and lifeless, like those of a stranded fish. No one spoke for several minutes then, "That's the strangest thing of all," Michael said to Stuart, indicating the dog curled at Lyndsay's feet, Mother Poole's dog.

"The old woman's disappearance, you mean?"

"Yes. There's still no sign of her."

"The police are still looking?"

"Yes, but not with a great deal of hope."

"They won't find her," Emelye said suddenly. "She's too clever for them. She'll . . ."

They looked at the girl, waiting for her to complete the sentence. She blushed and shook her head.

"She'll be back," Lyndsay said, looking at them all confidently.

"Meanwhile," Michael said, "the dog is absolutely devoted to Lyndsay."

"He was my first friend here," she said, leaning down to pat him.

"And the Hounds?" Stuart asked. "The Gabriel Ratchets."

"They're gone now," Lyndsay answered in a dreamy voice, without raising her head.

Stuart looked at Michael, puzzled, but Michael would not meet his eyes.

"I meant," Stuart persisted, "what were they? How do you explain them?"

Lyndsay shook her head as though the question were irrelevant or offended her.

Michael said, "It's interesting that some versions of the legend equate them with geese. They are supposed to take the form of geese."

"Quite," Stuart said, staring at Lyndsay, "but that doesn't explain what they are."

"You know what they are," Penelope said angrily, standing up.

"You've obviously done your homework, but more importantly you saw them. You were there. You saw them and what happened to them."

"But my dear Miss Clare, I can't . . . ."

Penelope turned away from him.

"Lyndsay, I must go now," she said. "If you'll excuse me."

Slowly, very slowly, Lyndsay turned toward her. Her eyes had a clouded appearance and she wore a puzzled expression as though she did not understand what was happening.

"Oh yes, of course," she said vaguely.

"Good-bye, Mr. Donne," Penelope said. "Take care, Emelye."

She nodded to Michael and walked quickly to the door before anyone could say anything. Stuart called after her, then sighed.

"Oh dear," he said. "I *am* sorry."

"You mustn't mind Penelope," Lyndsay told him. "She's very unhappy. We have to make allowances for her."

"Of course. I'm only sorry I upset her."

"It wasn't that," Michael said. "She finds any company difficult just now."

"Anyway Lyndsay," Stuart said, "I was actually asking you."

"About the Hounds?" she asked in a perfectly normal voice. "I can't add anything to what Penelope said."

"You agree with her?"

"Do you have a better explanation?" she challenged him.

"Alas, no," he admitted.

Lyndsay stood up. It was unmistakably a sign of dismissal.

"Well, Emelye," Stuart said as tactfully as he could, "we'd better be making tracks."

"I'll get my coat," she said, pushing her body awkwardly up from the settee.

"And I'll put your cases in the car," Michael offered.

"Thank you," Emelye said and went into the kitchen, pressing her hands to the small of her back.

Michael lifted the suitcases and took them outside.

"You'll come and see us again?" Lyndsay said, smiling at Stuart.

"I hope so."

"Thank you for all you're doing for Emelye."

"Oh no," he said, shaking his head. "It's we who must be grateful to Emelye. Without her and the baby to look forward to . . . Well, let's just say it has helped my parents enormously."

"I'm glad," Lyndsay said simply.

"May I . . . venture a word of advice?"

"Of course."

Stuart drew closer to her. Impulsively, he took her hand in his. He was surprised to find how cold it was.

"You're a very brave woman," he said. "But I think you should go away from here. I've been watching you . . . forgive me. I don't mean to be rude . . . you don't eat, you're very pale. In short, I don't think Ratchets is good for you, or Michael."

"All loaded and correct," Michael said cheerfully as he returned to the hall.

"Thank you," Stuart said. He looked at Lyndsay but she only murmured:

"Good-bye, Stuart. Drive carefully." She pulled her hand free and walked quickly toward Emelye. "And you mind you take care of yourself, you hear?" she said, embracing her. "And don't forget I want to know the moment Junior arrives, okay? And then, promise me, you'll bring him to visit?"

"Thanks for everything, Mistress," Emelye said, squeezing her.

Stuart looked sharply at Michael, who looked away.

"Come on now, we'll see you off," Lyndsay said, tucking her arm through Emelye's. Stuart and Michael followed them outside. While Lyndsay settled Emelye in the car, Stuart and Michael shook hands.

"If there's ever anything I can do . . ." Stuart offered.

"Thank you. I'll remember."

"Good luck."

"And you."

Through the open window of the car, Michael pressed Emelye's hand. She looked, he thought, more than happy to be leaving. Emelye would have no regrets, and he was glad of that. He stood beside Lyndsay, calling good-bye and waving. They watched until the car was lost to view. Lyndsay shivered and turned back into the house.

"What did Stuart say to you while I was putting Emelye's cases in the car?" Michael inquired, shutting the front door.

"Oh nothing. He was just saying good-bye."

"Leave those," Michael said. "Bryony will see to them." She began to collect up the glasses.

"Yes, you're right," she said, putting the glasses down. "Actually,

I'm bushed. I think I'll go and lie down for an hour. You don't mind?" She said it as an afterthought, from the foot of the stairs.

"I rather wanted to talk to you . . ." Michael began.

"Later, okay?" she said.

"That's what I was going to suggest."

"Come on, Dog," Lyndsay called. The dog rose, shook himself, and padded softly after her, up the stairs.

Lyndsay had put off moving into the master bedroom with Michael. At first he had needed to rest and recuperate. Doctor's orders. Then there had been all the turmoil and nervous tension of the investigation, the court appearances.

Those were the nightmare weeks when Lyndsay had grown despairing and cynical as one by one everybody implicated had shifted all blame and responsibility onto Bart. Everyone had some tale of coercion, blackmail, fear. It wasn't that she doubted the truth of these stories—although she certainly suspected a degree of exaggeration—but that something in her resented his being made a scapegoat. Only Cloris Poole had maintained any loyalty to him and, ironically, her statements had sealed his posthumous condemnation. By telling the truth she had confirmed everything else, even the wildest rumors. But at least she had defended him, as far as she was able. As a result, the villagers resented her. When she passed silently, dressed in deepest mourning, through the village to tend his unmarked grave, Lyndsay knew that they hated her, for she reminded them of their own culpability and weakness.

For a time, it had seemed that Cloris was determined to involve herself in any prosecution, but if that had been her intention, she had failed. Finally, it was only Patrick, poor silent, broken Patrick, who had been arraigned and sent to Warnford. Though found to have been an accomplice of Bart Poole and to have threatened his brother's life, he was, at least partly, exonerated on grounds of diminished responsibility. It had been a farce, Lyndsay thought bitterly. How wise Mother Poole had been to argue always against involving the police, people outside.

And when all that was over she had refused to move into the master bedroom until it was redecorated. Michael had taken it very well, she thought, but there was no way that she could conceal her pregnancy from him much longer. The constant effort to hide her revulsion to most foods and all alcohol, her sudden middle-of-the-night cravings for tomato salad or ginger cookies exhausted her. Her need to rest, the terrible lethargy which overtook her at times must soon make him suspicious. Meanwhile, she felt stranded, caught helplessly between the future and the past. If she had slept with Michael at the earliest opportunity then she might have been able to pretend. Other women were uncertain about dates, had conveniently premature babies. But she did not want to lie about it and she could not bear the idea of his touching her.

One question stood out from all the rest, haunting her. Had Bart won, after all? Did the fact that she was carrying his child mean that, in spite of everything, the Mistress was not supreme, not safe? She could not answer this question. She did not know how to proceed. She was not even sure if Penelope Clare knew of her condition. For a moment anger flared in her against Penelope, who had so weakly compromised her, who did not even bother to deny that she had allowed Bart free access to Lyndsay when she was staying, drugged, at Clare House.

Lyndsay turned, tired but restless on the bed, looking out the bright window. The dog, curled on the floor beside her, lifted his shaggy head and regarded her balefully. She knew why Mother Poole had gone. Throughout the nightmare weeks Lyndsay had waited for someone to say that he or she had seen what happened behind the mask that night in the chancel but nobody had. Perhaps only the old lady had seen, or was someone maintaining a conspiracy of forgetfulness, as they all had about Kenneth Donne? Mother Poole knew that Bart had not died by his own hand, and therefore she had abandoned Lyndsay, the Mistress. And without her, Lyndsay did not know what to do. She closed her eyes miserably against tears of self-pity. The dog whimpered, sat up, and placed his old head on the edge of the bed. Automatically, Lyndsay reached out to touch him. He licked her hand consolingly.

"You're right, Dog," she whispered. "I know you're right. This is no way for the Mistress to behave."

Michael worked for a couple of hours in the library. He had set himself the task of cataloging the books. Some could be thrown out, others sold. He would need space for his own books, since they were going to stay here. He felt depressed now that Stuart and Emelye had gone. Ratchets seemed more insulated than ever against the outside world. He forced himself to keep working, not to brood. And later he would talk to Lyndsay. Maybe there was a chance, still, of persuading her to leave. Or perhaps he would have to leave. There was more to it than just the place. They had to talk about their marriage, or what was left of it. That was really the crux of the matter: was there anything left? Did he still love Lyndsay? He waited for the answer to come spontaneously. There was no answer, none at all. They had been jerked out of their own world, where the answer to that question was simple and without doubt, and dropped down in another world like flies, caught in a sticky web. Only Lyndsay seemed able to adjust to it, or at least to have given up struggling. While he . . . He moved restlessly from the desk to the shelves. There was no point in thinking about it. He pulled out several fat volumes and carried them back to the desk. They must talk, be honest with each other and themselves. He picked up an old, soiled duster and began wiping the books. His hands were already stained gray with the accumulated dust of many years. After what they had been through, of course they would have to start again. He wanted that, was willing to try, but all his instincts told him that they would never succeed completely here, in Ratchets.

Sighing, Michael pulled his list toward him and opened the book he had just dusted.

The Book of the Ways
Being a complete history of the Mistress,
with a full record of the Ordinances
governing her Selection and Rule
by
Ezekiel Dolben

He slammed the book shut and pushed it away. His hands were trembling. They could never forget here, not when at every turn there was something to remind them. The way they still called her Mistress whenever they spoke to her; Cloris Poole's ostentatious mourning for her brother and the way she tended Bart's grave so that no one would ever forget.

He seized the book angrily. That was definitely going. It should be burned, was his first thought, but such destruction went completely against his grain. He hefted it in his hand for a moment, acknowledging that, dangerous though it was, it was unique. And then he had an idea which cheered him. It could be the start of reparation, something he and Lyndsay could do together to show that they were not trapped, that they could start again. And there was no time like the present.

Michael hurried into the hall, carrying the book. The fire had died down to a few embers. He put the book on the table and began to tend the fire, first with kindling and, when that had blazed up, with small logs. Just as he had got it going again he heard the clatter of the dog's claws along the gallery. He turned, smiling at Lyndsay. She was carrying her coat over her arm and did not seem to notice him.

"Feeling better?" he asked, standing up.

"Oh yes, thank you."

"You going out?" He looked at his hands, which were now even dirtier.

"Just to give the dog a run. I must speak to Bryony first, though." She seemed to drift toward the table, then stopped and looked down at the book. "You've been working in the library?" she asked. "How's it going?"

"Oh all right. Take a look at that, will you?"

He walked across to her and watched her face closely as she opened the book. It did not seem to disturb or even interest her.

"You realize what it is?" he said.

"Sure." She closed the book. "What are you going to do with it?"

"Well, I think I've had rather a good idea. At first I wanted to burn it . . ."

"Whatever for?" Lyndsay said, looking shocked.

"Because it's evil," Michael said, searching her face for some sign that she understood and agreed with him.

"Nonsense," she said. "You know books aren't evil. It's the interpretation people put on them." Her hand rested lightly but protectivly on the scuffed leather cover.

"Well anyway, I've solved the problem."

"I really don't see any problem."

"I thought it would be a nice gesture if we, you and I jointly, presented it to Kenneth Donne's college. I did promise to lend it to him and after all it does have some curiosity value."

"And have hordes of students coming here prying and asking questions? Haven't you had enough of that?"

He hesitated. There was a grain of truth in what she said, but he was determined that the book should not remain in the house.

"Let's talk about it, at least," he said. "Look, I must wash my hands . . ."

"Actually, you look as though you could use a bath. Your face is all dirty." Michael looked down at his clothes. They were stained with dust and dirt. "Why don't you have a bath and then when I've given the dog a walk, we can sit down quietly and talk?"

"I'd like that," Michael said. "You won't be long?"

"No. Go on. And I'll tell Bryony to fix something good for dinner."

Michael felt suddenly close to her. He reached out his arms to embrace her, but she pulled back as if shocked.

"Your hands, Michael," she said. "Go and wash."

"Sorry," he said, thinking that there had been a time when a little dirt would not have mattered. But there was no point in making an issue out of it. He walked to the stairs.

"Have a nice bath," Lyndsay called, pulling on her coat.

"I'll see you later," he said, climbing the stairs.

Lyndsay buttoned her coat and, calling to Dog, picked up *The Book of the Ways* and carried it into the kitchen. Bryony Dolben looked up from the chopping board on which she was slicing lean, bloody meat into long strips.

"You planning something good for dinner, Aunt Bryony?" Lyndsay asked.

"Aye. One of Michael's favorites."

"Good. Bryony, will you do something for me?"

"Anything, Mistress," she answered shyly.

"Take this home with you. Keep it safe, okay?"

She placed the book on the table. Slowly, Bryony wiped her hands, first on a damp cloth and then on a towel. She walked around the table and picked up the book almost reverently.

The two women exchanged a quiet, secret smile, then Lyndsay went out the back door and Bryony placed the book at the bottom of her shopping basket and covered it with her black shawl.

Lyndsay let the old dog lead her along the path beside the children's graveyard. She kept her hands stuffed into the pockets of her old woolen coat. It was far from dark yet, but the sun was already waning and the night promised to be cold. The leaves above her head were golden brown, dying. The dog snuffled happily among those that had already fallen. He never went far away from Lyndsay, and his short forays into the trees, on some elusive scent, always ended in swift, tail-wagging returns to her. She had become attached to the dog because he had chosen her and because she knew that he pined for Mother Poole as she did. She felt relief at having admitted her sense of loss at last. She did not know how to go on, how to be what the old woman had made her. Mother Poole would know and guide her.

Her brooding, rather heavy thoughts were interrupted when she came to the village green. Justin Dolben was there with Damon and several others. They fell silent as she drew close to them, the dog at heel. She greeted them and they spoke together of the coming winter, of the harvest which, all things considered, had been better than expected. Lyndsay smiled. The men were awkward in her presence and yet she sensed their gratitude. Their awkwardness stemmed not from resentment but out of their acceptance of her position. Each one unfailingly addressed her as Mistress. She thought that Damon looked less sad and reminded herself that she must talk to Penelope about him. There was so much that she should do but did not yet know how to do. Damon might think that she had failed him now that Emelye had gone.

"There she goes," Justin Dolben said suddenly, interrupting Lyndsay's train of thought. He had turned almost laconically and was staring up the village street. They all looked at the black-shawled figure of Cloris Poole as she paused to lock her door.

"Every night, sure as eggs," one of the other men commented.

Lyndsay suddenly had an idea. Smiling, she said, "Damon, why don't you walk along with her? After all, you're going that way." He hesitated, his face showing confusion. Lyndsay stared at him calmly, still smiling. It was a test, she knew, but if she could command Damon then the others would have to accept Cloris.

They were all watching him now, but it was only Lyndsay he saw. At last he bowed his head.

"Yes. Mistress," he said, "I'll say good-night then."

"Good-night, Damon. And tell Cloris hello for me."

The other men murmured their good-nights and watched as Damon set off up the street after Cloris. Lyndsay watched, too, holding her breath.

When he reached her, Cloris stopped for a moment and then they walked along together, their heads bent close, talking.

"Well, I'd better be going," Lyndsay said. "The dog's getting restless." She knew the men were bursting to discuss Damon's obedience but that they could not in her presence. It was a small triumph, she thought, but it was a beginning. It made her feel better. Damon could do worse for himself than Cloris, and Lyndsay could count on her. With a wave of her hand, she left the men who bade her goodnight. She did not look back at them. She knew that they would draw close together, whisper, and that soon everyone in the village would know that the Mistress had brought Damon Clare and Cloris Poole together.

The dog set off with an air of determination toward the oaks. Lyndsay felt a little daunted by the long climb up the hill, but she wasn't ready yet to return to the house and Michael. She had to get her thoughts in order. He would have to be told and somehow his objections must be overcome. She wondered what his reaction would be. Anger, pain certainly, but when they had passed . . . ? What terrified her was the chance that he might want her to have an abortion, or demand a divorce. He owned half the estate and would soon have control over Patrick's share. That was her child's birthright, all that Bart had striven for. If only she could make him accept her as the Mistress, then she could mold him. In time, she might even feel affection for him, but while he stood in opposition to her, a threat not only to her child but all she had to do here . . .

A sense of emptiness swept through her as, panting slightly, she reached the oaks. If only Mother Poole had not abandoned her. If only she had not precipitated Bart's death, but had allowed it to happen. She longed for the old woman's forgiveness, and yet was afraid of it. She stared at the grass beneath the trees. There was no sign now of the scorching. Only a practiced eye could make out the scar on the trunk of the oak. The earth had healed itself as it would, in time, heal all wounds. But how much time did she have? She wondered, as she walked between the trees and stood looking down at the roofs, at the curling wisps of smoke rising from the chimneys. She stared over to the dark mass of the chancel on its promontory beside Clare House and imagined Damon helping Cloris tend the grave. A cold mist was creeping down from the ridge and she shivered involuntarily. It was time to be getting back. She looked around for the dog but there was neither sight nor sound of him. She searched everywhere, calling and whistling to him, but he did not come. He must have taken off across the field, following the scent of a rabbit or something. But he had never done that before. Indeed, Lyndsay had thought him too old for hunting now. He never seemed to want to be far from her. He couldn't leave her, not now, she thought hysterically. She had to find him.

"Hey, Lyndsay. Remember me?"

Lyndsay spun around. The voice was familiar but just out of memory's reach.

"Lyndsay, sweetheart!"

There, standing on the road was, of all the people in the world, Mrs. Abernathy. With a cry of surprise and delight, Lyndsay stumbled across the grass into the old woman's plump and welcoming arms.

"Mrs. Abernathy," she said, holding her. "Oh it's so good to see you!"

"And you, too, honey."

"If you only knew how often I . . ."

"Never mind, just tell me how you've been."

"How on earth did you get here?" Lyndsay asked, looking in vain for a car.

"All in good time," Mrs. Abernathy laughed, pushing Lyndsay from her so that she could inspect her face critically. "You look wonderful," she pronounced.

"Thank you," Lyndsay said, smiling down into her bright, blue eyes. She was completely unchanged. The slightly ridiculous blue silk toque perched on her head, an unsuitable blue-checked coat pulled tightly round her soft, ample figure.

"Hey," she said, clasping Lyndsay's hand and drawing her back under the trees, toward the field. "Let me take a look at the old place."

Lyndsay felt herself being tugged along. She stood beside her friend, looking down at the village.

"Isn't that something?" Mrs. Abernathy sighed appreciatively.

"It's beautiful," Lyndsay agreed. "You can't imagine how attached I've grown to it."

"Oh yes I can," she answered, nodding her head.

Lyndsay looked at her.

"Now, Mrs. Abernathy, you owe me an explanation. Several, in fact. You know that hotel number you gave me? I couldn't find you.

And then, what are you doing here now?" Her face clouded suddenly. "I guess you read about it all in the newspapers," she said, her happiness fading at the thought of having to explain everything.

"I didn't need to, honey," she said levelly. "Come here." She still held Lyndsay's hand and now she drew her back into the shadow of the trees. "We don't have much time," she said.

"But you'll stay awhile. Oh you must," Lyndsay interrupted. "I couldn't bear to be parted from you so soon."

"First, you've got to understand," she said firmly. "Can you keep a secret, Mistress? The most important one of all?"

Lyndsay caught her breath. Her hand tightened on Mrs. Abernathy's.

"How did you know about that?" she asked, her voice trembling with fear.

"There isn't much time," Mrs. Abernathy repeated. "Trust me." She took hold of Lyndsay's other hand and pulled her round so that they faced each other. The old woman's smile vanished.

"Look at me," she said. "Look deeply into my eyes."

"What is this?" demanded Lyndsay, confused.

"Do it," Mrs. Abernathy ordered.

Lyndsay obeyed. Mrs. Abernathy's eyes were a bright, pale blue, but as she stared, mesmerized, into them they became larger and darker, darker until they were almost black. The flesh of her creased, plump face seemed to melt like wax and alter. It seemed that Lyndsay's vision became blurred, as though she were seeing through murky, lapping water. The grip on her hands tightened. She looked down at the hands which held hers. They were strong and knotted with veins and the dislocated joints of an arthritic condition. Mrs. Abernathy's hands were small, pink, and fat. Hardly daring to do so, Lyndsay looked up from the hands, to the woman who now stood before her, tall, straight-backed and black-robed.

"Mother!" she whispered.

"You called me, Mistress, and I came. It was time."

The strong, infinitely comforting arms went around her. Tears of relief welled into Lyndsay's eyes, but she felt afraid, too. She tried to pull free of the embrace. *Mrs. Abernathy?* Her mind could not take in or contain what she had seen, if she had seen it at all. Perhaps at last she had become mad. For a long moment her relief at discovering Mother Poole again made her forget her fear, the sheer impossibility of what she had witnessed. The old woman held her more and more

314

tightly, pressing her face down to her chest, soothing her, as if she were a bewildered child. Slowly, the indomitable strength of the woman prevailed over Lyndsay's fear and confusion. She felt drunk, light-headed.

"Oh why did you go away?" Lyndsay cried reproachfully as soon as she could speak.

"I never left you, Mistress."

"You did, you . . ."

"Think, Mistress. Think."

She spoke entirely without emotion, in a voice as bleak as winter. Lyndsay stared into her eyes and saw, or thought she saw, the dog reflected there.

"No." Lyndsay closed her eyes. "I can't believe . . . I . . . You're trying to drive me mad."

"I never left you," Mother Poole repeated. Lyndsay twisted against her hands. "Time's short," she said, holding on to her. "We must make our plans."

"I can't think straight."

"Yes you can. You know all now. And only the Mistress can witness my power."

"You really can . . . change shape? It's unbelievable."

"The dog ran off," Mother Poole said, shaking her slightly. "Just ran off. We'll not see him again. You understand?"

"Yes," Lyndsay nodded.

Her mind still whirled in its struggle to comprehend what she had seen, was seeing.

"How is it with you, Mistress?" Mother Poole asked tenderly.

"Bad. I think. That's why I needed you so much."

"I'm here. I'm here."

She reached out and laid a hand on Lyndsay's belly. A deep, gratified sigh escaped her. She closed her eyes.

"Yes," Lyndsay confirmed.

"What did I promise you?"

"Only life."

"Oh I feel it quicken. Oh this is good, Mistress, good."

"Is it? I'm pleased, of course, but there's Michael. How am I going to tell him?" Lyndsay asked.

"What does he matter?" she replied scornfully. "You must only think of yourself and your bonny twins."

"Twins!" Lyndsay exclaimed. "Oh no, come on . . ."

"How else should it be, Mistress? There are two lives in you. Trust my hands."

"Oh God, no . . . I . . ."

"Listen to me." Mother Poole caught her in a harsh grasp, forcing Lyndsay to look at her. "It will all be different now. You and me, Mistress. We rule here now. We can see to it all. There is no fear now. You called me back and I'll never leave you. Never."

"But how?"

"What could be more natural than that your friend Mrs. Abernathy should stay for a bit and grow to love the village? What has she got to go home for anyway? After a while, you'll suggest that she take over Mother Poole's cottage. Then she'll be near to deliver your babies and see that all's well with them. Soon now you'll say good-bye to this old carcass. It's time. I'm worn out. But you'll take Mrs. Abernathy home with you and she'll take care of everything."

"What about the baby . . . the babies?" Lyndsay asked desperately. "If Michael should ever guess . . ."

"You'll take care of that," she said certainly. "One way or another . . ."

"You lied to me," Lyndsay accused her, trying to resist the certainty in her voice, in her dark, dangerous eyes. *One way or another.* "You lied to me about Michael and about Emelye." She felt that she had to defend him against this woman. "Why did you do that?"

"I had to be sure of you. I had to be certain that you hated enough to be strong."

"Strong enough to kill Bart?" she demanded. There was nothing to be lost now. Everything had to be said, and besides she wanted to hurt the old woman, to show that she had some power against her.

"Bart killed himself."

"No. He wanted to but I . . . You *saw.*"

"He killed himself the moment he lay with you. He knew that it is written that the Priest must never lie with the Mistress. He did it in defiance, to break you and me, to subjugate all the women. But he did not know," she said softly, "that it is also written that the Mistress shall spill his blood and be forgiven in the act." Again she shook Lyndsay slightly. "You only did what you had to do, what was demanded of you as Mistress. And you'll be glad," she added, "when you've two fine boys, Bart's boys."

"You knew what he was doing," Lyndsay cried. "You let him . . ."

316

"I had to. You must see that. I had to let Bart destroy himself, write his own death warrant, and I had to keep my promise to you. The Mistress must be balanced by the Priest. Male and female, the one checking the other."

"But in a way he's won," Lyndsay said. "I'm carrying his children."

"There can never be complete victory. The battle cannot ever be won. The most we can achieve is harmony in all things. Harmony with the land, with ourselves. Men do not understand this. It's women's business. Men always seek the power for themselves. They think the seed is more important than the body which nurtures it. A moment's pleasure against a lifetime's nurturing. Which is more important, the seed or the earth? I needed you to break Bart, even though to do it nearly killed me. But that is the way it has to be. And now we are strong."

"I . . ." Lyndsay turned away. Her womb felt swollen, overcrowded. Her love for Bart revived and with it her fear, which now extended to the old woman. She turned back toward her, her mouth already shaping questions, but she never asked them. It was too late.

The strong, indomitable body trembled, seemed to fade. Lyndsay watched, open-mouthed, as other features took the place of Mother Poole's, fleetingly. She felt as though she were being sucked into a tunnel. One face after another formed and faded before her astonished eyes. It was like a trick photograph, one image laid on top of another, but none remained long enough for Lyndsay to fix it in her mind. The figures came and went, dissolving, forming, vanishing. The air itself trembled. All she knew was that the women grew younger and younger, even beyond age or time. And finally there was, long enough for her to see so that she would never forget, a woman of astonishing beauty and power. Strong and proud, black hair rippling to her waist, a benign smile curving her full, sensual lips but with eyes as hard as beads of jet.

"You . . . were . . . the first . . . Mistress," Lyndsay gasped, forcing the words out. "You cursed us all."

"Aye and will again," a voice answered as the figure faded. The words hung in the air, a terrible threat that would haunt and trap Lyndsay for the rest of her life.

"Well, honey?"

Mrs. Abernathy shook herself as though waking from a sleep. Smiling, she reached up to adjust her frivolous little hat.

"I don't know what to say," Lyndsay answered. Her head ached. She put her hand up to her forehead.

"I'm going to take real good care of you," Mrs. Abernathy said, linking her arm protectively through Lyndsay's. "And first of all we're going to get you where it's warm." She walked Lyndsay back across the grass and onto the road. Mrs. Abernathy turned her firmly in the direction of Ratchets.

Lyndsay thought, I don't have any power at all. It was an illusion. The only power is hers. She uses it through me. I am her creature. She tugged against Mrs. Abernathy's arm.

"What is it, Mistress?" she asked, stopping and smiling up at her.

"One thing you must tell me."

"Sure."

"That first day, on the airplane, was it you?"

Mrs. Abernathy laughed gaily. The sound seemed to fill the air and drift with the rapidly thickening mist out across the whole village.

"Well now," the old lady said, pulling Lyndsay forward again, "that's quite a question. Let's put it this way. Somebody had to make sure that you got here safe. Somebody had to take care of you."

Lyndsay found herself almost trotting down the steep gradient of the hill. Her fear screamed at her to break free, to go back, to get out at last. Mrs. Abernathy held her arm even tighter.

"Mrs. Abernathy . . ." Lyndsay began.

"Why don't you call me Mother Rose, Mistress. Heaven knows everyone else does." The blue eyes twinkled at her, benign and yet cold as ice. Lyndsay felt her will to resist thaw and trickle away.

"Yes, Mother," she said meekly, and let the old woman draw her along, down into Ratchets, where she would stay, she knew, for the rest of her days. She would never be certain who or what this woman was. But she could feel the babies moving in her body, living, and they were all that mattered.